Also by Gerald A. Browne

IT'S ALL ZOO

THE RAVISHERS
(with Merle Browne)

18MM BLUES*

19 PURCHASE STREET*

*Published by
WARNER BOOKS

GERALD A. BROWNE

11 HARROW-HOUSE

WARNER BOOKS

A Time Warner Company

WARNER BOOKS EDITION

Lyrics by Dory Previn copyright © 1970 by Mediarts Music, Inc. and Bouquet Music

Cover design by Diane Luger
Cover illustration by Danilo Ducak
Hand lettering by Carl Dellacroce

This Warner Books Edition is published by arrangement with Arbor House Publishing Co., Inc., New York, NY.

Warner Books, Inc.
1271 Avenue of the Americas
New York, NY 10020

 A Time Warner Company

Printed in the United States of America

First Warner Books Printing: June, 1995

*For Carl Rinzler, Jack Dreyfus
and especially Merle*

CHAPTER 1

Chesser had come to London ten times a year for the past ten years.

He always stayed at the Connaught, although not in the same corner suite, the one he now occupied. He was such a regular that the hotel no longer requested his passport when he registered and he knew many of the white-gloved, white-tied hotel employees by first name. They knew him as a more generous than average tipper.

This time Chesser had intended to be in London only overnight, to leave for Antwerp as soon as he picked up his packet. His business in Antwerp would require a few hours at most. After that he would be free to meet Maren in Chantilly, where he wanted to be.

But Maren's call had changed those plans. Through a bad, crackling connection that made her sound more distant, she'd said it was raining miserably in Chantilly and, although everything was now green and fresh, the workmen were still repairing the roof of her house, causing a mess. And the terrace pool hadn't been cleaned as promised. She wanted to be with Chesser. She wanted to be with him in London. It was her favorite city in May.

Chesser's first reaction was to console her and tell her to hold out one more day. He was confident enough to realize that most of Maren's discontent with Chantilly was caused by his absence. Her house there was one of the special places where they had truly shared one another, and Chesser thought to remind her of that. But he left it unsaid. He also held back telling her he would much rather be in Chantilly, how much he'd been anticipating the country peace and the indulgences permitted by isolation. London was too close to The System, too close for comfort.

No matter. With his love he couldn't deny Maren anything that might increase her happiness. She would arrive that afternoon on BEA from Le Bourget. Chesser's mind already saw her. He would meet her at the airport if The System cooperated by granting him an early enough appointment.

Now, he sat nude on the edge of the hotel bed, within reach of the telephone. He had to call them. He would have to lie to them about yesterday. He wished he'd gone in to The System yesterday, as scheduled. The reason he hadn't was vague, even to him. He had merely remained in his room, told himself he should get dressed, read the morning *Times* down to its society items, procrastinated until the time for his appointment had passed. And when it was too late he felt strangely relieved, more victorious than guilty, for some reason.

That was yesterday. Today he had to go in.

He quickly decided that the most acceptable excuse was to lie and say he'd just arrived. Conveniently, there was some sort of airlines strike in New York that he could put to use, although actually he'd come in from Nice.

He helped himself to a piece of sweet roll from his breakfast tray, spread it with butter that had gone very soft by now and dipped it into a cup half full of cold black coffee. He noticed the oil from the butter caused a silvery film on the black surface. He brought his mind back to the telephone, discarded the roll, and reached for the instrument.

He gave the number to the hotel operator. While he waited he brought his free hand to the socket of his other arm. He was perspiring. He resented that symptom of his anxiety. The number was ringing. It answered after the third ring, as was customary. He could have predicted it. A precise and ideal female voice wished him an automatic good morning instead of announcing the company's name. He asked for Mr. Meecham and was put through to Meecham's secretary.

She asked, "Who is calling Mr. Meecham?"

He told her. His last name.

"Mr. Meecham is conducting a sight," she informed him. "Mr. Berkely will speak with you."

Berkely was far down the ladder, under Meecham. Meecham was president of The System. Chesser, in all his ten years of dealing with The System, hadn't spoken to Meecham more than a dozen times. It was usually Berkely or someone else; usually someone else, in accord with the relatively modest value of Chesser's packet.

Finally Berkely came on the line. "Ah, Chesser," he said, as though finding something useful that had been lost. "We expected you yesterday."

"I was delayed." Chesser put off telling the lie. Fortunately.

"How was the flight from Nice?"

"Fine."

"I always prefer that late flight," said Berkely and then hesitated perhaps purposely. "You're stopping at the Connaught, of course."

"Yes."

A long moment's silence into which, apparently, Chesser was supposed to insert his excuse. However, he was using the time to invent another one.

Berkely prompted. "Let's see. Chesser, Chesser . . ." Evidently he was consulting a list. "You were scheduled for yesterday afternoon."

"I wasn't feeling well yesterday."

"Oh? Sorry to hear that. You should have rung us up."

"I meant to."

"Undoubtedly you had good reason for not calling." A half question. Then an indulgent sigh around Berkely's next words: "Now, what can we do for you?"

"I'd like to come in today."

"That may not be possible."

"I'll only pick it up. I won't need to look at it."

"I'm looking at the schedule. It's difficult, especially today. It's the last day for these sights, you know."

Chesser knew only too well. "Perhaps you could send my packet here, to the hotel."

"We'd rather not, in this case."

Shove the packet. Shove the whole System, Chesser wanted to say. He said nothing. It was a silent request for a pardon.

Berkely must have sensed that. "We'd prefer you came in."

"I understand."

"Promptly at three. Does that suit you?"

"I'll be there at three."

"You're feeling better, I take it?"

"Much better, thanks."

"Good," said Berkely, and clicked off without a good-bye.

Chesser placed the phone back onto its cradle but continued looking at it. He swore at Berkely but immediately directed his indignation more accurately at The System. Berkely was only an intermediary. It was The System that had just reprimanded Chesser as though he were a schoolboy caught playing hooky. He stood suddenly, attempting to cut his anger with sharp movement. But it stayed with him.

How the hell did they know he'd come from Nice? And the exact flight? For ten years he'd always kept his appointments. Ten times each year. What reason did they have to place him under such close scrutiny? There had only been that negotiation in Marrakesh, but that had been in 1966, years ago. It was impossible for them to know about that. The money from that had been in cash, and now it was represented only by a secret account number in Geneva. So, Chesser thought, it couldn't be the Marrakesh deal. What then? His affair with Maren? Possibly. But he doubted it. Besides, he and Maren had always been discreet. Hadn't they? He answered himself: More so in the beginning. Wherever they went together in the beginning they'd always taken an extra room in her name, although for the past year they hadn't been particularly careful. That was only natural.

He lighted a cigarette, inhaled deeper than usual, and blew out noisily, as though trying to eject more than smoke. He asked the distorted rectangle of sunlight that was hitting the hotel rug: Did The System always keep such close check on everyone with whom it dealt?

An hour later, after shower and razor, after he'd dressed in a conservatively cut suit of navy, because navy was this side of doleful black and the other side of casual brown, after he'd checked the contents of his dark blue alligator business case and snapped shut its pure gold catch, he still had the same question in mind. Really, did The System secretly observe everyone's behavior?

He decided he was being paranoid. He decided he was being absurd. The System wouldn't do that. Couldn't.

Chesser was wrong.

CHAPTER 2

In the *A* to *Z* London atlas and street index, Harrowhouse Street, EC1 may be found on page 64, reference square 3-C. To locate it on the map, the help of a magnifying glass is suggested, for the street is so short that the mapmaker was forced to reduce greatly and crowd his lettering.

Harrowhouse Street is near enough to Saint Paul's for an aesthetic if not reverent view. And even closer to Old Bailey. It is within easy walking distance of Fleet Street's churning urgency, and, in the opposite direction, there is the Bank of England, which was once considered the paragon of stability. Proximity to these formidable features is not, however, the significance of Harrowhouse Street, not the reason that address is known well by many affluent persons throughout the world.

The street itself gives no overt clue to its special importance. Like so many other streets in the maze of London, it is barely two carwidths across, and any vehicle stopped to discharge a passenger is apt to cause immediate congestion. Its sidewalks are equally unaccommodating. Persons walking in pairs cannot pass without at least one having to give way.

The buildings on both sides of the street are all of nineteenth-century quality, as much related in style as they are in space. There are no sheer contemporary facades on Harrowhouse. No neon lights, no plate-glass store fronts, no advertising of any sort. The feeling of the street has been preserved. That feeling is maturity.

Despite its appearance to the contrary, Harrowhouse is a street of commerce. The building numbered 12, for example, contains the executive offices of a maritime insurance company. Across the way at number 13 are the directors of Mid-Continental Oil. There is a dealer of rare books and manuscripts on the second floor of number 32. And the United Kingdom representative of an American plastics firm occupies a portion of the third floor at number 24. Plastics and oil, rare books and insurance. These four are the outsiders, the only trespassers among the other hundred or more companies on Harrowhouse that share a common pursuit of profits.

Diamonds.

From that, one might assume the street is merely a satellite of the ancient diamond district called Hatton Garden, located nearby. In Hatton Garden gems can be seen in abundance, glittering authentically in store windows, and there is the constant activity of independent dealers attached to the small, drawstring purses in which they carry their precious stones for trading. However, the relationship between Hatton Garden and Harrowhouse Street is the reverse of the obvious. Hatton Garden looks to Harrowhouse with established respect.

Number 11 is the reason.

It is also the reason why so many diamond merchants are eager to conduct business on that quiet, minor street. They are like particles unable to resist a powerful magnet. They feel fortunate to be there, as close to number 11 as possible.

Number 11 is one of the larger structures on Harrowhouse—a wider building of five stories, marked by four windows across at every level. The top floor slants to the roof, and the quartet of windows there is set back slightly, each with identical eaves. The building is painted black and crisply trimmed with white. Its entrance is only a degree warmer. Tall double doors of richly varnished oak. On the right-hand door is a rectangle of solid brass, originally chosen thick enough so that now it symbolizes durability and longevity after nearly thirty thousand polishings.

On the brass name plate there is no name. Only the words *number eleven,* in Spencerian script. Marking the headquarters of the Consolidated Selling System, or, as those in the business call it with no less veneration, The System.

It is here that The System maintains control of approximately ninety per cent of the world's diamonds, choking or releasing the supply according to its judgment.

It is a flagrant cartel, enjoying all the advantages of such an arrangement. From its own mines in South Africa and South West Africa comes sixty per cent of the world's supply. With this nucleus of power, The System either buys up or receives on consignment practically all the rough stones found elsewhere in the world.

The System has no competition. In its eighty years of existence there have been only a few challengers, and these have been swiftly dealt with, either dissolved or absorbed. Actually, no one in the business of diamonds wants to slay or even disturb the giant. It is better to have a giant, The System, in absolute control. Otherwise, there might be great fluctuations in price. Surely there would be underselling, and the entire market would be adversely affected. So, to the diamond merchant, The System plays a vital and rather heroic role. It stabilizes price. At least it dictates that the price of diamonds should go up and never down. And that seems to please everyone, including even those who finally purchase the cut gems for substantial investment or precious decoration.

While The System is a far-reaching and complex organization, its method of marketing is ingeniously simple.

Ten times each year invitations are cabled to a select group of two hundred diamond dealers and wholesalers. No one declines, for such an invitation is considered comparable to a gratuity. To be so included is a financial privilege, often handed down from father to son.

Prior to the arrival of these dealers, The System makes up individual packets of diamonds, choosing the stones from its inventory. One packet for each dealer. The size, quality, and number of stones in each packet are decided entirely by The System, and a price, also arbitrarily predetermined, is placed on each packet. Some packets are modestly valued—for example, at a mere twenty-five thousand dollars. Others have been known to be priced as high as nine million. Depending upon what The System dictates.

The dealer arrives at number 11. He is presented with his packet, and, if he chooses, he may examine its contents. Such an examination is called a *sight*. However, most buyers accept their packets without opening them. Not really a show of blind confidence. Merely an acknowledgment of The System's irrefutable terms, which are: No buyer may dispute what he finds in his packet, he may not utter a single questioning word about price, and he must accept all the stones in his packet, or none. If a buyer refuses his packet he is never invited again.

The System's volume is approximately six hundred million dollars a year.

On Friday, May 1st, at precisely two fifty-five P.M., a chauffeured black Daimler deposited Chesser at the entrance to number 11 Harrowhouse Street.

Chesser approached the door and reached for its imposing brass latch. Only the very tips of his fingers contacted the metal, for the door was immediately pulled open to admit him. He should have remembered that from all the previous times, but he was distracted, anticipating what his mind had developed into a confrontation. He didn't want to see Berkely, or even Meecham, especially not Meecham. He wanted to get his packet and get the hell out of there. Maren's plane was due in at six.

Chesser entered and was greeted by the one who always opened the door with such perfect timing. The man's name was Miller. A large man, evidently strong. He was a guard, although that was not apparent from his dress. He wore a black suit and tie. He might have been a funeral director. Miller's post had been the front door of number 11 as long as Chesser could remember. Miller was a friendly sort, always had a smile ready. But as Chesser saw him now he realized that the man would be formidable to anyone uninvited.

Chesser went deeper into the reception area, a wide, impressive center hall that led to a full-width stairway. He heard his steps on the patterned black-and-white marble floor. For some reason, his hearing seemed overly acute. He was also aware of his body's reluctance to move. He didn't want to be there.

He sat on a bench that was genuine Queen Anne and placed his business case beside him. He was minutes early. He preoccupied himself with the wall opposite, where a large painting was hung. A snowscape, well done in convincing soft whites, peaceful, glistening. He had the urge to smoke, but decided to wait. He noticed there wasn't an ashtray on the nearby table. Miller was standing in his place by the entrance. They exchanged friendly expressions.

"They know you're here," said Miller, reassuringly.

"Thanks."

Chesser glanced at his watch. It told him three exactly. He expected the door on the right to open, but then he heard voices and saw them coming down the stairs—Meecham and Sir Harold himself. Everyone referred to him as Sir Harold. He was the chairman of the directors, the very top of The System. His last name was Appensteig.

Meecham and Sir Harold flanked a short man who had hyperthyroid eyes and a gray suit cut to minimize a paunch. The man's feet seemed too small for the rest of him. Very small feet, like a dancer's. In obviously expensive shoes. Chesser immediately recognized the short man as Barry Whiteman, the American whose packet was usually valued in the millions. In the United States the name of Whiteman and diamonds were synonymous. Whiteman was carrying a black Mark Cross attaché case. He'd probably brought his bank draft in it. No doubt it now contained his packet.

Chesser stood when he saw them, an almost involuntary reaction. Although they didn't acknowledge Chesser, they seemed to know he was there. Whiteman was getting the important treatment from Meecham and Sir Harold. Chesser overheard them commenting on the lunch they'd shared.

They passed close to Chesser. Whiteman's eyes were aimed down, as though watching his shoes. They paused at the door. Whiteman touched his tie to verify that it was in place. Gray silk tie exactly matching a gray silk shirt. He made a remark about sherry. Meecham and Sir Harold laughed appropriately, and Meecham said he would see that Whiteman received some, *a case,* he said. Chesser thought it likely they were referring to a woman. Whiteman made Meecham promise. He extended his hand for two perfunctory shakes and was smiling when he went out.

Meecham and Sir Harold remained in place. Sir Harold was in his seventies, wore a suit of expensive worsted, black with an almost imperceptible blue broken stripe. In his youth his hair had been blond and his complexion English fair. Now what hair he had was a creamy-to-yellow shade, and his face was red from pressure, as though all the capillaries were trying to surface.

Meecham was a decade younger and about two inches taller. His mannerisms were sharp, alert, contradicting his rather indefinite, round features.

The two men spoke confidentially for a long moment. Sir Harold was faced away from Chesser, and Meecham was doing most of the talking. Once Meecham glanced over at Chesser, and that made Chesser feel he was their topic.

Finally, they came down the hall to him. They gave him automatic handshakes, first Meecham and then Sir Harold. Their hands felt dry and pulpy.

"Good to see you looking so fit," said Meecham, smiling. "Been in the sun, I see."

Chesser had a good tan from Nice.

"You've met Sir Harold before, I'm sure."

Chesser said yes and would have said more but Sir Harold broke in. "Of course I know young Chesser." The way he said it implied a compliment. "I knew your father very well," he added.

Chesser knew that was a lie. His father had never been important enough to receive any close attention from The System's director. Besides, Chesser remembered his father speaking of Sir Harold with only distant respect, as one might refer to a force rather than a living man. So Sir Harold's next words were unexpected.

"Your father always wanted to have a store, I remember. A first-class place on Fifth Avenue."

That was true.

"I suppose you continue his ambition?"

"Of course," lied Chesser.

"He was a fine man," said Sir Harold, with Meecham nodding concurrence. "Fine man," Sir Harold repeated, his attention directed vaguely down the hall. It was now evident that Sir Harold had given more than he cared to this inconsequential meeting. Chesser was no Whiteman. Never would be. Sir

Harold took the first step that started them down the hall together.

As they neared the stairs, Sir Harold moved from them toward what appeared to be a panel of blank wall. Immediately, as though anticipating his approach, the panel slid aside to reveal an elevator.

"Do see that young Chesser is cared for," instructed Sir Harold without turning, and entered the elevator.

Meecham said that he would.

The wall panel wiped Sir Harold from view.

Going up the stairs, Meecham remarked, "Sir Harold seems genuinely fond of you."

Chesser hoped he looked grateful.

"I'm surprised he didn't inquire about Mrs. Chesser. Can be a nasty thing, divorce."

Chesser had never discussed his divorce with anyone this side of the Atlantic except Maren. He assumed The System had learned about it the same way they learned everything, however that was.

Meecham continued: "They take divorce much too lightly in America. It's a serious problem."

"Actually, it's a solution," was Chesser's opinion.

"How's that?" asked Meecham.

"Like peace," Chesser told him. "Peace is a solution, war is a problem."

"You believe marriage is a war?"

"It can be."

Meecham grunted. Disagreement, particularly coming from anyone of Chesser's status, was insubordination. It wasn't done. "Thank the Lord we make divorce more difficult in this country," he said.

Chesser thought of Henry the Eighth's chopping block and almost said it.

"No offense meant, of course," said Meecham. "It's only that I've a personal prejudice against it. Married people should stick it out together, no matter what."

Chesser wondered how many demerit marks The System had on his ledger. As yet, Meecham hadn't said anything about yesterday's missed appointment.

By then they were on the second floor landing. Meecham

led the way into a room that was used exclusively for sights. It was a huge, high room. A pair of black leather Chesterfield sofas formed a seating area at one end. The walls were impressively paneled. Underfoot was a Persian rug, an authentic Kirman. At the other end was a long, sturdy table. The entire top surface of the table was covered with black velour.

The table was positioned beneath a large window that permitted exact northern daylight. This was *the* light for the entire diamond industry, considered such a criterion that electric illumination of precisely the same quality had been invented for use in diamond centers throughout the world. And in some important places the window itself had been identically duplicated in proportion and position, to standardize the examination of diamonds.

Behind the table was a man whom Meecham called by his last name. Watts. Chesser had seen Watts before in this room, at previous sights. The way he stood, Watts seemed more a fixture than a person.

On the table's black velour surface there was only one thing. Chesser's packet.

It wasn't, as might be imagined, a parcel elaborately wrapped and tied. No special ribbon or paper. It was just an ordinary small manila envelope.

Meecham asked: "Would you care to look?"

Chesser wanted to decline but decided it might be in his favor if he didn't. A show of interest. He took a seat at the table. Meecham went around to the opposite side and stood beside Watts, a position that allowed him to maintain his view of Chesser, from above and head on.

From his business case Chesser removed a loupe, tenpower, the type of glass most jewelers use. He placed it on the table and picked up his packet. He undid the flap and, rather ceremoniously, emptied its contents. Four squares of neatly folded tissue. He undid one. It contained five uncut stones of two to four carats.

Chesser picked up the largest and held it between his thumb and forefinger. He placed the loupe to his right eye and sighted into the stone, turning it for various angles. He saw that it was of excellent quality, good color, and had but a single carbon spot on one side, close enough to its perimeter. It would cut nicely.

"A beauty," Chesser approved.

He opened the other three folds of tissue. He sighted into several stones and then a few more, choosing at random, small and larger. All the while his expression remained set, and he made no comment. Finally, he refolded the tissues around the stones and replaced them in the envelope.

On the underneath side of the envelope's flap he saw the figure "17,000." He didn't react. He brought his look up and found Meecham's eyes upon him. He read Meecham's eyes. Superiority inviting defiance.

Chesser's packet had never been valued at less than twenty-five thousand dollars. This time he'd been presented with as many stones as usual but, with only a few exceptions, these were of inferior quality. He had seen the flaws in them, the inclusions, the bubbles, clouds, and feathers. The System was punishing him. But he knew if he complained there would never be a next time.

He took some of the edge off the moment by nonchalantly dropping the loupe into his business case. He picked up his packet, gave the envelope an extra fold and dropped that in also.

"I assume you're satisfied?" asked Meecham.

A nod from Chesser, and a forced smile. He felt transparent, as though Meecham were sighting into him for imperfections.

"Watts will complete the transaction," said Meecham. And with that he left the room.

Chesser was relieved by Meecham's departure. It improved Chesser's chances of making it out of there before erupting. He wrote out a bank draft for seventeen thousand. Watts gave him a receipt. Chesser knew it was probably Watts who had chosen those stones for his packet. Watts was in charge of grading, classifying the stones according to carat, color, and clarity. But he couldn't blame Watts. Watts was only a salaried employee, not an officer of The System. Just doing what he was told.

Watts verified that, as he handed the receipt across to Chesser. In a guarded, low tone he said, sincerely, "I'm sorry, sir."

*   *   *

Moments later Meecham, in his fourth-floor office, was using his absolutely private phone. After he dialed, and while the number was ringing, he moved to the window. He looked out at his most frequent view of London and did not really see the dome of St. Paul's, which dominated the horizon. He glanced down to the street and saw Chesser getting into a Daimler.

Meecham was certain that Chesser was cursing him personally and thought that perhaps Chesser's next packet should be even more of the same, for good measure. However, he had to admire Chesser's restraint. He would have wagered against it. He watched the Daimler drive off, and realized the number he was calling had rung more than enough.

Perhaps she was out, he thought, or more likely she was busy. He disconnected and tried the number again. He must have dialed incorrectly before, because now she picked up on the second ring.

After hello's, she said, "I thought it might be you, love."

He was pleased. It meant she'd had him in mind.

"It's been more than a week," she said.

"I've been busy," he said, not as convincingly as he might have.

"And you haven't been behaving yourself, have you?"

"No."

"You're a bad one, you are."

"Very."

"You deserve something for being bad. Don't you love?"

A yes, with calculated submission.

"I've got just the thing," she promised.

He was tempted but remembered Whiteman and had to sacrifice. He quickly arranged it, gave her the details, and told her he would be responsible for her fee.

When he said good-bye, he said it softly and, for the first time in the conversation, he referred to her by name, Sherry.

After the call, Meecham thought he might make another, similar, for himself. He decided to put it off until he'd had a sauna. One thing for sure, he'd stay in town tonight. Go out to Hampshire in the morning. A half Saturday and all of a Sunday would be almost too much wife and country.

CHAPTER 3

Chesser was at Heathrow Airport a half hour early. Information said BEA flight 36 from Paris would arrive as scheduled, not early as Chesser hoped. He went quickly to the upper level, his eagerness taking him.

He could have spent the time more comfortably distracted. There was a convenient bar. But he chose to wait standing at one of the large windows overlooking the dulled silver of planes receiving final service or being guided in. A flow of sibilant sound underscored the embraces he witnessed, the last of farewells and the first of welcomings.

Chesser and Maren had been apart only four days, but to him it seemed longer. Waiting, Chesser looked at his watch at least twice every minute and, finally, there was the black, crimson, and white of the BEA insignia on a plane taxiing in and swinging into position. He appreciated that plane. It was the one. Bringing her to him.

His eyes searched for the color of nutmeg. The shade of her hair. Viking hair, he called it. His insides did a catch when he saw it. She came out of the plane with eyes up, aimed precisely at him, as though she'd expected where he would be. She was wearing rich blue, ample-legged trousers and a soft shirt. Better for traveling. Among the other passengers in their wrinkled suits and dresses, she was outstanding, casually neat and fresh. She carried a Vuitton satchel. With her free hand she waved to Chesser. The wind chose that moment to take her hair across her face and she made no attempt to discipline it. That was very much like her.

He waited for her outside customs, a delay that seemed particularly cruel, as they were in sight of one another but not permitted closer. They gestured impatiently while she waited her turn in line. Then, oblivious to the public place, she came to him, against him full length. Without words, each reassured the other that everything was all right now.

When they arrived at the Connaught suite, she quickly unpacked, hung, and placed her things beside his. It seemed to him that she was decorating, dispersing loneliness. Even while she was in the bathroom putting her cosmetics and other personal necessities into proper transient place, he sat on the covered commode to observe her every movement. She did not stop to kiss him, knowing that if she did they would not stop, and, although the unpacking could have been done later, it served their mutual want with extra provocation.

When there was nothing more to unpack, she went to the window and gazed out toward Grosvenor Square. It was still daytime.

"Shall I order a drink?" Chesser asked.

Her reply was her hand on the drapery drawstring, pulling to make the room almost dark.

They never did their lovemaking in total darkness, for they also loved with their eyes. It helped each to know more surely of the other's needs. She liked him to undress her, particularly the first time in a new place. As now. She stood and he knew. He didn't hurry, proof of his control. And she didn't assist, which demonstrated her total willingness.

Across the large bed, in the kind half-light, they loved slowly and confidently. Afterward, they closed their eyes and floated on, feeling together. Her head on his shoulder, strands of her hair across his chest, her right leg overlapping both of his. He heard her breathing change and knew she was asleep. He needed to get up for the bathroom but didn't want to disturb her. Soon she shifted in her sleep, turned from him, and he had only to remove his arm from beneath her head to be free. He took care to be quiet. He didn't even flush the commode.

He sat in a chair near the bed and smoked. She was now in her usual sleeping position—on her side with both legs drawn up symmetrically and her hands, palm to palm, contained between her thighs. Chesser enjoyed observing her while she was so completely unaware. He thought, possessively, how deceiving her body was. When she was dressed she appeared angular, fashionably attractive but very thin. It led one to estimate she would be too thin when undressed. But there for Chesser to see was the naked truth. She was small-boned and her body had ample flesh in proportion. Ideally distributed. Each part of her curved nicely, just enough to define transition to her next part. No studding hipbones, as might be expected. Instead, a soft, rising line of hip that dipped gradually and then deeply to form her waist.

Her skin was northern pale, all over. She was Swedish, born and raised in a remote place far north, nearly on the Arctic Circle. Her ancestors had protected themselves from the harsh elements, so her paleness was inherent. She loved the sun, but it was too strong for her, burned her quickly whenever she trusted it.

The impression she created with her lean body and pale skin was fragility, perhaps a lack of stamina. She appeared to be the sort of woman who needed sanctuary, who would be at her best when dependent, relating passively to a man. Little more.

Chesser had thought that when he first saw her.

He had soon discovered how actively she contradicted that impression. At Gstaad she skied dangerously fast but very well. At Deauville she chose to ride the most nervous and challenging horses. En route to Le Mans she handled her sports car with alarming abandon and admirable authority. Once, in Monaco, on a day when a heavy mistral kept all small craft within the breakwater, Maren insisted on going out to pilot a speedboat through swells deep as canyons. Chesser went along merely because he preferred to drown with her. The boat smashed against the ridges of blown sea with such impact that at times it was nearly vertical. Maren was stimulated, while Chesser, reasonably enough, hung on.

He preferred to believe that she wasn't compulsive about it, that she didn't need to go from one dangerous challenge right to another. She merely took the chances as they came, and when something involved risk she seemed to enjoy it more. So he told himself.

Chesser, at first, was amazed and amused by Maren's unexpected agility and daring. But, as his love for her grew, he became alarmed. He considered her reckless, skillfully reckless he had to admit, but nonetheless reckless. The fear of losing her, the possibility of it, infected him. To taunt that possibility was foolish and thoughtless of her. He told her that: calmly accused her. In reply she told him that everyone was always competing against death for life.

They argued then, vehemently. Words such as stupid and coward were used as weapons, and they spent that night apart. Sleepless. The following day all that was needed for reconciliation was the sight of one another.

It taught Chesser not to restrain her.

She made a silent vow not to take so many chances, for his sake.

However, it didn't stop Chesser from wondering why Maren found danger so fascinating. Was it something left over from Jean Marc? Or had it always been there? He concluded the latter was most likely It had probably been a mutual quality, one of the attractions that had brought Maren and Jean Marc together. Surely it was the cause of their violent severance. Jean Marc crushed beneath the overturned Lotus, instantly dead at four in the morning on a wet road of the Bois de Boulogne. It was assumed that Jean Marc, the husband, had been the driver. Maren, the wife, was thrown clear and suffered only minor injuries. But she was hurt, indelibly, by it. Jean Marc had been very young and very rich. Maren's great beauty and youth were her equally important contributions. They had plenty of everything to spend together, until they gambled it all at once on a slick corner, taking it too fast for some extra exhilaration, just not matching that turn with a good enough turn.

Maren confided to Chesser that, actually, she had been the driver. Only Chesser knew. Maren didn't confess, merely told him in order to share it, and, although he looked for signs of guilt, he saw none, at least not on the surface.

A month after the accident, Maren went back to modeling. She was sharply criticized by Jean Marc's friends, who thought at least a year of secluded mourning was respectfully due. She defied them all with insouciance, and soon again was appearing on the pages of *Vogue Française*.

She needed the distraction, desperately, and besides, she claimed, during her personal communion with the spirit of

Jean Marc he'd given his permission. The temporal Jean Marc, however, had not been so liberal. His will, properly notarized, clearly stated that all his wealth and holdings should go to his wife, Maren. She was the sole heir, entitled to all the millions that had been handed down to him. With one condition. If she should ever choose to marry again, the entire fortune would automatically go to the lawyer-executors.

Chesser and Maren met a year after the accident. As soon as their relationship formed into a serious involvement, Maren told Chesser about Jean Marc's restricting condition. She believed it only fair that Chesser should know why it was impossible for her to just fly off somewhere and become Mrs. Chesser. It just wasn't practical.

Chesser agreed.

Maren took the same opportunity to make a condition of her own. She wanted to be able to speak of the late Jean Marc without inhibition, without fear of provoking Chesser's jealousy.

Chesser also agreed to that. After all, he reasoned, it was easy enough to compete with a dead man for a live, sensually demanding twenty-five-year-old woman.

So, it was not unusual for Chesser to be somewhere with Maren, at a restaurant or inn, for example, and have her remark, quite casually and often with tender reminiscence, "Jean Marc and I came here once." She never did it intentionally to irritate Chesser. It would just come out. Jean Marc used to do this or that. Jean Marc once told me. Jean Marc liked. Jean Marc detested. Jean Marc never. Jean Marc always.

It made Chesser uncomfortable at first. Then he got used to it. She was merely remembering aloud, he realized, and, after a while, Chesser began thinking of Jean Marc as an old friend. In fact, someone he knew well, though someone he'd never known.

Maren's verbalized memories of Jean Marc never created a problem. Chesser handled them with extraordinary confidence. What did become a problem, however, was Jean Marc's money. There was so much of it. There were the evident things, such as huge, beautiful houses, precious paintings and objets d'art, stables of thoroughbreds, yachts, and planes. Then there were the intangibles. Controlling interests in various companies, great blocks of stock and accumulated dividends. It was the sort of complex fortune that continuously nourished itself. By its size it increased at a rate that defied depletion. Maren could spend and spend while she became richer and richer.

She had only a vague idea of her worth as the widow of Jean Marc. Many, many millions was her nebulous estimate. Chesser, on the other hand, knew precisely what her financial status would be if she were to become Mrs. Chesser. His two hundred thousand dollars in the Swiss account, which he referred to as his fuck-you money, was a pittance by comparison. For his daily bread Chesser was dependent upon The System. Profit from packets brought him about a hundred thousand a year. Part of that went to ex-wife Sylvia; taxes took even more. The rest didn't approach buying Chesser's, not to mention Maren's, way of life.

Many of those to whom The System granted the privilege of receiving packets had built sizable fortunes. They spent most of their time dealing and exploiting their diamonds. Whiteman was a good example. He'd started small, squeezed off a few big deals, and now the value of his packet was way up. But such effort required a certain focused ambition that Chesser didn't seem to have. As ex-wife Sylvia put it just before the divorce, "You look good but you've got no goddamn direction at all."

At times Chesser wanted to prove Sylvia wrong. Usually on mornings after too much of everything the night before, he'd make a resolution to concentrate on business, to start dealing. But he really didn't want to, not enough. Each time Chesser picked up his packet from The System, he quickly disposed of it, usually without even opening it. He merely took a fair fast profit from a dealer in Antwerp or somewhere and forgot about diamonds for another month.

Sometimes, when he allowed it to get to him, Chesser felt like a bird on the back of a rhinoceros.

Money. Chesser and Maren discussed it only once. He told her exactly what he did and what he had. He didn't ask her to give up her wealth for him nor did he pledge to make a supreme effort toward financial success. She didn't volunteer to give up her wealth for him nor did she want him to try to become rich. She meant it when she said she thought his struggling to acquire a fortune would be an idiotic waste of time.

They reached an agreement. They'd spend his money and her money. But there'd be no distinction between the two. His limited funds would merely be mixed with hers, unlimited. It would just be money, for any purpose their love demanded.

So far, it had worked. Because Maren never felt the need to belittle Chesser. And he was not burdened by an oppressive conscience. The only problem was one they both felt but never mentioned in the fear they might just be foolish enough to do it and spoil the whole thing. The more they loved the more the felt it.

They wanted to be married.

That was Chesser's very thought now, as he sat in the bedroom of the Connaught suite and watched over Maren taking her after-love-making nap. He had the urge to hold her and suggest marriage. He prevented that by getting up quietly and going into the sitting room.

The windows there were open, and the light that came through them gave everything in the room an almost neutral cast. It was neither day nor nighttime. More correctly, it was time between, the effect of a hesitation or suspension. Chesser didn't turn on a light. He was nude and besides it was better to be able to see out while not being seen. He noticed it was just beginning to rain. He could hear the swift licking movement of cars on the wet street below.

His business case was on the sofa. He placed it on the floor and lay on the sofa with his head upon the arm rest. From there he could see chimney pipes on the roof of the building opposite. London, he thought. He glanced toward the bedroom, but it was too dark to see Maren. Meecham came to mind. He reached and brought his business case up, placed it on his stomach. He went into the case and, without looking, found his packet. Then into the packet for the tissue-covered stones. He ripped the tissues away to have all the stones in the cup of his left hand. The figure seventeen thousand repeated in his mind. He knew he'd be lucky to make a five-thousand-dollar profit this time. Maybe only four thousand dollars. To get five thousand, he'd have to haggle.

That pompous bastard Meecham.

The fucking System.

He let go. The diamonds spattered against the near wall. He lay there a while, trying to disregard them. He couldn't. He had to get down on his hands and knees and feel around to find them on the soft rug. As he searched, he heard Maren's voice coming from what seemed a different dimension.

"I had a weird dream," she said, standing in the bedroom doorway.

He was just below her. He got up and kissed her, held her. The diamonds were in his hand. He wondered if he'd found all of them. He'd see when there was light. He broke from her to put the diamonds back into the brown envelope. His hand was perspiring and a few of the stones stuck. He brushed them off and in. He sat on the sofa, expecting her to sit there beside him, but she was already in a fat, stuffed chair, curled up. She lighted two cigarettes and flipped one to him. She usually did that. This time he didn't catch it. The cigarette fell into the crevice of the sofa cushions and Chesser dug quickly to get it.

"It wasn't a dream," said Maren. "I think it was an astral trip."

"Maybe it was just a regular dream."

"No. I left myself. I saw you sitting in the chair and my physical body on the bed. My guide was with me."

"Which one?"

"Billie Three Rocks."

"The Chinaman wasn't around today?"

"Just the Indian. He showed me one of my past lives. It was as real as this room. I was a soldier. I think it must have been in Greece. It was, because there were marble columns and statues all around."

"A woman captain?" asked Chesser.

"I was a man, then. I told you how people change sexes from one life to the next. Remember? According to their karma."

Chesser nodded that he remembered.

Maren told him, "You were there."

"I suppose I was a woman."

"You were my younger brother. There was a celebration for you because you were a hero. You'd just come back from a battle."

Maren's great interest, second only to Chesser, was the supernatural. For her that included everything from spiritualism to Tantra. She'd read extensively on psychic phenomena, parapsychology, black magic, Tarot, the works. What evolved from all her research was a personal sort of orthodoxy which she felt somehow applied to all existence. No doubt her concepts were a throwback from her notoriously superstitious ancestors. In her native land the nights were always a half year long, so there was no lack of conducive atmosphere for dark and imaginative thoughts. Maren believed religiously in life after death, just as she believed emphatically that everyone had lived previous lives. She considered her and Chesser's love an important aspect of their mutual destinies. They had, according to her, chosen one another while in spiritual limbo.

Chesser never ridiculed her beliefs. He was wise enough to know that he didn't *know* what was true. Besides, he had no better philosophy to offer. At times he envied her faith and wished he could believe as strongly in anything. Because he never challenged or denounced her convictions, she tended to assume they thought alike.

"It's raining," said Chesser, for a different subject.

"We were having a lovely time," she went on. "It was a feast with everyone lying around gulping wine from golden goblets. Later on, you and I had a quarrel over a girl. A very pretty girl."

"And you won."

"No. It was settled most amicably. She wanted us both and had her way."

"Being the younger I was second of course."

"Simultaneously," said Maren. "It was very erotic." She thought a moment. "Perhaps it wasn't Greece at all. It could have been Rome. I don't remember what language we spoke."

"It's really raining. Are you hungry?"

"Starved."

"We can have dinner at Annabel's, if you want. And do some gambling later."

"What were you doing just then, on the floor?"

"I dropped something."

"What?"

"A couple of diamonds."

No reaction from her. Obviously diamonds were inconsequential.

By then it was night. They were sitting there in the dark

with only the reflection of car lights moving intermittently across the ceiling.

She said: "I don't know if I feel like Annabel's. I'd enjoy playing some roulette, though."

She got up, stretched, and came over to the sofa. She snuggled against him, submissively, in the cave of his arm. "Something's bothering you," she declared."

"No really."

"Diamonds?"

She wasn't clairvoyant, thought Chesser, just intuitive, adapted to his frequency. He tried to transmit another emotion.

"I love you," he said.

"I know."

"Shall we get dressed and go to dinner?"

"No."

Her hands were on him, not demanding, appreciating.

"You said you were starved."

"Order something up," she suggested.

"Be almost as easy to go to Annabel's. It's only a couple of blocks. We could walk."

"We could."

"In the rain."

"Want to?"

"Did you make a reservation?"

"No. And it's Friday night."

"Probably be packed."

"Every place."

She laughed, a conspirator now.

He said: "No roulette tonight, I guess."

"It's a shame, really, because I feel influential tonight. I'll bet I could will the ball into my number."

"We may be losing a fortune sitting here."

"My tummy's grumbling. Hear it?"

They had dinner in. The two waiters who brought it arranged the table in the sitting room and waited around to serve. Chesser dismissed them. Then he and Maren, after much difficulty unlocking the hinges of the extension flaps, wheeled the table into the bedroom. Chesser had put on a robe, but Maren remained nude. She suggested that he get undressed for dinner and he obliged. He'd ordered rare roast

beef for himself and Dover sole for her. She'd definitely re-
jected the idea of also having roast beef, making a face as
though she wouldn't be able to stand the sight of it. But now
she only nibbled at her sole and reached over to spear big
chunks of the beef from his plate. Her smile apologized. He
didn't mind. It wasn't unusual. If he'd ordered sole and she'd
ordered beef, she would have gone for the sole. Maybe it was
something from her childhood. She had a gigantic appetite.
She could outeat Chesser any time. She ate her Bibb lettuce
salad with her fingers, dipping the leaves into a server of mayonnaise. She asked Chesser if he wanted a taste of her sole.
She already had a large portion aimed for his mouth, and although he wasn't in the mood for fish he capitulated and said
it was excellent. For dessert she had two lemon tarts and half
of Chesser's strawberry ice cream.

Throughout dinner Chesser's look went from her eyes to
his food to her nipples. She had eyes of a color close to cobalt
blue, bright, as though they were backlighted. And there were
flecks of silver in them. Her nipples were erect. Chesser had
never known any other woman whose nipples appeared always aroused. Maren's announced their sensitivity with evident physical candor.

She wet her forefinger with her tongue and used it to gather
crumbs from her tart plate. Then she fell back on the bed,
complaining ecstatically about how full she was. She crawled
to the center of the big bed and lit two cigarettes.

He caught his this time, and she complimented him with a
glance.

"I forgot to bring the backgammon," she said.

"We'll buy one tomorrow."

Backgammon was their game. Her play was improving.
Now she owed him only nine hundred thousand. Last month
he'd been ahead by over a million. She always threatened that
she was going to pay him. In cash.

"I love you," she said.

"I know."

He got up and went into the sitting room. The light was on
and the drapes were drawn and he searched the rug near the
wall. He didn't see any diamonds. He looked under the table.

He must have recovered them all. He didn't regret having thrown them.

When he went back into the bedroom, Maren was sitting up with her legs crossed in the middle of the bed. She had a book with a frayed dust jacket.

"Let's do your *I Ching*," she said.

She was referring to the book, a translated edition of the ancient Chinese *Book of Changes*. *I Ching* is a method of guidance and prediction based on chance. It's premise is that everything is constantly in motion, changing. The sixty-four hexagrams of the *I Ching* are formed by broken and unbroken lines that abstractly represent objects and situations according to the intricate symbolism of the Chinese mind. Maren consulted the *I Ching* frequently for herself and for Chesser. It was another facet of her transcendental doctrine.

"Have you got three coins?" she asked.

Chesser knew he didn't. He always tipped his coins away. Maren told him to look in her purse. She didn't have any coins either. They couldn't do the *I Ching* without coins.

"Call down and have them bring up three coins," she told him.

Chesser had a better idea. He went in the bathroom and removed the blade from his razor. Then he went to the closet and used the blade to snip the three front buttons off his dark blue business suit. He tossed them onto the bed, and Maren said they would do fine. She designated the side of each button with a ridge around it as a head; the opposite, smooth side would be a tail.

Chesser tossed the three buttons six times, according to the ritual. Maren used an eyebrow pencil to record the results of each toss. His first throw was two tails and a head. Each of his next five throws was two heads and a tail. Maren consulted the chart at the back of the book and determined that this time his hexagram was number forty-three. *Kuai* / Breakthrough (Resoluteness). It was symbolized thus:

$$
\begin{array}{cc}
-- & -- \\
-- & -- \\
-- & -- \\
-- & -- \\
-- & -- \\
-- & --
\end{array}
$$

| above | TUI | THE JOYOUS, LAKE |
| below | CH' IEN | THE CREATIVE, HEAVEN |

She handed Chesser the book so he could read the appropriate passage.

This hexagram signifies on the one hand a breakthrough after a long accumulation of tension, as a swollen river breaks through its dikes, or in the manner of a cloudburst. On the other hand, applied to human conditions, it refers to the time when inferior people gradually begin to disappear. Their influence is on the wane; as a result of a resolute action, a change in conditions occurs, a breakthrough.

While he was reading, Maren kneeled behind him and massaged his neck and shoulders.

"Poor love," she said, "You've got so much tension."

CHAPTER 4

Every Saturday afternoon when the weather cooperates there is a promenade on King's Road, Chelsea. From Sloane Square to Beaufort Street, a distance of twenty blocks, the sidewalks stream with those who come mainly to be seen. Wear what you want is the code, and couples seem to be literally adorning one another, clinging. It is not unusual to notice authentically titled, long-haired young lords looking voluntarily indigent, while less fortunate common fellows are garbed in self-conscious elegance. As for the girls in their hot pants and see-throughs, high-slit midis and minis, they leave little for a voyeur to imagine.

Chesser and Maren were there among the walkers on that Saturday in early May. Maren had wanted to do other than the

usual things, and Chesser was willing. She'd thought enough
to bring him some casual clothes from Chantilly. A pair of
straight-legged denim slacks and a wide belt with a pure-gold
copy of a San Francisco fireman's buckle. A cotton jersey
Italian shirt cut narrow to his measure. He wore it unbuttoned
three down, with a figured silk scarf tied loose and low. He
might have been taken for a British nobleman with extreme
contemporary tastes had his hair been much longer. Anyway,
he appeared to be anything but a diamond dealer.

Maren contributed to the off-beat impression: mid-calf-
length skirt handmade in Pakistan, yellow, red, black, and
white. A sheer Indian cotton blouse of palest pink and several
woven Mexican sashes of various widths, in blazing colors,
which she'd tied on the side so they dangled long. Dozens of
tiny antique rings on her fingers. To further uninhibit this colorful mixture, her nutmeg hair flowed down freely. She was
confident, as always; in a higher mood than usual.

Others noticed them. They noticed others. They looked at
the windows of many boutiques, bought two large sugar
cookies in an old, good bakery and ate them as they went.
They laughed a lot, and Chesser didn't feel at all forty. Nor
did he appear to be, for he was naturally thin, and, according
to current values, fat was synonymous with old. By the time
Chesser and Maren had gone a dozen blocks they'd become
so conditioned that only the most bizarre costumes and hair-
dos caught their attention.

They came to the Chelsea Antique Supermarket and went
in. It was a deep building divided into many stalls where vendors offered all sorts of small, old things. It was there that
Chesser saw the huge man in black for the first time. Chesser
took casual special notice of the man, whose size was extraordinary. He was dressed entirely in black, suit, tie, and shirt.
A thick-bodied man a full head taller than everyone. He could
have been a retired professional wrestler. While Maren was
buying an old leather-and-ivory backgammon set, Chesser
happened to look down the aisle. The huge man's eyes were
on Chesser for a moment. Merely a glance in a crowd.
Chesser thought nothing of it at the time.

Later, when they were coming out of Arethusa, where
they'd had a late lunch, Chesser again saw the man standing

across the street. This time he and Chesser exchanged a long look. Chesser decided he was being watched. The System immediately came to mind. He steered Maren down the street and then glanced back. The huge man was walking in their direction on the opposite side, but now seemed to be taking no special notice of Chesser. Merely a coincidence, after all? But if The System did have him under surveillance, Chesser wondered what the report might be. That he was seen in unbecoming attire consorting with the counter-culture? How many demerits for that?

"I've never been to Regent's Park," said Maren, "or the Tower of London."

"Which would you rather do? It's getting late."

"Both," she said, which was what he expected.

Moments later they were on their way in the Daimler. Chesser looked back several times. He couldn't see if he were being followed. Traffic was very heavy.

It was a half hour before they reached the famous medieval castle on Tower Hill. They paid their way in at the Middle Gate and paused at Tower Green, where an official guide gave his memorized version of how Anne Boleyn, Lady Jane Grey, and numerous others had lost their heads on that very spot. The guide's monotonous, bloody description intrigued Maren. Chesser had to pull her away.

She told him: "I once knew a model for Givenchy who claimed she was reincarnate from the soul of Anne Boleyn. I believe she was. She had a particularly long neck and was always sucking on throat lozenges."

They went into the Wakefield Tower and found the room where the crown jewels were displayed. Maren was less fascinated by the precious glitter of the royal scepter and crowns. Chesser directed her attention to the Cullinan I, the largest diamond in the world, weighing five hundred thirty carats. And to the Cullinan II and III. Maren tried to appear interested when Chesser told her these huge diamonds had all been cut from a single rough stone about the size of a man's fist. He talked on while she was preoccupied with retying her Mexican sashes, explaining that the gigantic diamond had been found by a mine superintendent who was making a routine check of the Premier Mine in South Africa. The superintendent had noticed sunlight reflecting on something embedded in the wall of a shaft and he'd dug it out with his pocket knife.

"And that made him a millionaire," remarked Maren indifferently.

"No. The company gave him a ten thousand dollar reward, for which he was very grateful."

Chesser thought she would react with some comment about corporate injustice, but she only combed her hair back with her fingers and said, "Let's go to Regent's Park."

At that moment Chesser looked past Maren. Standing near the entrance was the same huge man in black. The excuse of coincidence was now impossible. Chesser's immediate thought was to leave, to get to the Daimler and back to the hotel and pack and get to the airport and out of London, out from under the eyes of The System. No matter how adamant Maren was about staying. He'd invent some story for her. He knew if he told her he was being watched she'd only consider it exciting.

Maren read Chesser's face. She asked him if he'd had too much *paté* for lunch. He looked as though he needed an Alka Seltzer.

He left her standing there and headed for the entrance. Tell Meecham up his was what Chesser intended to say, but when he reached the huge man and looked up, his more realistic side took over.

"You're following me," said Chesser, with what he hoped seemed convincing indignation. If the man appeared huge at a distance, he was near gigantic at this closer range. His neck was at least a size twenty-two. Waiting for a reply, Chesser took a half-step back.

The man said nothing. Chesser noticed he had brown eyes, unexpectedly soft and expressive. The man seemed literally to be trying to speak with his eyes. The man's hands went into his suit-jacket pocket and brought out an envelope, which he offered to Chesser. There was nothing for Chesser to do but take it. A regular letter-size envelope of expensive, heavy-quality vellum in a creamy shade. Chesser saw his own name on its face, scrawled in a quick flourish by a broad-nibbed pen.

Then Maren was beside him wanting to know what was

happening. Chesser told her he wasn't sure. As she looked on curiously, he opened the envelope and found a note written in the same scrawl.

> I want to see you regarding a business matter. My man will call for you at ten A.M. tomorrow.
>
> Clyde Massey

Chesser didn't believe it. He looked up to demand some sort of verification. But the huge man was gone.

"Do you know him?" asked Maren.

"Never saw him before. Big son of a bitch, wasn't he?"

"Not him. Clyde Massey."

Chesser shook his head. "It's nothing," he said. "Probably a joke."

"Why?"

Chesser's question exactly. He didn't know Clyde Massey, though, of course, he knew of him. The world's most publicized billionaire. While others in that financial category usually preferred to remain as anonymous as possible, Clyde Massey flaunted his monied status. His name had become common reference, representing the richest, as had Rockefeller's. Although Massey seldom made public appearances, he was on view and quoted nearly every month in one magazine or another. Recently, a major television network had devoted an entire hour to a report on the man, including a film tour of his spacious estate, with Massey himself doing the commentary. Massey was American, forced to be an expatriate by the divorce courts. He'd been married four times, the last three items to much younger women. Alimony had made him escape to England. A matter of principle rather than parsimony, claimed Massey. But now his ex-wives could only wave court orders at him from across the ocean, out of legal range.

Maren took the note from Chesser. She fingered its blind embossed monogram. "Feels authentic," she commented. "But tomorrow's Sunday. We're not open for business on Sunday."

Chesser agreed.

On the way out, Maren crumpled the note and from a distance of ten feet tossed it accurately into a convenient City of London trash receptacle.

They went to Regent's Park and enjoyed wildflowers along the Broadwalk. Then they returned to the Connaught, planning to dress and go out to dinner. Instead, they undressed and loved and had a late supper at Trattoria Terrazza. Following supper they gambled at the Pair of Shoes. Maren lost nearly twenty thousand dollars. She claimed negative forces in the atmosphere were opposing her. They got back to the Connaught at four. They played one game of backgammon for fifty thousand dollars. Maren won, immediately turned away and fell asleep, content. Chesser had to get up to turn off the bathroom light and open the window a crack. He got back into bed, fitted himself against her, and sent a hand over and around, gently, to hold one of her breasts.

In moments his fingers went limp with sleep.

CHAPTER 5

The miniature travel clock said three minutes after ten. It was from Hermes, had a twenty-one-jewel Swiss movement and was encased in genuine baby alligator with platinum-and-tortoise trim. Nevertheless, it was running three minutes fast, for the time was precisely ten o'clock when the telephone's ring pulled Chesser to consciousness.

It was the desk. "Your car is here, sir."

"Don't want a car," said Chesser, sleepy thick.

"It's Mr. Massey's car, sir, calling for you."

"Massey?"

With that name Maren was suddenly awake. She leaped out of bed. "Tell him we'll be right down."

Chesser asked her why.

"We've got nothing better to do."

"We could sleep. Besides, we don't know who the hell it is. Probably not Massey at all."

"All the more reason," she told him.

Chesser shut his eyes tight as possible, trying to get awake enough to cope. He was also gritting his teeth. Maren was already in the bathroom, beyond dissuasion. Chesser heard her humming the fragments of some song.

He reluctantly told the desk, "We'll be a few minutes." He hung up and stumbled into the bathroom. She left the shower on for him, urging him to hurry.

Out of the shower, he found she'd gone into the other room to get dressed. He felt as though he were an unwilling contestant in a race. He didn't even take time to change the blade in his razor. He scraped his face raw and splashed on some aftershave that was like salt on his wounds.

She was already dressed. He rushed to catch up. She stuffed her Vuitton satchel with things they'd need, such as her make-up and a hotel towel.

"Where are your diamonds?" she asked.

"Downstairs in the safe."

"We'll get them on the way out."

"What the hell for?"

He was buttoning his fly. At least, trying to. He had the third button on the fourth hole. She kneeled and helped him. "If it really isn't Massey," she said, "whoever it is might be after your diamonds. It occurred to me yesterday."

"That's ridiculous."

"My intuition tells me. Anyway, if we don't have them with us we won't be able to hand them over."

"So, we'll leave them in the safe."

"I'd rather get robbed."

He had to laugh, because she was serious. "You'd rather get robbed?"

"There are those who make news and those who only read it," she recited.

The driver of the car was the same huge man in black. The car was a white custom-built Rolls-Royce, a four-door convertible with white antelope suede interior. A glass partition separated Chesser and Maren from the large man. Chesser found the button that made the partition descend.

"Who are you?" Chesser asked.

No reply from the huge man. Not even a look back.

"Tell him I want the top down," said Maren.

Chesser leaned forward to say it loudly.

The huge man had Chesser's face in the rear-view mirror. He pulled to the curb and stopped. He snapped loose a pair of chrome catches on the top of the windshield frame, twisted a small chrome knob on the dash. The top folded back electrically and concealed itself within a flush enclosure.

When they were underway again with the top down, the wind felt cold. Chesser hunched to escape it and Maren snuggled against him.

"I need some coffee," Chesser said.

"So do I. Tell him to stop some place."

"I can wait," said Chesser rather than ask.

Maren moved forward and pushed a button on the seat panel facing them. A shallow compartment swung open to reveal a pair of identical plastic vials containing red capsules and blue capsules, a carafe of Evian spring water, and a cut-crystal tumbler. The base of each was inset for balance.

"No coffee," said Maren, closing the compartment, "but it's warmer when you lean forward like this." She demonstrated and then slid off the seat onto the plush, carpeted floor. "It's even warmer down here," she claimed.

Chesser joined Maren on the floor. They didn't know where they were going and now they couldn't even see where. They could only watch the sky and tops of some London buildings, and every so often high branches of trees.

"I don't think they're after the diamonds," stated Maren, with a trace of disappointment.

"Maybe we're being kidnapped," suggested Chesser for her benefit.

"I thought of that."

"You're worth a big ransom."

"So are you."

"Me? Who'd pay for me?"

"Me," she promised.

They kissed, because that called for a kiss.

The white Rolls took them about 45 miles down the A-2, remaining in the right lane and passing everything on the road, including signs that said: Hindhead, Liphook, Cowplain, and

Horndean. Just before Petersfield the car left the A-2 for 18 miles of smaller road. Between the towns of Petworth and Fittleworth in West Sussex it turned off for another three curving miles. Then it stopped. At the main entrance of Clyde Massey's mansion.

The driver was quickly out of the car to open the rear door. Chesser and Maren achingly uncoupled and stretched. Chesser felt paralyzed and nearly went down as he stepped from the car.

Maren was giving the house a fast appraisal. It was constructed of mellowed brick, three stories, authentic Georgian. Accordingly, the structure appeared to have sunk solidly into the land. Its first-floor windows were just above ground level. The slanted roof was slate and there were numerous wide chimneys, signifying many fireplaces. The house was beautifully preserved or, at least, conscientiously restored. Certainly it was well kept; its white trim fresh. Maren estimated thirty rooms, which was ten less than the correct number.

The entrance door opened and a servant dressed entirely in black hurried out to relieve Maren of her satchel. She refused to surrender it. The servant led the way into the house, through an impressive center hall into a large reception room. Without a word he left them there.

That room was extravagantly decorated. Tasteful pretension. The furnishings were mainly French Regency, but there was some Adams and Sheraton, and touches of Italian Provincial. A Savonnerie carpet covered a section of the floor. An Aubusson tapestry was hung on one wall.

Maren sat on a velour-covered Louis Quatorze taboret. From her satchel she removed her make-up and placed it beside her. She also took out a large Mason Pearson brush and swiftly stroked her hair neat. Then she began doing her face, using the antique mirrored surface of a nearby low table for reflection. It was difficult because her face was inverted and she was rushing to complete herself. As she smoothed on a very light foundation, she asked: "What does he want to see you for?"

"Who?"

"Clyde Massey."

Chesser teased. "You think it's really Massey?"

"Of course. I knew it all the while." She glanced at Chesser to verify his reaction.

He used the brush on his wind-blown hair but it wouldn't obey.

"Try some water," she suggested.

Chesser found several cut-crystal decanters on a side table. One contained a clear liquid. He removed the stopper from that one and was about to pour some into the cup of his palm when he thought to confirm it. He sniffed. It was gin. He noticed a silver mesh covered siphon bottle. He pressed its release carefully but the charged water spurted out, causing some mess. He rubbed the fizzing water on his hair. He brushed as best he could and presented the result to Maren.

"You look like Nick Charles," she said.

"Who?"

"The old movie detective. I saw him on television when I was in America with Jean Marc. We used to stay up late and watch." She went back to her make-up.

Chesser mumbled that he didn't care if he looked like a slick Spanish pimp.

He went to get a close-up of the Aubusson while wondering why he was there, in Clyde Massey's house. He thought probably Massey had him confused with someone else. He touched his hair and hoped it would dry quickly so as not to look plastered down.

Maren just made it. She was putting her make-up back into her satchel when the door opened. It wasn't Massey, just the servant in black, who gestured politely for them to follow him.

They passed from that room through several others equally impressive. Along the way, glimpses of a Bonnard, a Monet, a Pissarro, a Degas, a Vermeer, a large Lautrec sketch. Finally they entered what was evidently a huge sun room, what the English call a winter garden. Sides and ceiling of small glass panes slightly vine-covered so that sunlight dappled the pink marble floor. The room opened out onto a wide terrace overlooking spacious grounds. The grass was as finished as a spread of fabric. One could see where it had been electrically clipped in alternate directions, creating a pattern of precise swaths.

There was Massey. Standing on the lawn about fifty feet

away. A lean figure dressed in a short-sleeved, light-flannel jumpsuit of a creamy color. His slip-on shoes were the same shade of patent leather, and a pale yellow scarf made a splash of color at his throat. He was standing in profile to Maren and Chesser, who remained on the terrace. Massey didn't acknowledge their presence but apparently knew they were there.

Massey was observing dogs. Four braces of dogs held on leashes by four men wearing light blue laboratory smocks. The dogs were being led to run a wide circle, obviously for Massey's benefit. They were exactly matched pairs: Labrador retrievers, Kerry Blue terriers, borzois, and whippets. At a signal from Massey their running was discontinued and they were held in place, forming an evenly spaced line. Each pair was brought to stand before Massey, who examined them all around. The whippets were the last. They were shivering. Massey pointed to the Kerry Blues. The man holding that pair smiled briefly but gratefully. Then all the dogs were led away on the run.

Massey then approached Chesser and Maren. He was still a half-dozen steps away when he extended his hand. He said his name. Chesser introduced himself and Maren, but didn't say Maren's last name, merely, "This is Maren."

She smiled her best smile. And when Massey reciprocated Maren noticed that his teeth were too perfect, either completely false or totally capped.

"What splendid dogs!" she said. "Are you getting them ready for a show?"

"That was a show," Massey told her.

"But the dogs are all yours, aren't they?"

"Yes."

"And you were the only judge."

He nodded, matter-of-fact.

She laughed lightly. "You couldn't lose."

He was quite serious. "I avoid competition as much as possible. Especially when it comes to such unimportant things." He read her thought. "Not that I fear losing in an open competition, mind you. It's just that losing would be my fault, not the dogs'. It would be merely because of personal resentment toward me, my money; a chance to beat me that hardly anyone would pass up."

"But what if you won?"

"Then I'd consider it sycophancy. Either way, the dogs would not be judged on their merits. As it was, the Kerry Blues received the award, and they deserved it."

"Did they get a blue ribbon, or what?"

"The trainer received a one-fifth increase in salary. A more tangible incentive."

Massey started them walking down the terrace. He was between Chesser and Maren, but favoring Maren. A servant came with a white telephone, playing out its lengthy wire from somewhere inside the house. Obviously a call for Massey, who refused it with a gesture.

"I'm pleased you could come and share some of this lovely day with me," said Massey, breathing deep and sounding sincere. "I seldom get up to London, except when the theater offers something special. Did you happen to see Paul Scofield in Chekov's *Uncle Vanya* last year—or was it the year before?"

Maren was annoyed. "I personally adore anything by Polanski," she said with a mock sincerity Chesser recognized and saw through.

"He does films, doesn't he?" asked Massey, and again didn't wait for an answer. "We have most of the better films sent down and shown here, of course. But the ones they're making these days I don't find very entertaining. They seem involved with such unpleasant little subjects."

"I suppose you've seen Polanski's *Macbeth*?"

"No, but I will now that you've recommended it."

"I haven't," said Maren.

That stopped him. "It's bad?"

"It's excellent," she said, and smiled innocently.

Chesser made no contribution to the conversation. He thought about the wealth walking beside him. Massey and Maren. He knew she'd never seen Polanski's *Macbeth*. They'd never both been in the mood for it. Chesser looked up to a fluffy, isolated cloud. His stomach complained.

By then they had reached a corner where the terrace turned around a wing of the house and continued to a more intimate area. There, in full sun, were bright-yellow and white lounging chairs, and, to one side, a table, set for four for lunch.

Yellow cloth, laid with English silver and eighteenth-century Moustiers faience.

They sat in lounge chairs, Massey opposite Maren. A servant came. Massey asked what they would like to drink. Chesser was about to say coffee, but Massey suggested champagne. Chesser liked champagne in the daytime only when he was alone with Maren, but he didn't decline. He wondered who would be the fourth for lunch. Or perhaps he and Maren weren't even expected and the table was set for other guests. Anything was possible.

Chesser stayed on the perimeter of the conversation, which was pure trivia. Now their subject was flowers. Chesser remembered when Maren had put an avocado pit in a jar of water and had been astonished when it sprouted. She barely knew daisies from violets. However, she seemed to be holding her own now by letting Massey do most of the talking.

Chesser contrived a politely interested look while he studied Massey. The famous billionaire was past seventy. His complexion was well tanned, but that did not hide the different pigmentation of many age spots. Massey's nose: narrow, long, and slightly irregular; perhaps it had once been trimmed. Massey's eyes: pale green irises, as though faded with time; the whites were as creamy as his jumpsuit. Despite his age, he transmitted a surprising virility. There was nothing cautious or strained about his movements. No doubt the man was still quite active sexually. That impression was also supported by his voice, which did not sound old. An energetic voice that demonstrated the enduring acuity of his brain. Chesser thought of Massey's brain and all that was recorded and stored in it. The only true history of Massey was in Massey's brain, including how it felt as a young man to out-maneuver Supreme Oil, to cunningly victimize that great power. Massey had been just a salaried employee of Supreme. His job was to travel around and buy up land after it had been secretly surveyed by Supreme's geologist. Based on the geologists' findings and using Supreme's capital, Massey would make the purchases on behalf of the company. Massey had some capital of his own. Not much, a few thousand he'd saved and twenty-five thousand he'd inherited from his grandfather. He waited until he received a geological report that was an absolutely sure thing. Highly confidential information regarding a section of apparently worthless, cheap land in

Oklahoma. Then he went in and bought the land for himself. Of course, the oil was there, and that was the big start. He was a millionaire in less than a week. Mighty Supreme could only shout with anger. Massey only grinned and counted. Now there were fleets of Massey tankers, six Massey refineries, thousands of Massey service stations, and solid agreements with the honorable sheiks of Kuwait.

Chesser knew the facts regarding Massey's beginning because Massey himself had made them public knowledge. Nearly every time he was interviewed, the subject would come up and Massey would tell the story with complete candor. Premeditated strategy to avoid the criticism that he'd been devious, which of course was the truth. What better way to evade an exposé? Besides, that he'd managed to put one over on Supreme was something most people considered admirable.

Chesser gulped the champagne. He thought perhaps this might be the longest day of his life. He noticed that each time Massey wanted to emphasize a point in the conversation he turned his palm up, as thought expecting one's concurrence to be placed in it.

"Evidently you're not interested in roses, Mr. Chesser."

"He's unusually quiet," said Maren.

"I'm hungry," said Chesser. It just came out.

Maren consoled him, her hand found the back of his neck for a few possessive strokes.

"We'll have lunch soon," Massey promised. "I must say I'm enjoying myself immensely with your Maren. I hope you don't mind."

"Not at all," lied Chesser, and thought, *my Maren.*

"Women and roses," announced Massey. "According to Thackeray, 'if a woman is beautiful who shall demand more of her? You don't want a rose to sing?' " Massey sat up higher, obviously feeling he'd just made the go-ahead point.

Chesser imagined how many women Massey had bought during the past ten years. He also wondered how much the price of admission had increased.

"I like better what Oscar Wilde said," contributed Maren, hesitating for effect. " 'The only way to behave toward a woman is to make love to her if she's pretty and to someone else if she's plain.' "

"Marvelous!" exclaimed Massey.

Chesser remembered an old country cart road near Chantilly in the middle of last summer, in the middle of a day, when they'd been walking and Maren had read quotations aloud. He particularly recalled that one by Wilde which she'd just repeated. He resented having to share it now, as though that reduced its value. Christ, Chesser thought, we've been into dogs, movies, flowers, and quotes. Next will come acquaintances and risqué stories. Massey's summons had said business. Why the hell didn't he get to it?

"Do you golf, Mr. Chesser?"

"No." Chesser was tempted to say he didn't hunt either.

"Nor do I any more. I don't go around. But I usually take a few swings before lunch. To stretch the body."

It could have been a deliberate cue, for at that moment the huge man in black who'd driven the Rolls appeared with a golf bag and clubs. Natural-antelope bag with calf trim. The shafts and faces of the clubs were of a gold alloy.

Massey said the huge man's name was Hickey. My man, was how Massey categorized him. Hickey smiled at Maren and Chesser.

Massey got up. Hickey set a genuine ivory tee into the grass, placed a pale blue ball upon it, and handed Massey a driver. Massey didn't take any practice swings. In practically one motion he took his stance and hit the ball solidly.

The pale blue sphere shot away straight, was lifted by the clear afternoon air and became a speck of blue as it fell far down the hill. Massey remained in follow-through position, watching it. An excellent shot for a man Massey's age.

Three more balls were teed by Hickey. Massey hit each straight to about the same spot. Then he came back to his seat and took a sip of champagne, glancing over his glass at Chesser and Maren. They didn't compliment him as he expected. He liked them more for it.

Maren requested more champagne, but a servant, standing aside, remained in place until Massey instructed him.

"Such singular loyalty," remarked Maren.

"Not really," said Massey. "He didn't hear you."

Maren was sure she'd spoken loud enough. She said so.

"He's deaf and mute," explained Massey. "As are all my

servants. You'd be amazed what a difference it makes in efficiency. They rely on reading lips and gestures, so they must always be attentive. And there are other advantages, of course. Such as peace and quiet. Nothing worse than a lot of babbling help around."

It occurred to Chesser that such an arrangement was also fine for secrecy. No overheard phone calls or ears against doors of rooms where private conferences were taking place. And perhaps just as important, personal sounds could be as uninhibited as desired, day or night. Massey glanced up at the sun. "We'll wait a while longer for her," he said.

Maren and Chesser wondered who *her* was.

Massey answered their minds. He had a way of doing that. Making a statement to create a question he could answer. He told them, "Lady Gaye Bolding is joining us for lunch."

"Is she a neighbor?"

"An associate," said Massey. Another of those suspended statements. He waited for the inquiry in their eyes. Then he explained that Lady Bolding's husband was an executive in the legal branch of one of his companies. "Spends most of his time in the Middle East," Massey informed. "Speaks fluent Arabic and practically all the dialects. But what makes him most valuable is he thinks like an Arab." Massey paused and forced a small smile in tribute to Lord Bolding. "He thoroughly enjoys his . . . work."

"And what does Lady Bolding do besides be a Lady?" asked Maren.

"For one thing, she helped me acquire this house and most of its furnishings. She's excellent at finding things."

Chesser pictured Lady Bolding. The image that came with the name was a dropped-breasted, stick-legged older woman, resentfully past her prime because she'd made such poor use of her earlier opportunities. She'd be English stuffy and over-consciously correct. Chesser hoped she didn't show up.

"She functions more or less as my personal assistant," said Massey. "You'll find her quite interesting." He directed that remark more to Maren than Chesser. He looked up at the sun again. As though it told him the exact time, he decided, "We won't wait any longer."

They took their places at the luncheon table. At last, grumbled Chesser's stomach, as the hand of a servant snapped a napkin and placed it across Chesser's lap.

Caviar came first. Two pounds of largest gray Beluga in a silver bowl in a bed of shaved ice. Maren and Chesser heaped large portions onto their plates. They ate it the way they liked it—by the spoonful without garnish of any sort.

Now Massey's subject was food. He referred to it as gastronomy, which made Maren realize it was astronomy with a g in front of it.

According to Massey, the earliest gods and goddesses were invented as a direct result of food. Primitive man required someone to thank when the harvest was good and someone to appease when it was bad. Food civilized man. Not until food became available in quantity did the family table come into existence. Before that there was little more than selfish, individual, animal grubbing.

What a boring old bastard, thought Chesser, devouring caviar and nodding politely just often enough. He resented being a captive audience. Massey or no Massey, he decided, they'd leave. Right after lunch.

"Do you play backgammon?" Maren asked Massey. An attempt to detour.

Massey merely shook his head and went on. It was a lecture. A soliloquy. The memorized ramblings of a self-proclaimed expert. Early gastronomy, Massey said, might have been the primary cause of the polarity of the genders, particularly responsible for woman's inherent hostility toward man, which is so manifest today. When prehistoric woman became burdened with advanced pregnancy, she was unable to participate in the hunt. Therefore, in keeping with atavistic rule, she did not deserve equal share of the food. All she could do was huddle in a corner of the cave and snarl and hope that man might be generous enough to toss her a bone. She had to be grateful for whatever she got. She was dependent. But dependent with a vengeance. Soon, of course, she learned to get her share by using her own more personal weapons. Anyway, it was quite possible that was how it all began. Said Massey.

Maren growled at Chesser and stole some caviar from his plate.

Massey continued. He hurdled millenniums in mere sentences. He went from the eating habits of the Pharoahs to the culinary genius of Curnonsky and Escoffier.

Maren was on her third portion of the Beluga.

"Apparently you enjoy caviar," remarked Massey.

He'd caught her with a mouthful but she didn't hurry her chewing. When she finally swallowed, she told him, "I'm addicted."

"They claim it has aphrodisiac qualities," said Massey.

"So that's your secret," exclaimed Maren, aiming her words at Chesser, who felt them ricochet and find Massey.

"In that respect it's much like Burgundy," said Massey. "They say the women of Burgundy enjoy that wine most when their men have drunk it."

Next came Tournedos Rossini. Filets of beef set on sautéed bread, capped with fresh foie gras, crowned generously with truffles, and covered with Périgueux sauce. As an accompaniment, there were artichokes à la Baligoure.

Chesser was encouraged, feeling better now that his appetite was being so luxuriously pacified. Also, as a consequence, his patience was being restored. Maren pilfered some of his truffles and begged forgiveness with a smile. Chesser pretended he hadn't noticed and forked a bite of filet into his mouth.

Chesser's position at the table gave him first sight of Lady Bolding's arrival.

She was definitely not the lady that Chesser had pictured. She was under thirty. A blonde with a tan that announced leisure. She was the perfect English example of the difference between being merely bred and, as they say, having breeding. During introductions, she offered a languid hand to Chesser. That same hand became more resolute when she offered it to Maren, who examined it a moment before accepting it. Lady Bolding apologized for being late, said she was glad they hadn't waited lunch and explained she'd been playing tennis. The game had been at match point for a maddening number of times, she said. She declined the caviar in a way that made one feel it represented expiation for her tardiness. She was served the tournedos, so they were all on the same course.

"I've seen you in fashion magazines," she told Maren. Her tone so obviously admiring that Maren nearly said thank you.

Massey placed his hand upon the hand of Lady Bolding.

His way of letting Chesser know. Chesser thought it was like an old leaf covering a flower.

Lady Bolding brought up Wimbledon. She advised Massey that a box had been arranged for the tournament. The same as last year, she told him.

Perhaps, thought Chesser, the reason he felt the lady was so attractive was that he had expected much less. He told himself that was it, while he appraised her and realized it wasn't. Lady Bolding's features were fine and ideally distributed. She wore a minimum of make-up. There was a trace of petulance to her mouth, and her large, brown eyes suggested they had something delightful to reveal. She was, altogether, very well finished. Her gestures were delicate, extremely feminine, but without affectation. She knew exactly what she was doing. What she was wearing, for example. Full-length silk chiffon, Bianchini in a floral pattern that was see-through enough to say she was proud of her bare breasts. The way she was sitting, nearly profile to Chesser, he could make out the perfect underline of her right one. The calculated transparency of the fabric invited eyes to steal and Chesser, that moment, was very much a thief. He projected the intimate experience her body conveyed in its movements and attitudes. Her voice, as well, multiplied that impression. At least it did for Chesser. She had the sort of voice most serious actresses achieve only after years of training. Resonance without effort, a quality that was both mellifluous and pure. Chesser imagined her saying something erotic. In this house of Massey's she could scream it. There was no one to hear. Chesser glanced at Maren and found her eyes fixed on him. She created a little mouth expression that said jealous.

The four discussed various things Chesser now found more interesting, such as the Mare Moda, a water-fashions festival held each year on Capri.

Finally, Lady Bolding announced that she was going in to freshen up. She invited Maren to do the same. The two women went into the house, leaving Massey and Chesser facing one another. It seemed the women were gone a long while. A servant cleared the table except for Perrier and glasses. Massey looked off down the hill, as though he were trying to identify something in the distance. He asked Chesser how long it had been since he was in the States. Chesser told him three or four years.

When Maren and Lady Bolding returned and were settled once again at the table, Massey reached into the upper pocket of his jumpsuit. He brought out two gems. He rolled them, like dice, across to Chesser.

"Which of these is genuine?" he asked.

Chesser didn't pick up the stones. For one thing, Massey had caught him a bit off balance, and obviously this was a challenge of some sort. They were finally getting down to business, he realized. He let the stones lie there on the yellow tablecloth. He estimated they were each about seven carats, round cut, identical.

"Can you tell?" challenged Massey, insinuating that Chesser couldn't.

Chesser fingered the stones, respectfully but nonchalantly. They refracted equally brilliant flares in the sunlight. He picked one up and pretended to examine it. Then the other. He wished he'd brought his loupe. That would have added a professional touch.

"Well?" said Massey impatiently.

"Tell him, darling," urged Maren.

Lady Bolding remained silent, amused.

Chesser took his time. "I'd like some crème de menthe," he said. "Clear. And a tall glass."

Both were brought immediately. Chesser filled the glass with the liquor. Maren snickered. She thought he might drink it. Chesser placed the two gems in his palm and, with some minor ritual, dropped them simultaneously into the glass of crème de menthe.

The gems descended slowly in the viscous, syrupy liquid. One reached bottom before the other.

"That one," announced Chesser.

"Which?" asked Massey.

Chesser poured most of the liquor from the glass and picked out the gem that had descended more slowly. Crème de menthe dripped from its facets and his fingers. He rinsed them in a glass of Perrier, dried with his napkin, and handed the gem to Massey.

Massey had no way of knowing if this gem was the real one or not. He told Chesser that.

"The other stone is man-made," said Chesser, "probably strontium titanate, which has a specific gravity about one-third greater than a diamond. That's why the diamond lost the race to the bottom."

"Impressive," conceded Massey. But he was still dubious. Chesser could be inventing all this, putting on an act. "What if I told you they were both diamonds," said Massey, intimating that might be the case.

"They're not," said Chesser.

"There's a way of checking?"

Chesser removed the other gem from the glass. He rinsed, dried, and offered it to Massey. "Just scratch this one with that one," he instructed. "Of course, if they're both diamonds, you'll probably ruin one or the other, possibly both. It's a chance you'll have to take." Chesser was very confident. Now he was challenging Massey. Chesser knew the real stone was worth close to forty thousand dollars. It had excellent color and appeared very well cut.

Massey didn't hesitate. He took the stone from Chesser and scratched it harshly with the one he'd had. He looked at both and saw Chesser was right. The man-made gem was badly marred. The diamond not at all damaged.

"I congratulate you, Mr. Chesser." He threw the man-made stone over his shoulder. He tossed the diamond to the lap of Lady Bolding, who didn't even acknowledge it.

Massey sat back. It seemed a concluding movement. Chesser felt it was, but then Massey told him: "I want you to acquire a diamond for me."

Massey allowed time for Chesser's questions to form.

"No," he replied to Chesser's silence. "I don't want an already-famous jewel taken from the eye of some jungle idol. What I want is a new stone."

"How large?"

"What would you suggest?"

"Depends on how much you want to spend."

"Million and a half."

"Dollars?"

"Dollars."

Chesser felt the base of his spine glowing. Massey was serious.

"I want a quality stone, mind you. Perfectly cut. Big enough to become known as the Massey."

It came to Chesser that he might not be able to handle the deal. Here it was, falling right into his pocket, and he couldn't handle it. Because he'd have to lay out the money in advance for the rough stone and also pay for the cutting. He didn't have enough capital for that. He probably wouldn't collect anything until he delivered. Massey was overestimating his financial ability, thought Chesser. Evidently, Massey thought he was somebody like Whiteman.

Again Massey seemed to be tapped into Chesser's mind. "I'll give you a certified check for the full amount," he said, "today, before you leave. I'm sure in the million and a half there'll be some profit for you."

Chesser was also sure of that.

"Now," sighed Massey, rising, "let's all take a walk down through the orchard. The apple trees are still blooming."

Two hours later they were at the front of the house. The rear door of a Rolls was open. Hickey was standing by. It was a different car, a black custom saloon. Chesser and Maren were about to leave for London.

Massey took Chesser aside. He gave him the check, which was folded once. Chesser knew better than to look at it then. He inserted it into his jacket pocket.

"By the way, Chesser," said Massey in a low, covered tone, "you should realize something."

Chesser sensed a change in Massey. The two men were eye to eye.

Massey said, "All that running off at the mouth I did about women and flowers and food was nothing but bullshit. Understand?"

Chesser knew the Massey he now faced was the true Massey—competent, powerful, cool, and direct, laying it right on the line.

"I understand," said Chesser.

"I was concerned with your control," said Massey. "That was the thing."

They shook hands and went to the car. Maren was already

in the back seat. Chesser said his good-byes to Lady Bolding, who gave him an accepting smile as her parting grace.

"See you in a month," said Massey.

Then they were on their way. Chesser took out the check and looked at a million and a half, certified, made out to his name. Incredible.

He wanted to show it to Maren but money was the farthest thing from her mind.

She asked: "You think she's more attractive than I?"

"No. Definitely not."

"That's good. Because when we went in the house to freshen up, she kissed me."

"She didn't."

"She did. Right on the mouth, tongue and all."

"Really?"

"No. But she wanted to."

He had to laugh. "You're incorrigible."

"And intuitive," said Maren.

Massey remained in front of the house and watched the Rolls go out of sight. Well, he thought, that's phase two. He was very pleased. Phase one had been choosing the prospect. Phase two had been to determine whether or not the prospect had what it would take.

Massey was quite sure he had his man.

CHAPTER 6

The following day was one of those bad-looking London days with a thick threat of rain hanging over everything.

Maren got up at ten, glanced outside, and retreated to bed, covering her eyes with her hair.

Chesser called The System. He was told Meecham wasn't in. They wanted to put his call through to Berkely. Chesser didn't want Berkely. He got the same treatment when he called again, and it wasn't until his third try that the secretary said Mr. Meecham had just arrived. Chesser knew that was a lie.

Meecham came on. "Yes, Chesser, what is it?"

"I want to request a special sight."

"Impossible."

"I have a buyer for a large stone," said Chesser.

"Who?"

"That's confidential."

"What do you consider large?" asked Meecham sarcastically.

"Let's start with two hundred carats."

Chesser enjoyed saying that, especially the way he said it, as though he dealt with stones that size every day. Chesser saw three benefits in this opportunity. He could make a large profit. He could gain some respect from The System. And he could indulge in some personal retaliation. Right now his special pleasure was twisting Meecham's mind a bit.

"Two hundred?"

"For starters," said Chesser.

"You're in no position to handle a stone that large."

"I can handle it."

"You're talking about a sizable transaction, you know. It'll have to be in cash, as always."

"I can handle it in cash."

"You have a buyer, you say?"

Meecham was after the buyer's identity again. Chesser didn't go for it. He let his silence tell Meecham that.

"Come in around two thirty," said Meecham.

"Around two thirty?" Chesser emphasized the first word, letting Meecham know that such an approximate appointment was preferential treatment he'd not been granted before.

"Two thirty," snapped Meecham.

Chesser was tempted to tell him that four o'clock was more convenient, but he really couldn't afford to be too impertinent. He needed The System. They had the stones.

In the bedroom he saw that Maren was still drowsing. He said her name once, softly, and when she didn't stir he let her be.

He went out to the bank. The London affiliate of his bank in

Geneva. Presentation of the certified Massey check got him swiftly to the private desk of one of the bank's directors. Chesser told him what he wanted: to deposit the check into his Geneva account in dollars and be able to draw whatever he might need up to that total to cover a transaction here in London. The director said it would take only a day to arrange that.

Out of the bank and on the street, Chesser decided he'd walk back to the Connaught. He dismissed the Daimler and went up Regent Street with a step that matched his sense of well-being. He looked at almost every store window and felt in a buying mood. It was noon and many girls were out from offices. Chesser was very receptive. He thought there were more pretty girls than ever and he got a few reciprocal glances. He turned off Regent and went down Maddox Street, where he stopped in at a small shop to purchase a Victorian locket intricately engraved and enameled, with the appropriate initials *MC* entwined. After another half block, the rain started. No warning sprinkles from the sky. It let go all at once. Chesser's gray suit was spotted with dark drops. He took to the shelter of a doorway. He thought it might let up soon, but it was really coming down. He waited five minutes, which seemed like an hour, and then went out in it.

He had five blocks to go. In half that his shoes were squishing and his trousers sticking to his thighs. When he approached the Connaught he looked as though he'd fallen overboard. The doorman rushed out to rescue him with a huge white umbrella. Silly bastard, thought Chesser, but gave him a big tip anyway.

Chesser didn't expect Maren to be gone. She'd eaten her breakfast and left him a note.

Deserter!
I'm going to get the works at Sassoon's. Call me there if you can't avoid trouble.

He got out of his wet clothes and took a warm shower. By then it was one thirty. He thought about doing his *I Ching* but he didn't have any coins, and the valet had sewn the buttons back onto his navy suit jacket—fortunately, because now he needed to wear it.

*   *   *

He arrived at number 11 Harrowhouse Street a few minutes early. He remembered to let the door be opened for him by Miller, who, in his usual friendly manner, told Chesser he was expected to go directly to the sight room.

Chesser went up, believing he'd find Meecham already there, but the room was empty. He took a seat at the velour-covered table. He anticipated Meecham's entrance at any moment, and to create a blasé impression sat with his back to the door. He heard it open and close, heard footsteps coming to the table. He brought his eyes up. It was Watts.

"Good afternoon, sir," greeted Watts. He was carrying a black container proportioned like an ordinary shoebox, about half the size.

"Hello, Watts."

Watts was opposite Chesser now. He placed the box on the table. "I'm to show you some stones, sir."

"Won't Mr. Meecham be here?"

"No, sir."

Chesser felt cheated. He might never get another chance at Meecham. At least, not like this. He wanted to walk out. He was angry enough, but this wasn't the kind of business where you could take your business elsewhere. He thought of demanding that Meecham conduct the sight, but there was Watts and perhaps Watts would take that as an insult.

Fuck it, thought Chesser and smiled at Watts. "What have you brought for me to see?"

"Three stones altogether, sir," said Watts rather proudly. He removed the lid from the box and transferred three large, rough diamonds to the velour surface in front of Chesser.

Chesser put his loupe to his eye. He picked up the first stone.

"That's three hundred seventy-six carats, sir," informed Watts.

Chesser sighted into it. He knew what to look for but he thought he saw all sorts of things he shouldn't. The trouble was he wasn't accustomed to such large stones. Size created an entirely different dimension, it seemed. He couldn't determine whether the stone was good quality or not. He thought it had a great many feathers and carbon spots. From one angle the spots appeared to be inconsequentially on the edges, from another angle they looked deep and spoiling. Chesser wished he knew more.

He couldn't afford to make a mistake. Not this time. He started to sweat. Now he was glad Meecham wasn't there.

Watts said nothing all the while Chesser examined the three stones. He sensed Chesser's predicament.

"The one in the center, sir," said Watts.

"What about it?"

"Excellent color."

Watts was trying to help. He knew more about grading diamonds than anyone else in The System, or so Chesser had heard. But Chesser wasn't sure he could trust the man. Conceivably Meecham was trying to unload that particular stone on him. Via Watts. Chesser decided he didn't really believe that. He picked up the stone and examined it again. It was the smallest of the three, more rectangular, about three-quarters of an inch deep, a little more than an inch wide, and one and a half inches long.

"Two hundred five point sixty carats," said Watts. "I put a window on it."

Chesser located the small, polished area that allowed him to sight deep into the stone. He saw it was clear white, no devaluating yellow, and apparent imperfections.

"How do you think it will cut?" asked Chesser.

"The grain is right for an oval. If you don't mind my suggestion, sir."

"Not at all."

"You should finish with a perfect stone about half the weight. Perhaps a little more. Anyway, a real good one."

Chesser had to ask: "If it's such a winner, why's it still around?"

"It just came in with the shipment from Botswana. Even Mr. Meecham hasn't seen it yet."

Chesser believed him.

"My only instructions from Mr. Meecham were to show you a few stones in this size range, and I thought you'd particularly like this one. Of course, it may not meet your requirements."

"What's the price?"

"Seven hundred thousand."

Chesser listened to his intuition. "I'll take it," he said quickly. Watts's smile told him he'd made the right decision. Chesser was grateful.

"Shall we complete the transaction, sir?"

"Tomorrow. I'll come by with a certified check."

"If you prefer, we can deliver the stone to you. I can bring it around myself."

That appealed to Chesser, not having to come to number 11 again tomorrow. He told Watts that would be fine. "I'll have the check ready."

"What time tomorrow?"

"How about in the afternoon, say around two?"

"Very well, sir."

Chesser felt he owed something to Watts. He wanted to do something to show his appreciation. The only thing possible at that moment was to extend his hand for a shake. Watts was a little embarrassed by it. He hesitated and glanced toward the door uneasily. Then he took the hand that was offered.

Of all the people Chesser had met in The System, Watts was lowest on the official ladder. But Chesser liked him most.

At that instant, two flights above, Meecham was in a closed conference with Edward Coglin.

Coglin was head of The System's security section, a private police force whose routine responsibility was to guard number 11. It did so with such efficiency that there had been only one relatively inconsequential incident in the past twenty years, and none at all since Coglin took over. This admirable record allowed The System to conduct its precious business at number 11 with a high degree of confidence. Naturally, it was difficult to prevent past perfection from creating some complacency, a certain smugness.

Along with its regular protection duties, Security Section also performed another more extensive and complicated service, known only to those within the nucleus of The System itself. It functioned as a highly organized intelligence unit, employing, on an international scale, many of the tactics of contemporary espionage. It gathered and compiled in its computerized memory banks information on everyone in the world having anything to do with diamonds.

Especially kept under constant or intermittent scrutiny were those dealers who were regularly invited to attend sights.

Such as Chesser, even though he was far down the list.

It was extremely important to The System to know as much as possible about these men, their professional behavior and financial limits, as well as their comings and goings, habits and weaknesses. The System used this knowledge to predetermine precisely what amount and quality of diamonds it should include in each man's packet.

When all the information gleaned by Security Section was pieced together, The System was presented with an incredibly accurate picture of the world market, allowing it to cut down or increase the flow of diamonds accordingly.

Security Section did not operate out of number 11. With its massive electronic equipment and computers it occupied a separate building just across the way on Harrowhouse.

Thus, Coglin had come over for the conference with Meecham. The two men seldom faced one another as they did now.

"We haven't been on him," said Coglin.

"Apparently," said Meecham.

"Hell, there was no reason to be. He's small stuff. Always has been."

"Well, he's gotten into something big. While we weren't looking." Meecham was chastising, but with restraint.

Coglin resented taking any blame. He didn't have to. He'd been an inspector with the Yard, a good one, until The System offered him much more. Right from the start he'd seen the potential. Now, after fifteen years, Coglin was a living memory bank of everyone's activities, particularly their transgressions. An international string of informants, as well as his personally chosen staff, nourished the strength of his position. There were those high in The System who looked down on Coglin. They disliked him for his obscure background and lack of polish; however, they feared what he knew and what he might know. He was, so to speak, the J. Edgar Hoover of diamonds.

Coglin was a chunky, short man in his fifties, half Irish from his mother's side. The other half was probably also Irish, but even his mother wasn't sure. He had close-set, small eyes, a flat face, with a nose that must have been hit hard a number of times. One of Coglin's advantages was that he was more intelligent than he appeared.

Now he told Meecham, "We were never asked for more than a routine on him."

Meecham acknowledged this with a nod. He was glancing through a dossier. "Anything in here?" he asked.

"Only thing a bit off was back in sixty-six."

"What about that?"

"He has the money still tucked away in Geneva. Hasn't touched a penny."

"What's your opinion?" Meecham closed the dossier.

"Could be the girl. She's rich enough to buy herself a treat. Maybe that's all there is to it."

"I doubt that. By the way, what does she look like?"

"There's a snap of her in there," said Coglin. He leaned across, opened the dossier, and located the photograph for Meecham, who studied it for a full minute but made no comment.

"Well," Meecham concluded, "what we don't know we can find out, can't we?"

"You want him put under special?"

"Just to satisfy my curiosity."

"Remember that next time the board meets on budgets," said Coglin, and got up to go. As an afterthought, he mentioned Barry Whiteman.

"What bout him?"

"He was supposed to go back to New York day before yesterday, but he changed his mind."

"He's still in London?"

"Paris now."

"Why?"

"Not for the culture, I'll tell you. He took his own along with him. Tall, mean-looking bird."

Meecham, pretending indifference, busied himself with the daily report of production from Namaqualand, as Coglin, suppressing a smile, turned and went out.

"I'm sorry, the circuits to Antwerp are busy."

"Try again in a half hour."

Chesser was back in the Connaught suite. He felt good

about the diamond. Now he was after a cutter. There were more than fifteen thousand cutters in Antwerp, but Chesser was going for the best. Wildenstein. Chesser would feel safe with Wildenstein, though he doubted he could get him. Second choice was Kornfeld, but he wouldn't try for Kornfeld until Wildenstein was definitely out.

Chesser hardly dared consider the possibility that neither of these famous cutters would take the job. He was glad he didn't have to go through this every day. He doubted he could handle that, although people like Whiteman seemed to thrive on it. Perhaps, thought Chesser, one becomes habituated. The win big, lose big syndrome.

He called down for some Scotch. He also called Sassoon's for Maren. He was told she wasn't there, hadn't been, although she'd had an appointment. That worried him because it was unlike Maren to not do what she intended.

Chesser could only stay there and wait. The Scotch came but it didn't help. He tried reading yesterday's newspaper.

Shortly after five the phone rang. Ready with his call to Antwerp. Wildenstein was on the line.

Chesser introduced himself as best he could long distance, and was about to get into the proposition when Maren came in. She completely disregarded the fact he was on the phone, went right to him and kissed him on the mouth, a long kiss that left Wildenstein believing he'd been cut off. Wildenstein kept repeating hello's with increasing irritation.

Finally Chesser was free enough to talk again.

Wildenstein asked him what he wanted.

"I have a diamond I'd like you to finish for me."

"One moment, please. I'll see."

Chesser heard Wildenstein lay down the phone. He pictured the renowned cutter. Once, in Antwerp, Wildenstein had been pointed out to him. A scholarly looking man with a black beard. A Hasidic Jew in a long, black coat and black hat.

Wildenstein came back on the line. "Maybe in August," he said.

"I need it done now."

"I can't do it."

"I promised delivery in a month."

"August is all right."

"It's a two-hundred-carat stone. First quality."

Wildenstein hesitated, and Chesser felt encouraged.

"You bring it and I'll look at it for August," said Wildenstein.

Chesser decided. He had to risk insulting Wildenstein with an offer that would be buying him. "I'll pay a hundred thousand for the job," said Chesser.

"A hundred thousand what?"

"Dollars."

"That is too much."

"It's worth that much to me."

"You come to Antwerp."

"Does that mean you'll do it?"

"I need to see the stone."

"I will be there tomorrow afternoon. How late will you be at your workrooms?"

"I will be here," promised Wildenstein.

"Thanks. It means a lot to me."

"We'll see. We'll see when you come." Wildenstein said good-bye and clicked off so quickly Chesser didn't have a chance for another word.

It sounded as though he had Wildenstein. For a hundred thousand. Chesser believed it was worth it. Wildenstein would appreciate the stone. Chesser figured to clear seven hundred thousand dollars on the deal. The amount made him feel greedy, but he soon got over that when he realized that, actually, everyone was making out well. The System was getting seven hundred thousand for a stone that some black mine worker had dug out of the ground for mere pennies. Wildenstein was getting a premium hundred thousand, probably as much or more than he'd make on any stone he'd ever cut. And Massey was getting a perfect gem for which he might have to pay as much as two million dollars retail. So Chesser's profit was relatively justifiable. It equaled what he could make in seven years from The System's routine packets. Unless, of course, his packets were increased in value. That was a possibility, he thought, now that this deal was on record.

He went into the bedroom, thinking he'd tell Maren he was almost a millionaire.

She told him, "Oh, God, I'm famished. I didn't have lunch, just a cup of dreadful tea."

She'd just undressed, had everything off but her shoes, and that made her very good legs look even longer and better. She walked across to the dressing table for a pack of cigarettes. At least that was her excuse. She lighted two and, as usual, tossed him one, which sailed right by him. While he was picking it up off the rug, he thought he heard her say: "I talked to Jean Marc today."

"Huh?"

"I had a nice long talk with Jean Marc."

"Sure, you just ran into him on the street."

"In a way. I happened to see a card on one of those notice boards outside a tobacco shop. I was guided to it."

"By the Chinaman or the Indian?"

"One or the other." She sat on the edge of the bed. "Anyway, the card was put there by a medium. Her name is Mildred. She's a dwarf."

"A small medium," said Chesser.

Maren was too serious to smile. "Instead of Sassoon's I went to Mildred for a reading. She was incredible. She got right through to Jean Marc."

"Want to go out for a sandwich someplace, and then maybe to a film?"

"Jean Marc's very happy. He really likes it on the other side."

"Yeah. Everybody's dying to get there."

She disregarded his cynicism. "He said to say hello to you."

"I've got to go to Antwerp tomorrow," he told her, still trying to divert her. "You want to go with me or straight on to Chantilly? I can meet you in Chantilly, if you'd rather."

"One thing Jean Marc said really surprised me. He said we ought to get married. Imagine that."

Chesser imagined and thought Jean Marc ought to try getting that message through to his vulture lawyers, who were hovering around ready to get their beaks into the money. Or if Jean Marc was in such an altruistic mood, why didn't he simply dematerialize the original and all existing copies of his stupid will?

"Maybe we should," said Maren thoughtfully.

"Get married?"

"Meet in Chantilly. How long will you be in Antwerp?"

"A couple of hours."

"Then I'll go with you," she said. "You don't believe in Mildred, do you?"

"Sure. Why not?" he said, rather than argue.

"She doesn't even charge for a reading."

"Really?"

"If she charged she'd lose her power. That's what happens when mediums commercialize. Their power gets taken away."

"Who takes it?"

"The great cosmic force," she said, not as sure as she sounded. "You should see the depressing place where Mildred has to live. I felt so sorry for her. I gave her fifty pounds."

"She sacrificed fifty pounds worth of power."

"It was a gift. She's allowed to take gifts."

Keeping her eyes on his, Maren fell back onto the bed, her elbows supporting her, her legs still over the side.

Allowed to take gifts, thought Chesser. There was her intersection, made more prominent by her position, her fine nutmeg-colored floss offered up.

Afterward, he also gave her the locket.

CHAPTER 7

Watts delivered the diamond as promised.

He brought it in a small manila envelope in his jacket pocket, which was as safe a way as a bonded messenger in an armored truck, for no one would have thought this very ordinary-looking man could possibly be carrying anything worth seven hundred thousand dollars. He hadn't even taken a taxi; he'd come via the underground.

Chesser removed the diamond from its tissue wrapping and examined it, more to appreciate than verify it. He'd already given Watts a certified check.

"*Mazel* and *broche*," said Watts.

That was Hebrew for luck and blessings, the traditional phrase used throughout the diamond business by Jews and non-Jews alike. To seal a deal. Once spoken, the phrase officially bound a man to his word, and although it was not necessary for this transaction, Watts said it to convey his feelings. He got up to leave.

Chesser urged him to stay for a brandy, or whatever he preferred.

"I have to be getting back," said Watts.

"To hell with them," said Chesser. He poured the brandy, assuming Watts would stay. "Soda or water?"

"Soda, thank you," Watts said, and sat again.

The two men were alone in the suite. Maren had gone shopping. Chesser suspected she'd end up at Mildred's for another conversation with Jean Marc.

"How long have you been with The System?" asked Chesser, to start on common ground.

The question didn't warrant the charge of expression that came to Watts's eyes. "Twenty-eight years."

"Always here in London?"

"Five years in Johannesburg. Have you ever been to South Africa?"

"No."

"I began in Johannesburg."

Chesser thought Watts seemed depressed. Or it could have been bitterness. Perhaps the man felt used.

"Does Meecham know which stone I bought?" asked Chesser.

"Yes. He inquired yesterday afternoon, after you left."

"And?"

"He wasn't very happy about it. Gave me a lacing, actually. Said he'd rather someone such as Whiteman got that one."

Chesser was delighted to hear that. He'd gotten to Meecham, after all. But at Watts's expense. "I appreciate your help yesterday," said Chesser. "I'd like to show that somehow."

"No need, sir."

Watts used his empty glass to ask permission to help himself to more brandy.

"Really," Chesser told him, "I'm grateful for what you did."

"I was glad to do it," Watts said. Definitely bitter this time.

He was immediately self-conscious that it had come out so obviously in that tone.

"Why?"

Watts covered. "No particular reason, sir. I merely hoped you'd choose that stone."

Chesser nodded, but he saw through that half truth. He was intrigued. He speculated that perhaps Watts resented where The System had him after twenty-eight years' service. Certainly The System must consider Watts a valuable employee, but maybe Watts had higher ambitions. Chesser had some of that same resentment, although, of course, Watts's situation was different. Watts was staff. And loyal, too. At least until yesterday's minor act of dissension.

Chesser noticed Watts was downing the brandy too fast to be enjoying it. It was vintage very superior old pale and deserved more respect. Not that it mattered, really. Watts could pour the whole damn bottle in his shoe for all Chesser cared. It occurred to Chesser that he could at least share some of his feelings with Watts.

"I've never much liked the way The System does things," he said.

Watts nodded politely, but didn't comment.

"My last packet, for example," said Chesser with a short, derisive laugh.

"They're not always as fair as they could be," said Watts. He looked down, as though The System was there at his feet. "Granted, they've got to have regulations, but there's something to being human as well."

Chesser agreed. He remained silent, to encourage Watts to talk.

"Take this friend of mine," said Watts. "Been with The System just short of thirty years. January last the doctors at St. George told him he had cancer. Terminal. Nothing to be done about it. Scheduled to die before the year is up."

Watts stopped. Evidently that was all. Chesser didn't see how it was pertinent to The System. He put the question.

Watts was reluctant to explain, but he wanted to more than not. "The System has a thirty-year death or retirement benefit for all employees. My friend will die about a year short of the required thirty, but The System won't make an exception. My friend's family needs looking after, and there's not enough insurance. The wife's not well and there's also a daughter depending on him."

"He explained all that to The System?"

"Yes, of course. They were sympathetic but also said their thirty-year rule meant a full thirty years."

"The bastards."

Watts agreed with a thoughtful nod. "It required consideration by the board of directors, who decided to make an exception in this case, a generous compromise is what they called it."

"That was white of them."

"Twenty per cent is what they allowed. Perhaps adequate by their lights, but it doesn't seem right, does it? All those years for only twenty per cent of the benefits he was counting on. But I suppose big business must be run to form."

Chesser reviewed the words he'd just heard, how they'd been said, and was convinced the friend with terminal cancer was Watts. Kindly, Chesser changed the subject. He picked up the diamond. He said, "Wildenstein is going to cut it."

"That's marvelous, sir." Watts seemed genuinely pleased.

"He'll probably do an oval. That's what you suggested, isn't it?"

"Yes, sir," replied Watts modestly.

"I'd like you to see it after it's been cut."

"I'd enjoy that, sir."

"Tell you what. Leave me your home phone number. I'll call you when it's finished."

"When will that be, sir?"

Chesser was glad he didn't have to say next year.

Before nightfall, Chesser was at Wildenstein's workshop on Hoplandstraat in Antwerp. Maren preferred to wait in the limousine, more interested in reading a book entitled *Life Before Life and After Death*, which was a gift from Mildred. Chesser had said he'd be with Wildenstein a half hour, or an hour at most, and suggested Maren might use the time to see some of the city. She'd never been in Antwerp, but she'd already seen enough of it on the way in from the airport. She thought it looked bored stiff with itself. It seemed drab and unhappy. Maren was unaware that less than a hundred feet from where

she sat, just around the corner, was the house and studio
where the great master Peter Paul Rubens had answered his
call to the colors. And Van Dyck, as well, for some time, in
that very same house. Maren calculated that Chesser, knowing she was just waiting in the car, would take care of his diamond business more quickly.

Maren needn't have been concerned, for when it came to
business Wildenstein was a man of few words. Chesser found
him on the second floor of his workshop, sitting on a blue
enameled stool beneath a glaring, bare light bulb. He was
reading a Hebrew newspaper and sucking the juice from the
core of an apple he'd just eaten. He remained seated when he
saw Chesser, and, while Chesser introduced himself, Wildenstein calmly folded the newspaper and slid it into his coat
pocket. He asked to see the diamond.

He examined the stone under the illumination of a
Diamondlite, which provided an artificial light equivalent to
northern exposure on a clear day. He studied it for five minutes without saying a word.

"A beauty, isn't it?" asked Chesser.

Wildenstein merely nodded. He placed the diamond on a
nearby counter surface.

Chesser brought out a certified check for one hundred thousand dollars. He placed it next to the stone on the counter surface. Wildenstein looked at it. He picked up the diamond and
placed it on top of the check.

"Very beautiful," said Wildenstein. However, Chesser didn't
know whether he meant the diamond or the check.

"It has to be finished by the first of next month," said Chesser.

"Three weeks," said Wildenstein.

"Does it have enough depth for an oval?"

"Is that what you want?"

"Whatever is best."

Wildenstein scratched the side of his nose. He blinked several times, as though to clear his eyes. He squeezed the fingers of his left hand with those of his right. He returned to his
stool and sat. Out came the newspaper.

Chesser had hoped for more enthusiasm, at least more discussion. He wanted to hear Wildenstein say the stone was
going to cut into the most exquisite jewel he'd ever touched.

But, evidently, all that was going to be said had been said. Except good-bye. Chesser said that, along with a reminder that he would return on the first.

As he was leaving, Chesser felt the need to turn for a final look at Wildenstein. When he did, he found the old cutter's eyes were on him.

"Don't worry," advised Wildenstein, and resumed his reading, right to left.

During the next three weeks, Chesser thought as little as possible about the diamond. At times he was almost able to forget it completely. The town of Chantilly, old and small and easy, made that other world of Meechams and Masseys seem no more than a residue of memory.

Maren's house was not in the town proper but a short distance out, situated on its own private acres of land off the north road to Senlis. Jean Marc had left other houses to Maren. Those in Paris, Antibes, and Deauville, for instance, were larger and more luxurious. However, whenever Maren mentioned home, Chesser knew she meant the house at Chantilly. Built in the late seventeenth century as a royal hunting lodge, the house was actually used by certain members of the royal court less for the pursuit of game than for personal fun and games. Accordingly, what they in their style categorized as a lodge was by no means rustic. Rather, the structure had the pleasing lines and proportions of a relatively small château, and its twenty rooms were planned and decorated in a manner that verified its hypothetical purpose without sacrificing any creature comforts.

It was not difficult to picture the past: the carriages arriving from Paris with the necessary provisions, which were, of course, the most desirable choices of the court. Some of these young ladies had already been measured and found to be of adequate spirit. The others were indeed ready to experience initiation. All anticipated the delights of the chase. On the first pleasant afternoon, according to the rules, the pretty young things were sent scurrying into the woods in various directions, disrobing as they ran, leaving a trail of silks and laces and linens for the royal hunters. High hairpieces were knocked awry by low-hanging branches. Dainty slippers were left in the crotches of trees. Stockings streamed from the tips of saplings. And when the last, the most intimate of their female attire was left to mark the way, they themselves prevented the possibility of escape by revealing their locations with little cries of despair. Finally, feigning fatigue, each collapsed upon some carefully selected bed of moss or leaves, and waited to be overtaken. The stalkers were soon upon their quarry, whose ecstatic shrieks often frightened away such guileless creatures as birds, rabbits, and, sometimes, a doe.

Maren contended that some of these merrymakers still inhabited the house and its grounds. In their spiritual forms, of course. She claimed she could literally feel their presence. Once she found a length of pink ribbon in the woods and considered it to be a supernatural confirmation. The girls were still playing around, she claimed.

It was a provocative thought, that those lovely libertines and their gallant counterparts were scampering about the place. Certainly the premise was inspiring enough to make one want to believe. It didn't matter, really, that the ribbon found by Maren had actually been left there unintentionally just a few days before by a young girl of the town, who, while lovemaking, had released her long hair to please her partner. Maren did not know that, and even if she had, she would have said the girl had been prompted by the pervasive spirits.

Maren called London and asked Mildred's opinion. Mildred heard the facts and promised to ask around. An hour later, the little medium called back collect and confirmed Maren's perception. Yes, the spirits were there in considerable number. Mildred had communicated directly with several, particularly one named Simone who revisited every year from April to late September. Not more than a hundred yards from the house was a mossy glade where Simone had, with delightful compliance, taken and given her first with none other than the Monarch himself. An experience Simone could not repeat, naturally, but one so exquisite that she was irrepressibly drawn back to the place. Said Mildred.

The following day, without explaining to Chesser, Maren arbitrarily chose a direction and made him count off a hundred paces into the woods. Coincidentally or not, it brought them to a moss-covered spot. Maren was overjoyed. She circled the small area, respectfully. She transmitted some silent, sisterly communion to Simone, and received feelings she translated as invitation more than impulse.

Maren removed her shoes and placed them precisely on the peak of a jutting rock.

Chesser asked what she was doing. She didn't reply, so he shrugged and leaned against a tree to watch.

Next, she took off her skirt and blouse and, with some care for arrangement, draped them over a dipped bough. All that remained were her bikini panties. She got quickly out of those, bent a young, pliant tree and placed them on its highest point. She released the tree and the panties were swished up out of reach, high, like a guiding pennant.

Then she lay face down on the spread of moss, motionless for a long moment, pressed by her weight against the natural cushion. There was the sensation of countless tiny curls of touch. And her own of nutmeg color at her intersection coiled among those of the green.

She rolled over slowly, her eyes and her mouth open. From her came a prolonged sound of helpless submission. Her Viking hair fanned out around her head. Her legs arched up left and right and relaxed apart.

It was time for Chesser to get into the act. And he did. With appropriate spirit.

If the sybaritic Simone was observing them from her invisible vantage on the other side, no doubt she approved. For, naturally, it was quite exceptional.

Almost daily thereafter Maren made long-distance calls to Mildred, who soon got the picture and relayed directions. It seemed there were a great many mossy beds and grassy bowers within easy pacing distance from the house; ideal, lovely places, just waiting to again be put to use with the permission of a Geneviève, a Dominique, a Françoise, a Beatrice, a Sylvie, or Danièlle.

After a dozen days of such renascent behavior, including one twilight in a chill rain, Chesser looked forward to the more customary comforts of sheets and man-made bed. He didn't mention that to Maren. However, she shared that feeling because the previous time out, in the nice lap of an open field, she just happened to catch sight of a pair of farm boys peeking and ducking over a bordering rock wall. By then, of course, it was a bit late to feel self-conscious. Actually, much later than either Maren or Chesser realized, for there had also been another, more deliberate eyewitness to all their outdoor intimacies, an expertly quiet little man with a powerful long-distance lens on his 35-mm. Nikon camera.

From then on Maren and Chesser did their lovemaking indoors. Mildred validated that decision, conveying a message from the spirits, who said they were bored with the whole thing anyway. They were, after all, the type of souls prone to ennui. Said Mildred.

One night Chesser and Maren went into Paris for a soirée at the home of an acquaintance. They both had secretly looked forward to it as a sort of relief, but, after less than an hour of exposure to all the practiced remarks and thinly camouflaged unhappiness, they were eager to escape and went rushing back to Chantilly feeling even more grateful for one another.

Another morning, two Citroen-loads of lawyers arrived at the house with documents requiring Maren's signature. Chesser thought the lawyers all resembled rodents cautiously eyeing a big hunk of cheese and trying to devise some way of snapping it out of the trap. They were cordial to him, for he was, after all, their most promising means to a lucrative end. Maren invited them to stay for lunch and, when they expressed polite hesitation, she abruptly accepted that as their refusal and suggested a vague "some other time."

After the lawyers had departed, Maren and Chesser walked into town, down rue du Connetable to the Relais Conde, where they enjoyed double helpings of cold tiny crawfish taken from the local canal. They sipped Cassis and discussed such things as the universal need for contraception and the merits of various sports cars. Maren informed Chesser that she'd ordered a special Ferrrari 365 GTB and asked him to remind her to call and inquire why it hadn't been delivered as promised. From the Conde they went home the long way, around the Château de Chantilly, paying a franc each for entrance, and it was worth every sou because, as they walked by the moat, they witnessed the splashing, flapping, beaking mating of a pair of swans, one black and one white. It appeared more combative than amorous.

Nearly every night Chesser and Maren played backgammon. She threw many pairs but misjudged her advantages and doubled carelessly. As a result her gambling debt to Chesser increased to nearly two million dollars. Quite earnestly, she told Chesser she was going to have the lawyers issue him a check, because it was as valid an obligation as her account at Cardin or Saint Laurent. She was serious at the time but, apparently, it slipped her mind.

On the twenty-fifth, Chesser called Antwerp.

Wildenstein told him the diamond was ready.

"How does it look?"

"Fine," replied Wildenstein.

"How many carats did it finish at?"

"Come see and get it."

That same afternoon, Maren's new Ferrari was delivered. It was a convertible, deep blue in color, with a boldly designed body and enough horses under the hood to qualify for the Grand Prix circuit. She wanted to drive it immediately and Chesser knew it was hopeless to try to dissuade her. He thought she might at least take it slowly until she'd gotten the feel of the powerful car. But no. She started with a snapping getaway and put the machine through an excruciating test run over the narrow, unpredictable country roads. She handled the Ferrari as though it had always been hers, and when Chesser warned that she ought not put such a strain on the engine until it was properly broken in, she pointed to a temporary sticker on the windshield which stated that the car had already been run the prerequisite distance. Chesser, unable to think of another excuse, could only make sure their safety belts were fastened and pray nothing was coming around the blind curves.

CHAPTER 8

Everything was coming together nicely. Chesser could pick up the diamond in Antwerp, then go on to London and The System for his next sight. They had notified him by cable that his next appointment at 11 Harrowhouse Street was scheduled for Monday, June first, promptly at ten A.M. Underline promptly. While in London, Chesser planned, as promised, to let Watts have a look at the diamond before delivering it to Massey.

Maren's first suggestion was that they use the Fokker-28. The private jet belonging to the estate had been in repair but now it was ready to go. The pilots were always on stand-by. But her second thought, and the one that stuck, was to drive her new Ferrari 365 GTB. That would be more personal, she said, more leisurely. Chesser didn't agree but he consented when Maren assured him that she'd let him do some of the driving.

The decision to drive meant a change of plans. Instead of Antwerp-London-Massey, it was now much more convenient to make it Antwerp-Massey-London. That excluded Watts, but Chesser rationalized that perhaps Watts had expressed interest in seeing the diamond only out of politeness. Anyway, he'd explain to Watts when he was at The System.

The only problem was having to call Massey. Chesser had thought he wouldn't call until he'd seen the diamond and was absolutely sure it was right. Massey didn't expect delivery for at least another two weeks, but Chesser was anxious to get the deal over and done with. Out of courtesy, he had to let Massey know when to expect him.

He called.

Massey sounded pleased to hear from him. "You've seen the diamond?"

"Of course," lied Chesser.

"How is it?"

"Fine," said Chesser, borrowing from Wildenstein.

"How big?"

"Over a hundred carats." Chesser hoped it was.

"Then you'll be here the day after tomorrow?"

"Yes. We're driving."

"By we I assume you're bringing your Maren along?"

"She'll be with me."

"Good. It's only an hour or so from Lydd to here. Have you ever driven southern England?"

"No."

"It's a nice drive."

"I'm looking forward to it."

"See you Wednesday."

"Wednesday."

That's one hell of a great client, thought Chesser, as he dropped the phone receiver back into place.

From Chantilly to Antwerp is only about two hundred miles. However, until recently it was a long day's drive, an obstacle course of small towns. Maddening. But now the Auto Route du Nord is completed all the way to Lille, and from there on it's good Belgian highway. Another convenience is the speed limit. There is none. Only the rule that slower vehicles must remain in the right lane, leaving the left clear for those with the power.

So, once Maren got the Ferrari into high, she just stomped the accelerator to the floor and blasted everything out of the way with her horn. At first she enjoyed it but then she got bored and wished there were some corners to amuse her. When Chesser glanced over and saw the speed indicator at two hundred kilometers per hour, he had to fight against his impulse to tell her to go slower. After a while he became accustomed to the motion, and when a stubborn Peugeot blocked the way, slowing them to a mere one fifty kph's, Chesser felt they were crawling along.

They roared into Antwerp by early afternoon. On Kasteel-

pleinstraat they stopped long enough for Chesser to leave off
his previous packet at his usual brokers. No haggling. He didn't
even wait for payment, merely instructed the broker to credit
his account. It didn't amount to much anyway, and Chesser
was a bit self-conscious about that. From there they went on
to Hoplandstraat and Wildenstein's shop. Maren again preferred to wait in the car.

While Wildenstein got the diamond from his safe, Chesser
tried to read the old cutter's expression. It said nothing.
Wildenstein might as well have been going to the cupboard
for a piece of candy. He brought the stone to the Diamondlite
and offered Chesser the use of his loupe. An encouraging personal gesture, thought Chesser, who was surprised that his
own hand wasn't trembling as he held the stone.

Chesser sighted through the loupe and the diamond hit him
with its blaze. He'd never seen such brilliance. Even the
slightest movement caused the stone to shoot out dazzling
flares of rainbow hues. Actually, the stone itself had no color.
It was clear as water, as only the very best diamonds are. It
was oval shaped, and Chesser saw the table and facets of its
crown were in perfect relation to its total depth. Its pavilion,
the lower part of the stone, was also perfect. He turned the
stone slowly and appraised its most extreme outer edges. If
there was a cutting error, that was where it would be most evident—on the girdle. He saw that the edges there were smooth
and symmetrical, as they should be. Wildenstein had truly
lived up to his reputation.

"A beautiful make," complimented Chesser, referring in
the jargon of the industry to the diamonds correct proportions,
its finish and polish and the symmetry of its facets.

"One hundred and seven point forty carats," said Wildenstein.

Chesser continued sighting into the stone, hoping he
wouldn't see any spoiling inclusions. He didn't. "It looks
flawless," he said.

"It is," said Wildenstein, matter-of-fact.

Chesser straightened, relaxed the muscles around his eye
and dropped the loupe into his right hand. Over a hundred
carats flawless, his mind shouted. He felt like doing a tap
dance. He felt like hugging Wildenstein. He felt like kissing

that beautiful bearded old man. He restrained himself, and told him, "Congratulations."

Wildenstein accepted that with a nod. He took the diamond and dropped it into a small, soft, woolen drawstring sack. He pulled the strings tight and knotted them once. He handed it over to Chesser. Official fulfillment of his obligation. He also gave Chesser a little brown envelope containing fragments left over from the cutting.

Chesser was so enthused over the large stone he'd forgotten the fragments. Perhaps twenty-five or thirty thousand dollars worth.

"Thanks," said Chesser, genuinely grateful.

They shook hands.

Wildenstein almost smiled. "Don't worry," was again his only final advice.

Maren had the motor running. Chesser thought of suggesting they have a relaxing lunch some place there in Antwerp, but Maren couldn't get out of that city fast enough. She didn't stop until the third small town, where Chesser went into an ordinary bistro and got some Brie and sausage sandwiches and a bottle of chilled Chablis. To go.

They chewed and gulped straight from the bottle and sang Bacharach songs all the way to Ghent. It was the same road they'd come north on and the shortest way was to keep going farther south on it. But Maren turned off and headed across Flanders toward the coast.

Then they were on a road that offered more curves and Maren was relieved by that. Up to now she'd felt like no more than an engineer on an express train, but now she could use the gears some and feel integrated with the car and its course. Even when she took a curve a bit too fast and the car fishtailed precariously, Chesser didn't complain. He was so elated that danger seemed a suitable accompaniment. All he could think of was how he had it made.

He had, right there in his pocket, one of the world's great diamonds. He'd pulled off a deal worth seven hundred thousand dollars profit. He had The System in a position where now they'd have to respect him and come up with bigger packets. And he had Maren, with her long Viking hair in the wind and her dependable passion for him. Life was beautiful, big, capital letter *B*.

He took out the soft woolen sack and removed the diamond. Held it up, and it converted the sunlight into vivid, energetic glints. He called Maren's attention to it.

"Pretty," was all she said, inside a quick smile, and handed him her sunglasses with a request that he clean them for her.

In a short while they reached the coast. They bypassed Ostend and headed down by the North Sea, back into France again, past Dunkirk and Calais. The day was going and the damp air was chilling, but neither wanted to have the car's top up. They reached Montreuil-sur-Mer just before dark. They stayed in the best room of an expensive inn. For dinner they had platters of shellfish taken that day from the sea, and warm, fresh bread, and butter. Also some local cider that tasted much more innocent than it was.

Afterward, they didn't make love. They fell asleep thinking about it.

The next morning they were early enough for the first air ferry from Le Touquet. But the ticket clerk at Aeroport Paris-Plage informed Chesser no space was available on the first plane. What about the next one? No, there was nothing until one thirty that afternoon. Nothing? Nothing.

Chesser reported that to Maren.

She asked, "Did you wave money at him?"

"Of course," Chesser lied.

She thought a moment and then left him with the car. In less than ten minutes she returned with tickets for the first flight. She let Chesser believe she'd easily corrupted the French ticket clerk. Actually, she hadn't even tried. Just by chance, she'd found a pair of English hippies who were going home with their Mini Cooper only because they'd run out of money. They were delighted to exchange their places on the first flight for Maren's five hundred francs.

So the Ferrari was run up the nose ramp and into the belly of the transport. Maren and Chesser were in the passenger section, which seated only a dozen. The bulky plane lifted off and its frame seemed to twist under the strain of the turn it made to head toward England.

*   *   *

Back in the airport, there was a telephone call being made from a public booth to The System. Person-to-person to Coglin.

"He got on the first ferry, somehow."

"So why the hell aren't you on it?" Coglin wanted to know.

"There weren't any more places. He got on at the last minute."

"You're saying you've lost him?"

"Looks that way."

"Get a private plane and pick him up again on this side."

"Too late for that."

"Well, no doubt he's headed for London anyway. We'll get onto him here. Was there anyone with him?"

"Just the girl."

"Are you sure?"

"I'm sure."

"All right, come home."

"I take it you received the photos."

"They're a bit overexposed," said Coglin with a chuckle.

In half an hour Maren and Chesser were through British customs and the Ferrari had been cleared. Maren reluctantly surrendered the driver's seat to Chesser, who asked her to keep reminding him to drive on the left. Maren noticed that now they were traveling over the sort of roads she preferred; narrow, snaking, challenging. But she had promised Chesser he could drive some of the way. She thought maybe in a few miles she'd talk him out of it. She smoked and sulked and watched the countryside. She read aloud a sign that amused her because it announced the way to Fukham. She hummed parts of various songs. She got the *I Ching* from her satchel and, using the back of the book for a surface, tossed the three five-franc pieces she'd brought for that purpose. But two of the coins rolled off and fell between the seats. She wasn't in the mood to retrieve them.

"Let me drive now," she said. "Please."

Chesser let up on the accelerator. He downshifted.

There was a blinking amber light on a tripod in the middle of the road. A warning. With ordinary caution he steered around the next bend and a short straightaway presented itself.

Apparently the road was being repaired. A line of blinking

amber lights on tripods blocked the left lane. There were two men in fluorescent orange coveralls. One was signaling the Ferrari to stop. The amber lights were strung out all the way to the next bend.

Chesser figured traffic was probably being allowed to flow alternately in the right lane. But he didn't see any cars coming. He glanced over to Maren.

She was hunched forward, the *I Ching* book in her lap. She was staring straight ahead, as though her eyes were fixed on something unusual.

It never occurred to Chesser that anything was wrong. He merely looked to see whatever it was that had Maren's total attention. It was then he felt the sharp pain on the back of his shoulder. Like a hornet sting. And, immediately, a strange warmth flushed up to his scalp and down to his toes.

He tried to speak.

That was the first thing he found he couldn't do. His mind sent words to his throat but his throat wouldn't open and his tongue wouldn't work. He tried to bring his hand to his mouth but his hand disobeyed completely, remaining where it was. He couldn't turn his head. He couldn't move his legs. He couldn't even blink. His entire body was immobilized.

He wondered if perhaps he'd suffered some sort of sudden paralysis. A terrifying thought. But his head seemed too clear for that; no dizziness, not even a headache. He had a peripheral view of Maren, and she also seemed to be frozen in position. What the *hell* was happening? He could see, he could smell and hear. All his senses were normally sharp. But he couldn't move.

The two men in fluorescent coveralls were coming to the car. They'll help, Chesser thought. They'll notice something is wrong and help somehow. Maybe there is a hospital nearby, or at least a doctor.

One of the men opened the car door on Chesser's side. He switched off the ignition. Chesser tried to communicate with his eyes. The man looked right at him but didn't seem to get the message. Then a third man appeared from somewhere behind. The third man had a rifle. It looked to be a twenty-two-caliber with some kind of device attached to its breech. What the hell was a road worker doing with a rifle?

The man with the rifle reached to Chesser's shoulder and

withdrew something. Chesser saw it was a tiny dart with feathers and a point no longer than a push pin. That explained the sting he'd felt. Another man took a similar dart from Maren. What was it?

Chesser thought of something he'd seen recently on television: a documentary film on the black rhinoceros, how scientists in Africa were able to tag the ears of those ferocious animals. They used rifles to shoot darts carrying some sort of drug that temporarily immobilized the rhinos. Chesser recalled a portion of the film that showed a drugged rhino's eyes close up. Vicious anger exploding against the inability to express it. But what the hell, this was England and he wasn't a rhino.

One of the men searched Chesser's jacket pocket. He found the drawstring sack and removed the diamond from it.

No! Chesser silently protested. A burst of violence, full-force rage with no outlet.

The diamond went back into the sack and the sack went into the pocket of the man's coveralls. Then a truck with proper official markings wheeled into the open lane and stopped. Methodically, the men gathered up the blinking lights and tripods and put them aboard the truck. All the way down the road, until the way was completely clear and they disappeared around the bend.

Chesser and Maren could do nothing but sit there. Two cars passed. One came on them so fast it had to swerve to miss the Ferrari. The driver swore but didn't stop.

It had been perfectly planned, precisely timed. Obviously by someone who knew he had the diamond. Who? Chesser considered the possibilities chronologically, starting with Massey. He eliminated Massey on the basis of lack of motive. It was Massey's diamond. In another hour Massey would have had it. The System? He was tempted to put the blame there but logic told him that was ridiculous. The System had no reason to steal diamonds. They had diamonds. Next was Watts. Chesser felt sure Watts was incapable of such a thing. And the same applied to Wildenstein. However, along with Wildenstein came a possibility. Perhaps someone in Wildenstein's shop, one of the assistants, was an informant. Had, for a percentage, told professionals about the diamond. Those men in the fluorescent coveralls knew what they were doing.

Very professional. They'd probably tapped his phone conversations, knew exactly where he was going and when.

As remote and complicated as it seemed, that was the most likely explanation. Someone in Wildenstein's shop.

So what?

The realization that he really had nothing substantial to go on, that he'd never recover the diamond, hit Chesser hard.

Then came the big question: What to tell Massey? Massey was expecting the diamond that afternoon. Chesser had already told Massey he'd seen it and it was fine. There was no reason not to deliver. And if he didn't deliver he was ruined, thought Chesser. Massey would see to that. It would get to The System and there'd be no more packets. The name Chesser would be off the list forever. Everything was at stake.

Chesser thought maybe he could stall Massey. Go to The System for another diamond. Go through the whole thing again. Another diamond? This one had cost eight hundred thousand, including the cut. What he'd have to put out for another would just about break him, but it might be worth it. Maybe he could do it. He'd need cooperation from The System, Wildenstein again, and more patience from Massey than Massey probably had.

Chesser was desperately grasping for any solution.

He realized that and started feeling sorry for himself.

"I can move my toes," said Maren. Evidently now she could also speak.

Seconds later she had totally recovered.

"You look like a statue," she laughed.

Chesser needed sympathy, not ridicule. He felt like clobbering her but still couldn't move. Maren got out of the car and stretched, unperturbed, as though she'd just had a nice nap.

The effect of the drug was also leaving Chesser.

"They weren't very competent highwaymen," said Maren.

"They weren't highwaymen," said Chesser, glad to hear his thoughts spoken again.

"They didn't steal my purse, my virtue, or anything."

"Shut up!" snapped Chesser. He hadn't been that sharp with her since their one and only argument.

Maren came around to him. She smoothed the hair on his temples. "Poor love," she consoled.

"They got the diamond," he said, to hear it.

Chesser decided they might as well go on to Massey's. The best thing to tell him was the horrible, no doubt incredible truth.

Maren was driving now. She took a bumpy corner too fast. All four wheels left the road for a moment, then came down, shuddered and grabbed and went around. Maren glanced at Chesser for reaction.

Part of him didn't care if they went off a cliff.

CHAPTER 9

Massey presided. Behind a specious Directoire desk, beneath a Settecento chandelier, in front of a wide trompe l'oeil panel. On the ample surface of the desk were only three small objects: a gold and malachite Fabergé egg, an old Georgian watch, and a monogrammed Tiffany fountain pen, gold, circa 1930.

Lady Bolding was seated in a plush chair placed at an angle near a large window, allowing her attention to seem divided between indoors and out. She was holding by its stem a huge shocking pink peony, occasionally pressing the multipetaled bowl of the blossom to her nose but also including her mouth.

Maren was nonchalantly exploring the room, which was designated as Massey's second-floor study.

While Chesser related details of the highway robbery, Massey's eyes were steady on him. Not once did Massey look away, nor did he comment or indicate his reaction. So Chesser had nothing for measure along the way. He told it all exactly as it had happened, and when he'd gone over it once Massey still said nothing.

Nervously, Chesser began repeating himself and finally Massey broke the spell.

"I assume you carry insurance to cover theft," he said.

"No, I don't."

"Isn't that unusual?" asked Massey, implying stupidity.

Chesser had to admit that. His only excuse was he'd never handled anything big enough to warrant paying the big premiums. He hadn't even considered insuring this diamond. The deal had come together so swiftly and had looked so easy.

"What about The System?" asked Massey.

"The System?"

"Don't they help in such cases?"

Chesser was mildly surprised Massey knew about The System. Most people didn't. He supposed, though, that big business knew big business. Chesser was resigned to The System eventually learning how badly he'd mishandled this deal. However, he reasoned there was no need to invite their attention. He told Massey, "It's not their responsibility."

Massey seemed to accept that. "So what do you intend to do?" he asked.

"I'll keep my part of the deal."

Massey's eyebrows went up.

"But I'll need more time," Chesser added.

"We had a verbal contract," said Massey. "As valid as a written one."

"I know."

"You were advanced a million and a half in good faith. Now you can't deliver."

"I'll deliver."

"When?"

"In three to four weeks."

Massey compressed his lips. His fingers had the fountain pen, unscrewing and tightening its cap. He shook his head slowly. "You were to deliver," he said.

"I will."

"The point is you haven't. I'm unbending about commitments, Mr. Chesser. When we agreed on delivery in a month you could have disagreed. If you required more time you should have said so then. I'm not an unreasonable man." He sighed an old sigh. "Now my better judgment tells me to get out of the deal. You can return the amount I advanced, and that will be that."

That will be impossible, thought Chesser.

"Fair enough?" asked Massey.

"No."

"You think I'm being arbitrary?"

"Yes," replied Chesser, right at him.

Massey smiled. It was the last thing Chesser expected.

"We could notify the police," suggested Lady Bolding.

Massey quickly vetoed that with a glance. He asked Chesser, "What would you have me do?"

"Give me more time to come up with another diamond."

"I envy your ability to squander time." Massey picked up the old Georgian watch. He wound it and checked it against the one by Cartier on his wrist. Perhaps there was nothing more to be said. Finally he broke the silent tension. "Your theory is these men on the road were professionals and that someone in Antwerp provided them with information?"

"That's right."

"Perhaps. Who in Antwerp?"

Chesser shrugged. "Someone at the cutters."

"Do you know how difficult it would be to prove that connection? It's a flimsy conjecture at best. And even if it were true, even if we established evidence, would that get us the diamond back?"

"Maybe."

"Really?"

"I doubt it," Chesser had to admit.

"How would the thieves dispose of such a diamond? Quickly, of course, but how?"

"Sell it privately. Have it recut so it couldn't be identified."

"Why should they worry about identification? You're the only one who's seen it."

"And Wildenstein, the cutter."

"Hardly a multitude. Did you have the finished stone photographed?"

"No"

"You certainly know how to protect yourself, Mr. Chesser."

Chesser just took it. He had it coming.

"Describe the stone to me."

"It was an oval. Around a hundred and seven carats."

"On the phone you said it was fine. I believe that was the

word you used. By that I assume you meant it was first quality."

"I've seen better," lied Chesser.

"Then it wasn't perfect?"

"Not quite."

That set Massey back a bit.

Chesser reasoned that an accurate description of the diamond would only further irritate Massey. Better to depreciate the diamond some. Accordingly, he invented two flaws in the stone. "Carbon spots," he said.

"Doesn't sound worth owning or stealing," Massey said.

"Most large stones have minor imperfections," explained Chesser.

Massey jumped on that. "Another breach of our contract. My stipulation was a perfect diamond."

"Nature isn't always so obliging."

"But ignorance is," snapped Massey.

Chesser thought it best to say no more.

Massey turned away, completely away. Chesser looked over to Maren, but she was absorbed in a book she'd taken down from the bookcase. She was on the floor, sitting cross-legged. As usual, she found anything more interesting than diamonds. Chesser wished now he'd listened to her. To hell with being ambitious. He noticed Lady Bolding was now plucking the petals one by one from the peony and dropping them into her lap. From Chesser's point of view, Lady Bolding had a shocking pink crotch. He squinted to diffuse and heighten the illusion. He preferred to look at that rather than the back of Massey's old neck.

Still turned away, Massey asked, "What if our positions were reversed?"

Chesser answered truthfully, "I'd demand the money or the diamond."

Massey liked that.

He did an abrupt about face, revealing a much more agreeable expression. "Actually, Mr. Chesser, to be fair, I suppose you're a victim of circumstances. The more I think about it the more I feel you deserve perhaps a better shake. At least some effort should be made to recover the diamond." He hesitated thoughtfully. He touched the Fabergé egg gently with his forefinger. It spun a few times and then wobbled to rest. "There's an investigating firm in London, a good one, that does work for me occasionally. I'll put them on it and see what they come up with. Anyway, no harm in trying."

Chesser was thankful for any hope.

"Meanwhile," continued Massey, "I suggest you and your Maren stay on here. Relax a bit until we can get the matter settled one way or the other."

No choice for Chesser.

"I'd enjoy a swim," said Maren. Evidently, she'd been paying closer attention than Chesser had thought.

"I'll see that your luggage is brought up to your rooms," said Lady Bolding.

Chesser noticed she'd said rooms, plural.

"Splendid!" said Massey to everyone. Then, right at Maren, he said, "You swim and I'll watch."

Several giant willows hung around the pool area, drooping as though from ennui. The pool was set apart from the main house and was enclosed on three sides by luxuriously appointed and fully equipped cabanas. The rectangle of water was shaped by small Portuguese tiles resembling lapis lazuli, creating the more inviting illusion of pure and brilliant liquid blue.

Alone in one of the cabana rooms, Chesser found a selection of new swimming trunks. He chose a pair youthfully low cut. He couldn't stop blaming himself. He had the urge to smash the mirror because it reproduced him. He heard the laughter from the adjoining cabana. Maren and Lady Bolding.

Their gaiety irritated him. He was removing his socks and he threw one against the wall. It hit noiselessly. He should have thrown a shoe.

He went out and found Massey was seated at one end of the pool, like a monarch awaiting his subjects, the spread of water impeccable at his feet. Massey waved at Chesser to join him, but Chesser pretended he didn't see and went to a corner of the pool at the opposite end.

The surface of the water was undisturbed. Chesser shoved a foot in to test its temperature and splashed twice to spoil its perfection. He walked around to the other side and sat on the edge, to dangle his feet in. He glanced at Massey and wondered if the old billionaire might be offended by his remoteness. Chesser didn't give a shit. He noticed the nearby diving board and the adjacent higher diving platform. He thought of a ridiculous solution. He could go off the high platform, come up faking back injury and sue Massey for a settlement. But, hell, he had no reason to blame Massey. Massey was a fellow victim, if not an equal loser.

More of Maren's laughter from the cabana. Bitterly, he improvised a delicate figment of what might be going on in there and, for punishment, tried to believe it. He felt abandoned, isolated with his dilemma, quick to disparage anyone to relieve his misery a bit. Even Maren. He'd had a nice clean easy shot at a fantastic deal, and he'd botched it. By just not playing it carefully enough. Chesser thought how Whiteman would have handled it. Whiteman would have sat back and counted the profit while the Queen's royal mail took responsibility of delivering the diamond via registered package. Chesser knew why he hadn't done that. Ego. He'd wanted to be there for a moment of personal glory when Massey first saw that perfect, beautiful stone.

Massey should have chosen someone else to deal with, thought Chesser. He wished Massey had. Why, in the first place, had Massey chosen a Chesser for something so big? Instead of a Whiteman, for example? Chesser had wondered about that. For lack of any other explanation he'd made himself believe Massey was just giving him, an underdog, a break. But now that answer wasn't acceptable. There had to be more to it, Chesser realized. Massey had been altogether too easy on him, too readily cooperative about the loss.

Lady Bolding came from the cabana. Wearing a minimal white bikini. She walked effortlessly to one of several soft-cushioned lounge chairs and tossed her sunglasses onto it. She was very sure of her body and had every right to be. It was ideally proportioned, trim, with a tension that conveyed strength and activity. Her stomach appeared tight as a drumhead and her waist defined itself, easing deeply but softly inward. She shook her head to make her long, blonde hair swish loose.

From across the pool, Chesser, in his mood, tried to find some imperfection in her. He couldn't. But he remembered

Maren's insinuation about Lady Bolding's erotic preferences and he thought about that to diminish her impact.

Then Maren came out. In contrast to the sun-darkened flesh of Lady Bolding, Maren was creamy-pale in a bikini of black. She came to the edge of the pool and smiled whimsically at Chesser. He acknowledged her with a half-hearted wave. She turned abruptly to show him that the back of her bikini bottom was designed with a cut-out about the size of a large apricot, revealing that much of her right ass-cheek.

Chesser managed a broad but uneasy smile.

"Don't forget me," shouted Massey.

Noblesse oblige. Maren turned and received Massey's approval.

Chesser imagined he could hear the older man's eyes clicking like a camera.

Lady Bolding joined Maren at the edge of the pool, and after setting themselves they dove in together. Excellent, nearly identical dives that sliced the water and caused only the slightest splash.

They swam underwater. Chesser saw Lady Bolding approach the side of the pool to his right, make a neat turn and spring off to shoot herself back toward the other side again. Maren came up at Chesser's feet. Her hair was darker, wet, and adhering in strands.

She threw him a kiss with her lips. "Come swim with me," she invited brightly.

Chesser shrugged.

"Hey," she said. "I love you."

"I know."

Their eyes held for a moment, seriously.

She had been hanging onto the edge of the spillwater but now she playfully took hold of his left leg and tried to pull him in.

He braced and resisted.

She stopped pulling. She imitated his scowling face. She got his right foot and brought it to her. He thought she was going to kiss it, but she clamped a bite, sharp enough to make Chesser grimace and nearly cry out. "Crab!" she said.

She swam back across the pool, got out, and flopped face down on one of the cushioned loungers.

Meanwhile, Lady Bolding had been swimming, cutting the water with strong, meticulous strokes. Now, she also got out, squeezed the excess water from her hair, wiped her arms and legs respectfully with her hands, and lay on the cushion nearest Maren.

Chesser watched Massey get up and go over to the two women. There was some conversation, but Chesser couldn't make it out. A servant brought tall red drinks in frosted glasses. Chesser made no move to join them, Maren and Lady Bolding sipped, but Chesser wasn't invited over and the fourth glass, his, remained on the tray on the table. By now the water in the pool had calmed and become smooth again.

Chesser got up. He went to the diving board, walked out on it to the end. He hesitated. He'd never been a good diver. It looked like a long drop to the water. He was sure they were watching, expecting him to perform a damned jackknife of something. He sprung and went up and out and came down like a thrown log, making a smacking sound and a tidal wave compared to Maren's and Lady Bolding's neat entries. When he came up he thought he heard the trailing fragments of laughter.

He swam, beating the water with his hands and kicking the hell out of it with his legs. The opposite of Lady Bolding's bladelike grace. He swam with eyes open, alternately getting the sky and the tiled bottom of the pool as he turned his head for gasps of air. He did one length and another and a third and fourth and one more than he'd intended. He climbed out, using the chrome ladder instead of a more athletic pull-up on the edge.

He thought he felt better. His breathing was short and heavy, but at least some of his mental tightness seemed eased.

He'd join them now, he thought; go over and have his drink. He looked in their direction. Maren and Lady Bolding were motionless, lying on their stomachs with the straps of their bikini tops undone for the sun. He thought of warning Maren not to get burned. He saw Massey wasn't around.

Massey had gone to the main house, directly to his second-floor study, where he locked the door behind him. From the desk drawer he removed a Moe diamond weight gauge and a jeweler's loupe. From the desk surface he took up the gold-and-malachite Fabergé egg. His forefinger pressed the spring release, and the egg snapped open in exact halves.

In it, nestled nicely in a bed of cotton, was the stolen diamond. The Massey.

Expertly, Massey used the gauge to measure the stone—length, width, and from crown to pavilion point. He calculated that it was a little over a hundred and seven carats. As Chesser had said.

He took the diamond to the window facing north. He placed the loupe to his eye and sighted into the stone. This was the first opportunity he'd had to study it closely, and he was pleased to find it flawless, beautifully flawless. Not as Chesser had told him.

He smiled closed-mouthed. He could see the pool area from where he was standing. He rubbed the Massey between his fingers, as though it were a worry stone. Actually, the diamond didn't matter as much as the part it had played and what its quality told him.

More than ever he was now sure Chesser would do. That night Chesser slept better and longer than he thought he might. His room and Maren's were conveniently joined, so they mussed her bed to make it appear used. And then they really used his.

For having been sour and sharp with her, he made an active, loving apology, which she very sensibly accepted. Thursday morning they remained in bed late, letting an oblong of sunlight from an open window creep across them. They touched, listened to English country birds, and talked.

He told her: "I've got to go up to London Monday."

"I'll go along and visit Mildred. Why do you have to go?"

"Diamonds."

She said something in Swedish, then translated: "It may look like a boat with a hole, but it may be a hole with a boat."

"What's that got to do with diamonds?"

"It's appropriate," she said, lifting her chin slightly to underscore her words.

"And Mickey Mouse wears bright-yellow gloves," he intoned.

"So?"

"Well, that makes just as much sense."

"Why?"

"It does, that's all."

"No, I mean why does Mickey Mouse wear yellow gloves?"

"Because he lost his red ones."

"Or maybe," she said seriously, "he doesn't want to leave his fingerprints."

Chesser shook his head and gave her a dubious look.

"I've got so many things to ask Mildred," she said to the ceiling.

"Ask her who's got the diamond."

"I might." She nodded thoughtfully to herself.

Chesser observed her, adoring the priceless silver flecks in her eyes. He moved close and saw himself reflected in her pupils and hoped he was always there. He asked: "What was so amusing yesterday?"

"When yesterday?"

"In the cabana?"

"Oh. We were comparing ourselves in the mirror. Lady Bolding and I. Like two different pages in the same book. You know, side by side."

"And?"

"She's either a genuine blonde or a perfectionist."

Chesser got the picture. He was secretly intrigued. "You complement one another," he said, but as he did he realized it was more a private thing between them and he wasn't included. Some jealousy took over.

"We contrast nicely," she corrected.

"That's what I meant."

"I rather like her."

Chesser thought she might be trying to needle him, but she seemed sincere.

"She's very candid about herself," said Maren.

"Is she?"

"With me, at least."

"I suppose this time she didn't hold back. She just had to kiss you."

"On the shoulder."

He was sure she was trying to provoke him. He played along. "You didn't resist."

"I didn't see it coming."

"But you expected it, of course."

"Of course."

"Then what happened?" he asked.

"Nothing consequential. She tried to persuade me to wear a see-through bikini. For you, to cheer you up. I told her it wouldn't. Then she suggested I wear it for Massey's benefit. I said I didn't believe Massey needed any charity, even from me. That amused her. Then I told her I'd wear it for her if that was what she wanted."

"Why'd you say that?"

"Just to take her temperature."

"And it was above normal, of course."

"Of course."

"Better be careful."

"Why?"

"You might stir up more than you can handle."

"More than who can handle?"

"Ask Mildred," snapped Chesser.

She deliberately reached and found him, held him tenderly.

"I'm yours," she said pointedly.

"Yeah." He acted unconvinced.

"You've got nothing to worry about," she whispered, while touching him as she knew he liked best.

Despite Maren's reassurance, Chesser became especially aware of Lady Bolding. Indications that had gone unnoticed before now seemed obvious, magnified. Little things, as innocent as Maren seated close to her on a small plush sofa, alerted him. Any contact, no matter how slight, seemed erotically motivated, and the situation was made all the more complex by Chesser's own reaction to Lady Bolding's physical appeal. It was difficult for him to consider her an emotional opponent when he also found her so extremely desirable.

Chesser's contentious imaginings were actually the result of his annoyance at himself for having botched the Massey diamond deal. They served as both a diversion and a penance. No matter how much reassurance he might receive from Maren, it would not be enough. Because Chesser at this time just didn't like Chesser.

At night, alone with Maren, holding her, he was able to feel more positive. But only then. Whenever Lady Bolding was around, Chesser was tense, not assertive, on edge. He was even tempted to confront Lady Bolding, but he kept his misery to himself, allowing it to distort and expand.

It seemed to Chesser that Maren was encouraging an intimacy with the lady. She seemed to enjoy being the object of such attention, according to Chesser's point of view.

He was right to a degree. Maren was amusing herself; but merely that. She didn't realize just how upset Chesser was, and had no desire to be cruel to him. She never had. For her it was a relatively harmless distraction in a place she found rather dull, and was particularly welcome because her intuition told her Chesser was attracted to Lady Bolding. What better way to offset that? Besides, it gratified Maren's vanity in an unconventional way to be desired by such a superb beauty. Not to mention the slightly dangerous aspect of it, which, naturally, she found appealing.

What happened that Saturday afternoon was symptomatic. After a sumptuous lunch, Chesser said he felt like taking a nap. He thought Maren would join him, but instead she said she felt like taking a walk. Lady Bolding was also in a walking mood, and that made Chesser's alarm go off.

Pretending indifference, Chesser went to his room. From an upper window he saw the two women strolling leisurely away. Relax, he told himself, it was good to be alone for a while. He needn't be concerned about Maren. He was sure of her. Wasn't he?

He went down and out, to follow them.

They were not in sight but Chesser went in the direction he'd seen them going and soon he caught on the pink color of Maren's dress, along with the pale blue Lady Bolding was wearing. They were emerging from a strip of woods to climb a soft, green hill that was included in Massey's extensive acreage. Chesser kept them in view from a cautious distance, not knowing what lie he would use as explanation if they discovered him on their trail. Perhaps, he thought, he'd say he was bird watching, which was a metaphorical truth.

He watched them climb the hill and believed they were close enough to be arm in arm. And when they reached the crest he couldn't see any sky between them, so he decided they had to be at least side against side. They disappeared over the hilltop.

Chesser continued after them, noticing where their steps had bent the wild grass. Near the top he decided to crawl the rest of the way up and take a look over at them. At that moment, however, his self-respect intervened. He took stock of himself and realized how absurd his actions were. He stood abruptly and started back to the house.

What Chesser prevented himself from seeing was Lady Bolding and Maren lying in the deepest part of a small swale, the high grass partially concealing some of each of them. They were apart, stretched opposite one another, like the position of a clock's hands, pink and blue, indicating six and twelve. They were talking softly, while Lady Bolding's bare toes were paying attention, touching, just lightly stroking the sensitive bare underfeet and ankles of Maren, who didn't seem to notice, or mind.

Returning to the house, going up the open hill toward it, Chesser heard something whiz and hit close by. A golf ball. He looked above and found the figure of Massey addressing another ball and making another swing. Chesser ran, ducking, hoping to get out of Massey's range. He heard another ball whizzing in flight above him. It seemed as though Massey was taking intentional aim. He cursed Massey but quickly excused him, thinking perhaps the older man's eyesight was bad at such distances.

Massey's man Hickey was taking away the gold clubs and Massey was seated at an outside table when Chesser approached.

"Have a drink," Massey invited.

Chesser needed one.

"I just had a call from the investigating firm I spoke to you about. They seem to be on to something." Massey sipped his drink. "That's all they said. They were on to something. They're like that. You know, conservative until they have all the facts. Very competent people. They promised a full report by Monday the latest."

Chesser was concerned, of course, and anxious to know what was being done, but he'd decided it was best to wait until Massey brought it up. Even with Massey's resources at work he doubted the diamond would be recovered, but this information from the investigators seemed to offer some hope.

He still wondered, though, about Massey's forgiving attitude. It just wasn't right. Massey was being too cooperative for some reason.

"I understand you plan to go up to London Monday," Massey said.

"For business."

"To The System?"

Chesser nodded.

Massey told him: "One of my subsidiary companies has its offices there on Harrowhouse. Right next door to number 11, as a matter of fact. Mid-Continental Oil."

"I was wondering about that."

"Been there at number 13 for years."

"I mean, the way you referred to number 11 as The System. Usually only those in the trade call it that."

"Interesting business, diamonds," said Massey detached, looking off.

Chesser, despite some nagging misgivings, was now feeling much better. His drink tasted good and his confidence was returning. There'd be no more jealous lover foolishness. In fact, he was feeling so good, he thought he'd tell Massey a couple of diamond stories. Outsiders were always intrigued by them.

"Know what the ancient Persians said about diamonds?"

"Yes," said Massey.

It was as though he had clamped a hand over Chesser's open mouth.

"The early Persians," said Massey, "believed Satan must have created precious stones such as diamonds, because God made only useful things. Satan made diamonds to inflame men's avarice."

Probably the old bastard read that someplace and just happened to remember it, thought Chesser. From his repertoire he selected another story. The famous French-crown-jewel robbery of 1792. Included in that historic, politically motivated theft had been the Hope Diamond, known then as the Tavernier Blue. Chesser began, "In 1792 . . ."

"In Burma," interrupted Massey, "the word *chein* means both diamond and arsenic. Because the Burmese consider both to be fatal."

That was one Chesser had never heard.

"Many people feel that way about diamonds," said Massey.

"I'm beginning to," declared Chesser, lightly bitter.

"In the sixteenth century someone attempted to put diamond dust in a salad that was served up to Cellini, believing it would cause instant death."

"Mary Queen of Scots wore a diamond for protection against poison," Chesser managed to get in.

"Three diamonds," corrected Massey. "To ward off danger, disease, and poison. Unfortunately, she didn't have one for the axe." He smiled and again nearly gave Chesser time to speak. "When one considers the prominent role diamonds have played in murders and wars, perhaps the Persians were right about Satan. Wouldn't you say, Chesser?"

"I guess."

Chesser had expected to dominate this conversation, but evidently Massey knew plenty about diamonds. Chesser changed the subject. He asked about a good Klimt sketch he'd noticed on the second-floor foyer. Swift pen strokes capturing a pair of female lovers in a disheveled embrace. Where had Massey gotten it?

Massey ignored the question. "Well, if the Devil invented diamonds," he said, "then The System should thank hell for giving them control." He paused. Then added, with a touch of bitterness: "Perhaps they do."

That hit home. Chesser thought perhaps he and the billionaire had finally established something mutual. A dislike—for The System. However, Chesser doubted Massey's antipathy was equal to his own. No reason for it to be. It was even possible that Massey was baiting him for some reason. He might be a personal friend of Meecham or Sir Harold.

"I'll give you something to think about," offered Massey. "How many diamonds has The System taken in from its own mines and other sources, say, in the past twenty years?"

An indifferent shrug from Chesser.

"Keep in mind I'm only talking about gem quality stones, not industrial stuff. Care to guess?"

"I've no idea."

"About eighty million carats," said Massey.

"Is that your estimate?"

"An accurate figure."

"Based on what?"

"The System's own annual reports."

The sun chose that moment to go behind a small isolated cloud, dulling everything. Chesser smelled clover blossoms, a concentration of fragrance delivered by a slight breeze. He turned his head to accept and enjoy it. He was facing the house, his back to the slope.

Massey continued: "Now, let me ask you this. How many diamonds of gem quality has The System sold to the market over those same twenty years?"

"All they got."

"By no means."

"How many, then?" asked Chesser, concealing his indifference.

"Sixty million carats."

Massey allowed some silence to underline that figure. Obviously a point had just been made, but Chesser didn't get it. That The System had a lot of diamonds and sold a lot of diamonds didn't impress him.

"Subtract the amount sold from those received," instructed Massey.

"Twenty million carats."

"That's how many The System has held back. A monstrous inventory, growing at the rate of about a million carats a year. Now an accumulation of twenty million. It's a cardinal rule of cartels. Demand must always exceed supply to justify a continual rise in price. Since 1960, the value of diamonds has more than doubled. Comparatively, they've done much better than industrial stocks, for example, which have increased in value only about twenty-five per cent, little more than the cost of living."

"Which makes diamonds a good investment," Chesser said.

"At least they seem to be."

"A great many fortunes are tied up in them."

A nod from Massey. "And what a catastrophe it would be if suddenly those twenty million carats that The System has held back were to hit the market all at once, providing, of course, they were distributed by someone with the facilities to handle it."

"Never happen. The price would go down."

"The price would plunge. To almost nothing, overnight. Diamonds would be practically worthless."

"A good thing for The System it's able to keep its inventory well in hand. Twenty million carats just sitting there."

"Twelve billion dollars worth of diamonds. Twelve billion. Imagine!"

Chesser tried. It wasn't easy.

"Seventy bushel baskets full," said Massey, continuing to feed Chesser's mind's eye. "Over four tons of gem-quality stones."

Chesser was clearly stimulated now.

Massey knew it. "Where do you think they are this very minute," he asked, "all those diamonds?"

"Johannesburg," guessed Chesser.

Massey shook his head. "You've walked right over them perhaps a hundred times. At 11 Harrowhouse."

Chesser visualized Meecham and all those diamonds. Meecham perched pompously atop a mountain of diamonds worth twelve billion dollars.

"It's something to think about," said Massey, and immediately stood to greet Lady Bolding and Maren, who were returning from their walk, warm and thirsty.

CHAPTER 10

On the Wednesday before, when Chesser failed to arrive at the Connaught, Coglin ordered an immediate check of all the other best London hotels. When that didn't locate Chesser, Coglin made a conclusive written report to Meecham. In that report he did not mention that Security Section had abandoned Chesser's trail. He merely used the details his agents had supplied and fabricated liberally to get himself off the hook.

It was both easy and practical. Admissions of even minor discrepancies could accumulate into a major impression of incompetence. Chesser, in Coglin's opinion, wasn't worth such a penalty. Coglin also believed Meecham was overreacting to Chesser's having bought a large stone for someone. He suspected Meecham had a personal reason for wanting Chesser under priority surveillance. Some special, private interest. That being so, Coglin had been willing to accommodate. But now Chesser was lost and to concede the error was too much to ask. All things in proportion, thought Coglin. Chesser was small stuff.

Coglin's report included accounts from several of Security Section's most reliable agents: detailed, hour-by-hour documentation supporting the lie that Chesser's wealthy girlfriend was the recipient of the large stone Chesser had bought through The System. She had advanced the money for the transaction, and the diamond was now in her possession. The transaction had come about merely as a consequence of a personal relationship. Therefore, it was Security's opinion that Chesser was not deserving of any special recognition for having made the sale. Priority surveillance of Chesser had been discontinued, and the agents involved had already been reassigned to other, more pressing matters.

The report was inserted into Chesser's dossier and rush-delivered across the street to Meecham. Along with it, Coglin also sent four trays of color-photo slides that had been sorted and arranged in the order in which they'd been taken in the woods and meadows of Chantilly. Coglin was sure Meecham would consider the slides important enough evidence to require hours of careful examination.

As expected, in less than an hour Coglin received a call from Meecham, who expressed gratitude for Security Section's cooperation and was pleased to say that the report verified his own opinion of Chesser's limited ability and importance. Meecham also agreed it was no longer imperative that Chesser be under constant observation. "He's already received too much attention," was the way Meecham put it, a bit apologetically. As an afterthought, Meecham mentioned the photo slides, which, evidently, he'd already perused. He wished to keep them a while for further study.

Thus, Coglin got Meecham off his back, and, as a result, Chesser was out from under the sharp focus of The System's eyes.

CHAPTER 11

"I was only testing."

"Me or yourself?" asked Chesser.

"You, of course," said Maren. "People in love usually test one another."

"It's childish."

"To the contrary. It's very adult. You've done it to me."

"Never. When?"

"Lots of times."

"See, you can't even name once."

"Sure I can. I'm just deciding which incident to mention."

"It's a woman's game, testing like that. Men never do it."

"That obvious whore in Cannes."

"I don't remember any whore in Cannes."

"Hell you don't."

"Which whore?"

"That's a test! What you just said. *Which* whore? As though there were dozens."

"I meant exactly that. *Which* whore. I never talked to one in Cannes."

"Perhaps it was in St. Tropez. No matter. You stuck you hand inside her blouse and you weren't even sneaky about it. You wanted me to see you."

"Ridiculous."

"No. I remember distinctly because I reacted."

"You didn't say anything at the time."

"Of course not. That's what you wanted."

"She wasn't a whore. Anyway, she wasn't all that obvious."

"To me, she was."

"You're making something of nothing. It never occurred to me that you'd react."

"Oh, I see. You go about fondling whores, and I'm so blasé I'm not supposed to have any feelings about it."

"I was curious, that's all."

"Why?"

"She claimed she'd had silicone injections."

"At least admit you were testing."

"All right. I was testing. I was testing her."

"You were testing me. To see if I'd just take it or get angry. I knew what you were up to, so I just took it."

"That's how the game's played?"

"It's not a game. It's serious."

"Yesterday afternoon was serious?"

"Of course."

"I'd rather think it wasn't."

"Do you still love me?" she asked.

"I still love you."

"I know."

"But I didn't like them sitting there watching you perform bareass off that diving board. And when Massey asked you to do another swan, I felt like throwing him in, white flannels and all."

"That's precisely why I did it. To do it and have you not like it, but know that you still love me. That much. In spite. It was the same as your feeling up that whore."

"It would take more than that for me to stop loving you."

"How much more?"

"You'll never know unless it happens, will you?"

"Touché."

"Really, why did you do it?"

"You mean, besides as a test?"

"Okay, besides."

"Lady Bolding dared me."

"And the champagne convinced you."

"I had only two glasses, but thanks anyway."

"What did she say to you afterward, Lady Bolding?"

"Nothing consequential."

"I suppose she conveyed Massey's gratitude."

"Merely her own."

"Why should it turn her on? She'd seen you nude before."

"There are circumstances and circumstances."

"I don't believe she's as you say, not really."

"Well, she is. You just don't want to believe it."

"Makes no difference to me."

"Most men consider beautiful lesbians an awful waste."

"But women don't, I suppose?"

"Downshift, darling. Don't use the brake. Downshift."

"We're lucky we missed most of the morning traffic."

"Do we have to go back there tonight?"

"Yes."

"Why?"

"Massey wants me back."

"You work for him now?"

"He's getting a report on the theft. I want to be there."

"Anyway, we're going riding tomorrow."

"We are?"

"Oh, you can ride with us if you want. Lady Bolding might not mind."

"Stop testing."

"You're learning."

"I know what Massey and his Lady Bolding want. They want to dispense with me and disrobe with you. I'm beginning to feel like a chaperone, for Christ's sake."

"You're beginning to sound like one."

"I've got to protect my interests."

"I'm doing that for you, darling."

"Promise?"

"Cross my heart, legs, and everything."

"Will you be finished at Mildred's by noon?"

"Probably. I hope we get through to Jean Marc."

"I'm sure you will. I thought we might have lunch somewhere. You and just me, for a change."

"I'd like to kiss you right now."

"I'm all yours."

"I mean really kiss."

"Beg and I'll pull over."

"No. You've got diamonds on your mind. I can tell. I'm developing my psychic perception. Every day I get better at it. Mildred says I have extraordinary potential."

"I've always thought so."

"You know, the trouble with bucket seats is they're impossible."

"You could have specified a regular seat."

"Lack of foresight may well be my only flaw. I guess I'll have to settle for this, hmmm?"

"Do you feel more secure, holding on like that?"

"Depends on what you feel."

"I'll be letting you know any second now."

"That's good."

"Keep an eye out for trucks. Truck drivers are notorious voyeurs."

"Just don't let anyone pass."

"Okay, hang on."

"I love you."

"I know. But prove it anyway."

They made excellent time, better than expected, and the Ferrari pulled up before number 11 Harrowhouse shortly before nine thirty.

"The Ritz at noon sharp," said Chesser, surrendering the driver's seat to Maren, who climbed over the transmission hump with careless disregard for personal exposure. She lifted herself to straighten her dress under her, left her skirt gathered high in he lap. She put the car in first and promised, "I'll be there."

He leaned over for a brief good-bye kiss. She gave it, pressed her foot to generate approximately five thousand rpm's, released the clutch all at once and the powerful machine shot her recklessly away.

Chesser went into number 11 as he'd never gone in before—with an assertive nonchalance and a genuine bright smile for Miller at the door.

"I'm early," said Chesser.

"Yes, sir," Miller agreed.

"They might want to take me now. Would you call up and see?"

Miller got on the interphone.

Chesser remained standing nearby. Almost unconsciously he began humming a fragment of a happy song. He caught himself, cut the humming abruptly. He thought about how strong he felt, especially his legs. Capable of a high jump.

"Your appointment is at ten, sir," informed Miller.

"They want me to wait, then?"

"Yes, sir."

Chesser didn't mind. Probably they had Whiteman or someone of his importance up there, he thought. Probably they had scheduled sights early in the week for those who were to receive larger packets.

He sat on the Queen Anne loveseat and looked across at that same framed snowscape, which seemed to be whiter and more glistening than ever. He lighted a cigarette and watched the smoke violate the impeccable air of the foyer. He gave some thought to the Massey theft but didn't let it bring him down. Chesser was hopeful that Massey's private investigators would somehow resolve the case. Massey also seemed to think so. Although Massey hadn't come right out and said he believed they would recover the diamond, he had intimated as much. They'll get us the answers, were Massey's words, and that was enough to lessen Chesser's anxiety considerably, so that he could preoccupy himself with the consideration he expected from this sight.

He was truly looking forward to it. He was certain that his recent, very large transaction would affect his standing in The System. That was the way The System did things. Such a major deal warranted recognition: a larger packet, more stones, larger stones, better quality. Perhaps they'd double the amount of his usual packet. Maybe even do better than that, now that he'd proved he could handle big stuff.

Miller came over with an ashtray. He didn't place it on the table. Rather, he stood there holding it. Chesser flipped his ash and Miller stood there with a fixed smile. Chesser decided to hell with it and stumped out the cigarette.

It came back to Chesser then. What Massey had said about The System's inventory of stones. Twelve billion dollars worth. Where did The System keep them? Chesser glanced up because up was where he usually went to get his packet. Then he remembered Massey had said something about walking over them, obviously meaning the stones were kept somewhere below. Of course. They'd have to be underground in a vault. Chesser tried to imagine twelve billion dollars worth of uncut, gem-quality diamonds. The idea subdued him, made whatever quantity he was about to receive in his packet seem a pittance by comparison. He tried not to think about it, tried to get back the good high feeling he'd had. But he couldn't lose the image. It was too much. Twenty million carats, according to Massey. Over four tons of stones, just sitting there, being held back by The System, being doled out like candy to good boys.

Greedy bastards, he thought.

"You can go up now, Mr. Chesser," said Miller.

Chesser's legs had turned heavy. As he walked across the foyer, he had the irrational sensation that he might sink right through the floor and end up waist-deep in diamonds. Going up the stairs he wished he were going down instead. He'd sure like to get a look at, get at, those twelve billion dollars worth, he thought.

He expected to find Meecham in the sight room. But the only one there was Watts. Meecham would be along in a moment, thought Chesser. Meanwhile, this was an opportunity to make the apology he felt he owed Watts. He hurried right to the subject, anticipating Meecham's entrance.

"I'm sorry you didn't get to see that diamond after it was cut."

"It came out all right, sir?"

"Wildenstein did a beautiful make. Perfect. An oval, as you suggested. "

"I'm glad to hear that, sir."

"I had to send it registered delivery from Antwerp," lied Chesser. "You understand."

"Of course, sir."

"But I did want you to see it. I really did."

"Things can't always go the way one wants," said Watts.

Chesser thought Watts looked discernibly more haggard than when he'd last seen him. It had only been a month since they'd last met, but Watts looked years older.

"Your packet is ready for you, sir," said Watts.

It was on the black-velour-topped table. The usual small, plain manila envelope.

"We're waiting for Meecham, aren't we?"

"He instructed me to handle the transaction," said Watts. "If you don't object, sir."

That was a disappointment. Meecham's presence was part

of the reward Chesser had anticipated. Meecham usually handled the more important sights. To know he was accepted, Chesser needed to read the confirmation on Meecham's face. "I don't mind," he lied to Watts. "Not at all."

Chesser glanced at his watch. "Actually, I'm running a bit late. I don't suppose there's any reason why I should take a look. I've an appointment with a client, a good prospect for another big one." He smiled his best smile.

"Are you sure you don't want a look, sir?"

"No need. Thanks, anyway."

"As you wish, Mr. Chesser."

"How much?"

At the moment Chesser was asking the price, Meecham, in his office one story above, was inserting a photographic color slide into a portable 35-mm. viewer. He had been at the window looking down to see Chesser arrive. He'd noticed Chesser's crisp, confident movement, Chesser's lean, fashionable appearance, the rich vitality of the Ferrari convertible, and especially the girl, Chesser's beautiful, young girl, flaunting her desirability with bold indifference.

Meecham's imagination had worked on the girl. For a minute or so, he had the actual pale flesh of her thighs for raw material. As well as her unusual long hair. He had to believe she was erotically audacious—a demanding girl. One who would thoroughly enjoy being served, obeyed. His imagination remained fixed on the reality of her, until she drove herself away. Then, not wanting her gone, he quickly unlocked a drawer of his desk, hurrying to retain the impact of his imaginary concoction. He got out the viewer, inserted a slide, pressed for illumination.

All the slides Coglin had sent over did not suit Meecham's taste. He had culled them down to about twenty that were possibly relevant. Those that showed Chesser positioned above the girl disgusted Meecham. He disliked seeing the girl pinned down like that, and the idea that she was eagerly submitting was even more intolerable. Obviously, Chesser was an ingrate, thought Meecham, hadn't progressed beyond the schoolboy level of passion, didn't know how to express the proper humility toward such a lovely mistress. Chesser was an intruder.

Chesser had to be eliminated. It was most frustrating. The more Meecham looked at the slides, the more difficult it was for him to replace the image of Chesser with himself. Not only that. Even those slides Meecham had selected were losing their effect because he'd been over them so many times.

Now he had in the viewer what his senses considered the most inspiring slide of the lot. Taken with an extra sharp long lens. Maren in a full-length strong stance, legs slightly parted and head raised, looking superior, imperious. Her lips open, as though issuing a command. Only a portion of Chesser could be seen, out of focus and not identifiable, in the lower foreground.

As he studied the slide, Meecham thought he'd go out early that day and take advantage of the anonymity London offered. He'd had two consecutive days in the country with wife and visiting married children, an oppressively bland weekend. He decided he wouldn't call one he knew or even call for a referral. He'd go out and find a new one.

Preferably a redhead.

"How much?" was the question Chesser had just asked.

"Fifteen thousand," answered Watts, head lowered.

Chesser was certain he hadn't heard correctly. "Fifty thousand?"

Watts didn't want to say it again, but he had to, distinctly this time. "Fifteen thousand."

Chesser just stood there, silent. The back of his neck felt on fire and he had the impression that his hands were solid, heavy objects, dangerous, meant to be slung and exploded from the ends of his arms.

"I pass," he finally said, calmly.

"You what, sir?"

"I don't want the packet. I refuse."

"Perhaps you should have a look at it, sir," suggested Watts, trying to help.

"*No.* And I hope this room is bugged. I'm sure it is. Meecham can take those cheap lousy stones and shove them up his ass. That's probably what the bastard would like. The hardest thing in the world right up his ass."

Watts shook his head, not condemning but rather in sympathetic approval.

Then Chesser walked out of the sight room and down and, without a word, past Miller, who closed the main door to number 11 sharply behind Chesser, definitely and finally excluding him.

Chesser went to Holborn and got a taxi, told the driver to take him to the Ritz. He badly needed to see Maren then, needed her. He had just committed occupational suicide.

But it was only ten thirty and he knew Maren wouldn't be at the Ritz yet. He unknotted his tie and pulled it off with an emphatic snap. He shoved it into his jacket pocket and then also removed his jacket. He undid his shirtcuffs and rolled them up three layers. He was trying to fight the tight feeling, to get loose.

Incredible, he thought, what The System had done. Meecham had expected him to accept a packet worth even less than the last. Anyway, now there wouldn't be any more packets, not ever.

Maybe it was only a temporary side effect, he thought, but damn if he didn't feel good. Really good, matter of fact! However, as the taxi went west with the thick traffic, and along the street he saw people hurrying about their business, Chesser's mood descended. He hunched down and tried to think only of the good things. Telling Meecham to shove it had been a pleasure. He wondered if he'd have said it to Meecham's face. He convinced himself he would have. Anyway, he was sure Meecham had heard it.

From that, Chesser got a sharp image of his dead father. He decided that he'd just done something his father probably had wanted to do many times—would have done if he hadn't been so inhibited by responsibilities. Chesser needed to believe that.

"I'll get out here," he told the driver. It was Shaftsbury Avenue, a block past Charing Cross Road. Nowhere significant for Chesser. He just wanted out of the taxi he now seemed to be sharing with his late father.

He gave the driver a pound tip because right then his inner voice was saying *I don't give a shit*. He turned and walked along with his jacket hung by a fingertip over his shoulder, his business case in his other hand. He had the sensation that he was completely different from all the others on the street, who were too busy to notice.

He knew exactly where he was. He turned up Dean Street

and decided he'd pretend he was just another American tourist. Wasn't he, after all, only that—a perpetual transient? As though playing the part, he looked into every store window along the way. He read a small sign which said:

RUBBERWEAR MADE TO ORDER
One Flight Up

That made him feel, by contrast, considerably more normal.

He was in the heart of Soho now, and that district's preoccupation with all shades and forms of sexuality was so prevalent that even the air there seemed pressured with it.

What the hell am I doing here? Chesser asked himself, and quickly gave the excuse that he was only wasting time. It didn't occur to him that he'd purposely sought out the area, was inflicting himself with this lower level of commerce. Much more basic than dealing in precious stones: the selling of holes, the buying of holes.

He went into a penny-gambling arcade, where there were numerous electric games of chance. He wandered and watched for a while and thought it surprising that so many people were there at this time of day. He noticed their expressions, which remained the same, whether they won or not.

He went to the change booth and got a pound's worth of pennies. Two hundred and forty English pennies. He moved about, from game to game, spending a few minutes and pennies at each. Finally, he stood at the edge of a large table that had a flat rectangle of shiny brass isolated in its center. The idea of the game was to land a penny on any electric dot. Simple enough. The payoff was five to one. Chesser threw a few and came very close once. He paused to watch a man who was throwing from the opposite side. A man with very dirty hands, wearing an extremely stale suit.

Evidently the man considered pitching pennies a serious pursuit. Indeed, perhaps that was his calling, for he was quite good at it. He had a unique way of tossing—a graceful arm motion that culminated with a snap of the wrist. At least one out of every three pennies he threw landed on a dot, rewarding him with a nice little profit. Maybe if he threw pennies all day he came out enough ahead for a room and a pint and a pie.

Chesser tried to imitate the man's throwing technique, thinking perhaps that might be the trick of it. But he did it badly and it made no difference. His pennies seemed to avoid the dots magnetically, and he soon became discouraged. Impetuously, he threw the pennies he had left, a heaping fistful, all at once. Most rolled into the catching gutter. Others bunched up ineffectively. Only one or two landed on dots.

He left the place; wanted to be out of Soho. His watch told him it was almost eleven thirty, only another half hour until Maren. He'd go to the Ritz and wait.

He headed down Brewer Street, still in the Soho district. Now he was so eager to get to the Ritz that he disregarded everything. Unfortunately. Because at one point, if he'd happened to look across the way, he would have seen Meecham, might have recognized him, although Meecham was facing away, reading a public advertising board outside a pornography shop. Meecham's interest was concentrated on the hand-printed, four-by-five cards that were tacked up there. His imagination was trying to decide which of two was more promising:

Beautiful strict governess wants. pupils who desire advanced courses in discipline. Leather uniforms supplied. WEL-2894

or

Young girl, really masterful, with a commanding vocabulary, wants a temporary male domestic for housework. Binding contract required. CHE-9438

Chesser might have gone unnoticed in Soho, but he was the object of numerous disapproving stares at the Ritz. He took a seat in the lobby lounge, where he had an unobstructed view of the Piccadilly entrance, through which he expect Maren. However, no sooner had his Cerruti-trousered bottom come in contact with the damask-covered cushion of one of the Ritz's chairs than a member of the hotel staff informed him that he was not properly attired. Gentlemen, Chesser was told with the emphasis on gentlemen, were required to wear tie and jacket.

Chesser smiled rather apologetically and began rolling

down and buttoning his shirt cuffs. It was then suggested that he retire to the gentlemen's room, where he could privately make the necessary repairs. Chesser just didn't take the suggestion. He did his cuffs and tied his tie and put on his jacket right there, feeling many eyes on him. He turned to a full-mirrored wall behind him to make sure the knot of his tie was in correct position. There was no reason now why he should not be granted the privilege of purchasing a Scotch neat, with a side of Perrier. But it was not brought with the usual alacrity, no doubt as a sort of punishment.

He meant to sip the Scotch. Instead, he took a gulp that burned all the way down. Three swallows of the Perrier were quickly taken as an antidote. He looked at his watch, which said straight up noon. He looked to the entrance. No Maren. She'd be there momentarily, he thought. So he tried to keep his attention aimed in that direction, wanting to see her, needing to, that much.

For five minutes that seemed an hour he didn't take his eyes from the entrance, even as he brought the glass to his mouth. He emptied the glass and ordered another with a mere signal. Then, for the first time, he allowed the voices of those at nearby tables to get through to him. He caught fragments of a conversation between two elderly ladies on his left who were shaped like two well-dressed, supersize chicken croquettes. Their topic was those of their set who had recently passed away. On his right three younger married women were chewing over morsels of extramarital gossip.

When he was one small gulp from the finish of his third Scotch, Chesser's watch said twelve thirty-seven. . . .

"You'd better eat."

"I'm not as hungry as I was."

"You have to eat."

"I have to drink," said Chesser and tossed down the last in that glass. He flicked a finger at an attending statue-waiter.

"Why did you do it?"

"For the same reason . . ."

"What kind of answer is that?"

"Let me finish. I was going to say . . . for the same reason you never did. That's why. To save face. You know, pride and all that shit."

"Don't swear."

"Don't don't swear me."

"You're always saying you don't give a shit. Which indicates you do."

"Okay, I give a shit."

"You shouldn't have done it. You could have controlled yourself for five or ten minutes. That wasn't much to ask. After all, I—"

"Yeah, I know. You were controlled for twenty years."

"I convinced The System you'd be good. I recommended you."

"Why?"

"That was the most I could leave you. Don't you want to be something?"

"I'm something."

"Look at the friends you went to school with. Look where they are now."

"Serving life sentences."

"You could have been a lawyer but you quit."

"I would have made a stinking lawyer."

"You had a real chance with The System, to build something for yourself."

"I gave it ten years."

"You got too big for your pants."

"I sold a big one. Bigger than you ever sold."

"And somebody took it out of your pocket as easy as stealing a marble. You're so smart."

"You're right about that. But you were wrong to give so much to them. Instead of us it was always The System."

"What are you going to do now?"

"I don't know."

"Maybe you think you can live off your luck and looks forever . . ."

Allowing his dead father to have the final word, Chesser came out of it with a glance at his watch.

It was twelve fifty-nine.

He looked up and there, smiling her best, was Maren backdropped by a Ritz crystal chandelier. She sat, gave a hello kiss, and didn't apologize for being an hour late.

"We had a phenomenal session," she declared. "We couldn't

get through to Jean Marc. I don't know where in hell he was. But Mildred got someone else."

"Who?"

"Some woman named Babette, who took too many sleeping pills. She was in the original Follies."

"Ziegfield?"

"*Bergère*. I got some good advice."

"About what not to wear."

"Really, I learned a lot from her."

"About the other side?"

"No, this side. Did you eat?"

"I was waiting for you."

"Mildred fed me something."

"And you swallowed it."

"You've been boozing, haven't you? I can smell."

"Just a couple."

"You have to eat."

He wanted her to ask about his morning. He thought she'd be glad to hear he'd quit The System. She always seemed so indifferent to diamonds. The only jewelry she ever wore was antique, unusual, with small semiprecious stones. For her first birthday with him he'd given her a nice five-carat diamond, Tiffany set, and although she'd been excited and appreciative, she'd never worn it. "I had quite a morning," he said.

"You don't really want to eat here, do you? I didn't think you did, so I had them hold the car out front. Come on." She was already up.

Chesser figured five pounds would more than cover the bill. He left that much on the table, took a moment to slide an ice cube from his Perrier glass into his mouth and was sucking on it as he followed her. He thought she'd go out ahead of him to claim the driver's seat, but just as she reached the doorway she stopped, waited, turned and took his arm, lovingly. "We'll get you some pastries or something along the way," she promised. "I didn't have any dessert either."

CHAPTER 12

Between the fish, which was a Mediterranean lou, and the fowl, which was local partridge, Massey told Chesser, "I received the report from the investigators."

He said it in such an offhand manner that Chesser's hope took it to be good news. "What did they say?"

"I've no idea. I thought we'd look at it fresh together."

They were in Massey's main diningroom and, although the dinner was formally set and served, they were all casually dressed. "The best should be enjoyed at leisure," was the way Massey put it. For the several nights that Maren and Chesser had been at Massey's country mansion, this was the first time they'd eaten in this room. It was usual for Massey to order meals served wherever his mood dictated—on the terraces, at poolside, under a tree, in a gazebo.

After a choice of French cheeses, African fruit, or crème caramel, Massey led the way to a large anteroom. Coffee in demitasse and excellent brandy followed. Bolivars were offered, and although Chesser seldom smoked a cigar, he accepted one of these fine, plump, aromatic ones.

"I'll have one too," said Maren seriously.

Another was brought. Massey observed closely as Maren expertly prepared the cigar: smelled it, clipped it, and rotated it between her lips. Chesser, who had eaten too much and tasted too little of it, thought Maren purposely exaggerated her mouth for Massey's benefit. While Chesser was thus distracted, it was Lady Bolding who delivered a flame to the end of Maren's Bolivar.

They were seated in individual deep chairs. Lady Bolding
next to Maren next to Chesser next to Massey.

Massey gestured.

A panel at the end of the room slid apart to reveal a blank
white surface. The light dimmed. A film began, silent.

It was a street scene, apparently somewhere in London. Cars
and people. The focus was on a man in a dark suit. A brief, partially turned-away view of the man entering the underground.
A nearby sign registered the location: Seven Sisters.

"I don't know what all this is," said Massey.

The film jiggled erratically, went black for a few seconds,
and then came to picture again, now greatly obscured by the
grain of the emulsion, very grainy, as though enlarged. It
showed someone seated on the underground. The same man.
Several brief, indistinct views.

"Perhaps we're supposed to read this along with it," said
Massey with impatience. He brought up a letter-sized brown
envelope. Chesser watched him break the wax seal of its flap
and take out several papers. Time was taken for Massey's
reading glasses to be brought and the lights were turned up
enough for him to read by.

Chesser leaned to see.

Massey read aloud: "Identified as Max Toland, alias Marty
Toll, Manny Landers, Mister Maxwell. Age forty-five, height
five feet, eleven inches, weight about twelve stone. Last known
address 1567 Edgeware Road, a rooming house for transients.
Present address undetermined. Police record: 1968 arrested for
violation of National Code, statute 598, unlawful transportation
of property to avoid import duty. Served one year six months
Budney Prison. Nineteen sixty for armed robbery, served five
years at Bratingsgate Prison. Nineteen fifty-nine suspected
homicide, charge dismissed for lack of evidence. Marital status,
single. Nationality, Irish. Religion, Jewish."

While Massey was reading the description, Chesser applied
it to the man on the film. The jiggling and graininess made it
difficult.

Massey read on: "For the past four years Toland is known
to be—"

The film cut abruptly for a different view, evidently someplace outside again. A sharp, close shot of the man.

"That's him!" Chesser called out. "That's the son of a bitch who took the diamond from my pocket."

"Are you sure?" Massey asked.

"I'm positive. Recognize him, Maren?"

She puffed her Bolivar. "I suppose," she said rather passively.

"He looks different in a suit," said Chesser. "On the road he had on orange coveralls like the others. But I got a damned good look at his face. That's him!" Chesser was elated. Whoever Massey's investigators were, they were good. They'd hit it right on the button, first time.

The film continued, featuring various close-ups of the man. Massey went on reading, but not aloud. Finally, he said, "This is amazing."

"What?"

"According to this . . ." He read aloud again: "For the past four years Max Toland is known to have been in the pay of the Security Section of the Consolidated Selling System, engaged as a special informant. However, as the enclosed indicates, he has frequently undertaken more active assignments."

"The System!" Chesser's fury made him bite all the way through his cigar.

"Unlikely," said Massey.

"The goddamned System!"

"You're making a hasty assumption," said Massey. "This man, Toland, might have been acting on his own. Let's read what the investigator's conclusions are." He scanned another page, mumbling every so often. When he reached the bottom of the third page, he said, "Ah, here we are." He read quietly to himself, then looked up at the ceiling for a long moment, as though digesting what he'd read. He took a deep puff on his cigar and allowed the smoke to cloud thick around his mouth as he told Chesser, "Much as I dislike saying it, their conclusions are in complete accord with yours."

"The System?"

Massey nodded, handed over the report to Chesser, who skimmed it.

"So, what are we going to do about it?" Chesser asked.

"What do you suggest?"

"Nail this Max whatever-the-hell his name is. Make him confess."

"Have him arrested?"

"Certainly."

"Assuming that were possible, don't you think the publicity would be unfortunate? Especially for you. As for myself, in this case I'd prefer not being plastered all over the front pages. Besides," Massey continued, "what would really be the point? All we'd get out of Max is where the diamond is. We already know that."

"Do we?"

"Of course," said Massey. "Number 11 Harrowhouse. By now our diamond has surely been returned to The System's bulging inventory."

Chesser pictured and despised that. However, he still found it incredible that The System, with all its diamonds, should take the time and trouble to steal one. A big one, yes, but comparatively it meant little to The System. Then why? Chesser recalled that Meecham had been against his getting that fine stone in the first place. Meecham had been very annoyed at Watts for slipping it in. That was why Meecham hadn't even acknowledged such a big sale, and rather out of spite had deprived him of the recognition and fatter packet he deserved. Personal resentment. That had been at least part of it, thought Chesser. Also it would be very much like The System to consider it not really good business for a dealer of his standing to so suddenly break into the big time. The important dealers, such as Whiteman, might well resent it. And that being the case, Meecham would reasonably take the risk to see that he was kept in his place, below the salt.

Bitterly, Chesser imagined Meecham now in possession of the diamond. He hated the idea of Meecham smugly appreciating the perfect make that Wildenstein had executed; Meecham now enjoying the last laugh. On him.

Massey told him: "We must accept the fact that we'll never see that diamond again. Never."

"I'll see it," vowed Chesser.

"Forget it," advised Massey, with finality.

Chesser was standing. He just realized that. He didn't remember getting up from his chair, but evidently he had, during his excitement or fury. His head felt heavy, expanded. He let it drop, relaxed all at once—a physical indication of his spirit giving up. His eyes were aimed at Massey's feet. He thought irrelevantly how comfortable Massey's feet looked in Massey's white, light-weight slip-ons. Undoubtedly precisely made from a private personal mold. Probably an Italian or two had flown all the way from Rome to cast Massey from the ankle down. Down. It came to Chesser how down Chesser was now. Everything was negative. No income, no prospects, and he owed Massey a million and a half. Now that Massey was hopeless, Chesser was sure the next topic of discussion would be that million and a half. For the moment, at least, he was wrong.

"I'd enjoy watching a film," declared Massey. "I wonder what we've got in *our* inventory." Unlike The System's, it turned out to be worthless dross.

The following afternoon Lady Bolding and Maren had gone riding.

Chesser could have gone with them, had been nicely invited by Lady Bolding, but remembering Maren's remark about his acting like a chaperone, he decided against it.

Instead, he lay face up on a poolside cushion. The sun seemed to be pressing him down, personally broiling him. Eyes shut, he concentrated on the squiggles in the liquid between his eyelids and pupils.

Massey was relaxed on a nearby lounger. After a while, Massey said, "The million and a half I advanced you . . ."

Here it comes, thought Chesser, the heart shot.

"How much of it do you have left?" asked Massey.

"Seven hundred thousand."

"That was your margin?"

"Yes," admitted Chesser.

"About forty per cent," said Massey, implying it was disproportionate.

"Your diamond would have been worth a couple of million retail."

"Would have been," reminded Massey. From a black crystal bottle he poured some clear lotion into the cup of his palm and began slicking it on the skin of his stomach, chest, and the rounds of his shoulders. It smelled like ordinary baby oil.

"Ever hear of the Shorewater Project?" asked Massey.

Chesser said he hadn't.

"It was one of my enterprises," explained Massey. "Eight or nine years ago."

Meaning he owned it, assumed Chesser.

"My theory," said Massey, "was that the diamond fields of southwest Africa extended out into the sea. Got a few of my top geologists on it. They did some diving off the mouth of the Orange River and found I was right. So, I went to the trouble of buying the necessary government concessions from the top to a third of the way down. Had a barge built and towed there by one of my biggest tankers. Started dredging and the yield was even better than expected—seventy to eighty per cent gem-quality stones. All we had to do was suck them up and sort them. But we'd no sooner begun the operation than the barge was swamped and sunk by a storm."

"Tough," inserted Chesser, secretly enjoying his image of Massey's misfortune.

Massey continued, in a constrained angry manner that compressed his delivery, made it come out in a telegraphic manner. "Had another barge, bigger one, built and towed down there. Big enough to take any storm. Started dredging again. Barge caught fire. Completely destroyed. By then I had about twenty million dollars in the project. Wanted to go with another barge but was forced to stop."

"Why?"

"Government revoked permission. Went back on everything. I have reason to believe the burning of the barge wasn't accidental. There are now three barges working those underwater fields."

"Whose?"

"A subsidiary of The System."

"You believe The System sabotaged your barge?"

"And got to the government as well."

Chesser wanted to believe it but reasoned that even The System wouldn't push around a billionaire. "You're as powerful as The System," he told Massey. "More powerful, probably. As a matter of fact, you are a sort of System, aren't you?"

"Not in that area. Not Africa. Except Libya, of course."

Again, dislike for The System became the emotional hy-phen between himself and Massey.

"We're not being fair," said Massey. "Not really. I mean the way we're deprecating The System. It's not all bad."

Chesser admired Massey's tolerance.

Massey continued with it. "Consider the perpetual prob-lems they have keeping the price of diamonds up. I suppose they must resort to all sorts of measures, including some not so ethical. For instance, when the Russians discovered all that diamond-bearing ground in Kirensk a few years ago. Very high yield of gem-quality stones. Anyway, it must have been a touchy situation. But, as usual, The System prevailed."

"How's that?"

"The Soviets now deliver their diamonds to 11 Harrow-house for distribution. Through an intermediary, so it doesn't conflict with the persuasions they're making politically to the working blacks in Africa. Evidently, even the Kremlin real-ized how foolish it would be to buck The System and foul up the market. Smarter, more profitable to play along like every-body else. You know, my twelve billion figure of The System's inventory may be an underestimate, now that I think of it. With the Russian contribution, it may run closer to thir-teen billion." Massey sighed thoughtfully.

Chesser's mind's eye was seeing that horde of diamonds again.

Massey remained silent for a while. Finally he said, "Tell you what, Chesser. I'm willing . . . no, to put it more pre-cisely, I've decided to absorb the loss of our diamond fiasco. I expect you to return the seven hundred thousand, of course. But the rest I'll just write off."

Welcome words. Chesser suddenly felt so unburdened he actually liked Massey. No one had ever been so generous.

"That way we can start with a clean slate," said Massey.

Chesser wondered what he meant by that. Decided quickly that Massey was referring to their personal relationship. Chesser had always been of the opinion that billionaires were the sort of valuable friends one should, if possible, have. And Massey's wiping off eight hundred thousand dollars as non-chalantly as eight proved it.

Chesser relaxed, and let the cushion take all his weight. He was surprised how tense he'd been just moments before as he assessed it now against how loose he felt. Now the sun was something bright and kind upon him. He lay there enjoying relief and contemplating nothing more serious that what Massey might be serving for dinner that evening. I'll be terrific tonight, thought Chesser. I'll say all the right things and make all the right moves. Be a regular David Niven or Gregory Peck.

"Mr. Chesser, how would you like to make ten million dollars?"

Chesser was certain his mind was tricking his ears into pretending they'd heard those words.

"Would you?"

It was Massey, actually asking. He was still turned away, so Chesser couldn't see his face.

"How much?" asked Chesser.

"Ten million."

"Make it fifteen," said Chesser flippantly.

"All right, fifteen," agreed Massey, who now rolled over onto his back but kept his eyes closed.

Chesser sat up and tried to read Massey's expression. Massey's mouth appeared serious, but it was difficult not being able to see his eyes. It occurred to Chesser that perhaps Massey was letting him in on some spectacular inside deal. Being generous again. "What sort of investment is required?" asked Chesser.

"Time."

"Is that all?"

"Ingenuity."

"What do I have to do?"

"Steal."

Now Chesser knew Massey was merely playing with his mind. That was all right. Massey had eight hundred thousand dollars worth coming. Chesser went along with it. "Steal what?"

"Diamonds."

"That used to be my line," quipped Chesser. "Diamonds."

Massey sat up on the edge of the lounger, leaned his elbows on his knees, placed his palms symmetrically together so all his fingers were pointing at Chesser. He brought his look up so he was eye to eye with Chesser, level, steady. "The inventory," said Massey. "We must steal The System's inventory."

Chesser felt as though he were in the scene of a movie he was watching. "We?" he asked.

"I can't participate actively, of course," said Massey. "I would if I were much younger. But I am willing to finance such a venture to whatever extent is necessary."

"You've got to be joking."

"I'm not."

"Steal The System's inventory?"

"At least the bulk of it."

"Why?"

"We can get to all that once you've agreed."

"What makes you think it can be done?"

"Because no one has tried it and failed."

"That's peculiar logic."

"Perhaps. But I believe you can do it."

Chesser wondered why he was flattered. He shrugged self-consciously. "Hell, I don't know anything about stealing."

"A point in your favor."

"Why not hire a professional?"

"That would be entirely wrong. A professional would tend to overcomplicate the project. Surely he'd be less knowledgeable than you are about the subject, the place, and the people. You'll do much better."

Not really enough answer, thought Chesser, but nodded as though it were. "You actually have some sort of plan?"

"No."

"You must have given it some thought."

"It just occurred to me," lied Massey.

"Just now, out here in the sun?"

"Yes."

That amused Chesser.

"I'll pay you fifteen million," stated Massey, as though making a verbal contract.

"Just for the attempt?"

"No. You must be successful."

Chesser shook his head, definitely no.

"Why not?"

"I just saw myself behind bars. I'd make a lousy prisoner. I'm too fond of certain things."

"You wouldn't have to worry about the police. The

System's own methods guarantee it. The police are a pipeline for public information—the newspapers and all that. The last thing The System wants is everyone knowing how it operates, what its purposes are. Especially in regard to the inventory. The System would keep the police out of it."

"Maybe. But what about the heavies that work for The System? Like that guy Toland."

Massey nodded. "There are risks. In anything the risk tends to be in ration to the stakes. There's much at stake in this."

"Twenty million carats."

"Even more than that," said Massey.

Chesser had to admit to himself that the idea was appealing. Fifteen million for him and no more diamonds for Meecham to sit on. Chesser wouldn't have a money worry for the rest of his life. A man with fifteen million has a way of becoming a man with thirty million, et cetera. Meecham would have all the worries. The idea of stealing the inventory was absurd, of course, but it was a pleasant fantasy.

While these were Chesser's thoughts, Massey observed him closely, as though translating every nuance of Chesser's expressions. It was one of Massey's negotiating skills, something he'd developed over the years—the ability to read a man's fine print. He tried not to be misled by his own projections, to measure as accurately as possible how much his business opponent really wanted to agree. A crucial advantage. He'd seldom been wrong. He was quite certain he wasn't wrong now with Chesser. "Consider it a firm offer at fifteen million," said Massey, "plus expenses."

"I'll think about it," said Chesser, not really believing he would.

"Good," said Massey, resuming his position. He closed his eyes. "Give it some serious thought."

That night at dinner Chesser was on and he was good. He led the conversation just enough beyond risqué to make it more diverting for everyone. He traded stories with Massey, and, according to reaction, came out ahead. Lady Bolding seemed genuinely amused and contributed a few suggestive remarks of her own, while Maren, not to be outdone, told the truth about being a schoolgirl in a Swedish classroom so cold during winter that she and other pupils learned under blankets, and, once, when she was placed next to a young man she particularly fancied, the teacher had inquired about all the activity beneath the covers, and the young man had innocently replied that he was merely sharpening his pencil.

Following dinner, Massey suggested they view a film.

Lady Bolding was for bridge.

Massey capitulated.

They played in the library, men versus women, for a dollar a point. After the first hand, it was obvious that Massey took his game seriously, so Chesser respected that and limited his verbal cleverness to when the cards were being dealt and sorted. They played four rubbers and totaled. The men were ahead by two thousand three hundred and twelve dollars.

"Make it an even two thousand," said Massey.

Chesser hadn't expected, didn't expect, to get paid. It was only a game, like his perpetual backgammon match with Maren. However, Massey expected payment and said so.

"All right," agreed Maren. "Lady Bolding will pay you and I'll pay Chesser."

"No, no," Massey told her. "You pay me and she'll pay him. Otherwise neither of us will ever see the money.

"I'll give you a check in the morning," Maren told Massey.

"And I'll do the same," Lady Bolding promised Chesser.

It was then half past eleven. Massey said he was still in the mood for a film, but Lady Bolding's pretext was letter-writing and Maren did a yawn. Massey didn't wait for Chesser's excuse, merely said one good night to all, and headed for his exclusive late show.

As soon as Maren and Chesser were up in their room, Maren undressed with a carelessness Chesser knew from experience signified she was either passionate or tired. She discarded her clothes just anywhere, as though she would never wear them again. She didn't remove her shoes and crossed the large room three times causing Chesser to appreciate her movements and believe they were really for his benefit.

Then she flicked both shoes off with little kicks, sending them spinning awkwardly to the carpet. She sprawled gracefully on the bed, and Chesser thought it was significant she hadn't taken time to remove her eyelashes, which, with her eyes closed as they were, lay thick and full on the skin above her cheeks.

He undressed quickly, turned out all lights in that room, and partially closed the door to the adjoining room to create a kinder, softer illumination. He lay down on the bed, full length, close, next to her.

He gave her mouth a beginning kiss that she received with compliance but contributed to only slightly. Chesser took that to be a suggestion that she was in a taking mood. He was willing, was about to start, when she asked, "What did you do today?"

"Got some sun, swam a bit, talked with Massey."

"I had a jumper. Tall, beautiful beast. A dappled gray named Dover Mist."

Chesser moved only his hand, not abruptly, down to verify her want. Before it reached destination, her fingers intercepted, brought his hand up to one of her breasts. "Just hold me," she said.

She kissed him reassuringly near his mouth and they lay like that, very still, for a long while.

He told her, "I did the right thing."

"That's good," she said, detached.

"I never would have gotten anywhere with The System anyway."

She made a short agreeing sound. No further response from her, not a movement nor a word.

After a while he said, "Massey offered me a deal today."

"We rode through an orchard. Little green apples just coming out."

"You didn't even hear what I said."

"Uh huh. You should have been with us today. We jumped everything except the clouds. Brooks, bushes, and everything." She was delighting in the memory. "I'd like to buy Dover Mist. I wonder if Massey would sell him. Ask him for me. I don't care how much he wants. I want Dover Mist."

"You're not listening to me," said Chesser sharply.

She snuggled against him, perhaps her answer to his accusation.

Chesser's patience was running out. He separated from her but was still only a reach away. "Goddamn it, this is important, important to *me*. You just don't give a shit!"

"Shh," she told him.

"I quit The System. Don't you understand? I'm out of a job."

he gave her time to respond and when she didn't he sat up, his legs over the edge of the bed, his back to her. He heard her move and thought she was coming to him, to embrace him submissively, consolingly. But she had only turned onto her side in the opposite direction, and when he realized this he gave up, stood and went to the open window, looked out at the night. After a while the noises from outside separated themselves from the sound of Maren's breathing, which told him she had gone to sleep.

He put on slacks and a light knit sportshirt and shoved his feet into any pair of his shoes. He didn't try to be quiet, moved as though he were alone in the room. Found cigarettes and lighter on the side table and went out, closing the door surely with force enough to disturb her.

He went down to the main foyer, where he heard the voices and music of Massey's movie. He took care then to be silent with the multiple latches on the main door, neutralized their devices so he wouldn't be locked out. When he stepped outside he had the feeling alarms would sound—bells or a siren. He walked in any direction.

The night air was heavy, cool. There was a hazy ring around the moon. The night noises were louder, a cacophony of all the crawling, hopping, clinging creatures that were daytime cowards but giant brave at night. At least they sounded as though they were answering one another, thought Chesser, and continued on away from the house.

His eyes adjusted enough to the dark to avoid the shrubbery. He was sure of the well-kept expanse of lawn, so he walked full stride. He wondered where the hell he was going and his answer to himself was nowhere.

After a time he stopped and lighted a cigarette. It was then he sensed he wasn't alone. He turned to see a figure in white coming toward him, still about a hundred paces away. He could make out a short, white dress.

Immediately he thought: she's given in, she's come after me, she wasn't really asleep.

But it wasn't Maren.

It was Lady Bolding.

"I thought there was someone ahead of me," she said. "I saw it was you when you lit your cigarette. Do you have another?"

She took one from his case, feeling for it. Their fingers touched. When he lighted it for her the flame illuminated the beauty of her face for him.

"I felt like taking a walk," he explained, and glanced back to the house. Its few lighted windows told him he'd come farther than he realized.

"I walk nearly every night," she said.

"As late as this?"

Chesser had never been alone with Lady Bolding and perhaps that was the primary reason for the unreality he felt. He noticed she was barefoot. The night air held her perfume.

"Were you headed in any particular direction?" she asked.

"Just away."

"Shall we?"

They continued on together.

"To make the most of it," she said, "you ought to take off your shoes."

"Then I'll have to carry them. Less bother to wear them."

"We could share the burden," she suggested, "and carry one each."

He stopped and took off his shoes.

"A better idea," she said. "Leave them by that tree and we'll pick them up on the way back. Don't worry, I know the grounds well."

As he walked on, the damp grass under his feet felt refreshing. He stopped again to roll up his trouser cuffs. She waited silently.

Then they were going down an incline. It was slippery. She took his hand. He wasn't sure if she took it for support or to guide him, but when they were again on level ground she didn't let go.

He was receptive to the unfamiliar shape and texture of her hand; the newness of it was pleasant. For one thing, her hand was not merely placed within his for his to do all the holding. She maintained a pressure equal to his, far from passive.

Chesser thought they should talk, to establish as quickly as possible some sort of coalition. "Tell me," he said, "about you."

"What, particularly?"

"The more revealing, unimportant things."

"That's asking a lot." She laughed lightly.

He sensed she wanted him to continue on that tack. "I already know the unspoken important things."

"Such as?"

"You have a husband somewhere who works for the man you live with." He expected such directness might provoke her. It didn't.

"I don't really live with Massey," she said, not defensively. "I have my own home in Dorset. I only stay here because I prefer to. It's pleasant, no other reason. I come and go as I please."

Chesser thought that was a lie, but she sounded convincing. He asked about her husband.

"My husband is a homosexual."

Chesser nearly said something consoling. Instead he asked what he assumed was the obvious. "You discovered that after the wedding?"

"To the contrary. I've always known it. His name is Alexander. He's beautiful." Her tone was both empathetic and reminiscent. "He's one of those delicate persons, born, unfortunately, two or three hundred years too late."

Chesser asked what she meant by that.

"Alexander has to work to exist. It's unbearable for him. He's too sensitive to be competitive. Fortunately, Massey found a less distressing place for him. Have you ever been to the Middle East? Lebanon or Arabia?"

"No."

"Neither have I."

"I've heard things said about the Arabs," said Chesser.

"From what Alexander writes, they're probably true."

A sudden thought of Maren came to Chesser at that moment. He imagined her waking to find him gone. Would she be concerned? Probably not. His image of her tried to persuade him to return to the house, to her, but he countered it by telling himself she was still sleeping soundly, unaware of his absence.

"I told you a lie," said Lady Bolding.

About Massey, thought Chesser.

"When I told you I was just out for a walk," she said. "Actually, I had a destination."

"What?"

"The North Gate Cottage. Massey let me decorate it for myself. I often go there just to be . . . alone."

"Then I'm intruding."

She told him he wasn't by saying, "It's about another mile from here. Are you game?"

He definitely was. He broke pace then and laughed. "I just stepped on something squishy."

"A snail, no doubt."

"Out of his shell."

"Searching for food."

"Or maybe pleasure."

"They must come out to make love, mustn't they?"

"Otherwise it would be extremely crowded," said Chesser.

"And not nearly so comfortable," said Lady Bolding.

Encouraged by that exchange, his arm encircled her. And, reciprocating, hers went around him. They walked on like that, their sides touching. Chesser remembered how she had looked in the bikini at the pool. It stirred him some, but it also reminded him of Maren's remarks about Lady Bolding's lesbian penchant.

As though his mind had transmitted, she asked, "What has your Maren told you about me? Something, I'm sure."

"Nothing," he replied too quickly.

"Of course she has. She told you I don't fancy men."

"Maren's imagination is—"

"Maren's delightful! You mustn't say a word of apology for her. You should have seen her riding today. What a daredevil!"

"That's for sure."

"You must understand that women, especially beautiful ones such as Maren, have sensual antennae that help tell them almost immediately whether another woman such as myself is a friend, competitor, or potential lover."

"I don't put much faith in intuition."

"You should. Because everything I suspect Maren told you about me is true."

That didn't make sense to Chesser. It argued against all he was now feeling and certainly all he was anticipating. Logic, not intuition, now seemed to limit his prospects with Lady Bolding. He was suddenly, intensely disappointed.

Lady Bolding told him, "I've had my share of intimate experiences, but only twice with men and once with a boy." She paused, as though to allow Chesser to handle that, then continued in the same detached matter-of-fact manner. "The boy was first and, of course, was successful only in satisfying my curiosity. With the first man, it was trial. With the second, it was error."

Perhaps for psychological support she increased the pressure of her arm around him. Chesser was actually aware of her hand matching the curve of his waist. He thought he should contribute some thoughts of his own about women, perhaps make some statement to exaggerate his liberal attitudes, let her know that despite his heterosexuality he wasn't a sexual bigot. He decided to say nothing.

"When it comes to physical pleasure," she told him, "we're all pretty much reflexive creatures. Sooner or later we're irresistibly pulled to the particular part of the sexual spectrum that demands and offers the most intensity."

That sounded, Chesser thought, like something she'd probably read someplace and needed to remember verbatim. Excuses in the form of explanations were vital.

She continued: "Once one has finally accepted a certain identification in the erotic minority, it's very difficult to deny it. Even when one feels the desire strongly." She underlined that last phrase with her tone.

Chesser wondered what the hell she was talking about. "You mean . . ."

"Take a person such as myself. I've already accepted what I am. I know what I want. I enjoy a measure of self-confidence and personal well-being in that. I'm going along just fine. Then, suddenly, circumstances bring me to someone who causes contradiction in my sexual values. What should I do? Close off my feelings, tell myself it's not worth the agony of ambivalence?" She let the questions hang for a moment, then went on.

"Last night I gave it considerable thought. There I was in my bed, and, only steps away, there were you and Maren. My fantasies put me between the two of you. However, the more I thought of that, of sharing both you and Maren, the more I realized I was merely compromising, trying to camouflage my ulterior motive. You see . . ." She hesitated, out of diffidence or perhaps to add emphasis, and then said, ". . . actually, I only wanted to be with you."

That sent Chesser off-balance. Suddenly, marvelous possibilities. He said, "I'm flattered."

She didn't tell him not to be. "As long as I'm being so candid you might as well know I followed you out tonight. Purposely."

Chesser's ego was expanding. "I had no idea. Actually . . ."

"I know, I know what you thought. All along I was intentionally misleading you, as well as myself."

"You gave me no indication."

"As I told you, I couldn't. I felt the attraction from the first, but you were a man and I wasn't supposed to be susceptible, not at all. I honestly tried to block the compulsion, the chemistry, whatever it is. However, it increased."

They had been walking slowly all the while. He stopped them. He held her. She held. Against one another with a gentle full-length pressure.

Chesser was immediately aroused. She had to know it, perhaps acknowledged it when she drew her cheek across his and offered her mouth up. He kissed her very tenderly.

"Was your destination tonight also a lie?" he asked.

"No. We're almost there."

The North Gate Cottage. It was two stories and, in keeping with the main house, authentic Georgian. In daylight one would be able to see that its exterior of old brick was almost entirely covered with ivy. But now in the dark that growth, having eliminated all angles, made the cottage appear hulking, heavy set, and ominous.

Lady Bolding went in, preceding Chesser. She snapped a light on and immediately closed the drapes, an act that seemed to go with the clandestine circumstances. He remembered having told Massey he'd never stolen anything and thought this was a sort of stealing. Taking the forbidden . . .

"Would you like a drink?" asked Lady Bolding.

"Would you?"

"No."

She was across the room. The space between them created awkwardness. Their eyes met. She looked away. Before he could start toward her, she quickly excused herself and went upstairs.

He looked about the room. It was elegantly done in browns and creams, black, tortoise, leather, and valuable animal pelts. On the top of a desk he noticed a letter addressed to her in a strong, evidently feminine hand. He was tempted to read it. There also was some of her personal stationery, tastefully engraved, next to a simple sterling upright frame holding an enlarged snapshot of her, younger, flanked by two pretty dark-haired girls—leggy girls in short skirts. Their pose was arms around. Their expressions were identical, rather insolent. Chesser wondered. He heard her barefoot steps above.

For no particular reason he pulled open one of the desk's small upper drawers and was surprised to find a tiny nickel-plated revolver lying on some postage stamps. At first he thought the revolver was a toy replica, perhaps one of the novelty cigarette lighters, but when he took it out and felt its weight he knew it was real. He examined it, curious. As he replaced it in the drawer he saw a plain, wide, platinum wedding band. He closed the drawer carefully.

His eyes then came on another smaller framed photograph, propped up. This one of a slender young man, fair haired, fixed smile. Symmetrically featured, a bit too good-looking. Alexander. Chesser was sure.

He turned and was startled as a large tiger tabby came out from around a chair. It stopped, stretched, blinked, and spread its front toes, exposing its claws. The cat regarded Chesser with a disapproving stare, then sat and began licking itself.

Chesser heard Lady Bolding's movements above. He thought she might be coming down then, so he assumed what he considered an appropriately casual stance, turned partly away from the stairs. While waiting he noticed a clear, crystal humidor of cigars. Massey's. And an arrangement of fresh flowers—white daisies and cornflowers mixed with small pink roses in their prime. Saw, also, a glass paperweight with an iridescent blue dragonfly preserved forever at its center. Saw a portrait sketch of Lady Bolding, well done. He went closer to study the portrait. Lady in repose. Her breasts insinuated by the swift, intermittent pen strokes. Her perfect, languorous yet imperious face done in the same technique. Even in mere outline her fascinating blends and contrasts showed clearly.

Looking at her portrait, Chesser recalled with unease her saying that no man had ever pleased her. What made him so sure he would be the exception? How much of his past confidence with women had come from the knowledge of their ability to respond? Knowing they had previously experienced pleasure had always been a reassuring starting point. Usually, once desire was established, response was assumed. But not this time. This time he could assume nothing.

He heard her calling his name, the last syllable of it with a rising inflection; a request. Again she called. This time the last syllable was inflected down, softly but unmistakably demanding. He turned from the portrait and climbed the stairs.

The second floor was completely dark. Chesser put out his hands, felt walls left and right, and deduced he was in a narrow hallway. He edged his way along and collided with a table. She called again. He was headed the wrong way.

"Where are you?" he asked.

"Here."

"Something wrong with the lights?"

She didn't answer that, so he proceeded down the hall in the direction of her voice. His hands found the doorway to a room. "I can't see a thing," he said, a bit embarrassed. He expected her to say something then from inside that room, to guide him to her. But again her voice was coming from behind him, calling his name, this time with some impatience.

He turned and crossed the hall, got the opposite wall with his touch, felt along it until he located another doorway. He had the sensation that he'd gone blind.

"Where are you?" he asked again.

"Right here," she said.

At least he'd found the right room.

"Snap on a light," he said, and felt without success for a switch on the wall near the door frame.

"I'm waiting for you," she said.

That encouraged him to take some further steps. His legs came in contact with what had to be the side of a bed. He reached down and found the surface of a silk sheet, leaned over and moved his hand, patted until he came in touch with her skin, her bare hip.

She said nothing.

Chesser undressed. He wondered how large the bed was. When he lay down on it he decided it was king size. He rolled toward her and his forearm brushed her face. He apologized. He made out her position. She was on her back. He put his hand beneath her head so he could estimate where his mouth would find hers. He was slightly off the mark but immediately corrected that. He kissed her. He didn't bring her against him, although his chest and her left breast were lightly pressed. His free hand explored only the skin of her opposite shoulder where it made a soft transitional curve to her neck. She reciprocated in the kiss with an authority unfamiliar to him.

"Can't we have a light on?" he asked.

"No."

"I like to see what I'm doing."

"No." Definitely.

"Are there windows in this room?"

"I drew the drapes."

"Let's open them. There's a full moon."

"I prefer not."

She took the initiative, shifted onto her side and pulled him to her so they were front to front, pressed. Chesser was not entirely aroused, not nearly as much as before. He felt cheated. He was too accustomed to loving with his eyes as well.

They kissed again, and began their explorations. She gave his breasts important attention, applied her mouth, caused some well gauged apparently intentional pain. But her fingers handled him as though he were an unfamiliar object, either too fragile or dangerous.

Chesser traced his fingers over her, with long, slow-traveling touches, yet he felt the insufficiency of touch alone, wishing he could see all of her at once. He was forced to piece her together, using his memory for reference—her in the bikini at the swimming pool. He wished she would say something now to help verify her identity. He had to keep reminding himself it was she he was experiencing. He hated the blackness that added to the impression it was mere fantasy. The blackness was a handicap, and he wanted very much to be effective. He was tempted to get up, find the drapery pull, and get the help of moonlight, but he remembered how much she'd been opposed to that.

He resigned himself to it, resorted to technique. Reminded himself to be particularly tender, as he assumed her experience had been. Used his mouth delicately, his tongue, and wondered about the possible abrasive effect of his chin and cheeks.

He was encouraged when she sounded as thought he were pleasing her. And when she tightened as though it were true. When he hesitated she lifted to him for him to continue. And when he thought he'd done enough of that she held him there, her fingers reining his hair so harshly his scalp burned.

And apparently, after a long while, that was how she achieved. From the throaty animal sounds that came from her and the increase in her tensions, he was sure she had.

Finally her legs relaxed, left and right apart. He kneeled up. She must have sensed his intention to enter her then, because she quickly drew her legs up together and rolled onto her side.

Chesser crawled up and lay beside her again. He touched himself to assess the degree of his want. Her hand covered his hand. He quickly took his away.

She kneeled up close and he thought she might be about to return the pleasure. Expecting that, he concentrated to visualize her exquisite face. But then she pivoted on one knee and swung her other leg over, so he was beneath and between her. She found herself with him, exactly, and regulated the entering, gradually. Until he was entirely included and her weight sealed them. She remained motionless for a long moment. He heard her breathe in and out, shallow, as she waited to adjust herself to him. She was extraordinarily firm around him, clutching moist. He put his hands to her breasts, stroked them to their tips.

She began. Riding him.

Chesser thought of Dover Mist.

All the way to the finish, which for Chesser was not all that sensational.

Afterward he came down quickly, lay there in the dark with his right arm touching her. He reminded himself that he'd just fucked an authentic Lady. But he knew he hadn't really fucked her. She had literally been ascendant throughout. Not very D. H. Lawrence, he thought. He reached to his trousers on the floor, got cigarettes and the lighter. To be chivalrous, he also lighted one for her. "Careful," he cautioned as he offered it to her.

"No, thank you," she said, sounding distant.

He didn't have an ashtray, so he lay there and smoked both. "I've got to be getting back," he told her.

"You can't stay here, of course," she said as though he'd already left.

He got up, with the two cigarettes between his lips. His eyes smarted from unseen smoke. He grabbed up his trousers and shirt. He was fairly sure she didn't resent it when he didn't kiss her good night, merely said it. He groped his way downstairs, where he tossed the burning cigarettes into a huge, clean ashtray. The cat didn't look at him, only snaked her tail across the carpet twice. He dressed hurriedly and went out.

The moon was low now, going. What time was it? He hadn't worn his watch. He had only a vague idea of the direction back to the main house. He started off at a brisk clip, the cold, wet grass now not so pleasant under his feet.

As he walked he tried not to think of what he'd just done. And, of course, trying not to do that brought on Maren. Was she still sleeping? Sure she was. But perhaps not. If not, was she all right? Certainly. She wasn't alone. She was safe. There were others in the house. Massey was there. She wasn't alone.

Suddenly a despicable conclusion: Massey with Maren.

Chesser began to run. A race with his imagination, which said Massey had planned the entire thing. Lady Bolding had faked it. Under instructions from Massey to get him away so Massey could force himself on Maren. The lecherous old bastard.

Chesser didn't listen to the more rational thought that Massey with his years would hardly be even physically capable of raping an agile, violently resisting Maren. Nor did Chesser consider that his thoughts were at least partly a ricochet from his own guilt.

Chesser just ran.

To the rescue. Or, if too late for rescue, at least revenge.

He saw a distant light that he believed was the house. His legs ached and his breathing burned when he was close enough for the barking of many dogs to tell him it was only the kennels. He stopped, gasped for breath, and tried to figure which was the right direction. He guessed and ran on.

Finally he came to a continuous hedge, too high to go over and too dense to go through. He ran parallel to it, hoping it would lead to something. It did. An incline that reduced his run to a climb. By now his fears had transformed themselves into a sort of conclusive hysteria, which increased when he looked up and found himself at the rear of the main house.

He controlled his panic, decided against rushing in. Better to rest a moment, regain his strength so he'd be ready for anything. He sat on the terrace steps and let his head lie back to ease his breathing. The muscles of his legs were twitching. Sweat trickled down his temples and neck; his shirt was soaked with it. He advised himself that a forty-year-old man ought not to be out fucking and running around all night.

His breathing finally returned to almost normal. He got up and tried rear doors. All were locked. He went around to the front door he had unlatched earlier, but now it was locked and he took this as an indication of the plot against him. Determined, he backed off and braced himself in position to kick in one of the door's side windows. But he realized, just in time, that he was barefoot. While he tried to think of another way in, the front door was opened by Massey's number-one mute servant, Hickey, who smilingly motioned Chesser in. Chesser hesitated. Much of his resolve gave way to Hickey's size. With a false nonchalance, he stepped by Hickey and into the foyer.

He took the main stairs two at a time, hurried down the hall to their room. He had imagined crashing in, but now he carefully turned the knob, opened the door, and entered.

She wasn't in the bed. Despite his panic, he had held to the possibility she would still be sleeping. The bed was disheveled, but she wasn't in it. The bedside light was on. She wasn't in the bathroom. She wasn't in the adjoining room. She wasn't there. Her *I Ching* book and three half-crown pieces were on the floor. He got his watch from the dresser, saw it was four forty-five. At this hour she couldn't be anywhere else but with Massey. Against her will, of course.

He rushed out, along the landing. He didn't know which was Massey's room. Perhaps, thought Chesser, the old bastard sleeps the same as he eats, wherever, according to his mood. Or maybe he had a secret room especially equipped for such affairs. Chesser went down the corridor and around to a wing of the mansion. He tried doors, listened at doors, called her name but got no reply. He went back to the landing, intending to search the opposite wing. It was then he saw her.

She was coming up the stairs in a long, sheer silk Dior dressing gown, semitransparent. A palest blue color. Her long Viking hair was slightly mussed. She was carrying a glass of milk with a thick slice of well-buttered bread balanced on it.

Chesser was so relieved to see her that he couldn't speak.

"I woke up starved," she said. She hesitated when she came to him, extended her lips for a little kiss, and then proceeded to their room, sure that he was following.

She took a large bite of the bread. Chesser took her in his arms.

"I love you," he said with less intensity than he felt.

"I know," she said, chewing.

He had to wait for her to swallow. Then he kissed her. There was butter on her lips. She felt so good to him, so marvelously familiar.

"I was worried about you," he told her. He thought she might say the same.

"I did your *I Ching* for you," she said. "You got the Cauldron and Inner Truth." She broke from him so she could take another bite and a sip. She glanced down at his bare feet. His trouser cuffs were wet. Some blades of grass were stuck to his skin.

"I took a long walk," he explained.

"I thought maybe you were out playing cricket or something." She grinned.

"As a matter of fact, I got lost." A true lie. He hoped she wouldn't pursue the subject. He was so full of love and guilt he was afraid he would spill everything. "I'm sorry," he said.

"About what?"

"About before, losing my temper."

She didn't pardon him, except with her eyes. She sat on the bed, preoccupied with the slice of bread. She ate around the crust and drained the glass of milk. Then she looked thoughtful.

Chesser felt horrible. Foolish, tired, and dirty. Maybe if he took a shower he'd feel better. Wash the guilt away. He wondered if Lady Bolding would tell Maren what had happened. Undoubtedly she would. Beautiful women always inflict such things on other beautiful women. Chesser realized that his best chance was now, before tomorrow, to put so much of his love into and around Maren that Lady Bolding's words, no matter what, would seem ridiculous.

"I love you more than anything," he said.

"Why don't you take a shower," she suggested.

Chesser went into the bathroom. he hated himself in the mirror while he undressed, kicked his soiled shirt and trousers into a corner, got into the shower stall and turned on the cold for a momentary punishment. He adjusted the spray to a more benevolent temperature, lathered and rinsed and did feel better, cleaner.

Maren came in and helped. She used a towel to wipe his back and down the back of his legs.

"We're getting away from here tomorrow," said Chesser.

"To where?"

He wanted to say Chantilly but decided London might please her more.

"Business?" she asked.

"No more business," he told her, meaning it.

In the other room she lighted two cigarettes and tossed his with more force than usual. He caught it with fearless ease.

He thought he should say something to demonstrate his change of attitude. "You know, we ought to take up sky-diving," he lied. She'd suggested it once or twice, but he'd always vetoed it, adamantly.

"Why?"

"Oh, just for something different to do."

She gave him a long, suspicious look. "What was the deal Massey offered you?" she asked casually.

"You wouldn't believe it."

"I might. If I want to."

Chesser was sure that last remark referred to his most recent carrying-on. "Massey's deal is no deal," he said.

"Stop being cryptic."

"All right. He wants me to steal twelve billion dollars worth of diamonds."

She didn't laugh as he had expected.

"Isn't that absurd?" he said, sprawling on the bed. He was very tired.

"Tell me about it. Everything Massey said."

He told her, droning the words out.

She walked the room, back and forth, restless. She went to the entrance to the bathroom and flipped her cigarette accurately into the toilet bowl. Chesser heard the brief *phhht* it made as it was extinguished. He wished she'd come to bed. He had some crucial repairing to do. She sat on the floor, down from him. She separated half her hair into three strands and began braiding. The repetitive motion of her fingers was nearly hypnotic to Chesser's weary eyes. She told him, seriously, "It's a fabulous idea."

"Sky-diving?"

"No. Massey's deal."

Chesser scoffed.

"How else could you make fifteen million so fast and easy?"

Fast maybe, but not easy, thought Chesser. He told her: "It can't be done."

"Sure it can."

"I don't know a goddamn thing about stealing." He thought about what he'd just done that night.

"What about Marrakesh?" she asked.

"What about it?"

"Smuggling is a lot like stealing, isn't it? You already know how to smuggle."

That hit him. He was positive he'd never told her about the Marrakesh affair. How did she find out about it? He didn't want to ask her.

"Anyway," she went on, "stealing can't be all that difficult or so many people wouldn't do it. Perhaps we could learn, read up on it, get the advice of experts."

Chesser noticed the "we." From that and her exuberance he knew he was in trouble. "People get killed stealing," he said emphatically.

That seemed to increase her enthusiasm. "I'll bet it would be the biggest robbery ever. Twelve billion dollars."

"Let's go to sleep," he said, closing his eyes.

"I'm too stimulated."

He opened his eyes. "Okay. What do you want to do?"

"Beat The System."

"Nobody beats The System."

"We could."

"Nobody."

"I don't even hate The System and I want to do it."

"It's impossible."

"How can you say it's impossible? No one's ever not done it."

That, thought Chesser, was very much the same as Massey's reasoning. "Let's go to sleep," he told her.

"We'd make criminal history."

"We'd get caught. Or killed. Probably both."

"Not us," she said, as though together they enjoyed some special immunity.

"For Christ's sake, let's sleep," Chesser said.

"Not until you promise."

Chesser held out a while longer until he was too exhausted not to promise. Anything to get some sleep.

"No matter what," said Massey, "you must not contact me. Not for any reason."

"You'll want a progress report, won't you?" asked Chesser.

"No. I don't want to hear from you again until it's over. And then only after a respectable period."

"What's respectable?"

"Two weeks, at least. Remember my terms. If you bungle it you're on your own."

"I'm on my own."

Massey was delighted with Chesser's compliant attitude. It was one of the main reasons he'd chosen Chesser for this project rather than a professional. Massey was certain he could control Chesser, whereas a professional, no matter how competent, would have been difficult to manage, impossible to manipulate and, of course, unreliable. Chesser's amateurism was actually an asset. Chesser was clever enough to serve but not ruthless enough to betray.

Massey warned him, "Even if you do try to involve me, no one will believe you."

Even I don't believe me, thought Chesser, feeling ridiculous, actually standing there with a straight face taking Massey's instructions. He told himself the only reason he'd gone along with it this far was to pacify Maren. No one could possibly be serious about stealing twelve billion dollars worth of diamonds. Although Massey seemed to be. Perhaps, Chesser thought, the old billionaire had finally blown his old mind.

Massey contradicted that theory with a very sane, though faintly chilling, smile. "I've complete confidence in you, Chesser. I'm sure you'll pull this thing off. My only regret is that I won't be right beside you, enjoying the adventure of it."

"You're invited," Chesser said.

"My money will represent me," Massey said quietly.

"What about expenses?"

"It's all been arranged."

They were in Massey's study. Massey was behind the desk. He opened a leather-bound folio and turned it over to Chesser, who was seated opposite. "Sign this," Massey directed.

Chesser saw it was an ordinary application form for a checking account with the National Upland Bank of London. The form was pre-dated, July 18, 1968. Beneath the form was a sheaf of checks.

Massey started to hand across his personal old Tiffany fountain pen but thought better of it and got a white ballpoint from a drawer. Chesser took it and noticed it was imprinted "The Waldorf Astoria, New York, N.Y."

"Sign it M. J. Mathew," Massey told him.

"In my normal handwriting?"

"Of course."

"M-A-T-H-E-W?"

"M. J." instructed Massey.

Chesser signed the name on the application form. Massey took it from him. And the pen as well. "You'll notice I've managed to have the checks precertified," said Massey.

Chesser thumbed through the checks and saw they were officially perforated and stamped with certification. They didn't have any amounts on them. Chesser didn't know that could be done.

"In order," explained Massey, "that you may draw whatever funds are necessary. The bank will honor up to two million. That should be enough to handle it, don't you agree?"

"Should." Chesser shrugged. He decided he was becoming accustomed to huge figures. "Are you sure about this bank?" he asked.

"Absolutely," replied Massey. He had every right to be sure. He owned the bank, although his ownership was well camouflaged within the complex structure of his many enterprises.

Chesser thought a moment. "What's to stop me from withdrawing the two million and running?"

"Nothing except yourself."

"I could do that."

"You won't."

"What makes you so sure?"

"If you did, you'd owe me," Massey said. "Considerably more than you do now."

"So, I'd owe you."

"And I'd collect. Sooner or later, one way or another."

"What about my fifteen million," he asked. "How will that be paid?"

"However you want it."

"Dollars, negotiable bonds."

"How about Standard Oil of New Jersey, that sort?"

"That'll be fine," said Chesser, and demonstrated his confidence just for the minor drama of it. "Have them ready."

"You deliver, I'll have them."

Chesser stood and tucked the checks into his inside jacket pocket. Massey remained seated. Chesser was surprised to find he was now somewhat infatuated with the idea of giving this project a try. Maybe, he thought, insanity is catching. He also realized that fifteen million was not an incidental factor. He decided Massey didn't want to shake hands to seal the deal, so he started to go. When he got to the door it occurred to him that he'd forgotten something. He turned to Massey and asked, "Why?"

A quizzical look from Massey.

"Why do you want The System's inventory? You said you'd tell me."

"I thought you'd have guessed by now."

"It can't be for money."

"No."

"Revenge?"

"That's it exactly," said Massey, too quickly.

"Getting back at them for the Shorewater project?"

"That's it."

Chesser tried to believe it but couldn't. His expression told Massey that.

"I've another motive," Massey admitted, "but it shouldn't concern you."

"I want to know."

Massey didn't want to lose Chesser now. "It's a personal matter," he said.

Chesser waited.

"I'm a powerful man," Massey said. "But power, like most vital things, requires nourishment. This project, if successful, will allow me to make a personal statement, so to speak, in a unique and substantial way."

Chesser said nothing and kept his eyes steady

Massey told him: "There aren't many really important things left for me to do, short of causing a war, and I'm too old for that."

Chesser nodded and waited for Massey to continue. However, from Massey's expression, Chesser knew he wasn't going to get any more out of him.

No good-byes.

He just left Massey sitting there.

From the top of the stairs he saw Maren waiting in the main foyer. Lady Bolding was with her. They were talking in a serious manner. Chesser feared what he believed was probably the topic of their discussion. To spare himself from overhearing and perhaps provoking a confrontation then and there, he went down the stairs with enough noise to forewarn them.

"All set?" he asked, forcing a smile.

"The bags are in the car," said Maren.

"Last night . . ." said Lady Bolding.

Chesser braced himself.

". . . I promised to pay my gambling debt." She handed Chesser her personal draft for a thousand.

"I left mine on the bed for Massey," lied Maren.

Chesser hoped his relief wasn't too apparent.

Lady Bolding gave him her good-bye with swift cheek kisses. She gave Maren the same, left and right, and also an extra on the lips, a bit lingering, was Chesser's impression. But then, to him, everything seemed at that moment to be happening either too fast or in slow motion.

CHAPTER 13

In less than a week, Chesser and Maren were settled in London. They stayed four nights at the Connaught and then moved into a house in Park Village, N.W.1.

The house was bought for Maren by her French lawyers, who went so far as to sacrifice their native compulsion to bargain in order to expedite the purchase. They estimated that more was to be gained by encouraging the domestic inclinations of their most promising client. With typical French tenacity and faith in the persuasions of passion, the lawyers were waiting for Maren to marry her fortune into their hands. So, they believed buying a house, something she'd never done before, was a step in the desired direction. For that reason alone they paid the first price asked, and obtained immediate possession for her.

The seller of the house was a foppish, middle-aged, semi-aristocrat by the name of Philip B. Hinds, who desperately needed the money to spend. Actually, Mr. Hinds was merely a tenant in possession of a Crown lease and the property really belonged to Princess Margaret, who received a modest sum in ground rent annually. Ground rent meaning literally payment for that portion of earth upon which the house was placed. The Crown lease had ninety-two years to run, which Maren considered time enough.

The house, as all the other four on the exclusive, crescent-shaped street, had been designed and built by Nash. *The* Nash, who had so much improved the look of London with his concepts. It was a four-story structure, furnished in excellent taste, complete with private garden and grouchy, fastidious staff. The latter was dismissed immediately by Maren. She preferred not to pay for the idiosyncrasies of the former foppish tenant. She replaced his servants with a pair of au pair girls, attractive young Danes named Siv and Britta, who, Maren wisely judged, would be more involved with satisfying their libidos than anything else. Besides, she thought, it was more pleasant to have attractive help around.

However, with her Nordic female directness, Maren let the Danes know they were to care for everything except that between Chesser's legs. She alone, emphasis on alone, would care for that. Not that the girls need be prudishly self-conscious. Stimulation was one thing, culmination quite something else. Siv and Britta understood exactly where the line was drawn and went about their duties with their fair, pretty faces framed by drawn-back blonde hair, their braless blouses punctuated by nipples and their skirts amply exposing well-shaped legs and even more whenever they bent to pick something up or reached for something high.

Thus, on the second day in the house, when Maren announced she was going shopping, she confidently left Chesser alone with the help.

Maren's precautions were practical but really unnecessary, considering Chesser's frame of mind. Certainly he was aware of the pretty Danes, but that form of interest was superseded by thoughts of his new occupation: thief. Since leaving Massey, Chesser had the feeling he was observing everything from a different dimension. As though he had stepped from one existence to another, just like that.

Now the reality of what he had committed himself to do came to him sharply. Ambivalence pulled him tight. One moment he was convinced that he should laugh the whole thing off. The next he was a man with fifteen million. What finally convinced him to be more committed to the venture was the realization that he had no choice. He had promised Maren, and to her a promise was an emotional mortgage. Maren and the venture were now inextricably related and although it was possible that he could continue to have her without the other, he knew that would somehow cause a change in their close-ness—an important bruise, a flaw that might eventually have serious consequences. In theory he could, of course, walk away from the entire thing, including her, except that was something he knew he couldn't possibly do.

So, keeping the image of fifteen million in mind and push-ing away caution and pessimism, he decided to get on with it.

The next problem was where to start. Chesser didn't know. He tried to think as a thief and came to the idea that perhaps what he ought to do first was take a look at 11 Harrowhouse from his new, criminal perspective. For disguise he put on a pair of dark glasses.

He exercised good judgment in not going too near number 11, but observed it from the corner. It told him nothing. It was as it had always been, merely a building butted tightly against other, similar buildings on each side.

He walked around the block to see it from the opposite cor-ner, and all that presented was a view from the opposite cor-ner. Nothing inspiring. He walked down Andrew Street, which ran perpendicular to Harrowhouse, and discovered a mews, one of those comparatively wide back alleyways which make the maze of London more of a maze. A city sign said its name was Puffing Mews. It ran parallel to Harrow-house and would give him a rear view of number 11.

Chesser adjusted his dark glasses and strolled down the mews. He passed a parked Rolls-Royce saloon that was being wiped with routine affection by a uniformed chauffeur, who took no special notice of him. Chesser had difficulty ascertain-ing which building was number 11. But finally, when he saw a small sign that designated the delivery entrance of Mid-Continental Oil, he surmised that the next building was the one. It had to be. It was the only building on the mews with no rear entrance or windows, a sheer, five-story-high wall of brick.

He walked to the end of Puffing Mews, having learned no more than that the only way into number 11 was the front. Of course, it occurred to him another approach might be from above, the roof, but he had no way of confirming that.

He returned home. At least he'd accomplished getting started. He sprawled on a couch and tried for distraction with that month's edition of *Queen*. Siv voluntarily brought him a tumbler of very cold Aquavit and a warm smile, and he was thankful for both. He lay there, sipping the fiery yet frigid liquid, trying to get into what someone, via *Queen*, said was his horoscope.

Then he heard it.

A sound like a little sharp smack in a tight space. He thought nothing of it until he heard it several times at uneven intervals. It stopped for a minute or so and then began again. A unique sound that wasn't completely unfamiliar. It seemed to be coming from below.

He put his ear to the rug. It was definitely coming from below. He went to investigate, located the stairs to the cellar, and went down.

There was Maren.

She was standing solidly with legs apart, left hand on hip, other hand extended straight out. A perfect shooting stance with her body profile so that she was as minimal a target as possible for her adversary, which was an old, muslin-covered, headless dressmaker's dummy.

Chesser knew now that the sound he'd heard before was from a gun equipped with a silencer. He saw a bullet thump into the packed form of the dummy, where other bullets had previously hit, right where the heart would be. She took quick aim and pulled off another shot, which thumped in not a half inch off the same mark. She stopped to reload. Chesser had never before seen a woman with a gun, except in movies, of course. But never in the flesh. Extreme lethal attraction. He asked her: "Where did you learn to shoot like that?"

"Jean Marc."

"Oh."

She released the empty clip, picked up a loaded one, shoved it home and cocked a bullet into the chamber as though she'd done it thousands of times. "I'm not as good from the hip," she said, "not as accurate."

She turned and demonstrated, spent the entire clip rapid

fire. The bullets hit the dummy's chest, making holes no more than six inches apart, a sort of circle.

"See?" she said with a sigh, "not a good, tight pattern."

"Not bad," he said, and thought, Jesus, she's deadly!

"It takes practice. We must both practice."

"What for?"

"I got a Mauser for you too. Just like mine."

She indicated an identical weapon lying on the surface of a nearby packing crate. It also was equipped with a silencer. There were several cartons of bullets, a small can of oil, and some special cleaning brushes. What she had gone shopping for. His and hers weapons.

She told him: "I used to prefer a Beretta 380 Cougar until Jean Marc got me a Mauser. Jean Marc said a nine-millimeter Mauser Special could stop just about anything."

"Stop anything from what?"

"Living." She said it out of the side of her mouth, and it was so incongruous coming from her that Chesser had to laugh.

"We won't be needing guns," he told her.

"How do you know?"

"Because it's never going to get to that point."

"Supposing *they* have guns?"

"They who?"

She shrugged. "Whoever."

"Well, the best way to not get shot is to not have a gun."

"That's stupid," she said, and began reloading a clip.

"If you have a gun they may shoot because they think you intend to shoot. But if you don't have—"

"They might shoot anyway," she said.

"Never happen."

"Might."

"Even the British police don't carry guns. So it must not be so stupid."

"They carry guns," contended Maren.

"No they don't."

"They didn't use to but sometimes they do now."

She was right. Chesser remembered reading about the Bobbies now being frequently allowed to carry revolvers.

"Know why they decided to carry guns?" Maren asked

Chesser asked why, knowing she was going to tell him regardless.

"So they could shoot back for a change," she said smugly. Having had the last word she picked up Chesser's Mauser by its muzzle and handed it to him. In the transfer he almost dropped it.

He didn't particularly like the feel of it and he had to force his fingers to grip.

She gestured toward the dummy, offering him the target.

He stood wrong, full front, facing it, brought the Mauser up and jerked the trigger. The bullet missed the dummy entirely, zinged off the granite foundation wall behind it and ricocheted several times, making them duck.

"You jerked," she said.

He was surprised that he'd missed. Maren had made it seem so easy.

"You've got to squeeze the trigger," she told him. "I know you know how to squeeze."

She removed the clip from his gun and had him place his finger over hers on the trigger so he could feel what she meant by squeezing. She showed him how to stand and told him how his breathing could affect his accuracy.

Chesser told himself he was only humoring her by paying attention. After the fundamentals, she rammed the loaded clip back into the gun and cocked.

"The best way to get good at it is to pretend you're dead if you miss," she said.

He pretended that, really concentrated, and squeezed. The bullet thumped into the lower part of the dummy.

"Got her that time!" shouted Chesser.

"Yeah," said Maren, not impressed, "right between the ovaries."

"What's the difference?"

"Go for the heart."

He shot again and again. Maren loaded clips while he fired them off, round after round. Some hits. But mostly misses that zinged around their heads like deadly bees.

Half past noon the following day. Chesser was seated in a rear pew at St. Paul's.

About a hundred others were scattered throughout the vast

cathedral. They had chosen places most distant from one another, as though such separateness might bring them in greater proximity to God.

Chesser wasn't there to pray. He hadn't said a prayer since he was fifteen. He glanced up and was paying some respect to the structural genius of Christopher Wren when Maren sidled into the pew.

"You were supposed to meet me at one thirty. Outside." He said it at normal level but his voice seemed to boom in this well-built womb, where it is said one can hear a tear drop.

A few old heads turned to condemn.

"Shh," remonstrated Maren. Then she whispered, "I suspected you were meeting someone."

"I am."

"Who?"

"You don't know him."

"It has to do with our project, doesn't it?"

Chesser nodded. He'd intended to tell Maren about Watts. But not until afterward. Because Watts was a long shot, his best bet, but still a long shot.

"I want to be included in everything," said Maren.

Chesser shrugged. He took a prayer book from the rack in front of him, riffled its pages for no particular reason. He noticed part of one page had been torn out. He wondered irreverently if someone had done it to get rid of a wad of chewing gum.

"I talked to Mildred," Maren said.

"What did Jean Marc have to say this time?" asked Chesser, not really interested.

"I didn't talk through her, just to her."

"Oh."

"She's going to help us."

"You didn't tell her about our project, did you?"

"Not everything."

Chesser closed his eyes and shook his head.

"Don't worry," Maren assured, "we can trust her. If there's anyone in this world I'm sure I can trust, it's Mildred."

Chesser thought he detected some personal implication in that and decided he'd be better off not pushing the loyalty issue. Just because Maren hadn't mentioned his recent infidelity didn't mean she didn't know about it.

"Mildred won't tell a soul," declared Maren. "You do believe in Mildred, don't you?"

Chesser gazed at the far-away altar for a moment. He nodded.

That pleased Maren. "I keep forgetting that you've never met her. She talks about you so much. Anyway, I've asked her over tonight." She slid closer, to get arm in arm with him. "We can use all the help we can get. Mildred will put us in touch with someone on the other side who can guide us."

"What about your Chinaman?" asked Chesser, referring to Maren's invisible *aide-de-vie*.

A quizzical look from her. She hadn't given the supernatural Oriental a single thought since she'd started with Mildred. Now she glanced around as though expecting him to be there. "He hasn't been with me lately," she said, "and neither has Billie Three Rocks."

"I always figured we could count on dear, departed Billie," said Chesser.

"We can. He's just taking some time off."

"I suppose everyone needs a vacation, even a dead Indian."

Maren nodded. "He'll be around when we need him."

"Maybe they've both given up on you."

"No." She was sure. "They're supposed to see me through, all the way, to the very last."

Chesser saw Watts then, coming down the near aisle from the direction of the altar. Evidently he'd come in through a side entrance. He was squinting, searching for Chesser, who signaled discreetly.

Watts caught it. He came to the end of the pew, hesitated, then side-stepped in to sit next to them.

Chesser and Watts shook hands. Watts's skin felt extremely dry to Chesser. Maren was introduced. She had set a pleasant expression on her face, while her eyes studied this mild, ordinary-looking man. Her imagination had expected someone strong and insidious. Watts smiled gently and viewed her youthful beauty with respect.

Chesser got right to it. "I've a favor to ask of you."

"Yes, sir."

"Two favors, actually. The first is that you drop all the sirs."

"All right," agreed Watts, a bit embarrassed.

"I've been thinking," said Chesser, "about that friend of yours."

"Which friend?" Watts almost said sir again.

"You told me about him that afternoon at the Connaught. The one who had only a few months to live."

Watts didn't blink an eye. "What about him?"

"Well, I think we may be able to help one another."

"Help?"

"Yes. From what you told me, your friend has a financial problem caused by the unsympathetic regulations of the firm he works for."

A nod from Watts.

Chesser reached into his jacket pocket. Brought out a once-folded check. He unfolded it and put it on his left knee. It was one of the certified checks supplied by Massey and signed M. J. Mathew by Chesser. Made out for two hundred thousand dollars. Payable to Charles Watts.

Watts looked at it for a long time.

Chesser decided at that moment he was going to give Watts the check whether he cooperated or not.

From seeing his name on the check, Watts realized Chesser knew the friend was a figment. However, Watts chose to continue with it. It was better for both of them, more comfortable. He asked, "How can my friend help you?"

"By supplying me with some information about the place where he works."

"What sort of information?"

"As much as he knows. Especially about the arrangement of things beneath the ground floor."

"My friend knows all about that."

"I'm sure he does."

"But it won't be necessary to pay him. He'll be glad to do it."

A smile from Chesser. "I'm pleased to hear that's the sort of friend he is. However, I must insist on paying. It's worth it to me to know the details." He shoved the check into Watts's jacket pocket, which was already bulging with something.

"My lunch," explained Watts.

"I hope we haven't taken up too much of your time," Chesser said, and wished immediately he hadn't.

A polite smile from Watts. "I often come here anyway," he said, glancing toward the altar.

"When do you think I'll be hearing from your friend?"

"In two or three days, at the most."

"Perhaps by the weekend. How is your friend at remembering numbers?"

"Quite good."

"He should remember 387-9976."

Watts repeated the number aloud.

"He'll probably call from a public booth," suggested Chesser.

"I'll make certain he does."

That was that. Chesser and Maren got up. They left Watts there in the pew. From the aisle Chesser looked back and saw that Watts was already kneeling.

CHAPTER 14

Mildred climbed up onto the plush couch. She finally got settled against a back cushion, but sitting as she was, the couch was too deep for her. The front edge of it hit her about mid-calf, so her stubby little legs had to extend straight out, displaying her thick, rubber-soled shoes.

As though sensing Chesser's disapproval of her unsightly feet, Mildred complained: "Lor', there's nothing worse than foot trouble. Oooooh," she moaned, down-scale, "such suffering I've had—fallen arches, bunions, the lot."

Maren sympathized.

Mildred was inspired to continue. "Last month I was gimping about with a horrible ingrown toenail. My right big one, sore as blazes. Had to get me to the clinic at St. George's to have it properly fixed. Nice gentleman he was too, the foot doctor. Not all high-nosed and mighty like those Harley Street butchers who charge a fiver for doing nothing."

Chesser looked away and signaled Siv that he desperately
needed a drink. He tried to think of any excuse that might get
him out of the room but, to please Maren, he decided he'd better stay and suffer. His preconception of Mildred had not been
entirely wrong. She was just more grotesque than he'd imagined. An animate stump less than four feet tall; her torso and
limbs looked as though they had attempted to grow but had
been prohibited by some cruel compressing device. Only her
head was normal size; however, it appeared larger than normal. She had hyperthyroid eyes, lashes beaded heavily with
mascara, brows completely plucked to accommodate dark-
penciled lines drawn too high on her forehead. Extreme exag-
geration of the already bizarre. Face layered with white,
lavender-scented powder, cheeks smudged with orange rouge,
thin lips overpainted despite her large mouth, which resembled
that of a ventriloquist's dummy. And framing all this was an
abundance of her hair streaming down below her shoulders—
brassy, orangeish dyed hair that had been tortured by a curling
iron. She wore it middle-parted, lying open like a wound to reveal the pale flesh of her scalp and some darker new growth.

Chesser didn't like her. When he'd first looked down on her,
he disliked her and now he was totally repulsed. It wasn't because she was a dwarf. Actually it was a complete lack of that
sort of prejudice that allowed Chesser to feel, honestly, as he
did. Nearly everyone's reaction to Mildred was immediate pity
for her unfortunate proportions. But Chesser didn't give her
that advantage. He saw her as a person and believed there was
no reason for her being so garish and distasteful. After all, she
could have been a regular, nice-enough dwarf.

Understandably, the repugnance Chesser felt toward
Mildred affected his opinion of her claim to extraordinary
powers. Dubious to begin with, he was now certain that the
small medium was no more than a supernatural fraud. It annoyed Chesser that he had to put up with her. But he had to.
There was no alternative. Simply because Maren had already
confided in Mildred, had told her about the project, thereby
making Mildred a full-fledged accomplice. Chesser couldn't
imagine anything worse than trusting his fate to this loqua-
cious, unpredictable opportunist.

Now he tried not to look at those awful shoes. Maren was

on the floor near the couch, a position of homage. Siv came in, wheeling a drink cart. Maren asked Mildred's preference.

"Buttermilk," ordered Mildred, "with a spot of gin."

Chesser blanched.

"My old dad never drunk anything else," said Mildred, "when he could afford it."

"I doubt that we have any buttermilk," said Maren apologetically.

Mildred was disappointed.

"How about some Epsom salts and brandy?" suggested Chesser. That got him a quick disapproving look from Maren.

Mildred noticed and made the most of it. She acted victimized, lowered her eyes, shifted her bottom, and primped at the yellowed, tatted cotton bodice of her black dress. "Never mind," she murmured, subdued.

Maren's eyes sent a *now see what you've done* look at Chesser. Then she turned to Mildred and urged, "Do have something."

Mildred shook her head.

"How about some nice old Spanish sherry?" asked Maren.

Or some nice old Spanish fly, thought Chesser.

Mildred sniffled.

Chesser was handed a glass of his favorite Scotch by Siv, and barely managed not suggesting Mildred consider Lysol and vermouth, heavy on the Lysol.

"Please have something," entreated Maren.

Mildred finally raised her eyes to the drink cart and capitulated: "Just a touch of gin, then. Neat with no ice."

Siv, who Chesser felt was currently his only ally, poured Mildred a good four fingers of straight Tanqueray. Mildred took a delicate sip for an overture and then tossed down about half the gin in two consecutive gulps. She pretended polite dabs at her mouth with a napkin that she crushed into a ball as she brought her look to Chesser. A long, steady gaze. "How unusual," she declared.

"What?" asked Maren, eyes sparkling, sensing that Mildred was onto something psychic.

"He has the most amazing aura," said Mildred.

Chesser glanced down expecting to see his fly open.

"It's dirty red," said Mildred. "His nimbus, halo, aureola, and even his glory."

"Especially my glory," said Chesser.

Mildred clucked her tongue, rolled her eyes, and told him, "You ought to be ashamed of yourself."

"I wish I could see it," said Maren with sincere envy.

"See what?" asked Chesser.

"Your aura, darling," replied Maren, as though it was stupid of him not to know what that was. Rather intolerantly, she explained to him that every human body transmits a luminous radiation, but only those with mystical powers can see it.

"Actually, it's subsensible ether," informed Mildred, "related to the odyle."

"Oh," said Chesser, watching Mildred's mouth work.

"An exteriorization of energy," added Mildred, and finished her gin.

"The color of the aura indicates the character of a person," said Maren. "Isn't that right, Mildred?"

"My!" gasped Mildred, bringing stubby fingers to her cheek. "Even his karmic aura is dirty red." She continued to study Chesser. "Never saw the likes of it. Except once, around an Episcopalian bishop from Cardiff. But even his wasn't as intense as yours. Not nearly."

"At least it's not green," said Maren, sounding grateful for that.

"What's so amazing about dirty red?" asked Chesser.

"He's very neuropathic," diagnosed Mildred, squinting.

Chesser thought that sounded like an unkind reference to his mental condition.

"My aura is purple," Maren said with pride.

Mildred glanced quickly at Maren. "With a nice bit of rose at this moment, dearie," she said, and returned her concentration to Chesser.

He asked: "What's purple mean?"

"Spirituality," answered Maren.

"And rose signifies affection," said Mildred, beaming sweetly.

"And me," said Chesser, "old, dirty, red me, I'm nothing but lousy old, dirty red. Is that it?"

"You are what you are, darling," said Maren. "Auras don't lie. Besides, there's no reason to be ashamed of it."

"I'm not ashamed of anything. What does dirty red mean?"

"It means you're very erotic," said Maren.

Mildred chuckled. "That's putting it mildly."

Chesser was appeased. Maybe there was something to this aura thing. He imagined how entertaining and helpful it would be to see everyone's true colors. Rainbow people. He asked: "How far out does the aura usually radiate?"

"It depends," Maren said, because she didn't really know.

Mildred told him, "From six to twelve inches all around the body. Except when someone's about to pass over. Just the other day there was a young man on the L-bus. Looked to be in the prime of his time, he did. But the moment I laid eyes on him I knew he wasn't long for this world. Had hardly any aura at all. Probably one of those drug addicts. They burn themselves out, you know."

All the while she spoke, Mildred kept her eyes on Chesser, who was getting used to that by now. Abruptly but calmly she announced, "There's someone here."

Chesser looked around.

Maren asked who.

"I don't know yet," said Mildred.

"Maybe it's Jean Marc," said Maren enthusiastically.

"Lor'!" exclaimed Mildred, and told Chesser: "He's not very pleased with you!"

Chesser laughed a little, nervously.

"Ask Jean Marc where the hell he's been," said Maren. "Tell him I won't tolerate his chasing off somewhere without even a word."

"It's not Jean Marc, luv," said Mildred.

Chesser was relieved to hear that. Although he told himself he really didn't believe anyone was there. The damned medium was just putting on a show, mainly for his benefit.

"Well, if it's not Jean Marc, who is it?" asked Maren, disappointed.

"I haven't the faintest," Mildred said, concentrating.

"Ask him to introduce himself," suggested Chesser.

"I can't."

"Why not?"

"He's gone. Only showed himself long enough to let us know he was around. Didn't say anything, either. Just stood there, right back of your chair. He was scowling at you, real rankled, he was. Had on one of those overcoats with a velvet collar."

"A Chesterfield," said Maren.

Mildred nodded, "And a black Hamburg hat."

"Homburg?" Chesser said.

"That's what I said, a black Homburg. He was furious at you. Positively livid."

Chesser tried to visualize a ghost in a Chesterfield and Homburg. A lot more debonair than one in an ordinary old sheet, he thought. And then, for some absurd reason, he was presented with a fragment from the past. A black hat that Chesser had tried on when he was almost nine years old. A winter morning two days before his ninth birthday, to be exact. A Homburg hat that was much too large for him, that came down over his ears and eyes when he tried it on, alone in front of the hall mirror, before anyone else was up. The hat had just been returned from the cleaners in the special box in which his father always kept it. Then cleaners had done a special rush job on it because Chesser's father needed to wear it that day. His father always wore that Homburg when he flew across the ocean for business with The System. That time he'd be gone a week. Chesser was extra careful with the hat when he placed it back in the box and told it, with language he'd only said aloud when he was on the street with the guys, that he didn't give a shit.

But now, more than thirty years later, Chesser quickly dismissed the association, washed his mouth with the best available Scotch, and marveled only at the coincidence, giving Mildred or whatever Mildred represented at best the benefit of his chronic doubt.

By then Mildred was accepting her third double portion of gin. She smiled at Chesser, evidently confident that she had impressed him.

Chesser wondered if Maren would forgive him if he went downstairs to practice some shooting off the hip.

"Do you play?" Mildred asked him.

"Not anymore," he replied.

"She means the piano," explained Maren. There was a Wurlitzer grand in the corner of the room.

With difficulty, Mildred got down off the couch and toddled across the room to the huge, ebony-finished instrument. "My mum saw to it that I had lessons," she said, tracing fingers respectfully along the piano's side surface. She went up on her toes to peek inside at the strings. "She's gone over, you know, with kidney trouble, years ago. But she's very happy. Better off than she was here, I'll tell you that. A horrible shame, all she went through, having me, strange as I am and all. But that was her karma. She brought it on herself."

Maren thought to ask Mildred if her mother also was a dwarf, but she didn't know what words would be adequately tactful. With her absolute belief in Mildred's psychic abilities, Maren wasn't surprised when Mildred seemed to take her thought right out of the air. Mildred said: "I always looked up to her, my mum. She was almost six feet. Seemed tall as the bloody Post Office tower to me." She climbed up onto the piano bench. "Still she wanted me to have lessons, my mum did."

Mildred plunked a note several times and then attacked the keys. Her rendition of something by Tchaikovsky, which sounded more like "Camptown Races" the way she had to play it with her short fingers unable properly to manipulate both the black and white keys simultaneously. She also had to limit her efforts to the middle range because her arms were too short to reach lower or higher on the keyboard. And, of course, she couldn't work the foot pedals.

Mildred's performance brought tears to Maren's eyes. Chesser noticed and loved Maren for that. He also felt some sympathy for Mildred's incapacity, as she pounded her way through the piece, innovating and compromising to accommodate her limitations.

Both Maren and Chesser applauded at the finish. Mildred grinned, proud of herself. She toddled back to the couch, climbed up, resumed her former position, and was rewarded with another big helping of gin. "Let's talk business," she said.

Chesser preferred not to. He'd already decided he'd try to

buy Mildred off with a generous M. J. Mathew certified check when the time was right.

"Diamonds," said Mildred, "are one thing I've never had much to do with, except for a little stickpin I had once but lost down the loo. I've never been one for material things. Can't afford to be. They wouldn't like it if I was. They'd take away my power."

Chesser wondered who *they* were.

"I'm quite willing to help however I can, providing I don't get paid for it, you understand."

Maren nodded and admired Mildred's values.

Chesser merely nodded, skeptical.

Mildred continued, "I've already done a bit of groundwork, you might say. This afternoon I contacted someone on the other side who was very involved with diamonds. He said he was a crook. He's sorry now, of course, but nevertheless he was a crook."

"Who was?" asked Chesser.

"The someone this someone knows," answered Mildred, perturbed. "I didn't ask for names. They don't usually like to reveal their names, you know. Do you want me to go on?"

Maren urged her.

Mildred took a deep breath, sniffled some, fussed with her tatted bodice, clasped her hands, and told them, "I was given one bit of advice for you."

"What?" asked Chesser.

"I told you she'd help," said Maren.

"It's only three words," said Mildred. "Spirits usually communicate in as few words as possible. Perhaps because it's not easy for them. Anyway, 'black will oblige.' That's what he said. 'Black will oblige.' I suppose you know what that means?"

Maren didn't.

"Do you?" Chesser asked Mildred.

"Haven't the faintest," replied Mildred. "I thought you'd know, with your being in the diamond business and all."

"Think, darling!" Maren said. "Do you know anyone named Black?"

"Milton Black," said Chesser.

"Who's he?" asked Maren.

"First kid on my block who could masturbate. He was very

big in those days. Last I heard he was an interior decorator and handball champion of the entire upper East Side."

"He can't possibly be *the* Black," said Maren.

"Black will oblige," quipped Chesser, pleased with himself.

"It'll come to you," assured Mildred. "Anyway, I told that man on the other side I'd be in touch with him again. You don't mind if I go into a bit of a trance, do you?"

Maren was delighted.

Chesser was more tolerant now because he was feeling the Scotch.

Mildred knocked back what gin remained in her glass. She settled herself and closed her eyes. After a few moments her body went rigid. Her stumpy little legs looked as rigid as a plaster doll's.

Chesser was sure the small medium was about to give them the feature number of her act. But Maren eagerly anticipated some vital information from the vast spiritual limbo.

They waited nearly fifteen minutes. Nothing came from or through Mildred. She remained absolutely the same.

Maren was concerned. But she was afraid to make a sound, believing that Mildred's spirit was out in the astral world, trying to tap the cosmic force. Any abrupt sound, perhaps even a whisper, Maren believed, might disturb Mildred's physical entity without allowing time for her spiritual essence to return. If that happened, Maren had no idea how Mildred would be affected, but she knew it would be dreadful.

Chesser had had enough. While he was sitting there looking patient, he'd been thinking about number 11, how impenetrable it was. And wondering what information Watts might come up with. Chesser's opinion was that nothing Watts could tell him, no matter how secret, would really help his cause. He tried not to be such a pessimist, but it was difficult to be even slightly optimistic with the score 12 billion to zero. At least, almost zero. All he had in his favor were a dying man, a captious girlfriend, a fake dwarf medium and himself—an amateur everything.

He got up and, disregarding Maren's frantic gestures, went over to Mildred. He examined her closely and then tapped her on the shoulder.

Mildred's bulbous eyes opened with a start. "Lor'," she

said thickly, "I must have dozed off. You must think I'm daft or something."

Maren asked if she was all right.

Mildred nodded, rubbed her eyes with her knuckles, badly smearing her mascara. "It's just that I've been working too hard lately," she said pitifully. "The spirits take so much out of me."

She means the gin, thought Chesser.

"Poor Mildred," cooed Maren.

"Well, dearies," sighed Mildred, "I'm afraid we've had it for tonight. But I promise I'll do some work for you soon enough."

"I'll drive you home," offered Maren.

"Just toss me into a taxi," Mildred said.

Chesser was tempted to literally do that.

CHAPTER 15

Early Friday evening Watts called.

The information was ready. Should he bring it? No. Chesser thought it more prudent to have it delivered by regular taxi. Watts agreed and said he'd call again sometime during the week in case Chesser had any questions. They exchanged thanks.

Within an hour, a well-sealed, letter-size envelope was in Chesser's hands. It contained twenty-two neatly written pages, including numerous carefully drawn diagrams.

Maren and Chesser went over it together. While propped up by many extra pillows on their big bed. Munching on black Greek olives and red Irish radishes. No comments. They just devoured.

Watts had really done a thorough job of it. He had applied his obsessive regard for accuracy and detail, and it was all there, every physical characteristic of The System's facilities at number 11, as well as a precise timetable of operation.

Watt's diagrams were explicit, drawn in scale with the help of a ruler. Everything was clearly indicated, from the placement of worktables to the location of electric sockets. He had even noted measurements exact to the inch where it might matter.

Now Chesser and Maren knew what they were up against:

The System had two subterranean levels, accessible only by a small elevator—the same elevator that Chesser had seen Sir Harold enter from the ground floor foyer. Both subterranean levels ran the entire length and width of the building. The first level down was compartmentalized into various workrooms—receiving, evaluating, sorting areas. The lower level consisted of one huge oblong room which Watts referred to as "the vault." That was where the inventory was kept.

The elevator did not offer direct access to the vault. There was a shallow, boxlike antechamber preceding the vault door. The vault itself was enclosed on all sides as well as above and below by four-inch armor plate: a specially smelted combination of exotic metals that had been tested at an official armament-proving grounds and had been found to be impervious to a seventy-five millimeter shell fired at point-blank range. The thick vault door, made of the same material, functioned electronically and was programmed with an automatic timing device that opened it at nine each week-day morning and locked it at six each night. Whenever the vault was locked, various alarms and other security devices were irrevocably in effect. These were the primary reason for the vault's antechamber. A horizontal pattern of unavoidable electronic beams would set off an alarm if interrupted by anything. A complex heat-sensitive device, originally developed by space research, detected any living presence. And, as if all other precautions were not enough, another, even more formidable obstacle had been installed just outside the vault door—an arrangement of eight small mirrors, permanently and exactly set at congruent angles so that they reflected a network of laser beams. The contemporary death ray.

Within the vault, contrary to the great pile of diamonds Chesser had envisioned, the inventory was stored with extreme systematic care. Each of fifty matte-black steel cabinets accommodated thirty long, very shallow drawers, inner-lined with black velour. These contained the uncut gem-quality stones in more than two thousand classifications, depending upon the three *C*'s of the world of diamonds—carat, color, and clarity. For example, the white diamonds alone were graded to two hundred various shades, and accordingly categorized. There were special, deeper drawers for larger stones, but the bulk of the inventory, about ninety-five per cent of it, consisted of stones ranging from one-half to ten carats. Nearly all space in the vault was taken up by the storage cabinets. Even the middle space, where cabinets were placed back to back, forming an island and an all-around aisle arrangement.

Two of the cabinets against one wall were purposely shorter than the others and were used as work surfaces, upon which were situated a pair of Diamondlites, for standard quality evaluation. The Diamondlites were portable, merely plugged into regular wall sockets. As senior in charge of grading, Watts spent most of his hours right there, checking the stones that other graders brought down from the workrooms, making sure they were properly catalogued and put in their correct place.

There was a special note: a certain area of the vault was reserved for diamonds from Russia. A special inventory was kept for the Soviet, per agreement made during highly confidential conferences held in Moscow in 1968. Undoubtedly the Russians demanded this arrangement in case they might wish to withdraw their surplus at some future time, although, of course, their primary interest was to sell.

The roof of number 11 was sealed. No entry. The entire roof surface was equipped with a special pressure alarm that would be activated whenever anything weighing in excess of ten pounds came down on it. The ten-pound limit prevented activation by pigeons and other birds.

All alarms and prohibitive devices were set by and transmitted to a central control maintained by The System's Security Section on Harrowhouse, directly across from number 11. Security had a minimum of six men on duty at all times and kept various weapons ready for any emergency. Automatic rifles, side arms, and gas grenades. Security also operated a long-range radio on the unregistered frequency of ten and three hundred eighty megacycles. Every member of the Security staff was especially selected for the job and given extensive training. For example, taught to kill with hands. A sort of elite corps. Miller, who tended door at number 11, was rated expert by Security.

People: Sir Harold Appensteig was no longer active in day-to-day operations, was stepping aside, being phased out. Meecham, who was actually in charge, would soon be officially moved up to the chairman's post. The board of directors met twice annually at number 11. There were six outside members on the board. The major outside share was held by the Rathshield family, the same so prominent in international banking.

The final page of Watts's documentary was devoted to an estimate of the value of The System's inventory, based on current market prices as of the previous Friday.

Twenty-two million, four hundred thirty-two thousand, one hundred and three carats.

Worth twelve billion, five hundred thirty-two million, six hundred fifty thousand dollars.

Massey had been incredibly accurate.

Chesser blamed the radishes for the discomfort he had in his stomach. Maren felt suddenly empty, very small. They lay there in silence. Until nearly midnight, when Chesser finally stirred, grunted, got up and shoved Watts's report into the drawer of a Regency chest sticky bottom drawer, never used, inconvenient. Maren understood his reason for putting it there. Not to hide it as much as to try to disregard it.

For the next three days they tried to be content with routine diversions. They made no verbal pact not to mention the diamond project, but it was as though they had; neither spoke of it even once. And, significantly, they didn't once go down to the cellar for shooting practice.

They went out to see a play featuring better nudity than dialogue, to dinner at Alvaro's, to the zoo, to Sotheby's, where Maren bid on nearly everything just for spite and ended up owning a pencil sketch for eighteen thousand dollars, which, at that rate, Picasso had done for a hundred and forty dollars per second.

Or they stayed in and read anything, watched the telly without really seeing it, amputated yellow roses from the garden, played backgammon, and made so many ridiculous errors it seemed they were both trying to lose. No lovemaking, by silent, passive agreement.

Regardless of what they did they merely went through the motions. Frequently one would ask the other to repeat what the other had just said. They were each preoccupied with the same subject, which was, of course, the vault. That great buried tank of a room encased in four-inch special armor. Their separate imaginations attacked it from every direction, but its invulnerability defied them. There was simply no way into it, and even if they could get in, how could they carry off eight thousand pounds of diamonds without getting sizzled to death by laser or, at least, perforated by Security Section's sharpshooters?

Impossible.

That was Chesser's conclusion. But he hated giving up. He'd grown accustomed to the prospects of extravagant reward and maximum revenge. He'd call Massey that day and tell him it was no go. No need even to discuss it with Maren. Evidently she now realized how right he'd been when he'd told her nobody beats The System.

Chesser decided he'd take a walk first and, when he returned, place the call to Massey.

He went out, intending to be out ten or fifteen minutes at most. He turned up Albany Street, went across Gloucester Gate and into Regent's Park. The day was one of those big cloud days, with the sun frequently shut off. Everything was dull one moment and turned on bright the next. Appropriate, thought Chesser.

He claimed an empty bench. Sat there facing a vast open area of park grass, which was occasionally punctuated by children running around their mothers. And lovers horizontally together. Chesser noticed how the lovers used their bodies to conceal their hands between them. A park policeman came by, patrolling, sanctioning the mothers and dutifully delivering half-hearted warnings to the lovers, who pulled apart until he was past and then reunited, confident he wouldn't look back or come back, if he did.

Chesser started for home. But when he reached Prince Albert Road he gave way to impulse and went down Parkway to Camden Town. Along the way he looked at store windows containing mostly cheap things, stiff, dead fish, synthetic

dresses, and clear, plastic, female lower halves immodestly
inverted to show off pastel panty hose. At a bakery, scones
that looked as light as meringue tricked him into buying half
a dozen. They were heavy as plaster. He left the sack of them
on the step of a public doorway and felt sorry for the hungry
unfortunate who would find them.

He went back up Parkway loaded with depression. He told
himself to lose some of it along the way, not to take it home to
Maren. So he stopped in at a bookstore he hadn't noticed before.
Thumbed through an illustrated volume that made Portugal look
pretty and thought maybe he'd suggest to Maren that they just
take off for there. He perused a bound collection of photographs: nudes of a woman in the reach of the sea, *Naissance
de Aphrodite*, glistening beads hung in the mounded growth at
her intersection, the sockets of her thighs in tension, and all the
shapes of her skin dimensionally aroused. Chesser promised
himself and Maren much and better loving in Portugal.

His mood was rising. He brought his attention to an entire
wall of paperback books. He'd buy a few. His excuse for
being out so long. He was glad, though, that Maren was possessive. He chose three paperbacks at random. And it was at
that moment it came to him, just as Mildred had predicted it
would—the meaning of *black will oblige*. At least it was a
possible interpretation of that cryptic message. He took another paperback down from its place. Strange, he thought, the
way it had come to him, as though he had been guided right
there to suddenly experience a sort of revelation. Not that it
mattered now, but he was certain Maren would consider it a
vindication of Mildred.

Returning home, he found her in the main reception room.
She had some Led Zeppelin on the stereo and little more than
nothing on herself, just a huge square of that finest sheer cotton called lawn. She'd pinned it snugly beneath her chin so it
contained all her hair, framed her face angelically, but otherwise fell and gathered over and around her. She was on the
floor, her back against the sofa, with her legs arched up to sus-
tain a large sketch pad on which she was making notes. The
pages of Watts's report were scattered about.

She completed her thought before looking up to Chesser.
He knew immediately that her disposition had changed. She

was his irrepressible Maren again. He thought she also must have finally become resigned to the fact that the diamond-stealing project was canceled due to impossibility.

He sat down beside her and took her offered hello kiss. It was good to be really ensemble again. He told her, "I figured it out."

"You did?" She seemed disappointed.

"I think so. It just came to me."

"So, how do we get into the vault?"

"We don't."

"Exactly," she said.

"What I meant is, it occurred to me what *black will oblige* means. At least, what it might mean."

He took out one of the paperback books he'd bought. Its cover was a photograph of the author, a black man looking straight out, strong and belligerent.

"I used to know him," explained Chesser.

"He doesn't look very obliging," was Maren's opinion.

Chesser had to agree with her. He glanced at her sketch pad. She guarded it from his view. He only caught a glimpse of some of her handwriting in Swedish. He couldn't read Swedish anyway.

"I called Mildred," she said. "I asked her if she could do an apport."

"A what?"

"An apport. Making things dematerialize so they can pass through matter and be brought back to their original state somewhere else. It has to do with the transmutation of energy in the fourth dimension."

"I should have known that."

She agreed. "It's common knowledge."

"Done every day."

"It would have been the best way to get the diamonds," she said, "but Mildred can't do it."

"She's not much help."

"She does apports all the time but this would take too much power—you know, all those diamonds. She doesn't have that much power. It would have been interesting, though, doing it that way." She smiled thoughtfully, was silent a moment, then asked, "How much is a carat?"

"Seven thousandths of an ounce," he replied, "point zero zero seven."

"I mean how big."

He thought of several ordinary comparisons and then a better one came to him. He told her, "About half the size of your most very sensitive spot."

She had to grin. "No larger than that?"

"At its best," he added.

"Draw one . . . a carat for me," she said, handing him the pen and turning to a fresh page of the sketch pad.

He drew a circle about a quarter of an inch in diameter.

She studied it a moment. And ten times that is ten carats."

He drew an approximation of ten carats.

"That's not too big," she judged seriously.

"I've *got* to call Massey," said Chesser. He started to get up.

"You're not supposed to call, remember? Massey was emphatic about that. Besides, I just got through talking to him."

Chesser dropped back down. "He called you?"

"No. I told him to start renovating his building as soon as possible."

"What building?"

"His. The one he owns, on Harrowhouse next to The System."

"Renovate? Why?"

"To create a diversion, among other things. When there's a lot of unusual activity around the place no one will notice a little more."

Apparently she hadn't yet given up on the deal. Chesser admired her spirit but not her obstinacy. Calmly, unequivocally, he told her it was impossible to get into the vault.

She told him he was absolutely correct.

"So, let's just forget about it and get out of here." He then proposed Portugal.

"We don't need to get into the vault," she stated.

"We're going to apport, right?"

"In a way. At least that's what gave me the idea."

He saw she was serious.

"I haven't got it all worked out yet," she said. She flipped back to the page of the sketch pad on which she'd made her many Swedish scribbles. "You can make all the suggestions you want, but don't ruin it with too many improvements," she said, and began translating. . . .

CHAPTER 16

Harridge Weaver was the black man in black. The only white thing about him was the starched inch of clerical collar showing around his throat. Except for his teeth and eyes, of course.

He was waiting his turn at Immigration, standing there in line, looking patient and serene. He had shaved his beard, moustache, and sideburns, and wore gold wire-rimmed glasses he didn't need. Altogether, his identity coincided unquestionably with the photograph that was officially embossed in the Algerian passport he was carrying, issued February 20, 1969, to the Reverend Gerard Pouteau.

The Immigration officer nodded to Weaver that he was next. Weaver crossed over to the podiumlike desk and presented his papers, which a sign had instructed him to have ready. First the officer ran a check on the name Pouteau, methodically referring to an alphabetically compiled list of undesirables, such as wanted persons and tax delinquents. Then the officer asked the Reverend how long he planned to stay in the United Kingdom, where he would be staying, and the purpose of the Reverend's visit. Weaver answered all three questions routinely with believable lies.

He was passed through Immigration and customs without trouble. This was the only time in four years that he'd put himself on the line, his freedom. At least as much freedom as he had. He didn't trust white law, and therefore couldn't rely on the British law, which stipulated that political prisoners were excluded from the extradition agreement between the United Kingdom and the United States.

Although Weaver considered himself a political fugitive, the FBI and CIA and all the other great white hunters had him differently classified. According to them, he was wanted for murder and flight to avoid prosecution. The murder part wasn't true, but that was how they had labeled him and that was the crime he would have to pay for if he ever went back, or was taken back.

Four years of exile had changed Weaver considerably, had driven his determination in deeper, inside, where it really counted. From his remote vantage across the ocean, he was able to observe the violence of his brothers and see more clearly why such confrontations were necessary and also why they were futile. Weaver would sit in the striking North African sunshine and view more rationally and painfully what he and his brothers had tried to accomplish. Were still trying. But how naïve they'd been at times in the past, so open in their actions, demanding their black rights, taking a position to the far Left, trying to stay just inside the line of the law. Realizing soon enough that the law could be lopsided, could come at them from any direction, and even if they found a loophole it was easy for the whites to plug it up by merely creating another white law.

Early in his exile, Weaver's perspective had not been so objective. He was full of the humiliation of having had to run from his inevitable death. Run to escape white guns or their gas chamber or, at least, one of their cages, in which they would put all of his life.

Earlier Weaver would pace in the punishment of the North African sunshine and see only as far ahead as revenge and only as far in the past as that night in Newark when five thousand rounds of lawful bullets of various calibers and singular intent had torn around him and had blown the heart out of his good brother George. They murdered and then accused Weaver of it, and he knew they could make the charge stick because, as one of his brothers said sardonically, they had all the glue.

Weaver remembered his flight as only a blur. Of being cramped in the hole of an automobile trunk, of being transported like precious black shit, of hunching down in the rear seats of various cars, being transferred from car to car for precaution. Of riding a speedboat south from a small Florida coast town, the unfamiliarity of being on the sea a relief for him all the way to Varadero, Cuba, and on via jeep to Havana, where he stayed a week and was treated well enough.

When he got to Africa, where he would stay, he was grateful for the immunity. However, as much as he appreciated being out of reach of his enemy, he hated his enemy being out of his reach. He suffered through adjustment to his new environment, eased somewhat by many letters, a flow of the Movement's newspapers, and infrequent visits by brothers. The latter usually left him depressed. It was as though they were coming to pay respects to a handicapped veteran of the fight, who would probably never fight again. Whenever he spoke to them about his return, they warned him with their eyes while they patronized him with their words.

What really got him through that bad time was his writing. Despite his new lack of faith in words, he turned to them. He sat in the broad blade of the North African sunshine and sent his voice into the microphone of a cassette recorder. When he played back what he felt, he felt and believed it all the more. Expression opened him, let him see his past errors. Not only the minor ones but also the principal one: the confidence that black would fearlessly, automatically follow black. Weaver believed the theory was still valid and eventually would prove itself, but for the time being it was an unrealistic expectation. Persuasion was necessary, along with dramatic examples. No past revolution could be used as an example. The structure of past revolutions, with their martyrs and swift massive overthrow, were now passé, made ineffective by the intricately organized, scientifically complex manner by which contemporary tyranny fortified itself.

A man with less resolve would have yielded to the circumstances and transferred his energy to making his own life more comfortable. But Weaver accepted the compromise, kept his basic optimism, and more intelligently channeled the force of his hate into his writing. He wrote two books and made contributions to any medium that would voice his beliefs. His spirit was catching and he believed the time would come, perhaps in his lifetime.

Exile had made Weaver a wiser man.

And much more dangerous.

That latter quality was hardly apparent as he got out of a taxi in front of the rectory of St. Edwards Church, Hanover Square. He gave the driver a beneficent smile along with a humble shilling tip, and pretended to be consulting directions that were actually an Air France pamphlet on survival under ditching conditions. Until the taxi pulled away. Then he picked up his luggage and walked across the street and down to where Chesser waited in the car.

Weaver opened the door on the passenger side and threw his luggage into the space behind the seats. No hello. Nothing. His ecclesiastical disguise surprised Chesser, who wasn't immediately sure this was the same man he'd met with in Paris just two days before.

Locating Weaver hadn't been difficult for Chesser. He had put in a call to the Moroccan Ministry of Public Affairs in Algiers and requested Weaver's telephone number. He didn't get it, of course, but the Ministry official was polite and suggested Chesser's call might be returned. Chesser gave his name and London number and two days later Algiers was calling and it was Weaver. Chesser thought Weaver might not remember him, but Weaver did, right off. However, from Weaver's guarded tone, Chesser thought it wise to forgo any old buddy routine and got directly to the proposition, outlining the general nature of it without revealing any details. Weaver was cautiously interested. He insisted on an interim meeting in Paris to hear the entire proposition face-to-face on neutral ground, instead of coming directly to London and risking everything.

Chesser and Weaver had hit it off well enough in Paris. Weaver hadn't asked as many questions about the project as Chesser had anticipated, but he'd checked out Chesser and hadn't found a white trap. In the Paris hotel room, while Chesser revealed the scheme, they'd drunk vintage Château LaFitte straight from the bottle. Two separate bottles, actually. About half way through, they'd exchanged bottles, which signified Weaver's acceptance of Chesser's offer. A million dollars.

Now they were suffering through West End traffic. Weaver removed his glasses, rubbed the bridge of his nose, and tight shut his eyes a couple of times. He also released his stiff collar, ripped it off and made a sound of relief. "That fucking thing was killing me," he said. And that was all he said for several blocks of stop and go. He just sat there observing the people on the street, particularly the girls.

Chesser remembered how outgoing Weaver had been back in 'fifty and 'fifty-one. A big, first-string tackle who should have been majoring in law rather than physical education. He had all the prerequisites, except the meaningless ones they demanded on a high-school record.

At that time Chesser was living off campus, and the girl who frequently stayed overnight and caused him to miss morning classes was Jessica, an aggressive, challenging girl out to prove how liberal she was, in mind and body. It was through Jessica that Chesser had met Weaver, when he got in with her radical element, whose big cause then was integration.

Naturally, Chesser was for integration; he'd never felt any prejudice. For him it was as uncomplicated as that. Unlike most of his companions, he didn't feel any guilt demanding active involvement. That was probably the reason he let others make the speeches and didn't show up at many meetings. They needed it; he didn't.

Weaver must have sensed that quality in Chesser and liked it, found it a relief from the tension of being the object of a cause. From the first they found they could relax together. Weaver would drop by Chesser's place anytime, get some law second hand, and borrow books. Conversely, on Saturday afternoons Chesser, from his stadium seat, felt some vicarious satisfaction in the violence he watched Weaver perform.

By the time the football season was over and Weaver had gotten through nearly every law book Chesser's father's money had bought, they were truly comrade opposites. Different colored brothers-in-law is the way they humorously put it, because by then the girl Jessica had really overcome and made the transfer to Weaver's bed.

It was a good winter for Chesser; one of the best in his young life. Weaver was what made it so good. However, when it was over it was definitely over. Weaver didn't come back from spring vacation. He'd stolen a car and filled its trunk with a harvest of marijuana and broken three ribs of the arresting state policeman. Weaver wrote Chesser one letter from prison, a sort of angry apology, not really defending himself. Chesser sent off a long reply immediately but, after that, Weaver was in prison and Chesser was in and out of law school and they were on divergent courses.

Now, nearly twenty years later in London, Chesser told him, "I read your book."

"When?"

An unexpected question. Chesser had to decide quickly not to lie. "Last night."

Weaver nodded to himself, confirming a judgment. No doubt related to Chesser's degree of interest in the black versus white supremacy problem. Weaver's book had been on the stands for more than eight months. A highly charged book that exposed the visceral issues in such a blunt and impatient manner that it made even some racists' skin crawl. It had sold well but had not appeared on the bestseller lists. Worse than that, the proceeds from the sales of the book had been impounded, withheld from the exiled Weaver on a technicality enforced by the United States government, Weaver's indicated enemy. Regardless, he had just finished writing another, he told Chesser.

"What's the new one about?" asked Chesser.

"It's a sort of handbook for revolutionaries."

"Fiction?"

Weaver wasn't amused. They were stopped in traffic. He watched a pale and pretty English girl get into a Lotus Elan. She had to pivot her ass on the low bucket seat to swing her legs up, so the teasing split of her midi skirt exhibited the entire length of her inside thighs. Weaver's view was cut off when she closed the car's white door. He told Chesser, "You haven't changed much." He intended the remark to be light, but it came out like a criticism.

"You have," retaliated Chesser.

A grunt from Weaver.

Chesser was ill at ease, as he'd been to some extent when he was with Weaver in Paris, but then the wine had helped and he'd also been able to blame some of it on self-conscious reunion. Now he knew what it was. Weaver was causing it, wordlessly communicating his blackness, making Chesser feel it so much that he couldn't possibly disregard it. Weaver's mere presence generated that force, magnifying their difference. Chesser could have met Weaver blindfolded and still felt it. There had been none of that way back in the other days, and Chesser didn't see why there had to be any now.

Weaver reached around and got his smaller bag. He put it on his lap and unzipped it. He was after cigarettes, although he could have asked Chesser for one.

Chesser caught a glimpse of a gun. A black thirty-eight.

Weaver closed the bag and kept it on his lap. He used the cigarette lighter on the dash panel. "You're not into politics at all, are you?" he asked.

"I won an election bet once."

"Nixon?" Weaver hated just saying it.

"Miss Rheingold," replied Chesser.

That brought out some of the Weaver that Chesser remembered, and Chesser was relieved to see it, suspected there was a lot more of the same beneath Weaver's facade.

Weaver brought up his large hand, as though he were stopping something. He was trying not to laugh. "Look, man, all I want is to do the job, collect my bread, and get the fuck back. You dig?"

"Sure."

Chesser knew Weaver had good reason to be edgy. If Weaver was arrested in England he was a dead man. They'd kill him legally but they'd kill him. Weaver might be resigned to dying but he at least wanted to do it in a more useful way.

"Be best for both of us if we don't get into any political shit at all," Weaver said.

Chesser agreed. "Actually I didn't read your book. I got through the first part but I fell asleep."

Weaver wasn't offended. Rather, he considered it a point in Chesser's favor. He didn't know any other white man who could fall asleep while being kicked in the balls by black hostility. It was perversely reassuring to Weaver that that was the sort of man to whom he was now literally trusting his life.

At that moment, Chesser's thoughts were involved with that future sometime when and if the blacks got what they wanted and more. He hoped Weaver would still be alive then, to vouch for him. Thus distracted, Chesser was looking ahead but not really seeing the parked lorry. Until it was almost too late. He had to brake suddenly to avoid hitting it. Defensively, he resorted to blowing his horn, several staccato blasts. He kept on with it, grinned over at Weaver. "You know what I am, don't you?" he asked, really blasting the horn.

Weaver shrugged.

"A honky bastard," declared Chesser, still trying for a laugh.

He got it this time. A full out laugh that made Weaver choke on his Gauloise. Finally, recovering enough, Weaver asked, "Know what I am?"

Chesser nodded.

Weaver told him anyway. "One big, mean, black mother effer!"

CHAPTER 17

Most people are better at taking things apart than putting things together.

Marylebone, Ltd., claimed to be adept at both these functions. It displayed on its letterhead, as well as its trucks, the tradesman's coveted symbol for having performed services to the high standards of royal demand: crowned lion on the left and fairy-tale unicorn on the right hoofing and clawing at a crest with *Dieu et mon droit* inscribed across the base. No matter that the most important major royal commission ever received by Marylebone, Ltd., was when Queen Victoria gave it the nod to convert an atrocious bath at Windsor Castle into an even more atrocious aviary.

When Marylebone received a call on behalf of Clyde Massey, it caught the scent of big money and acted with dispatch. Preliminary blueprints and some exaggerated perspectives in full color were rendered overnight. The executives of

Mid-Continental Oil were evacuated just barely ahead of all furnishings, and the following day Marylebone began tearing at the insides of number 13 Harrowhouse Street with such ambitious fury that it might have been mistaken for wrath. Interior walls were smashed down, fixtures yanked out, floors were mercilessly mistreated. Nothing escaped the specialized destruction of Marylebone, whose catechism was: whatever was destroyed at the client's expense would have to be repaired at the client's expense.

However, it had to be said in favor of Marylebone that it destroyed with dignity. It made efforts to minimize the inconvenience caused to others in the area. For example, as soon as windows were ripped out, Marylebone sealed the openings with a clear plastic material to prevent the float of dirt and plaster particles. Rubble was swiftly taken away, and the drivers of the various Marylebone vehicles were instructed to do their loading and unloading only at the rear of the building, on Puffing Mews.

Despite such discretions, those in the immediate vicinity had to tolerate a considerable amount of dust and noise. And a continuous stir of unusual activity. Therefore, shortly after dark on the night of June twenty-seventh, it was not inconsistent for a white panel truck bearing the understated Marylebone name and mark to turn into Puffing Mews and park close to the rear entrance of number 13. The three figures dressed in Marylebone work uniforms would not have created suspicion had they been seen. The only unusual thing about them was their gloves. Each wore snug latex surgical gloves to prevent fingerprints.

With the casual attitude of workmen, they removed their tools from the truck and entered the renovation site. They went up from floor to floor, slowly, using the carefully aimed beams of powerful flashlights to help avoid such things as ladders and sawhorses and stacked bags of plaster. All the way up to the fifth, the top, floor, where they played their beams of light on the ceiling.

It was Weaver who found the recessed rectangle that offered access to the roof. Accommodated by one of Marylebone's taller ladders, he climbed high and pressed upward with all his strength. But the horizontal trapdoor refused to give way. Chesser shone his light up and Weaver saw the reason. Only a simple spring latch. He released it and effortlessly shoved the door up. He climbed up and out. Maren and Chesser followed.

As they crouched together on the roof, each had the sensation of being apart from the world, above it, with numerous silhouettes of chimney pipes forming a rather surrealistic vista. And far off were the higher buildings of London, landmarks such as the lighted dome of St. Paul's, only vaguely discernible through the night mist.

Maren was first to stand. She walked over to the low brick ledge that joined number 13 to number 11. Mounted on the ledge, solidly inset, was a steel mesh fence about seven feet high, topped with huge, overhanging burrs of sharp spikes. An unexpected obstacle. Watts's report hadn't mentioned it. The fence ran the entire length of the building, there and also on the opposite side. It extended out on each end to prevent circumvention.

"Don't touch it!" warned Chesser.

Maren had been about to do just that. She jerked her hand away.

Weaver got a pair of insulated gloves from his satchel of tools. He put them on and used the raw metal face of a pair of pliers to make contact with the fence. No sparks.

They played their flashlights on the roof of number 11, scanning. The roof seemed to be flat, no interruptions or protrusions of any sort. They examined all the edges and corners. Maren discovered the only irregularity. On the outer rear edge, adjacent to the dividing ledge opposite. A symmetrical outcropping of bricks that might possibly be housing something.

"Even if it is something," said Chesser, "how the hell do we get to it?"

Maren investigated further. Her flashlight revealed a gutter drain attached to the roof's outer edge. Merely an ordinary galvanized tin drain about five inches wide that ran the entire width of the roof, about thirty feet.

"It's worth a try," Maren said.

"Have to be a fucking tightrope walker," Weaver said.

"I'm good at it. Even better than Elvira Madigan was," boasted Maren. She was inspired by the danger of it, wanted to do it. Also, as the lightest of the three she obviously was the logical choice.

Maren asked Weaver: "Can you cut through the fence?"

With a pair of long-handled wire-clippers he snipped vertically and horizontally and bent back a section of the fence.

Maren climbed through the opening. She used the fence to help make her way quickly to the edge of the roof, where she hesitated and looked down on Puffing Mews.

Watching her, Chesser had a clutch in his stomach. This could be the great all-time loss, he thought, and at that moment wanted to call the whole thing off. But he realized from knowing her that nothing he could say now would persuade her to stop. It was too wonderfully risky.

Maren removed her shoes and recklessly tossed them back over the fence. If one had dropped onto the roof of number 11 it might have come down with enough force to set off the pressure alarm, bringing Security Section's gunmen. She raised her right foot and softly placed it into the drain gutter. She gradually shifted more of her weight onto that foot. All her weight. The drain gave slightly but then proved it was strong enough to support her.

She began her perilous walk, took several precise steps, and paused. After several more steps she paused again, remained absolutely frozen. Because she'd caught the movement of someone in the Mews below. One of Security Section's men making his patrol. If he looked up he would certainly see her. He didn't. He went past and away, down the mews. Maren relaxed. Too much. She lost her balance. If she fell to the right she would plunge five stories, to the left, she would activate the alarm. She steadied herself with her arms out, palms flat, like a plane using its wings for control and when she continued on, she kept her eyes level ahead and pretended she was merely walking a sidewalk curb. Until she reached the other side.

Chesser breathed normally again.

Weaver was also relieved.

Maren examined the outcropping of brick. She peered over the edge and saw that it ran all the way down the rear of the building, evidently serving some purpose. But it gave no indication of what it contained. She related that in a whisper-shout to Chesser and Weaver.

"Come back," Chesser instructed.

She refused. "I'm sure this is it," she insisted.

An unconvinced shrug from Weaver. It was up to Chesser. He climbed through the fence opening and out to the edge, feeling as though he wasn't in the same dimension as his body. He stepped out onto the drain gutter, and his greater weight caused it to tear away from where it was lightly bolted to the edge of the roof. For a moment it seemed about to collapse completely, but then it held. Chesser steadied and tried to swallow. When he could feel his legs again, he continued on and made it across. He acted nonchalant, but at that moment he wanted very much to take Maren in his arms.

Weaver started across. It was more difficult for him because he was carrying the satchel of tools. This also wasn't the way he wanted to die. Chesser and Maren silently petitioned fate to be kind, and Weaver made it across safely.

Together they examined the brick outcropping and agreed it appeared promising. Weaver immediately went to work on it with a chisel, appropriately diamond-edged, that cut easily into the mortar between the bricks. In less than five minutes he had one brick out. Maren eager shined her flashlight into the hole and saw the metallic inverted U of a pipe.

"May be from a toilet," she said.

"It's all toilet," said Chesser. Weaver continued with the chisel until eight bricks had been removed. That exposed enough of the pipe for them to see that it emerged from the roof and was connected to a wide elbow which reversed its direction. Housed within brick, apparently the pipe ran straight down the building and into the ground below.

Weaver looped a diamond-covered filament around the pipe and connected it through a portable, powered instrument. A special type of vibrating saw. He switched it on and the filament began cutting through the steel as if it were mere wood. He was careful not to cut too deep, so as not to sever whatever the pipe contained. The saw made only a faint gritting sound.

A quarter hour later a large enough section of the pipe was lifted away.

The pipe contained five electrical conduits. Each identical, two hundred forty-volt size. Weaver took the opportunity to cut open each of them. Then he replaced the bricks, so that nothing appeared out of place.

They retreated as they'd come, cautiously but more confidently, back across the drain gutter and through the fence to the roof of number 13. They took time to bend the section of fence back into its original position. They replaced and latched the trapdoor after them before descending all the way down and out to the Marylebone truck.

No one had seen them.

They were, of course, greatly encouraged by the success of their reconnaissance. As soon as they arrived home, they rewarded themselves with some chilled Tattinger and a delicious supper served by Siv and Britta.

Those two pretty au pair Danes. Chesser detected a distinct change in their attitude since Weaver had come. An obvious increase in provocativeness unmistakably directed toward Weaver. Siv and Britta were not competing with one another. Rather, they seemed consolidated, as though performing a purposely choreographed pas de deux.

Chesser's initial reaction to it was some resentment, jealousy. He figured that Siv and Britta had held back on him, and if that didn't deeply would his vanity, it did bruise. For consolation he reminded himself that fair-skinned Nordic girls, being naturally free of prejudice, find dark-skinned men extremely attractive.

Maren was well aware of what was going on. She understood why Siv and Britta were aroused by Weaver. She was even tempted to let Weaver know that with some flirting of her own. But she checked the impulse in deference to Chesser's possessiveness. Now she sat closer to Chesser. "You were wonderful tonight."

He nodded. To hell with modesty. "We all were," he said, and raised a toast.

"What about the pipe?" asked Weaver, not trying to deny his partial distraction by what Britta's see-through blouse didn't quite conceal.

"Five to one's not good odds," Chesser said. "Be okay if we have five shots at it, but we've got only one."

"Could be worse. Could be ten to one," said Weaver.

"Actually," reminded Chesser, "we don't know if any one of the five conduits is what we want."

"Man, there's no way of telling."

"There must be," hoped Maren.

For a long moment each tried to imagine a solution.

Weaver watched Siv's walk, a rear view. He asked Chesser, "What you said about the Russians, is it true?"

"Sure."

"That pisses me, man," said Weaver. He knew the hopes the Communists were pouring into the black ears of Africa, playing on the truth that the blacks had pulled their own riches out of their own earth and handed them over to the whites in return for just pennies and a bed and a bottle of beer a day. The blacks of South Africa got shafted, spent their bodies, and got nothing out for themselves, even when they stuck stones up their assholes. All they got was apartheid. Action against that injustice was one of the primary reasons Weaver had come in on Chesser's project. Now he had another, knowing that the Communists were stirring with one hand and dipping into the pot with the other. Fucking hypocrites, thought Weaver, glad he'd never really been a Communist. He'd almost joined the party once, in prison, because a very persuasive cat was proselytizing. But about that same time he'd gotten into his own black thing. He was only a little surprised to learn now that the Communists were users, just like all the whites.

Weaver decided he didn't want any more champagne. He just wanted what he had coming, what he could handle, including Siv and Britta, a double helping, which was only fair enough.

The next morning Maren announced she was going to visit Mildred. She reminded Chesser to pick up the special equipment they'd ordered. They'd also need a stopwatch, she said, because Watts was coming over the next evening for a final briefing and rehearsal.

Chesser went out to do his chores, mildly resenting having to do them alone while Maren enjoyed a *tête-à-tête* with an astral body and Weaver stayed home for some less incredible heavenly response from the generous Danes.

Chesser had to wait more than an hour for the men at the shop to make a few final adjustments on the unit. It was a bulky thing, nearly the size and shape of a fifty-gallon drum. He'd placed the order under the name M. J. Mathew, and volunteered that he'd be applying the unit at his factory in Belgium. He paid for it with cash. At the other place the flexible hose was ready when he got there. Three hundred feet of it, not as heavy as it looked. He loaded it into the car and drove home feeling conspicuous with the top down, the unit on the seat beside him, and the huge coil of hose sticking up from the rear space. He was almost home when he remembered the stopwatch. He drove back to Baker Street and tried three places before he located one at a camera shop. Even then he arrived back before Maren.

He didn't see Weaver anywhere about. Nor Siv. Nor Britta. Chesser shouted that he was there. No answer. Also no help. He went out and unloaded the car, struggled the unit and the hose into the house.

He was hungry, irascible. He fixed himself a Scotch, got a hunk of cold chicken from the refrigerator, stuffed his mouth with dried apricots, and went out to the garden. He was staring into the unfolded face of a giant yellow rose when Maren appeared on the terrace and called to him. She'd been rather pensive when she'd departed but was returning exuberant. She hurried down the terrace steps to him, kissed him a nice, open kiss. He still had the chicken and the Scotch in his hands, so she had to do all the hugging.

"I solved it!" she exclaimed.

Chesser assumed she meant the pipe problem.

"It was easy."

"No assistance from the other side?"

She shook her head. "But Mildred was a big help."

"How?"

"Which reminds me, darling, I forgot to tell you, my Indian's back. I knew he'd be around when he was needed."

Chesser glanced around, asked with a straight face, "Is he here, right now?"

"No, but he's around somewhere."

"How was Mildred a big help?"

"Well, we were sitting there in Mildred's room, that dreadful, shabby place where she lives, and no sooner had I explained the problem than there it was, the answer, right at our feet."

"Mildred put it there?"

"In a way."

"And what was the answer?"

Maren took time out to pay tribute to one of the giant yellow roses. She inhaled deeply and sighed appreciation before telling Chesser, very precisely, "*Blatella germanica.*"

She had seven of them. Two spares. She had them isolated in individual small plastic prescription vials, with pin holes punched in the tops so they wouldn't suffocate. They weren't a special, rare sort. Just ordinary cockroaches.

She and Mildred had captured them alive at Mildred's bedsitter, where there were plenty more, if needed. Maren had stopped off at the British Museum to do some research on the insects. A very accommodating entomologist had told her some amazing things, which she now passed on to Chesser.

For example, did he know that the cockroach is one of the oldest living inhabitants of the world? Three hundred and fifty million years ago it was running around and doing damned well without kitchen sinks and Chinese restaurants. Roaches preceded dinosaurs by a hundred and seventy million years, and even those heavy-footed monsters failed to stomp them out. Roaches have five eyes, six legs, two antennae, and no birth control. They can swim if they must and fly as well. They thrive on such goodies as chocolate cake but can survive on nothing more than cardboard. Caviar or soap, it's all the same to them.

By compressing its exterior skeleton to a wafer-thin dimension, a roach can squeeze through the slightest crack. Said Maren.

That particular ability was now most significant, Chesser immediately realized.

Maren placed the plastic vials on a table, along with a roll of adhesive tape, a pair of scissors, five containers of Dior nail enamel, a sharp-pointed sable eyeliner brush, some cotton, a felt-tipped pen, and a bottle of chloroform.

First she cut strips of the tape, which she affixed to the vials. She printed names on them to give the roaches identity.

Lea.

Ingrid.

Deanna.

Lily.

Marika.

Chesser asked how she knew all the roaches were females.

"Did you ever know a man named Lily?" she replied, and continued her task, step by step, obviously having thought it out in advance.

Into each vial she stuffed a wad of cotton saturated with chloroform. In seconds the insects were unconscious. Then, using the brush, she applied a tiny dot of nail enamel to the back of each roach. A different color for each—pink, white, orange, fuchsia, and true red. She explained to Chesser, "Cockroaches clean themselves much the same way as cats. That's why I put the spot there, where they can't reach it. Otherwise they'd clean it off. And I only put a speck because it's toxic and might kill them." Advice gleaned that day from the entomologist, no doubt. Although she said it as if she'd known it forever.

Chesser remarked that the roaches already looked dead.

Maren scoffed, but then wasn't sure. She picked up one of the vials to examine closely the roach it contained. "I hope I didn't overdose them," she said. She uncapped the vial and prodded the roach gently with the tip of the brush. The roach didn't stir. It leaped. Up the side of the vial and off onto the rug, easily beating Maren's reflexes. She jumped to capture it alive, attempting to come down over it with her cupped hands. The roach did a comparative four-hundred-meter dash in what may well have been world's record time, reached the wall, flattened itself and squeezed through a crack, out of sight and out of danger.

"Damn!" exclaimed Maren, and directed her exasperation at Chesser. "You stood there and let it get away."

Immediately she admitted it really wasn't his fault by smiling the smile she always smiled whenever she wanted to be forgiven.

She had to substitute one of her spare roaches and once again repeat the procedure of labeling, chloroforming, and painting. On the strips of adhesive, next to the name of the roach, she dabbed an identifying color and finally, on a piece of paper, she made up a master key of colors and names.

By then all the roaches had recovered from the anesthesia and were waving their long antennae, shaking their legs, and searching for a way out of the vials.

Chesser didn't want to waste any time. It was important that they solve the pipe problem as soon as possible. So, after dark, they again drove the Marylebone truck to Puffing Mews and parked at the rear of number 13. Dressed in their Marylebone uniforms, they went in and up to the roof. Weaver bent open the section of fence.

Both Weaver and Chesser volunteered to make the trip across, but Maren wouldn't have it. It was her idea, therefore she deserved to see it through. She already had a lightweight mesh sack slung over her shoulder, containing the roaches in their vials and two extra rolls of adhesive tape. Not waiting for any further protest or demonstration of superior male valor, she climbed through the fence opening and sidestepped to the roof's edge. She didn't hesitate this time, walked right out and across the narrow ridge, making it look easy.

She removed the bricks and then systematically transferred the roaches, one into each of the five narrow openings within the pipe. She peeled the labels from the vials and stuck them on for designation. Using the spare tape she sealed the openings tight. Then she replaced the bricks.

She had the urge to whistle for a show of extra nonchalance as she walked back over the drain gutter. Also because she was delighted with herself.

As usual, Watts carried his simple lunch to work the following day. A sliced egg sandwich with mayonnaise and lettuce, an apple, and a thermos of tea.

The first thing he did each morning when he arrived at the vault was place his lunch in the far right corner on the cabinet surface upon which he'd be working with the Diamondlite. Same place, never fail. But this day he broke the habit. He placed his lunch on top of a high stool just to his left, within full view.

Watts would be there in the vault all morning, checking the contents of packets. But from noon on Meecham expected him upstairs to help conduct sights.

From nine until eleven he examined various stones under the Diamondlite, confirming their weight and other qualities, folding tissue neatly around them, collating them into packets. Although he appeared to be concentrating on the diamonds, he was very preoccupied with his lunch. At eleven o'clock he interrupted his work to undo the wax paper wrapping and partially expose the egg sandwich. He also took one large bite from the apple. Perhaps that would help, he thought.

At precisely eleven forty-five a cockroach of the *Blatella germanica* species flattened itself enough to make it through a sliver of space, between the wall and the face-plate of the electric outlet into which the Diamondlite was connected. The insect had spent the previous fourteen hours on a one-way trip confined within the corrugated metal of a conduit. When the roach's highly sensitive antennae had detected a slight flow of air, it had intelligently headed downward toward it. And then, when the odor of food came from the same direction, it just followed its nose. Now it emerged from behind the outlet, crawled down the wall, and hesitated there, cautious. Temptation overcame fear. It scooted across the floor, climbed a leg of the stool, and waited several minutes in an inverted position on the underside of the stool seat. Five minutes before noon it decided to make a try.

Watts saw it. He was careful not to cause a sudden motion. He merely leaned over and noticed that the roach enjoying his lunch had a tiny spot of color on its back. Pink.

It was Marika.

To the delight of everyone concerned, Watts reported that fact when he arrived at the Park Village house that night for the rehearsal. The caution that had previously prohibited such direct contact with Watts was now eliminated by necessity. They could only hope Watts was not under The System's surveillance and they believed there was no reason why he should be. After nearly thirty years of loyal service, didn't one deserve absolute trust?

One also deserved full death benefits, thought Chesser, but he didn't say it.

Chesser regretted having to implicate Watts to such an extent, to risk compromising the man. Chesser had already written Watts another certified check, bringing Watts's compensation up to an even million, equal with Weaver's. That didn't relieve Chesser's conscience as much as Watts's attitude, which was unqualifiedly cooperative. Evidently Watts was having his own vendetta in his own way.

The rehearsal went well. Maren's insistence that they have it was justified. Among other things, they learned that the hose fit snugly but had enough slip to it, and the unit worked well. Maren used the stopwatch to time Watts's efforts. With crushed gravel substituted for diamonds. After several trials, Watts improved his speed, but that was as fast as he could do it. They multiplied his best time and calculated they wouldn't, at that rate, get all the diamonds. But they'd get most of them.

Mildred attended the rehearsal at Maren's request. She sat and watched, fascinated, and was unusually quiet while the others went over the plan. Finally, Chesser was satisfied that everyone knew everything. Then the only question was when. Maren contended there was no need to wait. They'd do it the next night. Agreed.

Watts departed. But Mildred stayed on, expecting Maren to drive her home. Chesser was grateful for the opportunity to settle matters with the small medium. He had a certified M. J. Mathew check ready, made out to her, for two hundred thousand dollars, an amount he considered generous. He was sure she'd grab it eagerly. So, no preamble. He just held it out and offered it to her.

Mildred gazed at it, bewildered for a moment. But then she suddenly recoiled, as though his hand were a cobra about to strike.

"Lor'!" she exclaimed. "I told you not to try giving me money. As much as I need it, I'd rather keep my powers." She raised her eyes. "I don't want it," she wailed. "I want to keep my powers."

Maren was furious.

"I thought she could use it," explained Chesser. "After all, she did help with the cockroaches and things."

Maren snatched the check from him. She tore it into little pieces that she dropped into an ashtray. Chesser observed Mildred closely as the two hundred thousand dollars she could have had was being destroyed. Mildred didn't even wince.

Maren put a consoling arm around her spiritual confidant. "He just doesn't understand. You must forgive him."

Mildred whimpered.

Chesser would have bet anything on Mildred's accepting that check. Maybe, he thought, he was wrong about her. Anyway, he found himself telling her, "I'm sorry."

Mildred managed a forgiving smile. "I'll be sending out some strong positive thoughts tomorrow night," she promised.

CHAPTER 18

The night of June thirtieth was the sort of night motion-picture people either pray for or try to duplicate when they're filming a mystery, murder or monster. The sky was dark angry with great erratic balls of clouds rolling around in turbulence. The atmosphere was too agitated to settle into a rain. However, a consequence of all its commotion was a convulsive wind, coming to earth in whipping sheets and fistlike gusts.

It was perhaps amateurish, certainly audacious, for Chesser, Maren, and Weaver to make their attempt on such a night. Actually they'd been misled by the official weather forecast, which had predicted mere cloudiness with only a twenty-percent chance of showers and no mention of high winds. Perhaps that afternoon these winds had been headed in a different direction. Anyway, by the time Chesser, Maren, and Weaver realized the extent of the handicap, they were committed.

The two huge dump trucks marked Marylebone, Ltd., were parked strategically close to the rear of number 13, and the unit was brought in and up to the second floor along with the cumbersome coil of hose.

More important, Watts was already locked within The System's subterranean vault.

At exactly five twenty-five that afternoon he had gone to the sorting area on the first subterranean level. Five thirty was quitting time and all the classifiers were preparing to leave. Watts usually remained a while to avoid the delay at the door on Harrowhouse, the only way in or out of number 11. There was always a jam-up of fifty or more at quitting time.

But this day at five thirty Watts went with the others, rode the elevator up to the main foyer, where The System's secretaries and various office workers were already a shuffling crowd, eager to get to the door and be through. Their flow was restricted by the narrow width of the door itself, and by Miller of Security Section, who was checking everyone out.

Watts looked ahead and observed Miller's procedure. Miller had a personnel list on a clipboard, marking departures according to the faces that passed by him in twos and threes, irregularly. Watts saw how automatically Miller was doing it, no doubt from having done it so many times before.

Watts had counted on that. He reached the door simultaneously with two of his fellow workers.

Miller's eyes recognized him.

Watts hesitated there.

Miller's eyes left Watts and went to the list.

And, during that moment, Watts stepped aside and busied himself with adjusting his hat while those who had been behind him filled in, continued the flow, became the faces for Miller's attention.

Watts turned partly away and glanced aside at Miller; saw through the spaces between those now going out that Miller was entirely preoccupied. Apparently, as far as Miller was concerned, Watts had gone, checked out.

Watts went back along the fringe of the remaining crowd, entered the elevator, and took it down to the vault, where he remained.

At precisely six, he watched the vault's automatic door close and heard the electronically controlled tumblers of its internal locking mechanism click its intricate combinations. He had three hours for preparations. Ample time. He had purposely not read the *Morning Telegraph* that day, had brought the newspaper with him to enjoy during his spare time. But now he again postponed reading it, decided he'd first do what was expected of him.

He took off his suit jacket and hung it over the back of a chair. From a pocket he removed a pair of ordinary gloves, a sterling penknife with his initials engraved on it, a small roll of electrician's black tape, and a two-hundred-foot length of five-hundred-pound test nylon fishing line gathered into a compact circle. He got down on the floor, disconnected the cord of the Diamondlite from the wall outlet and used the dull edge of the knife's blade to twist out the single bolt that held the outlet's face-plate in position. He did it with care not to make any marks. He placed the face-plate and its retaining bolt on the floor nearby where he could easily locate it when the time came for that. Then he slipped on the gloves for insulation and went to work on the outlet box itself, unscrewing the pair of bolts that held the double-plug unit in place. No trouble. He released the wires connected to it and placed the plug on the floor.

Next he taped the two exposed ends of the wires, so they wouldn't contact and cause a short. He made the ends of the wire into a loop. He tied the fish line into a loop and led it through the loop of wires, so the wires and the fish line were securely attached. He placed the fish line on the floor, right there, ready.

For the next hour and fifteen minutes he prepared the cabinets that contained the sorted diamonds. He pulled out the many wide, shallow drawers to leave them all in open position. The drawers were well-balanced, made with ball bearings, and came out easily, smoothly.

That done, Watts took notice of the time. He had just a little less than half an hour. He sat and relaxed with the newspaper.

At that moment Weaver was unlatching the horizontal door to the roof of number 13. He pushed it up, and the wind nearly tore it from his hands. Weaver and Maren climbed out onto the roof and found out how really bad the wind was. They stood with legs wide and tried to lean into it to keep their balance, but it was sporadic, blowing with varying intensities from one direction and then another so there was no way to dependably compensate for it.

Chesser came up with the end of the hose. Weaver took it and began pulling it up swiftly hand over hand. The wind caught the hose, and Chesser and Maren had to control it by pressing it down onto the surface of the roof with their bodies. When enough of the hose was pulled up, Weaver took the free end of it to the fence and secured it there. He bent open the section of fence.

Chesser told Maren, "There's no need for all of us to go across."

She glanced at the roof of number 11, at the drain gutter.

"Let's go together," she said.

Part of Chesser wanted to argue about that, wanted her as safe as possible. But another part told him that was the best way to go. Together.

Chesser went first. Maren was right behind him. He could sense her there, and it helped, just as it helped her to have him leading the way.

The wind was their enemy now, a deadly, unpredictable element that slapped against them like a powerful, invisible hand, pushing one moment, pulling the next, swirling and sucking, letting go all at once only to come smashing back again with renewed force.

They inched across the narrow drain gutter, making more progress during the intermittent lulls. A fall either way meant death. They didn't step foot over foot, as they'd done before. Now they slid their feet along the drain, maintaining contact with it, front foot forward a length, back foot forward an equal distance. Slowly.

When there was a little more than a yard to go, Chesser had the desire to leap the rest of the way, just lunge and grab for safety. He didn't because he thought it might cause Maren to lose balance, the suddenness of it. So he continued to slide his feet until he was across. He immediately turned and reached for her and she got his arm and he pulled her to him.

They held against one another. "I love you," he said. He'd never meant it more than at this moment.

"I know," she said.

A blast of wind hit them with reality. They kneeled together and began removing the bricks.

There was the pipe containing the five electrical conduits. Maren shined her flashlight to determine which of the corrugated tubes bore the adhesive strip marked with pink. They undid the tape from that one, exposing the pair of wires it contained. Chesser worked the wires up with his fingers until he had enough to grasp. He pulled hard. The wires came. Hand over hand he brought them up the corrugated tube, feeding them to Maren, who gathered them. Finally, there was the end of the wires, and with it the fish line that Watts had attached. Now they were ready for the hose.

The plan had been merely to lead the hose across the roof, but now the wind prevented that. Weaver improvised. While Chesser and Maren were busy extracting the wires, Weaver had searched the rooms of number 13 and found some adequately heavy twine left by the Marylebone workmen. Several pieces, which he knotted together. He tied one end of the twine to the hose and the other to a wrench. He knew he'd have only one chance. If the wrench fell short onto the roof of number 11 it would set off the alarm.

Weaver took a wide stance and whirled the wrench above his head. When it had enough momentum, he released. The twine played out. The wrench cleared the near fence, spun and fought the wind above the roof of number 11 and, by inches, cleared the opposite fence which separated number 11 from the next adjacent rooftop. Chesser retrieved it, untied it, and pulled the twine to him until he had the end of the hose in hand. He pulled the hose across, not without difficulty, because the wind snapped and twisted it erratically.

Meanwhile, with methodical caution, Maren disconnected the fish line from the wires.

Chesser removed the twine from the end of the hose and Maren secured the fish line in its place.

From her pocket Maren brought out a tiny brass pellet. She dropped it into the corrugated tube. Hopefully it would communicate a signal to Watts, seven floors below. It did. In a few seconds the fish line went taut. Chesser fitted the end of the hose into the corrugated tube. For some reason it wasn't as snug a fit as it had been rehearsal. It slipped in easily. Weaver played it across and Chesser and Maren guided it in and down.

Below, in the vault, Watts kept just enough pressure on the line to help bring the hose down. When the tip of the hose appeared in the hole of the wall socket, Watts guided it out and detached the line. He carefully gauged how much pull he should apply to the hose and, as it came to him, he arranged it on the floor in a neat coil, the same as he usually did at home with his gardening hose when he'd finished watering his lawn or roses.

After a while he decreased his pull, judging that he now had nearly all the hose they could allow him. And, yes, the hose soon went taut. Watts hoped he had enough. To determine that he picked up the end of the hose and walked it down an aisle to the farthest end of the vault. He found it reached, with some to spare. He put its open end against the palm of his hand. Nothing. He waited what seemed a long time and feared that it wouldn't work, now, after all this. But then he suddenly felt the suction begin. He tested it again on the skin of his palm and it was strong.

Watts had a lot to do. He began at the far end of the vault, the top drawer first. Perfect white stones of highest quality, all of eight carats, give or take a point or two. Watts knew exactly how fine they were; he had classified them. They lay crowded in the wide drawer, completely covering its black-velour inner lining. Watts extended the end of the hose to the diamonds and sucked them up. Until the drawer was empty. He pushed it closed and proceeded with the next. And the next, and the next.

Above, Maren and Chesser tended the hose where it emerged from the conduit, while Weaver was on the second floor of number 13 looking after the unit. The unit was much like a very powerful industrial vacuum device, except it was specially constructed to receive and discharge simultaneously. In that manner it was more like a pump. The hose that came down from the roof conveyed the diamonds into the unit. Coupled to the unit, on its opposite side, was the hose that evacuated the stones. This hose was directed out one of the second-floor windows and down to one of the dump trucks parked in the Mews. The truck was enclosed by canvas over a high frame. In the top center of the canvas was a hole through which the hose fed, and blankets had been spread on the bed of the truck to inhibit noise.

The first diamonds fell into the truck at precisely ten twenty-three P.M.

At two A.M. the diamonds stopped flowing. Weaver thought something had gone wrong, but then decided it was only because Watts was taking a break. That was correct. In ten minutes the flow resumed.

By six A.M. Watts was extremely tired. He had to take another rest. His legs ached, his arms and shoulders burned with fatigue. His eyes felt as though they were shrunk and asking too much of the muscles that held them in place.

He sat on the floor. He looked at some of the cabinets he'd emptied, their drawers now closed. He lay back on the floor, stretching, and tried to go limp. But he had too much tension. He told himself it would be all over very soon.

Less than an hour to go. And he still had a lot of work. He hadn't labored this hard in years. He hadn't thought it would require this much energy. He got up, stiff from having rested, and began on the drawer of the cabinet he knew contained unusual pink stones. Fancies, they were called. He saw them disappear under the suck of the hose, giving the illusion they were dissolving.

Watts was determined to finish. He hurried, but didn't sacrifice efficiency. At five minutes to seven the hose sucked up the final diamond from the final drawer. He suddenly felt better. He wished it were possible to take the larger stones. They were all that remained. The rest of the cabinets were empty. Ninety-five per cent of The System's inventory had been cleaned out.

Watts fastened the fish line to the end of the hose.

At seven A.M. Chesser and Maren pulled the hose up and transferred the line to the wires. Watts pulled the wires down, untaped their ends, attached them to their connections, and bolted them into place. He rolled the used tape into a tight ball and wound the fish line over his fingers, knotting it compactly. He shoved both into his trouser pocket. He screwed the face-plate into position and plugged in the Diamondlite. Then he put on his suit jacket and sat where he usually sat.

Outside, the wind had gone, as though despite all its wild blustering it was afraid of the sun. Dawn was coming. The eastern sky was announcing it with some mauve.

Weaver pulled the hose across. Chesser and Maren replaced the bricks and came across the drain gutter, stepping swiftly now, confident as a pair of veteran performers. They bent the section of fence back and went down from the roof of number

13, latching the trap door, taking the hose and the unit down and out and tossing them into the back of one of the trucks.

Each of the two trucks contained about two tons of diamonds. Chesser and Maren got into the cabin of the lead truck. Weaver would drive the other. They started off. The rear end of Weaver's truck cleared the corner and was out of the Mews just in time. Five seconds later an authentic Marylebone plasterer in an authentic Marylebone vehicle turned into the Mews at the opposite end.

Maren navigated. Using a map Chesser had marked in advance. They kept to major streets, where truck traffic was common early in the morning. By seven forty-five A.M. they were on the outskirts of London. They picked up the A-2 and headed south on it at a speed just below the limit. All the way to their predetermined turnoff. After another six miles of regular highway they got off onto a smaller road, and then onto one that hadn't been used in over a year.

There it was. Their destination.

Where would one hide four tons of diamonds? Professional thieves, imitating themselves, would have probably made a get-away to an abandoned warehouse to keep constant watch over the haul. The place Maren, Chesser, and Weaver had selected was more original. It was, in fact, an unhiding place, right out in the open, where it was reasonable to assume no one would think of looking.

An abandoned sand and gravel pit. Which the National Department of Highways had used temporarily while constructing the M-3. It was isolated and very inaccessible. The only road to the pit was about a quarter of a mile long and so overgrown it did not appear to be a road at all. Low-hanging branches and clusters of crowding bushes naturally camouflaged it, and grass had grown up in its tracks. A short distance in, the road was interrupted by a narrow but formidable gully, making the pit even more unapproachable. On a previous day, Chesser and Weaver had brought in some four-inch-thick, twelve-foot-long planks and had laid them across to make a serviceable bridge.

The pit itself was just a gouged-out, gaping hole in the countryside, located five miles southwest of Hindhead, conveniently less than twelve miles from Massey's West Sussex mansion.

On the floor of the open pit were several mounds of crushed rock, of various sorts, including some quartz which, except for size, resembled uncut diamonds. Not quite as transparent, but almost. Also there was a metal shack in the pit, dilapidated and rusted.

Maren got out to direct Chesser and Weaver, who maneuvered the trucks into a nearly tail-to-tail position. The rear gates were released and the hydraulic dumping mechanism put into operation. The diamonds came pouring out and down onto the ground, sliding, clicking against one another. A minor avalanche of twenty million carats, forming what appeared to be merely a pile of worthless, ordinary stones.

The trucks were pulled forward and their engines cut. Chesser and Weaver jumped out, eager to see.

There were many things they could have said at that moment, but nothing was adequate. So they just stood there, all three speechless, shocked numb by their total success. It was difficult for them to accept what they'd done. As Maren had prophesied, they'd made criminal history, pulled off the greatest robbery of all time.

Delighted as she was, Maren couldn't help also feeling a considerable letdown. The concentrated risk, the intense stimulation, was over.

Weaver's thoughts transcended the diamonds. He saw all the black hands that had scratched them from their own earth. And how he could now, finally, pay them back.

Chesser was trying to convince himself that what he was seeing wasn't an illusion. Look at all those fucking diamonds. Repeat. Look at all those fucking diamonds . . .

Chesser broke the spell by rushing forward and climbing up to sit on the summit of the twelve-billion-dollar heap, assuming what he had always resentfully visualized was Meecham's unique position. He got diamonds in his shoes. He felt them hard and gritty under the cheeks of his ass. It made him lightheaded.

Chesser had heard often enough that one's status in this life depended greatly upon were one sat. At that moment, Chesser was on top.

*   *   *

It was nine A.M. The door to the subterranean vault at number 11 performed all its electronically timed intricacies. Its alarms were deactivated, and the door itself swung slowly open.

The plan had called for Watts to make his exit from the vault as soon as possible. He was to take the elevator up to the second floor and then come down the stairs to the main foyer, where he would sit reading the newspaper, as though he'd just arrived. More often than not he got to work early and had to wait for the vault to open before going down to it. So his behavior this day wouldn't be considered unusual. He would merely be running a few minutes behind schedule, and was supposed to set his watch back to explain that.

Because Watts was normally the first one down in the vault each morning, he would discover and report the robbery. They wouldn't suspect him. His loyalty was taken for granted by The System and his consistently mild deportment placed him, so to speak, beneath suspicion. No, they wouldn't suspect Watts. If they considered him at all, they would consider him incapable of such a thing.

Watts wasn't to pretend excitement or act extremely upset when he reported the robbery. Rather, he was to inform Meecham in his customary understated British manner. If he was nervous, that would be understandable.

That was the plan.

But it was impossible.

Watts had known all along that it was impossible, because whenever he arrived at number 11, early or not, he had to be checked in by Security. No exceptions. Security was even more conscientious about checking in than they were about checking out. Watts had chosen not to reveal that restriction to Chesser and Maren. He felt it was his prerogative not to do so. He reasoned that he was scheduled to die soon anyway. So it wasn't much of a sacrifice, really. When his watch said eight thirty, he removed a small blue capsule from his vest pocket and placed it in his mouth. He had difficulty swallowing it. His throat was dry, wanting to reject it. He managed, though, to get it down.

He'd been told it would be relatively painless and would take twenty minutes to kill him.

That information was correct.

One of the classifiers discovered the dead Watts and notified Meecham. Meecham was astonished and annoyed. He immediately informed Coglin and hoped this incident wouldn't interfere with the important sights that were scheduled for that day.

By the time Meecham arrived down in the vault, Coglin was already there with several of his specialists. Watts's body wasn't covered. It was stretched out on the floor. Meecham tried not to look at it.

"Suicide," was Coglin's opinion.

"Why the hell didn't he stay home and do it?"

"He was in the vault. When it opened this morning he was already here."

"Impossible."

"He must have been in here all night."

"He was checked out yesterday afternoon, wasn't he?" asked Meecham.

"He was checked out," replied Coglin, subdued.

"Your section fucked up." Meecham was very upset. He never swore, except under the most intimate circumstances.

Coglin took the blame with a nod.

Meecham pressed his advantage. "The least you can do now is see this mess is handled discreetly. I assume you can get the police to cooperate?"

"Of course."

"Today of all days," Meecham continued, "we've got packets to make up." In his mind he was already appointing the next most senior classifier to fill Watts's position.

"You don't know all of it," Coglin said.

"What do you mean?"

"The inventory is gone."

"Please don't be ridiculous."

Nevertheless, Meecham pulled out one of the drawers of the nearest cabinet, and saw it was empty. He didn't believe it. He pulled out another, and then went from cabinet to cabinet, his hysteria increasing as he saw they were all empty. He rushed up and down the aisles, grabbing drawers open, cursing their emptiness, slamming them shut. Finally he turned his anger on Coglin. "You incompetent son of a bitch."

Coglin couldn't deny it. He told Meecham, "I personally checked out the electronic log."

"Like you checked out Watts."

"All alarm systems were functioning last night, all night, continuously."

"What does that prove?"

"No one got in through the vault door."

"I don't give a damn how they got in. It's what they got out that's important. Every carat, the lot. Incredible."

"The time locks on the vault door are not retractable," said Coglin, and shook his head sharply as though to clear it.

"The inventory just evaporated, is that it?"

"I don't know how it was done. Not yet." Coglin glanced over at Watts's body.

"This could ruin The System," said Meecham, realizing the potential consequences for the first time.

"We'll get the diamonds back," Coglin said.

"We'd better." Meecham felt like vomiting. "If word of this gets out the entire industry will panic. We can't mention it to the police."

"Only the suicide," promised Coglin. "We've got to act as if nothing has happened."

"*Nothing has happened*," repeated Meecham. He tugged at his shirtcuffs and smoothed his tie, as though his appearance were important to maintaining the lie.

"It's obviously a professional job," Coglin thought aloud.

Meecham agreed. He was feeling so desperate he would have agreed had Coglin said it was the work of trained bears.

"That being the fact, we're sure to get them," said Coglin.

"We have sights today."

"Cancel them."

"That's impossible. Whiteman is scheduled in this afternoon. What precisely am I going to tell Whiteman? We don't have diamonds for his packet."

"Tell him anything but that."

"How long do you estimate it will take to get the inventory back?"

"A couple of days, no more than a week," said Coglin with what he hoped sounded like total confidence.

Meecham reconsidered. "I suppose we could postpone the sights. Not cancel, just postpone. I'll use the excuse that Sir Harold is critically ill, or something."

"I'll have to stall Whiteman, of course, keep him occupied."

"That shouldn't be difficult."

"Evidently, you know Whiteman," Meecham said.

Coglin nodded. He knew Meecham too, he thought.

"I'll get cables off to the others," said Meecham, "rescheduling their appointments."

"Good idea."

Meecham created a smile. "My apologies," he said.

"For what?" asked Coglin, knowing but wanting to make Meecham say it.

"Security has always done an excellent job. I'm sure this wasn't caused by any lack of efficiency on your section's part." He, of course, didn't mean it, but needed Coglin's help now more than ever. Everything depended on Security getting the diamonds back.

"You were in shock," said Coglin. "I still am," he added generously.

Meecham took out a handkerchief and wiped his hands dry. "Keep me posted," he requested. "And when you apprehend whoever did this I want them appropriately punished. Severely." Thus, having obliquely assigned the extreme penalty to those who had disrupted The System and caused him such personal anguish, Meecham composed his mask of unconcern and left the vault.

Coglin remained there with his specialists.

He ordered a thorough search of Watts. They stripped the body completely and placed the contents of Watts's pockets neatly on the floor. Included were the small, crushed-up ball of electrician's tape and the fish line. Coglin realized the incongruity of those two items but, as yet, did not know their significance.

He gave the vault a perfunctory examination and found nothing out of place. He opened the cabinet which contained larger stones. Intact. That they hadn't been stolen, he suspected, was in some way significant.

He briefed his men and put them to work. First, all cabinets against walls were moved from their places. Coglin was doubtful that anything could cut through the armored skin of the room, but it was a possibility that had to be eliminated. Meanwhile, one of the men called Coglin's attention to the velour inner lining of an empty drawer. A strong side light revealed a pattern of strokes on the nap of the fabric. Evidently something had been swept back and forth across it.

Coglin kept that in mind. He went to the far end of the vault and studied the entire length of that wall. It was perfectly sheer. Except for the two electrical outlets. Coglin ordered the face-plates of the outlets removed.

Within a half hour, Coglin had it figured out. The roof, the fence, the gutter drain, the replaced bricks, the two-hundred and forty-volt electrical conduit. He had to admire someone's courage and, even more, someone's ingenuity. He was still convinced that he was up against some very sophisticated professionals. He'd get to them. He counted on the dependable imperfection of the criminal mind, its compulsion to boast and confide within its own element. For that very reason, Coglin had developed a good scattering of bad characters as informants. While waiting for one of them to bring him a lead, he would investigate Watts. It was regrettable that he hadn't had Watts under surveillance. That would have made it easier.

Coglin didn't report his progress to Meecham. He decided to let Meecham sweat it out. Long ago Coglin had learned that handicaps frequently offer opportunities.

CHAPTER 19

The night after the robbery, Chesser, Maren, and Weaver found some lighthearted release in the verbal replay of their adventure. Most amusing, and mutually reassuring, were admissions that beneath surface displays of calm and bravery had been some very human feelings ranging from fear to terror to near panic. Only Maren wouldn't admit it. However, she did laughingly remember that she and Chesser, in their anxiety, had forgotten to carry their guns. And after all that practice. Weaver said he hadn't forgotten his, had carried it under his Marylebone coveralls, stuck into his belt, where it had caused his groin considerable discomfort.

At this time they hadn't yet learned of Watts's death and they wouldn't know about it for some time to come. Chesser was tempted to call Watts, just to find out how things had gone. Not because he was worried that Watts's early-morning act hadn't been believed. What Chesser really wanted to hear from Watts was how Meecham had taken it. Chesser happily imagined Meecham having an immediate nervous break-down, a total collapse.

Fortunately, Chesser didn't call Watts: he thought better of it. Fortunately, because Coglin had already placed a twenty-four-hour monitor on Watts's home line, along with a special set-up to make voice prints. For the past five years Coglin had been making voice prints of everyone who came in verbal contact with The System. It would have been relatively easy for him to identify Chesser.

Chesser was also tempted to call Massey. His ego wanted him to tell Massey the good news, and there was the matter of fifteen million dollars he had coming, but he remembered Massey's explicit instructions about not calling.

They went to bed early. Chesser couldn't sleep.

He tried to tell himself he ought to be finally content, sat-isfied. He virtually had fifteen million dollars, didn't he? His reply to that was, no. More accurately, he had twelve billion. He wanted to awaken Maren and talk it out with her, but she was deeply asleep and he needed more than a few sleepy mumbles. So he lay there and tried to work it out alone, jump-ing back and forth from millions to billions. He was ex-tremely tired, his body demanding sleep, but his mind expanded, hyperaware of those opposing figures, bringing him to a nearly psychedelic state where fantasies became in-distinguishable from realities. Until, eventually, there were only realities, and shortly after three A.M. his mind and body joined and allowed him the relief of unconsciousness.

He slept through the morning and missed Maren's depar-ture by a half hour. Siv served him warm buttered scones and Irish bacon, and relayed Maren's message: she had gone to

Mildred's for lunch. Chesser imagined all the *Blatella germanica* also lunching.

Weaver came down the stairs. He was packed to leave, again dressed as the Reverend Pouteau although he hadn't yet put on the benevolent expression that went with the costume.

"Want some coffee?" invited Chesser.

Weaver declined but helped himself to half a scone and two strips of bacon from Chesser's plate. Some excess flour from the scone fell onto Weaver's black clerical vest.

"What time's your plane?" asked Chesser.

"Three fifteen."

"I'll drive you out."

"No, man, don't bother. It'll be a drag."

"I was going out that way."

"Okay."

Chesser wondered about Weaver's million. He didn't want Weaver to have done all he had for nothing. He asked about it.

"No hassle," replied Weaver. "I got verification this morning." That meant Weaver had his money safely deposited in his bank in Africa.

"How's it feel to be a millionaire?"

Instead of answering, Weaver asked: "What are you going to do with yours?"

"I haven't decided," lied Chesser. Almost incongruously, he suddenly remembered that he hadn't sent ex-wife Sylvia her payment that month. Chesser could pay her a lump sum now and sever that final, oppressive tie. Sylvia would hate that. He couldn't remember himself with Sylvia. She had ordered pencils with their name on them and sent Christmas cards bearing a snapshot of them. The only reason Chesser could remember for marrying her was that she felt good at the time. It had been more than that, of course, but now that was the best, acceptable excuse.

"We better split," said Weaver, taking the last slice of bacon from Chesser's plate. Weaver, Chesser thought, owed a good-bye to Siv and Britta, but Weaver didn't go find them to say it. Just picked up his luggage and went out to the car.

On the way to Heathrow Weaver was in an up mood. He talked and laughed a lot and recalled old times. Chesser believed the change from the Weaver who'd come and the

Weaver now leaving was the million. Whether Weaver wanted to admit that or not.

Going through the underpass, approaching Heathrow, Weaver told him, "Don't take me all the way in."

Chesser turned off onto a lane which served a public parking area. Remote enough, no traffic that day, no people that far away from the terminal. Weaver got out with his luggage. Chesser wondered if he'd just walk away. Weaver dropped his luggage on the pavement and leaned back into the car, offering his hand and a grin.

Chesser matched him as well as he could, hand and grin.

"Thanks."

"Ever get to Africa?" asked Weaver.

"Could. Used to."

"Say good-bye to Maren for me. I didn't get a chance."

Chesser nodded. "Good luck, Reverend."

"Keep the faith."

Weaver slammed the car door shut, picked up his luggage, and started walking toward the terminal. Chesser watched him going. He'd be home by dark. But not home, really. Chesser also thought of himself as an exile.

He swung the car around and accelerated away from the airport. He headed south in the direction of Massey's. He got off the A-2 and drove into the town of Hindhead, were he found the bright red booth of a public telephone. He called Massey station to station.

A servant answered and said Massey wasn't there.

Chesser identified himself.

Massey came on.

Chesser pictured him.

"I hope you've good reason for calling," said Massey.

"I'm in a pay booth," assured Chesser. "No way of tracing this call."

"Well?"

Moment of truth. Chesser told him, "It didn't work."

Massey didn't say anything. Chesser anticipated an angry or disappointed reaction, but he couldn't even hear Massey breathing. "No go," said Chesser, "but we came close."

"That's unfortunate."

"Yes."

"You must tell me what happened."

Chesser had the story ready, actually what had occurred, except for a false twist at the end. He was about to start on it when Massey said, "You and your Maren should come spend next weekend here."

Chesser read suspicion behind Massey's words. One thing for certain, he didn't want to face Massey now. He said the first excuse that came to him. "We're going to Scotland."

"How long will you be away?"

"Ten days, maybe longer."

"Then perhaps when you return."

Chesser tried to appraise Massey's tone and decided it was too normal considering the circumstances. He told Massey, "You'll be glad to hear no one was caught."

"Then why not give it another try?"

That suggestion encouraged Chesser to believe Massey was accepting his story. "Can't. Not now." said Chesser, intentionally sounding apprehensive.

"We never have much luck doing business together, do we, Mr. Chesser?"

"Not so far."

"You seem to specialize in failures."

Chesser managed a resigned sigh. "I guess nobody beats The System."

Massey clicked off.

Chesser said good-bye anyway.

He tried to convince himself that Massey had bought the lie. But he wasn't sure. It had cost Massey a good two and a half million dollars.

Chesser placed the phone back on its hook and argued against his conscience with the likely possibility that Massey had made that much during the time it had taken to lose that much. Also, there was Massey's true reason for wanting to steal The System's inventory. Chesser had felt from the beginning that Massey's motive was more than revenge against The System for the Shorewater Project. Massey himself had implied as much. At first Chesser had suspected that Massey was out to get financial control of The System, planning to use the diamonds as leverage to gain that advantage. But when he thought more about it Chesser decided that wasn't it.

Twenty, perhaps even ten years ago it might have been, but
not now. With his seventy-odd years and billions, Massey
wasn't about to involve himself with a new operational problem that huge and complex. Why then was Massey so eager
to get his hands on those twenty million carats?

A memorial to his power. A more durable monument than
anything his money could build of stone or steel, more indelible than any altruistic gesture he might grandly bestow
upon mankind. History, Massey knew, was redundant with the
forgotten altruistic gestures of men desiring permanent mem-
orability. At best, only a few ever attained even the trivial,
often temporary distinction of having a street, a square, a
structure named after them. It seemed the world was more
lastingly impressed with tyranny.

The diamonds, Massey realized, were an opportunity for a
final, sweeping, backhand display of despotic but unforget-
table power. He intended, systematically, to flood the market
with those twenty million carats. The annual world market demand was about three million carats. At that rate, scarcity was
maintained. Thus, twenty million sudden carats would deval-
uate diamonds sharply, pull them down to the semiprecious
category. A unique and mighty show. Huge fortunes would be
wiped out in an instant. Everyone who owned even one of
those hard little valuable stones would feel the impact.
Massey would strip the petty romantic values off all the fingers in the world. Massey apparently reasoned it was better to
be remembered as the man who ruined diamonds than be another Ozymandias fading into obscurity.

Knowing these were Massey's intentions helped Chesser to
justify his own behavior. He told his conscience that double-
crossing Massey was actually doing the world a good turn.

His conscience cooperated.

Chesser left the phone booth and walked up the street of
Hindhead. He went into the local version of a Woolworth
store and purchased the first thing he saw that would suit his
purpose. A cheap plastic satchel with a zipper opening. He
also bought a half pound of chewy butterscotch that tasted as
though it contained disinfectant. If only half the things in the
world were even half as good as they appeared, wished

Chesser, and discarded the bag of candy out the car window on his way out of town.

He stopped at the entrance of the small road leading to the sand and gravel pit. After a car passed and the way was clear, he drove in. When he reached the pit he saw the sun reflecting off the huge pile of gems. He had to do something about that.

But first he filled the satchel, scooping up double handfuls of diamonds. About ten pounds of them. Then he went to the metal shack, where he found a rusted shovel which he used to distribute a layer of sand over the diamonds, dulling their effect.

On the drive back to London he thought about how he might communicate with Meecham without giving himself away. He considered and dismissed numerous complicated notions before settling on what seemed a good simple plan. He stopped at a Regent Street corner and bought two copies of every London newspaper.

Maren was home. Chesser found her in the bathroom seated before an ultraviolet lamp. She had her hair piled untidily atop her head and a pink clay beauty mask on her face. It exaggerated her eyes, nostrils, and mouth. He knew she was depressed; she inflicted such elaborate rituals on herself only when she felt down. Usually her depression was concurrent with boredom. He wondered if now was the time to tell her his change of plans. He sat on the edge of the bidet and remained silent, just observing her, for a long while. She was nude.

He told her. Everything. Including, word for word, his telephone conversation with Massey.

While he was speaking she kept her mouth and eyes set, so as not to spoil her mask. But finally she couldn't contain herself. Her lips opened and the clay cracked. She smiled and exclaimed, "Darling, that's fabulous!" She forgot entirely that her face was caked and rushed to demonstrate her approval with a kiss that made Chesser lose his balance and fall back against one of the bidet's control knobs. Water swirled into the basin, soaking the seat of Chesser's trousers.

Maren laughed and peeled off the mask. Chesser removed his trousers. She helped dry him and got him a robe.

The prospect of renewed excitement brought Maren immediately out of her doldrums. They went over the details of his entire plan. She especially appreciated the way Chesser had chosen to communicate with Meecham. "Clever," she complimented, and Chesser agreed immodestly. In practically the same breath, she disapproved of the demands Chesser intended to make on The System in exchange for returning the inventory.

"You really want those things?" she asked.

"Sure."

"What the hell for?"

"For a change," he said with some annoyance.

"I think you should think more about it."

"I have."

"You're letting spite get in the way."

"I don't think so. It's what I've always wanted, something substantial under me."

"I'm substantial."

"I've never had a definite direction."

"But, darling, you do. You have marvelous direction."

"Hell I do. Half the time I don't know where I'm headed."

"So? We're going together, aren't we?"

Chesser nodded, not ungratefully.

"Obviously you haven't really thought it out."

"I've given it plenty of thought."

"Then why, when you have them at such a disadvantage do you want to end up owing them?"

"Owing them what?"

"Valuable things. I mean truly valuable things, like attention, worries, time. You'll have to be here, you'll have to be there. You won't be able to be just anywhere you might happen to want to be. How restricting and horribly dull."

With her usual directness Maren had hit on Chesser's central quandary. What she said seemed logical to the part of him that especially valued the benefits of personal freedom, the good irresponsible life. Conversely, another part of him was hungry for proof in the form of fulfilled ambition. That part suspected her argument was biased by her own unique motives.

"Call it a matter of self-respect," he said.

Her eyes went up.

"I can't just play around all my life."

"Why not?"

"A man should work, have a goal of some sort." The cliché made him wince.

"You've got us."

"That's something else."

"It's not. It's something to work on. And it's a full-time job too. At least it ought to be. The trouble is you're going by rules that don't apply any more. At least not to us."

Chesser wondered what his father would have said to that, and knew his father wouldn't approve no matter what he decided. Extorted success was worse than no success.

Maren went on. "You know what most people do. They don't. And when it's too late they look back and cry about it."

"You forget, not everyone has the money to do just anything."

"Maybe not. But even those who do usually don't," she said. "Anyway, if that's how you want to end up, just tell me."

That had the ring of an ultimatum, and between anything on earth and her, he'd choose her every time.

What Chesser had intended to demand from The System was irrevocable control and sole legal ownership of their newest and most productive mine in Namaqualand. Plus, a percentage of shares from each of The System's major stockholders, giving him membership on the Board as a director.

"All right," said Chesser, "what do you suggest I ask for?"

"I don't know. Ordinary ransom, I suppose."

Chesser was glad she'd used that term. He related ransom to kidnaping and his conscience could handle that easier than extortion. Kidnaping diamonds seemed more quixotic than criminal. "How much ransom?"

"Enough to make it interesting."

Chesser now wished he'd stuck to the original plan, turned the diamonds over to Massey for fifteen million dollars. He would have been out of it by now. Irritated with himself for having complicated the deal, he arbitrarily increased the amount and said, "Fifty million."

That settled that.

They composed the ransom note. Carefully selected words. They searched the pages of the various newspapers Chesser had bought. They found *The Times* most accommodating.

They had to rephrase their wording some, but finally that newspaper contained everything they wanted to say. Using a bright red, felt-tipped pen, they merely circled corresponding words on the printed pages of *The Times* and numbered each circle. So all one needed to do to get their message was to read the numbered words in sequence, one through sixty four.

We have your diamonds. You can have them back for fifty million dollars. Unless you agree to these terms we will destroy the market value of diamonds by creating a disastrous surplus. On July 5th you will arrange for the clock in Victoria Tower to strike thirteen times at midnight. This will signify your willingness to cooperate, and we will then issue further instructions.

To have the Tower Clock toll incorrectly was Maren's idea. She believed that less trite than a reply in the personals column of the classified section. Chesser thought it was a bit of corny dramatics, although it would create some extra scurrying for Meecham. Also, there was rebellious appeal in causing that famous old timepiece, Big Ben, to make a mistake. Considering British regard for efficiency, it had probably never occurred before and might never again.

CHAPTER 20

So far, Security Section had come up with nothing. Not a fingerprint, footprint, strand of hair, or whisper. Nothing.

Coglin was sure that Watts was involved. However, an extensive investigation of Watts's personal and financial affairs revealed not a single fact or rumor to contradict Watts's loyal, conservative reputation. Every report concluded that Watts, a temperate man of modest means, had never done anything questionable. Coglin personally attended Watts's funeral on the remote chance that a suspect might turn up. The funeral was small and sad, and the most suspicious-looking person was the thin-lipped Episcopalian minister, who routinely uttered insincere final tributes.

Coglin's efforts were hampered, he believed, by the need to keep the robbery confidential. That prohibited him from using the full power of his international force. Perhaps one of his sources in Beirut or Dublin or San Francisco might nose around and come up with the vital lead, but there was no way of knowing. Those few men on his immediate staff who knew about the theft were his best, but it was impossible for them to cover enough ground. As it was, they were working day and night, infiltrating the London underworld, discreetly pumping every source. Coglin was still convinced he was up against highly adept professionals.

On the fourth day following the robbery, when every effort had drawn a blank, Coglin sat alone in his office with a bottle of ten-year-old Irish whiskey, and contemplated failure. For not preventing the robbery in the first place, he was already at fault. And now, he realized, even if he succeeded in getting the diamonds back he'd still have to suffer for permitting the theft. As soon as the inventory was safely returned to the vault, Meecham would exonerate himself by presenting a detailed report to the board. Undoubtedly the report would censure Security Section, most specifically Coglin. The board would ask for Coglin's resignation. So, inventory recovered or not, Coglin would lose. That is, if he allowed the situation to run its seemingly inevitable course.

Coglin's interphone rang. The light on the instrument indicated it was Meecham's direct line. Meecham again. He'd been calling almost every hour, anxious to know of any developments. Coglin had put him off with cryptic insinuations of progress, but had actually told him nothing. Often he just hadn't bothered to answer. He decided he would this time.

"Something just arrived in the post," Meecham said.

Coglin forced interest, asked what.

"A message of some sort. Come over."

Coglin hadn't seen Meecham since that morning in the

vault. Now he found the man had the drawn look that results from prolonged tension, his eyes pinched and darkly receded, his entire face tight and tired. Meecham eagerly showed Coglin the copy of the London *Times* he'd received. With the red-circled, numbered words.

Coglin realized at once what it was. He quickly transposed the message, writing it out on a yellow pad.

"They must be insane!" Meecham said.

"Clever, actually," was Coglin's opinion.

"Fifty million dollars! That's ridiculous. No one in their right mind would demand such an amount." Meecham raked the heel of his hand across the newspaper, as though that might wipe it from sight. "Do you think this is authentic?"

"They could have asked for more. After all, they do have twelve billion dollars worth."

Meecham turned abruptly and looked out the window without seeing the view. He closed his eyes, squeezed the bridge of his nose with a thumb and forefinger. "Can you arrange this Tower Clock nonsense for tonight?" he asked.

"Of course, but—"

"I'll have to ask the board," said Meecham.

Coglin didn't want that. Not yet. "Why involve the board?"

"To raise the fifty million, of course."

"That won't be necessary."

"But if those people do what they threaten to do . . ."

"They won't," Coglin assured him. "They want the money more than they want to ruin The System."

"That's true, isn't it?"

"Certainly."

"So what shall we do?"

"Nothing for the moment. We'll call their bluff and see what happens. My guess is we'll just receive another note."

"You're onto something, aren't you?" asked Meecham hopefully.

"Yes," lied Coglin. "We should have them and the diamonds before long now."

"When?"

"Soon."

"Can't you be more definite than that?"

"No. But we do have a schedule. For God's sake, Meecham, you've got to relax."

As though obeying, Meecham collapsed into his plush swivel chair. "You've identified those responsible? You know where they are?"

"We know who they are," was Coglin's empty reply.

"So what the devil are you waiting for?"

Coglin invented. "With patience we can finish off this whole thing quietly and neatly. An abrupt move now would be premature. Unless, of course, you want those twenty million carats scattered around the globe. Because that's exactly what they'll do, you know, if there's a chase, just throw the stones away and run."

The mere idea of that made Meecham shudder. He managed a weak smile in appreciation of Coglin's expertise in such nefarious matters.

Coglin folded the newspaper and the note and slipped them into his jacket pocket. "How's Whiteman?" he inquired.

"I've been with him for the past three nights. Right now the damn fool is at the Dorchester with a pair of Welsh girls."

"That should keep him a while."

"Not really."

"Then send in some fresh supplies."

"I'm going to schedule the sights," said Meecham. "I'll have Johannesburg send up enough from their reserve. They can fly it up and have it here by tomorrow." It was a recourse Meecham had kept in mind since the day of the robbery, but he'd been putting it off until it was absolutely necessary. To request this large a shipment from Johannesburg, especially on such short notice, was irregular and would certainly cause speculation. However, he had no choice now. Replenishing the inventory, even partially, was the only way to remove the immediate pressure and make The System appear to be operating normally. It would also get Whiteman out of the way, and Meecham would be thankful for that.

"I'll schedule sights for next week," he said, "beginning Monday. That will allow time to make up the packets."

"And that should give me the time I need," said Coglin, leaving Meecham to signal his secretary and place a call to South Africa.

*   *   *

Early that night it began to rain. Not a short, hard storm but a steady, persistent drizzle.

Maren and Chesser were keeping their rendezvous with Big Ben. It seems reasonable to believe the tolling of that great clock's chimes can be heard nearly anywhere in London. But the fact is one must be in its near vicinity to hear it at all. So Maren and Chesser were parked at the southwest perimeter of St. James on the wide way known as Birdcage Walk, only three blocks from Parliament, within easy hearing distance of Big Ben. Although no parking was allowed along any of the streets in the area, they had to chance it. They kept the motor running. They had nearly half an hour to wait. The rain beating on the car's top sounded like fingertips nervously tapping a drumhead. The wipers performed precise sweeps across the windshield, contrapuntal to the London Philharmonic music that came from the radio.

Maren was hunched down in the seat, her cheek pressed against the side window. She gazed at the jewel-like drops that hit on the outside of the window, noting how they lost their individuality when they became too heavy and were transformed into rivulets.

She remembered times.

Times of childhood when the weather had kept her indoors, when she'd looked out across the desolate flatland and imagined beyond. She hadn't then appreciated the smell of baking embroidered by the contentment of her mother humming. Rather she had disliked the tranquility because there was constantly only that. And even when the most pleasant sort of day opened the house and she went out along the deep blue mirrors where the sea was almost locked in and she ran beneath the glide of white birds that seemed to be scratching the perfect sky with the points of their wings, she still felt confined and promised herself that someday she would escape. The sky and the sea would open for her and she would go between.

The car's windows were steamed opaque by their breath. Chesser drew a wet, lopsided heart on the windshield. Maren acknowledged it with a very soft smile that made him want to touch her. He reached for her hand, but at that same moment, unintentionally she reached over to the radio and dialed for some livelier music.

Someone rapped on the window on Chesser's side. Chesser pressed the button to lower the window. He didn't realize immediately that it was a policeman in a long black rubber cape, shiny wet. Chesser tried to appear at ease, managed a friendly, inquisitive look. Rain dripped from the policeman's wrist as he touched his hat in a salute and inquired, "Something wrong, sir?"

"No, everything's fine."

"There's no stopping alone here, sir."

"We were uncertain about the way to Old Paradise Street." That street had come to mind because he'd once stayed overnight in the bed of a young blonde actress who lived on Old Paradise. That was before he met Maren, just before.

"Old Paradise is straight ahead," the policeman said, "across Westminster Bridge." He took out his official street directory and flashlight. Its beam swept once across Maren, illuminating her. Chesser thought the policeman did it intentionally, to get a look at her. Why? Had The System alerted the police? Perhaps they had the entire area covered. Chesser recalled Massey's confident opinion that The System would never involve the police. It had seemed reasonable at the time, but even Massey could have been mistaken.

Chesser put the car into gear and thanked the policeman, who saluted again and stepped back. As the car pulled away from the curb, Chesser's guilt made him feel the officer's eyes reading the rear license plate.

"London has the nicest policemen," commented Maren.

"Nosy bastard."

"He wasn't. He was just doing his job."

"He got a good look at you, me, the car, and everything."

"So?"

"Nothing. Forget it."

"He was wet and lonely, that's all."

Chesser doubted that. He turned right and then right again onto Old Queen's Street. No parking along there either. Only a single vehicle was standing about half way down the block. A police car. They went by it at normal speed and Chesser took the first cross street to get out of sight. His hands were perspiring and gripping the steering wheel too tight. He glanced to the rear view mirror and saw they weren't followed. No matter, he decided to leave the vicinity, drove through a maze of narrow one-ways until he was headed toward the Thames. He committed the car to Westminster Bridge and a glance at his watch told him eleven fifty-five. He'd have to hurry not to miss the chimes. The river had never seemed so wide, but finally they reached the other side, where Chesser took the first right, which led them to St. Thomas's Hospital. He pulled into a parking area above the Albert Embankment, facing across the river.

He cut the lights and motor and quickly wiped the windshield with his hand, erasing the heart he'd drawn. He couldn't see well enough. He got out of the car. So did Maren. She came around and stood next to him, close.

Across the river the Houses of Parliament were bathed in ochre spotlights, bizarrely diffused through the murk and rain. They couldn't make out the hands of the clock, only the lighted circle of its face on the tower. The drizzle pounded noisily on the car and the pavement and their heads. Chesser put his arm around Maren and drew her close. He wondered if they'd be able to hear the chimes at this distance, considering all the handicaps. Maybe it was already past midnight. It seemed they'd stood there more than long enough.

A tugboat on the river blasted its horn three times.

Chesser cursed it.

Then Big Ben began to toll.

They heard it easily. The wet night actually amplified its sound. They counted. One to twelve, and waited for the thirteenth ring. But it didn't come. Chesser reasoned that perhaps the clock needed to be reset in order to ring once again, or perhaps its limit was twelve and some intricate manipulation of its mechanism was required. They waited, stood there against one another and got thoroughly soaked. Until twelve ten, when they gave up and got back into the car.

Trickles of rain ran down the backs of their necks. Their feet squished in their sodden shoes and their clothes stuck cold to their skins. Maren kneeled up on the seat and squeezed rainwater from strands of her hair.

Chesser wiped his face with both hands, hard. He was enraged. Never in his life had he been so furious. The System had refused to yield, even now, when he surely had the upper hand. The System wouldn't even signal it was willing to negotiate with him, wouldn't give him even that much satisfaction. But he would show them. He'd bend the bastards.

"Maybe they didn't receive the newspaper," said Maren, hugging herself, chilled.

"They just didn't get the message," Chesser said bitterly. He started the car and turned on the heater, and Maren didn't wait to take off her clothes. She was completely nude, and warmer that way, by the time they were back across Westminster Bridge, heading home.

They didn't go home to stay. Only long enough to dress in dry clothes and swallow some brandy. Then Chesser took them out again to drive London's streets, which because of the rain and the hour were mostly deserted. They quickly reached their destination.

Hatton Garden, the diamond district.

All the store windows were dark and protected by latticed steel gates stretched and locked in place across their fronts. There wasn't another car in sight, and no one along the sidewalk.

They cruised the area and then repeated that route with the window down on Maren's side. She had the satchel of diamonds on her lap, the ones Chesser had taken from the gravel pit. He drove slowly and told her when to begin.

She shoved her hand into the satchel and came up with as many diamonds as she could hold. She flung them out onto the rainy street, laughing, finding it exhilarating. Chesser shouted encouragement as she threw handful after handful to the gutters and sidewalks of that diamond-obsessed district.

Altogether, she tossed away more than twenty-two thousand carats. Worth approximately twenty-five million dollars.

CHAPTER 21

At seven fifteen that morning, Sterling Griffin didn't believe his eyes.

He was on his way to work on a ten-carat gold mount for a cheap topaz ring he'd promised he'd have ready first thing that day. Alone on the street, just walking along with his right hand in his trouser pocket privately comforting. Sterling stepped on one. He stopped, turned and looked down at it, pushed at it some with the toe of his shoe. Although he knew what it appeared to be, he didn't pick it up right away, because it was an impossibility. Sterling was a disbeliever by profession. He had his own jewelry business, specializing in anything. That is, he paid monthly for a small booth with six feet of enclosed counter space at the Wilcox Diamond Arcade. Safe privileges included. Not that Sterling required much protection. Currently his stock consisted of:

> 3 tourmaline rings
> 1 diamond chip stickpin
> 2 tortoise-shell pill boxes
> 4 turquoise-and-silver odd pieces
> 1 silver cigar clipper
> 1 tray of assorted cheap earrings
> 1 Queen Victoria souvenir fob
> 1 Spiro Agnew wristwatch
> Some gold bits and pieces worth their weight.

At one time Sterling featured antique jewelry but now his only vintage possession was a dream. Of having his own store spotlighted to the advantage of abundant first quality gems. Each of the men who rented space in the Wilcox Diamond Arcade had that same dream. When business was slow as usual, they would talk about it.

Now, Sterling bent down to the sidewalk and picked up whatever it was. No harm in looking. He held it in the palm of his hand and squinted at it, dubious. He shrugged and dug into his jacket pocket for his loupe, which he twisted into the socket of his eye. It couldn't be. Not a diamond. Not about five carats, just there on the sidewalk begging to be found. Sterling gazed around, sadly, expecting fate to reveal what sort of joke this was. But he was alone on the street.

Sterling made a tight fist around the stone and shoved it into his pocket. He wanted to run, but then his eyes caught upon another diamond on the sidewalk and another in the gutter. He pounced on them. And another. It occurred to Sterling that perhaps he hadn't really gotten out of bed that morning, that maybe he was still there, dead there, and what he was now experiencing was the promised land. He bit his lower lip sharply and felt reassuring pain. His throat was suddenly dry and his legs drained. He got down and crawled along the gutter, finding diamonds and hoping his heart held out.

Similar experiences occurred throughout the Hatton Garden area that morning. Those who came early to work scooped up the most, but everyone who could distinguish an uncut diamond from pigeon droppings got in on the melee. By ten what they had was a full-scale riot. The streets of the diamond district became a battleground for those fighting over the diamonds that had miraculously come from somewhere and belonged to no one.

By eleven the streets had been picked clean and the panic seemed to be over. But then someone got the inspiration to investigate a sewer drain, pried off a heavy iron gate, and found a considerable cache imbedded there in city grime. That caused a reprise of the struggle at every corner. After that the district retreated to lick its wounds and count its blessings. Until noon, when bargaining began and sellers were surprised to discover that what a carat had been worth yesterday was not what a carat was worth today. Too many of those who'd found stones were eager to turn them into cash. They were willing to undersell. Prices on the London market dropped as though racing to reach rock bottom. They would stabilize in due time, of course, unless there just happened to be another catastrophe.

That possibility was not overlooked by the British press, which reacted characteristically to the event, its members delighting in the opportunity to stretch their imaginations and demonstrate they are all Lewis Carrolls at heart. If, for example, a phosphorescent flying sea serpent a half mile long is sighted off the Irish coast by a dipsomaniac, a good British reporter can and often will do eight credulous, straight-faced columns on it. It's excellent for circulation.

Understandably, the mysterious Hatton Garden diamond rush provided welcome journalistic fodder. It had all the necessary fantastic ingredients to warrant special editions and loud shouts of extra from the news vendors sandwiched between their hand-printed headline boards.

Each of London's twelve daily newspapers expressed its version of the incident. One took the position that the phenomenon was an act of ecological vengeance by Mother Earth. Another offered the possibility it was a test conducted by creatures from outer space, who created the episode to study our avaricious behavior.

DIAMONDS RAIN DOWN!!

was one headline above insinuations that what had occurred was a miracle because, apparently, the precious stones had fallen from the atmosphere along with the preceding night's rain. Perhaps the diamonds were miraculously solidified raindrops, that paper implied. What it failed to mention, however, was why the miraculous rain had fallen only in Hatton Garden and only on the streets. There was also a lengthy opposing interview with the Archbishop of Canterbury on the subject of miracles in general, including some of those performed by Our Savior, for instance.

Sir Harold Appensteig, board chairman for The Consolidated Selling System, contributed: "We are accustomed to unusual occurrences." And Reginald Meecham, president, was even less responsive. "No comment," was his brisk reply to every question from reporters, who were of the opinion that

Meecham appeared worried. Some suggested that Meecham was concerned with the General Electric Corporation's recent announcement that it had successfully reproduced genuine flawless diamonds by artificial means, ready-faceted stones of any size. Although G.E.'s process was still experimental and too costly to be widely feasible, it demanded consideration as a future threat to the marketing of natural diamonds.

The *Evening Bulletin* went all out for the human interest angle. It featured a large, front-page photograph of one Sterling Griffin grinning above his double-cupped hands, which contained his new-found fortune. Obviously, Mr. Griffin had gotten into the thick of it, for he had two swollen black eyes and was missing one and a half teeth.

The colorful news of raining diamonds caused some reactions outside Britain.

In Paris the skies were promisingly overcast. Many were inspired to close shop early and be out praying in the streets with skirts, hats, and the like held up ready to catch. However, not a drop nor a carat descended. French commerce suffered, as did French pride when the storm clouds drifted in a northeasterly direction, perchance to unload riches upon already prosperous Germany.

The monarch of a minor European principality took a good, hard look at his crown jewels and seriously considered selling them and using the money to construct several resort hotels. His loyal subjects might appreciate his foresight, but he would have unhappy pouting from his nice blonde American wife, who had learned to adore her authentic crown.

In Beverly Hills, an aging right-wing scion opened his secret floor safe and removed a small, flag-wrapped package of first-quality gems. He'd been accumulating them for years, but now he had the feeling that unless he died very soon he'd chosen the wrong way to beat the inheritance tax.

Owners of famous diamonds were apprehensive. Such as a superstar married couple. Superstar husband, two years previous, had literally exhibited his love to the entire world by purchasing for superstar wife a perfect seventy-carat pear-shaped diamond. Reportedly for two million cash. The brilliant stone was often photographed in its resting place within the ample cleavage of superstar wife. It became emblematic overnight, that jewel. It was *her* diamond, *the* diamond, and the public queued up to get a glance when it was placed on display in Mr. Roussel's, the famous gem dealer's window. The believers believed. But there were those in the diamond world who were skeptical. They didn't say anything, because, what the hell, it was all good for business.

The top men, but only the top men, at Mr. Roussel's knew the truth. In 1968 the diamond changed owners for seven hundred thousand dollars. Only two years later, when it was put up for auction, Roussel's outbid everyone and paid a million and a half for it. Immediately superstar husband bought the diamond from Roussel's, who, it was assumed, made a profit. The inside truth was: Roussel's and the superstars made an agreement in advance. Roussel's purchased the diamond for as much as it could. The firm actually had several representatives bidding against one another in order to hike up the price. That was part of it. In turn, superstar husband didn't really acquire the diamond from Roussel's. He only said he did—told the world he'd bought it for his super-loving woman. As a result, both Roussel's and superstars received more publicity than would be given to the wife of the President of the United States if she had her hair styled Afro. The flashing stone demanding attention between superstar wife's attention-getting breasts was only a good copy. No matter. People saw what they wanted to see. For Roussel's it was, of course, an excellent investment. Not only in publicity received. The value of this diamond could no longer be appraised on an intrinsic basis. It was now a *famous* diamond, and the desire to possess it now far surpassed its intrinsic market worth. Some day soon, according to the agreement, superstar wife, in an acute fit of ennui, would publicly announce that Roussel's had bought the diamond back. And Roussel's would swiftly sell it to the highest bidder, who couldn't afford not to own *the* diamond, *her* diamond.

Understandably, the press now wanted to know superstar couple's reaction to the rain of diamonds, and for that purpose a special press conference was held aboard their yacht moored on the Thames.

Superstar wife appropriately wore a sheer, white, silk jersey jumpsuit decorated with the celebrated seventy carats. She sprawled on soft cushions on the afterdeck and answered reporters' questions with ease, while superstar husband was nearby, exposing his chest hair, gulping Scotch.

How did she feel about the Hatton Garden incident?

"I think it shows what greedy shits people really are," she replied, as Nikons clicked and Aireflexes turned. "I mean, how ridiculous, the way those people fought and maimed one another over something so superficial."

What if much more of the same happened and the value of diamonds were really affected? How would she feel then?

"Wouldn't make any goddamn difference to me," she replied, looking away. She unconsciously fingered the seventy-carat stone. "Everyone believes the reason I love my diamond is because it's worth two million. But they're mistaken. I only treasure it because of the thought with which it was given, the love it represents. It's a matter of values. My values. Ours. Nothing could ever destroy that. Besides," she laughed and displayed the pretty pink pillow of her tongue, "what's a couple of million?"

At that moment superstar husband got up abruptly and, without a word, went below deck. Superstar wife brought the seventy-carat object up to her mouth and, without apparent intention, played it casually upon and between her lips. She impatiently answered two more questions and then excused herself graciously to also go below.

She walked forward down the yacht's mahogany-lined passageway to the master cabin, where superstar husband lay nude on a slant board, his eyes closed. "Fucking creeps," she complained as she took off the diamond. "Have somebody go up and tell them to split."

Superstar husband did a sit-up on the slant board, lowered half way and held, until he was red-faced and straining.

"C'mon," she said, as she dropped the seventy carats on superstar husband's own sizable and precious jewels, "roll us a joint. I think I feel like balling."

Chesser watched for the BBC television early-morning news.

He anticipated the pleasure of observing the object lesson he'd administered to the almighty cartel. However, as he watched his satisfaction gave way to the terrifying consequence that he'd brought on himself in his eagerness to antagonize The System. Massey. Surely now Massey had to know he'd been deceived. Surely Chesser would be the target of the billionaire's vindictive wrath. Massey had probably already dispatched some of his forces, large Hickey, for example. And others.

Chesser cautiously looked out one of the front windows to see a man in black standing across the street. Just standing there. A glum, sallow-faced character, definitely evil and dangerous, was Chesser's appraisal. Perhaps it was already too late. Well, at least they would make a run for it.

He found Maren downstairs in the main reception room. She appeared ready to go out, probably to Mildred's. No time for that. Chesser began explaining the circumstances.

Maren interrupted, calmly told him, "Siv and Britta are already gone. I gave them a year's vacation with pay."

"Let's not bother to pack."

"Everything's packed."

"How did you know?"

"She parried that with, "The car's all serviced. All I have left to do is call Mildred. I've been trying to reach her since ten but her line's been busy. I hate to leave without at least saying good-bye to Mildred." She went to the nearest phone and started to dial. Chesser grabbed the phone from her, slammed it down, and pulled her away from it.

They went quickly through to the garage. Maren insisted on driving. "In case we have to lose someone," she said.

She backed the car out fast, nearly to the opposite curb, where the sallow man in black was standing. He was faced away, acting preoccupied with the sky.

Chesser wondered why Maren hesitated. "Let's go," he said.

Maren called to the man, who turned, blinked, and pointed to himself quizzically.

"Come here," ordered Maren.

"Pardon," said the man, approaching.

"*Ça va?*" inquired Maren.

"*Ça va,*" the man nodded.

"*Nous allons,*" said Maren brightly.

"*Pourquoi?*"

Maren told him in French that she and Chesser were on their way to be married.

That last word was magic. It excited the man so much he seemed about to jump out of his clothes. "*Vraiment?*"

"Really," smiled Maren, and then changed and added defiantly, "but you're going to have to prove it!" She had the engine doing about five thousand rpm's, so she just let the clutch out all at once and the car shot away, leaving that spy of the French lawyers with his mind in a knot.

She headed out of London, going southeast, disregarding speed limits. Chesser glanced back frequently, but when they were out of the city proper and there was only clear road ahead and behind, he relaxed enough to ask where she was going.

"The Fokker-28 is meeting us at Biggin Hill," she said, meaning her private jet and a small airport about fifteen miles out. "I called early this morning to arrange it."

That suited Chesser. But he got to thinking. "First I want to go to Hindhead," he told her. "To the gravel pit."

"For what?"

"No reason why we should go off empty handed."

"It's the same whether we do or not."

"Not to me it isn't."

She sighed. "All right, if it means that much to you." She downshifted sharply and turned right to change their route. "Stupid diamonds," she muttered.

"I want at least a satchelful," said Chesser. "Then know what I'm going to do?" He'd just decided.

"Be a millionaire again," said Maren, exaggerating her indifference.

That reminded him he'd blown fifteen million by double-crossing Massey and was now running away from a possible fifty, settling for a couple. Considerably better than nothing, he decided. Much better than dead. "I'm going to call The System and tell them where the diamonds are."

"You're not!"

"It might get them off our tails."

"No."

"At least then we'll only have Massey to contend with. Which is more than enough."

"It won't be half as much fun," she protested.

"Okay, which do you want, Massey or The System?"

"Both."

She acted victimized, then angry, then petulant.

Chesser remained firm, and in a while she began humming—her signal that she'd accepted his decision.

That made it definite. He'd call The System. He disliked letting Meecham off so easy, but got some gratification in the suffering he'd surely caused Meecham the past week. And one day, Chesser fantasized, he'd confront Meecham with the whole inside story, with special emphasis on the fact that the inventory had been returned and the entire diamond industry preserved only as a result of his, Chesser's, benevolence.

Actually, Chesser was relieved by the mere idea of the diamonds being back where they belonged. He already felt twenty million carats less responsible.

He asked Maren, "Why didn't you try to stop me from throwing those diamonds all over the street?"

"It was good for your anger," she replied.

"And better for your pleasure. You enjoy the prospect of being chased, whereas I don't find it at all amusing. As a matter of fact, I'm scared shitless and I don't mind admitting it."

"I'm not."

"You never are. And that's not normal."

"Normal what?"

"Behavior. Even animals avoid danger when they can."

"Not all animals."

"Name one that doesn't."

She tried to think of one but couldn't. After a moment of silence she asked, "Have you ever thought of leaving me?"

"No," he answered too quickly.

A disbelieving side glance from her. "I've never thought of leaving you either."

He was pleased to hear that, but doubted it.

She leaned forward over the steering wheel and stretched her shoulders. "Why didn't you?" she asked.

"Just never have, that's all," he lied.

"No, I mean, when you thought about it, why didn't you leave?"

He said what he thought was an absolute truth. "I've never stopped loving you."

"Sure you have."

"Never."

"Love is full of stops and starts."

"Not mine."

"Yours is so exceptional?"

"Definitely."

"What's so exceptional about it?"

"You."

That succeeded, got a soft, pleased laugh from her.

He asked, "When did you last think of leaving me?"

"About ten minutes ago."

"Why? Just because I wouldn't let you have your way?"

"Of course."

"Do you stop loving me often? Actually stop loving me?" He wanted her to deny it.

"For maybe a second or two. Never longer."

A second or two, he thought, might begin a chain reaction into forever.

"It's good," she contended, "because when I start loving you again it makes me realize how very much."

"One thing for sure. We ought to stop lying to one another."

"We might some day," she said thoughtfully, "but I hope not."

"You hope not?"

She nodded. "I can't imagine not caring enough to not want to lie at least a little. Can you?"

"No," he said because it sounded good, even if it was an excuse. He looked down at his hands and thought how fortunate they had been for having ever touched her. He looked up to appreciate her profile. She knew that was what he was doing, so she relaxed her mouth open to make it appear even more sensual.

"Do you lie to me often?" he wanted to know.

"Can't you tell?"

"Not always."

"I can with you. Always. I have my own natural lie detector."

"Your ears ring, I suppose."

She laughed. "No. My love lights up."

"Do you know when other people are lying?"

"Only you," she said meaningfully.

"I love you to hell and gone," he declared, shaking his head, helpless.

"To hell and gone," she echoed, and her foot made the speedometer climb another ten mph's, to a perilous ninety on that narrow black ribbon of road.

They vroomed through Hindhead as though it were on the Grand Prix circuit, and arrived a few minutes later at the turn-off to the gravel pit. Going in, the makeshift road was still a mucky slime from the recent rains, obscuring some tire tracks, which neither of them noticed.

She didn't stop until she'd wheeled a fast, full-about turn, and, at first, Chesser thought that swift, blurring change of direction had disoriented him. He got out, carrying the empty satchel. He saw piles of crushed rock and piles of sand.

But no pile of diamonds.

There, right there, was where they had been, where he now stood, struck speechless. He could barely manage a gesture to Maren, wanting her to get out and verify what he didn't want to believe. She remained in the car.

Chesser examined the ground. There were some broad, smooth impressions obviously made by a mechanical shovel. Someone had come in and just scooped them up, he thought, every goddamn carat. Except a few that were partially imbedded in the damp soil.

He squatted and dug them out, not knowing really why he bothered. No more than a dozen. He looked around, went over to the equipment shack. Everything was the same. Only the diamonds were gone. *Where?* It was too incredible to accept. He had to look again at where they'd been, a long look, before he finally got back into the car. "They're gone," he said, empty.

"So I see," said Maren.

"But who? Who could have taken them?"

She shrugged. "Maybe somewhere England now has the world's most valuable strip of road."

"You mean, someone mistook them for ordinary gravel?"

"I said maybe."

It was a tormenting, ironic idea, and not very plausible, really. This was an unused, out-of-the-way pit. That's why he'd chosen it. He shook his head sharply.

"Got a better explanation?" she asked.

"No."

"Actually, it's really quite funny when you think of it—"

His hard look stopped her. He opened his hand and looked at the few diamonds he'd picked up. "I don't give a shit."

She agreed and suggested, "Let's just forget about it and remember us." She leaned to deliver a soft, pacifying cheek kiss.

That helped some. He told her, "I think we better start running."

"From everyone," she said, her enthusiasm renewed.

He put the diamonds in his shirt pocket, thinking he would keep them as mementos. But, feeling bitter on the way to Biggin Hill Airport, every few miles he flipped one out the window.

Until he had none.

CHAPTER 22

The yellow and silver Fokker-28 came in perfectly on runway one. Nearly everyone there at Nice's Areoport du Plage took notice, for such an expensive private plane would surely be carrying someone worth seeing.

Maren and Chesser disembarked, and, as they hurried through the terminal to a waiting dark blue Mercedes limousine, many inquired who they were. Some knew.

The limousine took them to Cannes and Maren's yacht, which was moored at the new marina. Of all the boats there, hers was the most noted. It was longer at a hundred ninety feet, more imposing in design, impeccably black, and fitted with polished chrome rather than the usual brass. Displayed on its stern was its name, as designated by Maren. *Après Vie.* And properly below that was Panama, where, for tax advantages, the vessel had been legally registered at the advice of Jean Marc's lawyers. The *Après Vie* had a cruising speed of fifteen knots, an eight-thousand-mile range, slept twelve lux-uriously, and was served by a permanent crew of twenty-two. Its captain was a rust-bearded Englishman, who contended that a ship of such quality was better maintained through use, a theory that justified long cruises to various warm and pleas-ant places, whether the owner was aboard or not—not being usually the case. Thus captain and crew enjoyed a life style above their means, one they were anxious to perpetuate.

Going aboard, Maren attracted the attention of everyone within seeing distance. She made sure she exposed an ample length of her fine legs when she made her exit from the lim-ousine and she walked up the gangway with an air of exag-gerated *haute*. At once, she demanded a half-hour private conference with the captain. To discuss sailing plans. Then she and Chesser dressed for an evening ashore.

First they had drinks on the terrace of the Carlton at the most advantageous table, not to be missed by numerous ac-quaintances who stopped by to give and get meaningless cheek kisses and doses of flattery. Maren was extremely ani-mated, exchanging comments freely, gaily. To all appearances neither she nor Chesser had a worry between them. They were just ideal lovers loving every minute of the ideal life. Of course, they were asked where they'd been, where they were staying, and, most important, where they were going.

From the Carlton they went to the Voile du Vent for an ex-cellent dinner. There they met others who knew them. Always the same questions.

But not always the same answers.

After dinner they strolled the Croisette, leisurely, with arms around, intent on one another. As they passed the outside cafes, they were recognized by many from past seasons and other desirable places.

When they'd walked all the more active section of that boulevard, they signaled to their trailing limousine and were taken to dance at Whiskey A-Go-Go. This time there Maren displayed extraordinary abandon. Her mouth was almost con-stantly open, as if she were screaming. Her long Viking hair swished wild and whipped in the musically pressured atmos-phere. She pranced savagely. Her body sporadically tightened and released, caught and delivered. While Chesser, just a

reach away, did correct, restrained moves, Maren competed
with all the lovely, libidinal extroverts, made extreme physical promises, performed a vertical mime of limitless passion
punctuated with slinging pelvic thrusts that hit upon the thick
beats as though they were invisible phallic targets.

The Whiskey was tight with people. Maren's beauty, however, cut an exhibitionistic swath through the crowd, demanding maximum regard, deserving it.

All things considered, their behavior that evening was
strange for two people on the run. Circumstances called for
obscurity. Instead, they flagrantly intruded on the Cannes
scene and established their presence. They seemed to be deliberately declaring to anyone seeking them: Here we are.

They did it with purpose. They hoped their pursuers would
come, make inquiries, and be told by reliable sources that the
man known as Chesser with the wealthy, beautiful woman
Maren had just departed for Tangiers, the Greek Islands,
Portugal, Capri, Majorca, Venice, and elsewhere. False desti-
nations that Maren and Chesser had distributed generously
into many ears throughout that evening.

According to plan, at ten next morning the *Après Vie* pulled
out of the marina and headed seaward, cutting diagonally
across Cannes harbor. On its way it passed close by the
United States aircraft carrier *Shangri-La*, which, along with
several escort units of the Sixth Fleet, had anchored in port at
dawn. Perhaps merely for the sake of reconfirming that
wealth could still equal might, the yacht's captain ordered a
visual salute, thereby demanding the same be returned by the
huge warship. And, yes, from the *Shangri-La*'s gigantic su-
perstructure came the signal of recognition.

Good morning war.

Good morning money.

The yacht proceeded at half-speed out and around the Ile
St. Honorat, then altered its course and headed due east.
Almost immediately from leeward came a Riva speedboat,
which ran alongside for a ways, gradually reducing the width
of water between it and the yacht. The speedboat came closer
in, dangerously close. And finally tangent, to receive Maren
and Chesser, who had to jump for it.

As soon as the transfer was made, the yacht increased its

power to full and swung out in the direction of the open Mediterranean. The Riva continued straight on, then made a wide, hull-slapping turn back toward the bay of Cannes. Within ten minutes it deposited its two special passengers on the Ile Ste. Marguerite.

That island is shaped like a severed foot with its sole parallel to the Cannes coastline a mere three miles away. On its heel is a four-hundred-year old fortress-prison that once held in one of its cells the celebrated man in the iron mask, whose facial covering, truthfully, had been a more comfortable velvet. On the island's opposite end, the toe, are deserted Nazi fortifications, and on its arch, facing inland, is a cluster of modest homes, several temporary stands selling ice cream for double price, a repair yard for small boats, and a hotel by the most likely name, Masque du Fer. There are no roads, and therefore no vehicles, which tempts one to consider the island unspoiled. But partially spoiled and not developed is a more accurate description. From the fourteenth to the seventeenth centuries, the town of Cannes rented the island from certain monks, who were paid six silver coins and two chickens annually. Perhaps handicapped by this precedent, the place has never been valued enough to inspire investment, despite its proximity to the flourishing mainland.

At irregular intervals each day the island is served by public ferryboats to and from the port of Cannes. They are wide-beamed, awkward vessels that arrive, especially on holidays, loaded to the gunwales with bourgeois families in desperate retreat from extravagance, having been literally driven out to sea by the high cost of everything on the Côte d'Azur. One can read the money panic on their tight faces. However, on Ste. Marguerite they find nothing to suit them, no plastic bistros, no pinball machines, no garish shrines or old churches offering free absolution or holy water. There is nothing to ride or to sit at, not even any free sand to lie upon, for the island is entirely fringed with small, pain-inflicting pebbles. So, after a swift, apathetic glance into the historic cell of the fortress, most visitors wander back to the public wharf and wait impatiently for the next return boat. On days when the mistral causes the bay of Cannes to become even slightly ruffled, the ferry crews are quick to discontinue service, thereby

placing anyone wanting to reach Ste. Marguerite at the mercy
of speedboat owners, who dubiously appraise the sea and confidently quote fees of a hundred francs or more, depending
upon how the wind blows.

Maren and Chesser were met on the landing. By a beautiful teenaged gypsy boy named Petro, who was barefoot and
topless, wearing a pair of cheap woolen trousers that hung
with insolent precariousness from the studs of his hipbones.
While Petro tossed their baggage onto a wheelbarrow, he
looked steadily at Maren's body. Chesser caught him at it and
looked at him with annoyance. Petro immediately presented
his appeal to Maren, wordlessly requesting her preference.
She expressed forgiveness but withheld permission. Petro
shrugged, as though it was her loss. He lifted and pushed
ahead of them to the Hôtel Masque du Fer.

It was a two-story structure of creamy, weathered stucco.
The entire first floor was a dining room and bar, with many
windows, many tables covered with oil cloth, and folding
metal chairs. No customers.

The guest rooms were above. Six in all—five regular and
one special. Only one of the regulars was occupied, so Maren
and Chesser got the special. They found the only reason it was
special was that it had the hotel's only bath. That is, it had a
sink, a bidet, and a tub. The other necessary fixture was down
the hall for everyone.

"It's clean," said Maren optimistically.

A weak smile from Chesser. "It's safe," was the best he
could say for the place. He was positive no one would ever
believe they were there. As yet, he didn't.

Maren kicked off her shoes. The floor was linoleum painted
over with a dozen or more coats of high-gloss enamel. A dark,
reddish-brown. The last coat was recently applied and still a
bit tacky. Maren disliked the squeaky, sticking sensation of it
under her bare feet, but she didn't complain. She pulled aside
two straight panels of printed cotton that served inadequately
as drapes over a pair of windowed doors. "We've got a private
balcony," she said, but then she opened the doors, looked out,
and saw the balcony was really just a rooftop with a railing
around it, and it was shared with two other rooms.

Chesser was testing the bed. He found it was two pushed

together and covered by a faded brown chenille spread. The sheets were very white but overstarched and felt as though all the detergent hadn't been rinsed from them. Beneath lumpy mattresses were raw springs, which the damp sea air had corroded so that they practically squealed when Chesser bounced. A measure of that revealing noise was caused by even the slightest movement. "Have to do something about that," said Chesser.

"What for instance?"

"Oil or abstinence."

"I'm for oil," declared Maren.

"That's what's good about us," said Chesser. "Our matching preferences."

He got up and placed their bags on the bed. He zipped them open and, there, right on top, were the pistols, the Mausers, his and hers. He hadn't packed them. Maren must have. He hadn't even known she'd brought them along. He saw they already had their silencers attached and clips in and he assumed they were loaded. The sight of them stopped him for a moment, and he knew she'd noticed, so he picked them both up, pretending he enjoyed the feel of them. All the while, his mind was turning over the reason for bringing them, the possibility of having to use them to prevent death by causing it.

"They need cleaning," said Maren. "I was going to do it but I didn't have the chance."

He tossed the Mausers carelessly onto the bed.

It was like her to do whatever had just occurred to her. She got the service kit from the bag and sat on the floor with the pistols, her splendid fingers preoccupied with caring for them.

Chesser observed her for a long moment—his love, sitting there in a yellowish slash of late afternoon sun, playing with deadly things. He cut the thought and went into the bathroom. He suppressed the urge to urinate into the bidet, had to go out and down the hall to the common toilet. In there, he kicked the cover and seat up and saw the commode was like a gaping mouth with a throat hole that went at least two stories down.

Their idea was to spend two or three days on Ste. Marguerite. At least time enough for all their adversaries, whoever they were, to overrun them by chasing after the yacht. But Chesser, gazing down at the wall dispenser which doled out individual slips of cruel, slick, French toilet paper, doubted that Maren could take it that long.

That night, when they went down to dinner, there were three burly islanders at the bar, drinking *vin ordinaire.* The son of the fat woman who owned and ran the hotel was serving whatever his mother had cooked to a young woman seated at a corner table, her back to the room. Evidently she was the other guest.

Maren and Chesser took a table near the window. The islanders at the bar made some off-color remarks about Maren in such rapid jargon only they understood. The flavor of their laughter, however, told Chesser their subject. He ignored them.

The fat hotel owner rushed out of the kitchen to serve her two special guests personally. She brought a steaming platter of *moules.* There was no menu. One could eat what had been prepared or not at all.

Chesser didn't care for mussels, though he'd often heard they had supercharging aphrodisiac benefits. Maren loved them, started right in on them, and ate more than her share. She insisted they were delicious and forced Chesser to swallow three and take a big taste of the broth, which, she claimed, contained concentrated goodness. The fat owner grinned insinuatingly, as she came to remove the platter and leave two fluffy omelettes and some sliced fresh tomatoes in vinaigrette.

A few minutes later, the hotel's only other guest got up, having finished her meal. She was dressed casually but tastefully. Her attractiveness was the sort most plain French women know how to attain. Dark eyes subtly exaggerated, dark hair cut in a contemporary style to appear slightly, intriguingly undisciplined. She was unmistakably French, however, characteristically so from the waist down, with hips and buttocks a degree too thick and legs lacking in length. As she turned and saw Maren, she hesitated, unsure. Then she recognized her, smiled around a cordial hello, and went upstairs to her room.

That caused Chesser to choke. Some wine vinegar went down the wrong way, burning.

"She's from Paris," informed Maren.

Chesser gasped, wheezed, and managed to say, "She recognized you."

Maren nodded, blasé. "From when I was modeling. Her name is Arlette or Colette, or something like that, I think."

"What's she doing here?"

"The same as we're doing probably—trying to get away."

It really bothered Chesser that anyone there should know them. He was so disturbed he couldn't eat. He just sat, trying to clear his throat every so often.

Maren helped herself to some of his omelette, even had some *tarte aux pommes* for dessert and twice remarked to Chesser that he didn't know what he was missing.

After dinner, to assuage Chesser's anxiety, Maren went alone to visit the young woman. After nearly an hour, Maren returned to their room with some comforting facts, which she related to Chesser.

The young woman's name was Catherine. She was the first assistant to one of the leading Paris fashion designers; had been with him for five years, in love with him for all five. A *très intime* relationship complicated by the ambivalences of the designer's libido. He was, it seemed, more consistently inclined toward *les hommes* but required sporadic expiation of a sort and that was provided by Catherine. For her, it was a futile, humiliating alliance. Not always but more often than not. She had just recently made up her mind to sever herself completely from it. With more conviction, she claimed, than all the other previous times. However, when she'd informed the designer of her decision, he'd pleaded for reconsideration and fortified his new vows with an acute display of hetero-virility. As a result of that, Catherine was now pregnant, and, in turn, the designer was suddenly, madly, concurrently in love with a young man he had happened to meet. It was all so complex, said Catherine. She was in her seventh week now and the reason she'd come to Ste. Marguerite was to decide alone upon an abortion or not. She had arrived there self-convinced that she should have the child, although, thank God, she wasn't Catholic. She had been there two days and was now vacillating. In ten days she would meet the designer in St. Tropez and tell him her final decision. She supposed she would have the abortion and continue working for him. They were so close, so very close. She was already missing him, feeling cut off. If she had the child she would never see him again, because, as he'd put it, he would never see her. She thanked Maren for listening. She needed so much to hear another woman's opinion, Catherine had said.

Chesser was relieved. Apparently, Catherine had problems enough so that she wouldn't be a problem. He asked Maren, "So what did you advise her?"

"Nothing."

"She asked for your opinion."

"No, she didn't. She only said she needed it, but she didn't actually ask for it."

"Okay. So, if she had, what would you have told her?"

"You're testing."

"I'm not testing."

"You just want to know if I am for the abortion or not."

"Or the baby."

"Let's play backgammon," suggested Maren.

"You're slippery, you are."

"How can you tell from way over there?" she grinned, unashamed.

They were eye to eye for a long moment.

"Let's play," she chose.

Chesser got out the portable backgammon set, while she got out of her clothes. She didn't take off everything until he was watching.

"Your aura is showing," he told her.

"You can see it?"

"Sure. It's very turned on."

"What color is it?"

"Red as hell."

"No it isn't. It's lavender," she contended demurely.

"Not tonight," he said, reaching.

"Backgammon," she reminded and began arranging the white and red discs on the board he'd placed on the bed. "How much do I owe you now?" she asked.

"Three million."

"I thought it was more."

"No, that was it. Three million."

"Let's play one game, double or nothing."

He shook his head. "The limit's a million."

"You don't think I'm good for it?"

"Did you pay Massey the thousand you lost at bridge?"

"No," she admitted.

"You're a welcher."

"That's better than a freak."

"Who's a freak?"

"Old man Massey."

Chesser believed it with a laugh. "What do you suppose his hang-up is?"

"Money."

"I mean his sexual hang-up."

"That's what I mean."

"Money?"

Instead of explaining, Maren tossed one of her dice for first. She got a one, the lowest. She quickly grabbed it up. "That was practice," she said and tossed again. A six this time.

Chesser let her get away with it. He was still thinking about Massey, picturing the old billionaire literally relying on money for sexual support, perhaps even having to go as far as using a tight, thick, hard roll of thousands as a fitting extension or substitute.

By then Maren had taken two turns consecutively. Chesser allowed her that advantage. They played two games for five hundred thousand. He won one and let her win the other.

Then she turned out all the lights.

It was too dark.

"I can't see your aura," he said. He switched on the bedside lamp. It was too glary. He draped a towel over it to make it right.

He found out immediately that she was in an aggressive mood. Her fingers and mouth declared that. And they were both well into it before they realized how loudly and discordantly the bed's corroded springs were accompanying them.

Chesser held her very still. He heard the laughter of the islanders downstairs at the bar, directly below. Maren didn't care, tried to continue, but now, for Chesser, the screeching rhythm of the springs sounded greatly amplified and he was certain that it was the reason for the laughter of the islanders. He cursed the bed and tried again, differently, but the springs were relentless, and, to make matters worse, the two beds split apart. Chesser's knees plunged between them, thumped hard on the floor.

A burst of laughter from below, with exclamations in French that sounded pertinent.

Chesser got up, angry, and went out onto the roof balcony. He leaned far over the rail, attempting to get a glimpse of the people in the bar below, but all he could see from there was their lower legs and feet. He stood out there a while, looked across to Cannes, saw the distant symmetrical streetlights of the Croisette and a bunch of brightness that was the Casino. The carrier *Shangri-La* had lights strung all over its super-structure, festive-looking. Chesser wondered why. A speck of red moved across the water a few hundred feet out. A small boat. He heard its engine, a nice sound, really. The most unpleasant thing was the jabbering of the islanders.

His passion having subsided adequately, he went back into the room. The bed had been ripped apart. Maren had removed the mattresses and placed them on the floor, made them up neatly. She was kneeling there, waiting.

It made a world of difference. They didn't even need the lamp on, because the night's natural light was enough, and kinder, and they could lie there and see the water and the individual glints of Cannes three miles away, and the sky seemed nearer.

Despite all previous intrusions, when they were connected it was exceptional.

I am in you was the normal way it began for Chesser.

I am around you was the normal way it began for Maren.

But soon such definition became less distinct, less and less, while sensations increased. Until *I am you* is what they both felt. There was then no beginning nor end for them. All was entrance and entering for both of them. They were extended into one another, open to one another, and their separate roles were surrendered, lost in the loving. All the way to the ultimate testimony that they were equal and blessed with the ability to transcend aloneness.

CHAPTER 23

Meecham was in much better control now.

The Hatton Garden incident was a minor example of the monstrous catastrophe that would occur if those twenty million carats were poured all at once onto the world market.

It shocked the panic out of Meecham, snapped his mind clear, and sharply regenerated those politic skills with which he'd achieved the top echelon of the business.

His most serious error, he now realized, had been not reporting the robbery to the board immediately. The board would resent having been kept uninformed of such a major crisis, and the time gone by was indelible testimony against Meecham. Each passing day incriminated him the more. Meecham blamed himself, and hated Coglin for that. Coglin, with his daily assurances of progress, had taken advantage of Meecham's panic and hope.

Meecham still had faith that Security Section would recover the stolen inventory. He had to believe that. It was now, for him, the only clean way out of it. Once the diamonds were back in the vault, he would make a full personal report to the board, understanding the desperateness of the situation, casting indictments at those who rightfully deserved them, and magnifying the efficiency with which he, Meecham, had handled the emergency. The board's reaction would more than likely, for self-serving reasons, be favorable, a collective need to feel an even greater sense of almightiness.

All that, of course, was contingent on the stolen inventory being returned, an eventuality Meecham expected but something he would no longer depend upon as an immediate solution. Interim measures were necessary, he decided.

First, most crucial, The System's supply of stones had to be replenished so that operations could continue in a normal manner. Nearly all the reserve from Johannesburg had been used for the sights earlier that month. The next scheduled sights were less than three weeks off.

Meecham estimated that shipments due into The System from its various regular sources might supply enough stones for those next sights. If all packets were cut to a minimum. However, at the same time, he noted that the summary of international market conditions indicated an upward demand. Normally under such circumstances The System would press its monopolistic advantage to the limit. To skimp now, Meecham reasoned, would be inexplicable, tactically wrong.

He personally communicated with The System's own mines and instructed the managers to increase production by all possible means. He ordered into immediate operation a new, rich claim in Damaraland that had been held in abeyance. He sent official word to The System's dredges working the underwater fields off the mouth of the Orange River to extend their work day to all daylight hours, seven days a week, until further notice. Every facility was told emphatically not to wait until regular shipment dates. Gem-quality stones in their yields were to be forwarded to number 11 on a daily basis.

Meecham also contacted all The System's major affiliates. Except the Russians. He thought it better not to disturb the Russians. Via crackling long-distance lines to remote places, Meecham negotiated skillfully, careful not to reveal any urgency in his tone, apparently dealing from strength as usual, giving the impression it was The System that was being accommodating by offering to receive on consignment whatever gem-quality stones the affiliates presently had on hand.

Two additional calls Meecham made were particularly irregular, but strategic. To The System's undercover agents in Freetown, Sierra Leone, and Monrovia, Liberia. These agents, whose actual loyalties were known only to the highest echelon of The System, were deeply involved in the marketing of illicit stones—those diamonds smuggled out of the mines or taken from unauthorized diggings. It was estimated that traffic in illicit stones totaled about a hundred fifty million dollars a year, and the purpose of The System's agents was not only to inform, but also to frequently purchase these black-market diamonds and channel them into the hands of The System. A matter of preserving control.

Now Meecham sought to seriously tap this source, and the agents were quick to assure him that he could count on sizable shipments from them.

"Gem-quality," Meecham specified.

"Only the best are stolen," was the agents' guarantee.

Within forty-eight hours diamonds began arriving at number 11 from Luderitz, Capetown, Mwanza, Swakopmund, Accra, Luluburg, Pendembbu, Bahia, Berberati, and elsewhere. As soon as received, the stones were classified according to size, color, and quality. Meecham was greatly pleased with himself, when he went down to the vault and saw many of the shallow, velour-lined cabinet drawers again layered with diamonds. Over six hundred million dollars' worth had already arrived and there were still more to come. Enough inventory for several future sights.

Meecham reviewed the list of dealers who were scheduled in. He especially noted the amounts and quality of diamonds recommended for each man's packet. With bold calculation, he increased the contents of all packets by twenty per cent and issued instructions that every stone in every packet should be first quality. This time the dealers would not have to take any bitter with the sweet. The dealers would be delighted, of course, and their enthusiasm would sift down through the entire industry. Meecham reasoned it was excellent insurance at this time against any qualms or speculations.

Whiteman's packet, in particular, would cause plenty of healthy talk. On Meecham's order, it would contain forty thousand separate diamonds of various sizes and one three-hundred-ninety-six-and-a-half carat stone of exceptional quality. The price on the packet would be eight million, two hundred thousand dollars, and, at that, Whiteman would consider it preferential treatment.

While all this was going on at number 11, across the way on Harrowhouse Security Section was coming up with nothing.

The important lead anticipated by Coglin had not materialized, despite the fact that he was now directly piped in to the underworld elements of every major city in the world.

Coglin silently concluded that these thieves were smarter, tighter-mouthed than average. He preoccupied himself with looking in another potential direction.

The renovation of number 13.

He'd always believed there was more to that than coincidence. It was possible, of course, the thieves had been waiting years for just such an opportunity to present itself, but more probably the tearing apart of that next-door building had been a premeditated part of their scheme.

Coglin got a fast rundown on Mid-Continental Oil. It wasn't very encouraging. All it led to was Clyde Massey and the fact that Massey himself had ordered the renovation. A seventy-year-old billionaire was hardly a prime suspect.

He turned to Marylebone, Ltd.

It was like flipping over a rock and looking in on a colony of desperate, scurrying insects.

The owner of Marylebone, Ltd., was a young man of twenty, a contemporary, long-haired type caught in the ambivalence of being for or against his own establishment. His main interest seemed to be finding ways to keep the company in debt, an ability that was perhaps a genetic contribution from his late father, for Marylebone's balance sheet had been predominantly red for the past fifty years. At the present time it was just a nudge away from falling into bankruptcy. All of Marylebone's assets, including its fleet of six dump trucks and four panel trucks, were mortgaged to the limit. It was, altogether, a disorganized, horribly managed old firm attempting to maintain an appearance of solidity by overemphasizing tradition.

Seventeen persons were employed by Marylebone on a permanent basis: office personnel, interior designers and construction/destruction supervisors. However, at various times, depending on its commissions, Marylebone had as many as thirty to forty more on its payroll. Laborers as well as various specialists from the building trades such as plumbers, carpenters, masons, roofers, and electricians.

The electricians in particular stimulated Coglin's suspicion. He had in mind the manner in which the diamonds had been extracted from the vault via that two-hundred-forty-volt electrical conduit.

Coglin ordered a full-scale, in-depth investigation of Marylebone and everyone who'd been connected with it during the past two months.

It paid off quickly.

One of Marylebone's temporary employees was a man named Frank Rosilli. Rosilli had a criminal record for robbery. Twice during the past twelve years he had been Her Majesty's guest in Dartmoor Prison. Rosilli's other trade was electrician. Security Section found Rosilli in his room at 481 Shandy Street, Stepney, E1. When they broke in he was seated at a kitchen table examining some rough diamonds. Twenty-two uncut stones, to be exact. Deaf to his wails of innocence, Security Section took him roughly into custody, and Coglin personally conducted the interrogation.

Rosilli claimed he had found the diamonds in the street, a lie obviously inspired by the Hatton Garden melee. Coglin put the pressure on him. Rosilli glanced furtively at the fists being made by two of Coglin's biggest men and quickly changed his story. He'd found the diamonds in one of the Marylebone dump trucks. With the strange affinity diamonds have for grease, they'd stuck where the tailgate mechanism was heavily lubricated. He'd noticed them while riding in the back of the truck. Marylebone supervisors used the company trucks for personal transportation to and from work and around town. Sometimes they gave the workers a lift home. Rosilli said he hadn't recognized the stones as diamonds right off, not until he'd seen the photographic coverage of Hatton Garden in the *London Illustrated News*.

Coglin almost believed him. "Which truck?" Coglin demanded.

"The white one," replied Rosilli.

All the Marylebone vehicles were assembled in the parking area next to the firm's headquarters. They were each identical, stark white. However, instead of six dump trucks, there were now eight. And five panel trucks instead of four—a discovery which astounded Marylebone's young owner, who believed it incredible that he'd overlooked something that could be mortgaged into spending money.

It required the better part of an afternoon to search the company's disorderly files and find the registrations of the authentic vehicles. Engine numbers were matched and, through elimination, it was determined which of the trucks were the extra three.

Coglin stared at them intensely, as though hoping for a miraculous after-image of the person or persons who had been behind the steering wheels of those trucks on the night of June thirtieth. His face skin felt tight and the hair in his ears tingled. He was, he believed, getting closer.

His specialists went over the trucks. They vacuumed and brushed, tweezered, magnified, and microphotographed. They worked all night in their laboratory.

The following morning Coglin was presented with a fact sheet.

There were fifty-two different finger and thumb prints on the three trucks, twenty-five clear, and the rest partial or smudged. Four were prints of women. None matched any in Security Section's memory bank.

Eighteen hairs had been recovered, of which fourteen were from males and four from females. Three were from an area other than the scalp.

Analysis of dirt particles taken from the tires and under-chassis revealed nothing exceptional, just ordinary English dirt.

Blood stains, type O, ten days old, definitely female, were found on a handkerchief stuffed beneath the seat of the panel truck.

Also recovered were several cotton and wool fibers, miscellaneous metal and food particles, tobacco shreds, four cherry pits, eight nails, and two paper matchbook covers from a Soho strip club called The D-Cup.

Conclusion: the extensive and varied use of the vehicles since the robbery prevented any clear determinations. Coglin turned the fact sheet face down on his desk. He'd hoped for more.

An hour later he got it.

M. J. Mathew, 1096 Uxbridge Road, Shepherd's Bush, W12.

That was the name and address that appeared on the official registrations of the three trucks, according to the National Bureau of Motor Vehicles.

Coglin examined photostat copies of the three separate registrations. The signatures were dissimilar, back-slanted, extreme vertical condensed, and large-looped loose. However, Coglin's experienced eye strongly suspected they were all made by the same hand.

Getting somewhere, he thought.

But a computer check on the name got nothing. Mathew had never been connected with diamonds in any way, legitimate or otherwise. And the Uxbridge Road address turned out to be a Catholic bookshop.

Coglin sat there at his desk and gazed across at number 11. He encouraged himself with three swallows of straight whiskey from a sterling, old-school tumbler he'd bought from a Portobello Road tinker. He didn't feel any inside glow from the whiskey; he was that distracted. He slouched as though pressed by defeat but immediately recognized that old enemy and pulled himself up out of it.

For consolation he created a mental panorama of the robbery and credited his ingenuity with the pieces that were already in place. To fill in a couple of the blanks, he asked himself where the thieves had kept the trucks when they weren't using them. A garage or warehouse, he decided. Actually, to avoid such complication, they'd parked the trucks on a minor street in the vicinity of Marylebone, Ltd., close enough not to seem out of place, yet where Marylebone itself might not notice them. And after the robbery. Coglin was right about that. The thieves had abandoned the trucks at the Marylebone parking area, where they became part of the confusion of the Marylebone fleet.

Coglin reviewed the fact sheet and decided the direction of his next move. He noted that lab had determined the original color of the three extra trucks. Black. That meant somewhere they'd been given a professional paint job. Agents were already questioning the firms where the trucks had been purchased. The paint shop would provide verifying identification.

A full, accurate description of M. J. Mathew was forthcoming, Coglin believed.

His agents reported in.

M. J. Mathew was gray-haired, about fifty, stoop-shouldered, wore a built-up shoe because one leg was shorter than the other.

M. J. Mathew was red-haired, about forty, blotchy complexion, with bifocals, prominent nose, bad smoker's cough, tattoo of anchor and halyard on left bicep.

M. J. Mathew was black-haired, with mutton chop sideburns, full moustache, overgrown brows, spoke with a stutter, did not have total use of his right arm.

M. J. Mathew was a Negro, dark West Indian type, had two diagonal scars on left cheek, gold filling in upper front tooth, walked very knock-kneed.

M. J. Mathew had, in every instance, paid cash.

M. J. Mathew, whoever he was and whatever he looked like, was a bloody smart professional son of a bitch, brooded Coglin.

Rosilli was released. He'd come out honest on his lie-detector test, even after being injected with a double dose of sodium pentathol. Not really knowing what he was into but sensing it was too deep, Rosilli forfeited the diamonds he'd found and gladly accepted one hundred pounds for signing without reading a document which exonerated The System of any charges he might make, including abduction.

CHAPTER 24

More than a week had passed. But neither Chesser nor Maren mentioned leaving Ste. Marguerite. As so often happens, especially with lovers, they began claiming their surroundings with their experiences.

Each night they transferred the mattresses from the beds to the floor. A personal ritual kept secret by their remaking the beds first thing each morning.

The fat hotel owner turned out to be remarkable. A woman with abundant energy devoted to pleasing them because their love was so apparent to her. She had been in *la résistance* during the war and always wore a tiny, soiled Legion of Honor rosette pinned over her heart. She cooked special dishes she hoped Maren and Chesser would like, even gathered fresh thyme and rosemary for their seasoning. Her son voluntarily took time to squeeze cold fresh raspberries into a thick juice. For them. Pure and quenching.

The other guest, Catherine, did not intrude, kept to herself, sat in the sun, pensive, and took long, thoughtful walks. Only one night did she join Chesser and Maren for dinner, and the talk was mainly about fashions. She ate with the serious efficiency typical of her nationality. Frequently, she was seen using the hotel's only telephone, which was located in a little hallway between the kitchen and the bar. Calling for mercy, was Chesser's opinion.

Each day it was the same island, but each day Maren and Chesser discovered it. Lemons hung like bright decorations from branches, and a big, old fig tree next to the hotel had a ladder propped up into it so the higher fruit, sweeter and ready to drop, could be picked for spontaneous eating. There were untended geraniums along paths, and the entire outer side of the island was a grove of tall spruces, bedded with years and years of aromatic needles and scattered with huge fallen cones.

One morning, early, Maren and Chesser stood on the roof-balcony and watched pairs of islanders in ordinary rowboats poling slowly in the waveless shallows. It was explained that they were after squid and that it could only be done early when the sea was placid enough for the bottom to be seen. After that, Maren and Chesser watched with greater interest, hoping that the men would have good luck and expressing delight whenever they saw it come true.

The sea had never offered so much—not Biarritz, nor Portofino, nor the Costa del Sol, or anywhere of that sort. Unlike those resorts where the sea served as an excuse for everything else being there—merely the major element of the setting—on Ste. Marguerite the sea was, for them, an intimate explanation of anemones and sea urchins, bulby fragments of strange weeds, water-bleached sticks, and not extraordinary pebbles, all of which had to be taken up and closely examined.

One day they climbed to the fortress, up the steep rise of hundreds of shallow steps to unscalable old walls and into it, where an underfed dog came running at them, barking, followed by a little skeleton of a lady-keeper yipping remonstrations in French and brusquely calling attention to the sign that proclaimed the site historical and stated the legal visiting days and hours. As soon as a twenty-franc note was in the woman's bony hands, the dog discontinued its threats, as though its behavior were conditioned to that condition. Without smile or gratitude, the keeper and dog went off somewhere, leaving Chesser and Maren with the run of the place.

They found the fortress and its inner grounds delightfully unkempt. Either the government made no appropriation for maintenance or, more likely, such funds were intercepted by hands money couldn't possibly pass through. Thus the fortress structures were being allowed to deteriorate, and acquire more valid character. Tall, yellow grasses overgrew, thistles clumped up, brambles reached, knotted, and spread. There were wild blackberries everywhere. In the sunlit air shiny, flaxen particles floated amidst the natural frenzy of bees and flies. It was all much more pleasant than if the place had been restored and self-consciously manicured.

Such things contributed to the reason why Maren and Chesser, on the morning of the fourth day, were happy to notice that the *Shangri-La* and all the other units of the Sixth Fleet were gone from the bay. Maren fancied that she'd made them disappear, erased those grim, gray war things. Because she had been silently telling them to go.

Late that same day, they were on the toe of the island. Nearby were the Nazi fortifications they had previously explored. An enclosed concrete bunker, above ground, evidently once the placement for a coastal artillery gun, and adjoining that, a long rectangular underground bunker that must have served as quarters for the German soldiers. More recently, according to evidence noted by Maren and Chesser, both bunkers had been used frequently for acts of love.

About a hundred feet from the bunkers was an unusual rock formation. Connected sections of granite, diagonally upright, like individual troughs. It was as if some powerful giant hand, when slipping back into the sea, had clawed them out with its fingers. Slanted as the rocks were, and smooth, and warm, Chesser and Maren found them a pleasant place to lie.

They relaxed there, confronting the Mediterranean, with isolated pools at their feet.

"What day is it?" asked Maren.

"July something. I don't know exactly."

"I mean, Tuesday or Wednesday, or what?"

He guessed it was Friday. "Why?" he asked. He thought she might be getting bored with the place.

"No reason," she replied and stretched langorously. "It's indulgent not to know, but it's nice, isn't it?"

For a long while they said nothing. Their hands were joined. Chesser turned his head and marveled at Maren's eyes, which were aimed at the sky but fixed with thought. He asked her what she was thinking.

"About time," she answered. "You know what I believe?"

He truly wanted to know, was fascinated with the way her voice was coming to him then, with the sea's sounds underscoring it.

She told him, "I believe love is the reason we live lifetimes rather than one long endless forever."

"Go on."

"That's what makes time precious. We're eternal, of course, but the doubt that we're not is important. If we knew for certain we'd never die, time would be meaningless and then lovers would have nothing of value to give one another."

The idea of living forever, together, just as they were, seemed ideal to him. He wished there was some guarantee of that eternity.

"Time is the currency of love," she said. "Each lifetime is an allowance for us to spend in love."

"You make me feel wealthy," he told her, "despite my recent loss."

"Let's make a promise," she suggested enthusiastically. "Right now, this time."

"All right."

"Next lifetime you be me and I'll be you."

"Maybe that's what we're doing now," he said. "Maybe we promised that to one another last time."

She considered that. "It's very possible," she murmured and brought her look around to him.

"Anyway," he said, "we might as well promise, just to be sure."

"I want you to feel everything I feel. Promise?"

"Promise," he vowed.

He thought more about her philosophy. "Is that why you're never afraid?" he asked, believing it was.

"There's nothing to be afraid of."

"There's dying."

"Did you ever think that perhaps people are even more afraid to be born?"

"Perhaps," he conceded.

The sun was going, its circumference defined. It looked like a big precise hole punched in the sky. They could gaze directly at it without squinting. The sea was acting up a little, just entertaining itself some with the wind before it calmed for the night. Maren was wearing only a long shirtdress of lightest georgette. Pale pink patterned white. Chesser could see her nipples firm through the fabric. He cared that she might be cold.

"Shall we go back?" he asked.

"Not until after dark."

"You're not chilled?"

"No. Give me a cigarette. I just want to stay here and watch the night take over."

They were out of cigarettes, he told her.

"I want one."

"Then let's go back and have a drink before dinner."

"You go. Fetch the cigarettes. And you can also bring us a drink if you want."

"You'll be all right?" He didn't like leaving her, even for that short time, even in that idyllic place.

"Hurry," she urged, sending him off and thinking how very much she loved him as she watched him pick his way across the rocks and up to land, past the concrete bunker, which cut him from her view.

*   *   *

He walked at a brisk pace, not taking time to appreciate things as he did when he was with her. He chose the path that was the shortest route to the hotel—about a half-mile.

He just happened to look inside before entering. He almost walked right into them. They were seated at a table in the dining room, drinking beers. One had a face Chesser had said he'd never forget. From the highway robbery and the film Massey had shown. Max Toland.

Chesser moved quickly to one side of the hotel entrance, where he crouched below the window level, out of their view. He wasn't altogether certain they hadn't seen him, and expected them to come rushing out. He wondered if he should run now while he had the chance. However, he doubted that he could run, the way his legs felt—as though he didn't have legs.

He remained there in a crouch. They didn't come out, and Chesser decided he hadn't been seen.

The System, Chesser thought. Toland was working for The System. Massey's investigators had stated that in their report. Toland on Ste. Marguerite meant The System was on to everything. But how? How had they known where to come?

No answer. No time now for answers. Chesser's stomach felt inverted and he heard his own breathing, like a balloon inside him being blown up. He ran in a crouch below the windows and around the corner of the hotel to its only windowless, solid side. He kept close against the building for a few moments, but knew he was vulnerable there if they came searching. Some scrubby growth a short distance away offered better concealment, and, when he was behind it, he positioned himself so that he had a view of the hotel's entrance, an advantage because from there, if they came out, he would see them first.

He tried to organize his thoughts. He had the urge to get back to Maren, but he decided she was safe where she was for the time being. But how could they get off the island now? It was almost night. No more ferries to the mainland and no way of calling for a speedboat to come over and take them off. No way. The island that had been so good to them was now their inescapable trap. He thought if they could make it through the night they might get on tomorrow's first ferry, and, although Toland would undoubtedly be watching for that, it was the only chance. He reviewed his impression of Toland and the other two men. From the brief glimpse he'd gotten, they appeared tough, dangerous. Hired by The System.

He waited there until dark, then he went stealthily around to the front of the hotel, the long side that faced the bay. He took a cautious peek in through one of the windows. They were still there at the same table, and he watched them long enough to realize they were growing restless, particularly Toland's two companions. One, he noticed, was extremely thin, had ominous, gaunt features. The other was stocky, had blond hair; Prussian-looking, with a full, sort of little-boy mouth and round cheeks that made him appear as if he had something stuffed into each jaw.

Chesser sighted up to the roof-balcony. There was no easy way up to it. A drainpipe ran down the side of the building, but he decided that would be impossible without too much noise. Then he remembered that ladder against the fig tree on the far side of the hotel. He hoped it was still there.

It was. He propped it up and found it was just long enough.

Everything was extremely difficult because his sense of touch seemed lost, numbed by fear. He climbed the ladder, not believing he could but knowing he must. Up all the way and over the roof-balcony railing. He paused, saw the double doors to their room were open as they'd been, and the room was dark. He took one full-weight step and heard gritting beneath his shoes. He retracted the step and removed his shoes, placed them there, and walked quietly into the room. He listened a moment and believed he sensed someone's presence in the hall. Yes, someone was there. Now he definitely heard a movement. Someone waiting, posted outside the door. That meant four against him.

He couldn't turn on a light. Fortunately, he knew where Maren had put them. In her Vuitton satchel. He found it and removed the Mausers, one at a time, tucked them snugly into his belt. He dug into the satchel and his fingers identified the cellophane wrapping and shape of a pack of cigarettes. He quickly put it into his pocket and again felt in the satchel to find the box of extra cartridges, heavy, compact. What he didn't realize was that the end flap of the box was partially open and, as he brought the box to him, several cartridges fell from it, landing sharply on the hard enameled floor. As soon as they hit, his instinct told him to hell with caution. He ran out through the double doors. Someone immediately shoved open the door from the hall and was after him.

Chesser leaped over the balcony railing without thinking of the drop. He landed on the dry, packed ground with such force it felt as though he'd come down directly on two long blades, piercing all the way up to his knees.

But there was no time for pain. He ran around the end of the hotel, through the scrubby brush and across the path, and kept on running until he estimated he could afford a glance back. He didn't see them but was sure they were hunting for him. So, instead of taking the shortest route back to Maren and possibly leading them to her, he hurried in the opposite direction to the fortress. Then he circled back on the outer side of the island and was relieved when he came to the spruce grove, because his bare feet were badly bruised and cut. He hoped to God Maren's impatience hadn't made her return to the hotel. She couldn't possibly still be way out on those rocks in the dark.

He reached the point, sighted out, searching desperately for her. He couldn't risk calling out. He didn't see her out there where he'd left her.

She was sitting safe and quite content on the top of the bunker, not more than ten feet from him. She let him know she was there by singing a fragment of a song they shared.

> He lives all alone
> in his great big house
> with his Jacobean chairs
> and his marble stairs,
> and he sleeps . . .

He hushed her, and she climbed down quickly.

He told her what had happened and his idea of trying for the first ferry in the morning. She thought what they'd better do was swim out to one of the yachts that usually anchored in the channel between Ste. Marguerite and its brother island St. Honorat. They'd noticed there were usually one or two vessels there, using the channel as a stopping place. And many more on nicer days, because owners would sail out from Cannes especially to stop there, swim, and have lunch aboard rather than in crowded Cannes. It was the thing to do.

The channel was only about a quarter mile across. Maren and Chesser would have to swim a hundred fifty to two hundred yards at most. Easy. And it certainly wasn't beyond Maren's physical talents to persuade someone to take them aboard and give them passage back to Cannes. Then, at least, they'd have running room.

Chesser agreed to it. The channel was just around the point. At dawn they'd make their way along the rocky shore, and if the tide was out it would be even less difficult.

For the night they'd take shelter there in the above-ground bunker. They went in and sat on its concrete floor, against the deepest wall, facing the entrance. The bunker had three other openings. The largest was in the wall at their backs, above them, the opening through which the muzzle of the Nazi artillery gun had once extended. Now that space was completely overgrown by brambles, inaccessible. The left and right walls had rifle ports, horizontal slots approximately thirty-six inches by ten inches, too narrow for a man to squeeze through. So, for Toland or any of his men, the entrance was the only way in.

For the moment, Chesser and Maren felt relatively safe. It was night. They could be anywhere on the island. Toland wouldn't know where to look, probably wasn't even aware of the bunker's existence. But tomorrow—tomorrow would be a different matter entirely.

Chesser placed his gun at hand on the floor. Maren held hers in her lap. Both off safety. One thought was turning over in Chesser's mind. Finally it came out: "How the hell did they know where we were?"

Nothing from Maren.

"They couldn't have figured it out."

Maren remained silent.

"Someone must have told them."

"Yes," she said, low.

"But who?"

After a while, she told him, "I called because we left London without even saying good-bye."

Chesser knew immediately she meant she'd called Mildred. He was suddenly too angry, so angry that at that moment he stopped loving Maren. She was stupid, careless. To hell with her. And that Mildred. He'd been right about her all along. No wonder she'd refused the certified check he'd offered her. She was holding out for a bigger pay-off. From The System. The fucking phony runt, thought Chesser bitterly. The small medium had done them in.

"I didn't do it purposely," Maren said, her voice discernibly controlled to keep from breaking.

Chesser began loving her again. He felt what she had to be feeling. Perhaps there is no pain as excruciating as when faith is shattered. He put his arm around her, drew her against him. His hand brushed her cheek and found it wet. He was glad it was dark so he couldn't see her tears. But he felt them and hated the hurt they represented, hated Mildred more for that than anything.

"I really didn't do it for any other reason," said Maren, meaning this time she hadn't invited danger just for the excitement of it.

"I don't believe it was Mildred who told them," lied Chesser.

"You don't?" hoped Maren.

"No," lied Chesser. "She had too much to lose, her power and all that." He invented quickly. "I think it was Catherine at the hotel. She was on the phone a lot, wasn't she? She probably just happened to mention to the wrong person that we were here. Her kind of friends are a network of gossip."

"Catherine?"

"Sure," said Chesser with exaggerated conviction. He let her think about it a while.

It helped. Maren didn't completely believe it, but instead of expressing her doubt she accepted its possibility and used it. It was better than nothing.

Chesser remembered he'd brought the cigarettes. He lighted two. "My feet hurt," he complained, trying to distract Maren's thoughts.

"Poor baby," she soothed.

He drew his legs up and she touched his feet tenderly. "You're always losing your shoes," she remarked.

He recalled the last time. The Lady Bolding night. He changed the subject. "I'm thirsty," he said.

"Try not to think about it."

It was all the running he'd done. He was really thirsty and said so again.

"Suck on something," she advised. "That's what they do on the desert when they're lost. They put a pebble in their mouth for some reason." Her fingers found one of the buttons on her dress. She tore it off and put it in his mouth.

"Hell of a place to spend what might be our last night," he said.

"It won't be our last."

"They're killers, Toland and the others with him. They had the look."

"At least it's better than dying in bed."

Chesser scoffed.

"Really." She was serious. "Too many people just lie there and let death happen. They just die out, when actually there are so many better ways. I think people should meet death, not let it come and get them."

It's coming to get us, thought Chesser.

"I never told you about my uncle, did I? My old Uncle Olan?"

"No."

"They put him to bed and said he was going to die in a few days. Uncle Olan knew it was true, so, rather than just lie there, he got up, put on his best clothes, went to Stockholm, got half drunk, shoved his way into the National Assembly, cursed the government, was thrown in and out of jail, got more than half drunk, went to bed with three sixteen-year-old girls ensemble, ate everything most expensive at the best restaurant and refused to pay because he didn't have any money, robbed a bank of fifteen million kröner and was killed making his get-away in the direction of the most famous sauna bath-whorehouse in all Sweden."

Chesser had to laugh. "What a lie."

"It's true," insisted Maren. "Well, some of it."

"You probably never had an Uncle Olan."

"Yes I did. He used to tell me bedtime stories. When he wasn't out trying to get killed."

"It would be ridiculous to die here, for this," said Chesser.

"It's a good enough cause."

"The cause doesn't bother me," he told her, "as much as the effect."

"You'll never learn," sighed Maren.

She slept some in the cave of Chesser's arm. He didn't once close his eyes, kept them almost constantly on the upright rectangle that was the entrance opening contrasted by the lighter outside. He had time to think, couldn't stop it. Fragments, quick changes . . . women he had known, vague first names, nebulous bodies, intimacies experienced and forgotten, as forgotten as meals. Sylvia doing her dance costumed in only a sanitary belt. Followed by Meecham and Weaver and Watts and Lady Bolding and Massey. A big-as-life revue, building to the main attraction. His father, who started a remonstrating soliloquy, but Chesser beat him to the word, brought up the subject of mother, forcing father just to stand there on stage, with his mouth open. Chesser claimed she'd died from malignant lack of attention. He'd never seen his mother, that he could remember, not even a photograph. That was how much she had been eliminated. There must have been photographs, at least. He'd studied his birth certificate once and that inscription of her name officially linked with his caused him to imagine her more vividly. She must have been beautiful, too beautiful, and not really unfaithful, which was the eventual claim that replaced her death when he was old enough to be allowed to understand such things. He had never confronted father with the subject, but this time he brought mother into it and father couldn't take the blame, did an abrupt exit threatening never to make another personal appearance, ever.

The contrast in the rectangle began to increase. Chesser knew dawn was about to happen.

Maren was sleeping so nicely against him that he put off waking her, to give her a few more minutes of peace. Now, in the predawn light, he noticed fondly that she had her legs drawn up to get as much as possible of herself in warm touch with him. Her hands were clasped together, fingers interlaced, as though she was wishing very hard. She stirred her cheek against his chest and resumed sleeping, but it was full dawn by then. He whispered her name twice and she opened her eyes. "Good morning," she greeted softly.

He doubted the first of those two words.

She stood and stretched, arched her back, and extended her arms straight up. It looked a bit strange because she had her gun in her hand. "I don't know how those *clochards* do it every night," said Maren, referring to those homeless human bags of rags one sees sleeping on the sidewalks of Paris.

Chesser had difficulty rising. He'd remained in one position so long that his hinging parts, especially his lower back and knees, felt crystallized. Painfully, he flexed them back into working condition.

Meanwhile, Maren was checking her gun. She released its clip, examined it, saw the full gray noses of the cartridges it contained. She told Chesser he'd better do the same.

He did. And then they were ready to go for the channel.

Chesser went out first. He took three steps before his eyes caught a movement on the perimeter of the spruce grove, about two hundred feet away. A figure in black. It was the one with the Prussian face.

Chesser retreated into the bunker, silently indicating the situation to Maren. They went to the rifle port on the right wall, looked out and saw there were now two figures in black. Prussian Face and the Gaunt One. The two men were standing on the edge of the grove, surveying the area. They couldn't help but notice the bunker; its concrete structure obviously contrasted with everything around it.

Prussian Face and Gaunt One each had a gun. They spoke quietly to one another, then proceeded warily toward the bunker, taking opposite, flanking approaches.

Maren went to the rifle port on the other wall to take position there.

Chesser saw Toland then, coming down the path to the left. And following Toland was the fourth man, a head taller than Toland and, from Chesser's vantage, the two men created the illusion that Toland had two heads, one atop the other. When Toland stopped to call attention to the bunker, the fourth man came into full view.

Chesser recognized the fourth man immediately, the huge man, *Massey*'s man. Hickey.

Hickey and Toland? That meant . . . that Toland was also Massey's man. . . .

Suddenly Chesser understood, saw it all. Massey's deceit,

his treachery and manipulation. The preplanned highway robbery. The phony film report from the private investigation, which probably never existed in the first place. The way Massey had set him up, duped and used him from the beginning. Chesser felt so much anger he thought he'd explode with it.

At that precise moment a face presented itself on the other side of the rifle port, not more than twenty-four inches from Chesser, as though it were a close-up shoved into place by a slide projector. Prussian Face.

Chesser squeezed and heard the silencer's spitting compression. He saw the nine-mm. hunk of bullet enter Prussian Face just above his upper lip, smashing flesh and teeth roots and bone, tearing through the soft matter inside his skull, and, having spread itself without spending half its velocity, carry flesh and brain and bone with it as it made its larger exit.

In that split second, Chesser noticed the gray blue eyes of Prussian Face petrified, like the incapable eyes of a store-window dummy. He saw Prussian Face's head blown back six feet, the impact so great that it snapped up the rest of the body. Chesser believed Prussian Face had screamed, but not because he'd heard it.

Chesser turned to Maren to see if she knew what he'd done. Just in time, as the Gaunt One jumped down from the thick roof of the bunker and appeared in the entrance opening. Again that same impression of merely a projected image within the linear confines of a rectangle. Chesser wasn't ready for it.

Gaunt One's aim was right, but he hesitated for a fraction of a moment because of the darkness inside the bunker.

Time enough for Maren to shoot him, as she had the dressmaker's dummy in the London cellar, exactly where his heart was, blasting him back from the entrance way and into a tight net of brambles that held him partially upright, not looking as dead as he was.

Now they were equal as before. Maren and Chesser. They both had killed. And now the odds were also even. Two against two.

Hickey and Toland stood just beyond range, reappraising the situation. They'd expected some resistance, but not this much, not this violence, and the bunker was an unexpected obstacle. Massey's orders had been explicit. By no means were they to kill both Chesser and Maren. If possible, both were to be taken alive. However, if things got rough, Massey had said, all he needed was one, preferably Maren. To reveal where the twenty million carats were hidden.

Toland glanced at his watch. In another two hours the first public ferry would arrive and the island would be scattered with tourists. Toland studied the bunker a moment and decided, "We'll gas them out."

Hickey read Toland's lips.

"You hold them in while I get it. I'll be back in less than an hour." Toland turned and hurried away.

Hickey remained where he was, even more alert now that he was alone, his eyes ready for any movement.

Observing from the bunker, Chesser thought Toland was going for reinforcements. He told Maren that.

"Or a flamethrower," was her sardonic opinion.

"We could make a run for it."

"One of us might make it," she estimated.

Chesser was afraid he would be the one. He glanced at the entrance, had the urge to make the dash alone, confront Hickey. Maren could go for the channel while he kept Hickey busy. He imagined Maren telling some future lover about the somebody named Chesser who'd gone to meet death rather than wait for it to come get him.

A much less quixotic plan prevailed. Maren went to the rifle port in the left wall. She reached through, gripped the outer edge and made her body rigid. Chesser grasped her ankles and lifted so her entire length was on a horizontal plane with the narrow port. He pushed slowly, and, when she was partially through, she was able to help herself the rest of the way. She was just thin enough to clear the dimensions of the port and drop outside on the growth of brambles, which almost made her cry out.

Chesser went to watch from the right port. He saw Hickey was still in the same place, his attention on the bunker's entrance. He appeared gigantic to Chesser, larger than ever.

Soon Chesser noticed a movement of white that was Maren deep in the spruce grove. She was running crouched, traveling swiftly, disregarding noise because Hickey couldn't hear.

But if Hickey happened to look even half way around he would see her.

Afraid for her, Chesser had to restrain himself, and, finally, she reached the point that was his starting signal. He shoved his gun into his belt and walked outside, his arms straight up in obvious surrender.

Hickey saw him at once, withdrew his gun from under his jacket.

Chesser took ten steps, counting them aloud, then halted. Hickey, uncertain, waved him forward, but Chesser remained where he was, still out of range. "Move, you fucking dumb giant," shouted Chesser.

Hickey only motioned Chesser forward with his free hand, his other hand holding the gun ready, leveled.

Chesser had planned to stay there, not get into range, make Hickey come to him. But Chesser dared ten more steps and kept his arms raised and that started Hickey walking slowly forward.

Hickey seemed completely diverted now, as they had hoped. But then, with the instinct sharpened by his handicap, he suddenly turned and saw Maren, in the clear, no more than thirty feet to his left.

He fired twice.

She went to the ground, flat. Almost simultaneously she squeezed off her first shot. It seemed to have missed. It was incredible that she could miss so large and close a target. Hickey loomed there, in position to fire again, his gun aimed at her, but he didn't pull the trigger. There was a spreading splotch of red on his shirtfront covering his stomach.

Maren's second shot was more accurate. Above and slightly to the right of her first, going for the heart.

Hickey's legs crumpled as though they were paper. He toppled over backward in a contorted position.

Maren lay there. She was bleeding. Chesser rushed to her, kneeled beside her.

She moaned, sat up, and examined her legs and arms. "Goddamn brambles."

They couldn't linger there. Toland might return any moment. They went directly to the shore of the channel and saw three yachts were anchored midway across. Reluctantly, but so as not to appear threatening, they discarded their guns, dropped them in the shallows as they waded out. The salt water wasn't at all kind to Maren's bramble wounds. She grimaced and dove in to swim ahead.

When she approached the yacht, a handsome blond man dressed in casual white for sailing looked down at her. She floated on her back, treading. He smiled appreciatively, the water having made her dress almost completely transparent. She asked if by any chance he was ever going into Cannes. He told her he would take her anywhere. He was obviously American, a West Coast type. He noticed Chesser, but that didn't seem to affect his hospitality.

Maren started for the yacht's boarding platform; however, at that moment a Riva speedboat came full speed down the channel. It cut between Maren and Chesser and abruptly reversed its engine to idle there.

Chesser recognized Lady Bolding at the wheel of the Riva. Lady Bolding alone. She regarded Chesser in the water with a brief, passive glance and turned her attention to Maren, who now disregarded the sanctuary offered by the yacht and climbed up into the Riva's front seat.

Immediately the Riva's engine roared in neutral, and the fear that it would pull away, take Maren away, made Chesser swim hard around its stern, close to the boiling suck of its propellers, to the other side where a rope ladder was hung. He grabbed it and got it just as the Riva went into gear and nosed up with the suddenness of full power.

Chesser was being dragged and the water was slashing at him, trying to rip him from his hold. He had to hang on. The thought of Maren being torn from him gave him the extra strength to pull himself up the slick varnished side of the Riva and tumble down into the rear seat. Then he stood up and the air the boat was cutting through hit him. At the same moment his face was also slapped by the long trailing ends of the orange silk scarf Lady Bolding was wearing to confine her hair.

"Massey's in Cap Ferrat," she shouted.

They were now clearing the channel. Cap Ferrat was down the coast, east of there. Lady Bolding swung the Riva in the opposite direction, west, around the seaward tip of St. Honorat and steady upon a diagonal course to the mainland.

Maren turned to Chesser and smiled almost smugly.

Chesser sat to avoid the silky orange slaps.

Lady Bolding got them safely to the village of Le Tayas.

Chesser knew the extreme risk that Lady Bolding was taking. He also knew her reason, made amply clear by the long, deep look she gave Maren before she left them on the public landing.

CHAPTER 25

The Watts family had been and still were under constant surveillance.

Security Section agents were ready to move at the first sign of elevation in the family's life style. However, the widow Watts and her daughter continued to be very frugal, choosing cheaper cuts at the local butcher's and only the less costly essentials in small quantities at the greengrocer's. They never went beyond their neighborhood, remained home nights to watch the telly. The assigned agents were suffering from acute ennui.

The break in this direction finally came from an informant in Lichtenstein.

Watts had deposited a certified check for one million dollars in the Fritzmeiten Private Bank one week prior to the robbery. The deposit had been made via registered mail along with a letter of instructions from Watts stipulating that precisely one year from the date of deposit the bank was to notify Mrs. Edwina Watts, or her surviving heirs, that the money was available to them.

The informant in Lichtenstein had obtained a facsimile of the check and the letter, and Coglin considered this evidence so important that he ordered it brought to him by hand rather than trust the intercontinental mail.

Coglin expected the signature that he saw on the check.

M. J. Mathew. And once again his expertise told him it had been made by the same hand. More pertinent was the fact that the check was drawn on the Upland Bank of London, which, Coglin reasoned, would certainly be able to help identify such a large depositor.

Coglin and two of his best men arrived at the Upland Bank a few minutes before closing. The bank's senior vice-president, a Mr. Franklin, heard Coglin's request and instinctively refused it on the grounds that such information was confidential. However, he obviously recited that code with excessive conviction, and, when Coglin threatened to obtain a subpoena, that was all the pressure needed to obtain Mr. Franklin's cooperation.

Coglin was shown to the bank's records department. A reel of microfilm was brought from the files and projected for his benefit. Coglin watched as the reel whirred and the microfilm blurred on the screen, speeding to the section where M. J. Mathew would be revealed.

The reel stopped.

It showed the details of a Morris J. Mathew of Chelsea, whose balance had never exceeded seventy-two pounds, seventeen shillings and who was now overdrawn one pound six.

The microfilm was run forward and back several times.

Mr. Franklin looked on and Coglin made impatient fists behind his back.

There was nothing on the reel pertaining to *the* M. J. Mathew.

"Maybe you've got the wrong reel," Coglin said.

The bank's man in charge of records double checked and insisted on his efficiency. He also took time to examine the microfilm with a 20X magnifier and was perplexed by what he discovered. He showed it first to Mr. Franklin, who remarked, "That's quite irregular," before showing it to Coglin.

The microfilm had been spliced. The section containing a record of the M. J. Mathew account had been removed. As far as the bank was concerned, they had no proof whatsoever that there'd ever been such an account.

Coglin cursed modern banking methods and went back to headquarters on Harrowhouse. On his desk he found the fact sheet he'd asked for regarding the Upland Bank. He noted some of England's most influential men were listed as directors.

Coglin wasn't looking for the name Clyde Massey. And it wasn't there.

That same afternoon Meecham had two very unwelcome visitors.

Victor Keeling and Rupert Leander.

They came without appointment, without even phoning in advance, merely showed up at number 11 and arrogantly demanded to see Meecham.

Keeling and Leander were known Communists, but in no apparent way were they the stereotype. From the expensive cut of their correct city suits, shirts from Turnbull and Asser, the deft way they handled their bowlers and gloves, Keeling and Leander appeared to be true English gentlemen rather than Party members, self-confessed since 1953 when they'd both finished at Cambridge.

Actually, as the London intermediaries for the Soviet Committee of Natural Resources, Keeling and Leander enjoyed the best of both possible convictions. They received a fractional commission for acting as a link between the Soviets and The System. A legitimate yet hypocritical arrangement, which allowed the Russians to market their diamonds to best advantage without dealing directly with those they publicly designated as capitalist exploiters. Keeling and Leander for their part were guaranteed one-tenth of one per cent on all the stones they handled, seemingly a modest enough commission but actually a rate that had made both millionaires.

Meecham received them in the private conference room, a relatively small room, impressively paneled and decorated with conservative elegance. They sat in deep brown-tufted leather chairs and were served fine port and Havanas.

Keeling began: "We received an urgent communiqué from the minister this morning."

"How is Minister Konofsky?" inquired Meecham.

"Skeptical," answered Leander.

Meecham sensed a crisis but kept level to ask, "Why?"

"Certain recent actions by The System have been quite unorthodox," said Keeling.

"You called up the reserve from Johannesburg," Leander pointed out.

"Routine," said Meecham, passing it off, although he was surprised that the Soviets knew about that. He wondered how much more they knew.

"You increased production," said Keeling.

"You ordered additional output from your underwater fields," said Leander.

"You've been buying up all the illicit stones you can get," said Keeling.

Meecham was in a cross-fire. He decided to let them use up their ammunition.

"You," accused Leander, "requested extensive consignments from all your affiliates."

"Except us," said Leander.

Keeling gulped port. Leander puffed a cloud. Their eyes remained on Meecham, whose expression admitted nothing while inwardly he resented the accuracy of their knowledge and realized what a grave misjudgment he'd made in excluding the Soviets from his emergency negotiations for more stones. He could invent excuses for everything but that. With what he hoped seemed cold indignation he told them, "The System is hardly obliged to explain its activities to the Kremlin."

Keeling and Leander looked at one another.

"What we do is our business," Meecham continued on the offensive.

"Surely, however, you can understand the minister's concern," inserted Keeling, somewhat milder.

That encouraged Meecham. "As for Johannesburg, as I said, it was routine. Merely a transfer of inventory, which is something we do from time to time. The rest were merely actions intended to stimulate the industry."

"You're stimulating the sale of illicit gems?" asked Leander.

"We're attempting new tactics in that area," said Meecham, "to temporarily divert the flow of illicit stones via Beirut and Tel Aviv. Affording us the opportunity to cut it down altogether. Although I doubt very much your Soviet friends will appreciate that. As you well know, most of those illicit stones end up behind your curtain—and then on to us."

Meecham was sharp, with an edge of outrage.

"Despite your formidable sources of information," he continued, "you must concede that The System knows the intricacies of the world diamond market rather better than either of you or your somewhat excitable minister."

Keeling glanced down at the expensive black antelope business case Leander had placed by his chair. Leander brought the case up, snapped it open, and removed a single sheet of pink-colored paper.

"Perhaps," suggested Meecham, "I should call Minister Konofsky and personally assure him."

That was disregarded.

Leander consulted the pink paper. "According to our figures, you're presently holding three million, one hundred twenty-five thousand, six hundred fifty carats on consignment from the Soviet."

"That would be correct," said Meecham.

Keeling asked, "The Russian stones have been kept in separate inventory as stipulated?"

"They have," said Meecham.

"You're familiar, of course, with the terms of the agreement made between The System and the Committee in Moscow in 1968?" said Leander.

Meecham had negotiated that agreement, knew it well.

"The Soviet may withdraw its diamonds from The System at any time without giving prior notice," reminded Keeling.

"That was the purpose of the separate inventory," said Leander.

"Get to the point!" snapped Meecham.

"The minister now wishes to exercise that option," said Keeling. "The entire Soviet inventory is to be returned to Moscow. You are to ship in individual lots of three hundred fifty thousand carats every third day. Via Aeroflot, of course. We'll make those arrangements. In all it should take not more than a month."

"Very well," agreed Meecham, retaining external composure, while crumbling inside miserably, knowing there was no possible way to do what the Soviets were now rightfully requesting. Exposure was inevitable now. The System was ruined. *He* was ruined. There would be repercussions on a high level, possibly a diplomatic crisis between the governments. He told them, "We'll prepare to commence shipments immediately."

Keeling drained his glass.

Leander crushed out his Havana.

"I do hope the minister finds a more expedient and profitable means of marketing the Soviet diamonds," remarked Meecham.

"I'm sorry," smiled Keeling, "we didn't make that point quite clear. Returning the diamonds to Moscow is only a temporary measure, for the sake of reassuring the minister. I'm sure he has no intention of permanently severing the arrangement between the Committee and The System."

Meecham uncrossed his legs and recrossed them the other way.

Leander explained: "If, after a month or two all is well the Soviet inventory will be returned to The System and we'll be doing business as usual."

"Is that satisfactory?" asked Keeling, confident that it was.

"No," was Meecham's reply. "In keeping with the terms of our agreement, when you withdraw your consignment you relieve The System of any further obligation."

"But—"

"A completely new agreement will have to be negotiated," said Meecham.

"But . . ."

"The board will have to take it under consideration. And, out of fairness, I must warn you there are certain directors with conservative sensibilities who from the start were much against our having any dealings at all with the Soviet. Anyway, by no means should you take for granted that you'll be able automatically to resume marketing through The System."

Keeling fussed with his shirtcuffs.

Leander stared thoughtfully into the depth of his shallow business case.

Meecham stood abruptly and without a good-bye left them sitting there.

He returned to his office, where, in privacy, he didn't have to suppress his trembling. He removed his suit jacket and realized he was soaked under the arms. He sat at his desk and placed his hands on its tooled leather-inlaid surface, palms down. To stop his hands. He lifted them after a moment and, detesting the moist imprints they'd made, swiveled around to look out and find the distant dome of St. Paul's. He silently petitioned for some miraculous, merciful intervention.

A half hour later he received a phone call.

It was Keeling.

Saying: He'd just heard from Moscow. Unfortunately not in time to prevent his and Leander's visit with Meecham that afternoon. Unfortunate because by that time Minister Konofsky had already convinced the Committee not to recall the Soviet diamonds. The minister's faith in The System had, of course, never for one minute been anything but positive.

Meaning: Keeling and Leander had called Moscow and told the minister the outcome of that afternoon's meeting with Meecham. To preserve their own profitable arrangement, they had supported and validated Meecham's explanations regarding The System's recent activities. What had really persuaded the minister not to withdraw the Soviet diamonds was the prospect of having to renegotiate and possibly lose the substantial benefit of The System's marketing power.

Meecham's bluff had worked. It was the most crucial sleight-of-hand business he'd ever attempted. And, although he was greatly pleased, he couldn't manage a smile.

He was too drained.

CHAPTER 26

Gstaad in midsummer is a pretty, and unlikely place.

For those two reasons Maren and Chesser chose it for their next sanctuary. Though they'd dealt once with Massey, he

was far from out of the way, and they believed they also had
yet to contend with The System, a most complex, resourceful,
and proficient enemy.

They thought it better to avoid airports. So Maren used her
name to purchase a new Aston Martin DBS and drove them
furiously over the Alps. The snaking, high-ledged roads had a
neutralizing effect, reassuring them that they weren't, at least
for the moment, being closely pursued. Now, for some reason,
no matter how recklessly fast Maren's driving was, Chesser
didn't hang on. Actually, he napped most of the way, she noticed.

They had, of course, been together in Gstaad several times
before, but always during high season. Now, on the opposite
side of the year, everything looked unfamiliar, particularly the
houses and other buildings that they'd always seen humped
down, half hidden in deep snow. Now all those structures
seemed strangely taller and too angularly defined.

Maren's chalet, built in Jean Marc's final year, was located
in the desirable section called Oberport near the Palace Hotel.
It had a grand duchess for a left neighbor, a baron on the right,
and an earl just across. Unlike the other private chalets of the
area, which were relatively traditional in design, Maren's was
outstandingly contemporary, linear in the style of Mies van
der Rohe, composed of expanses of thermal glass firmly supported and narrowly framed by brushed steel. Its interior
motif was in perfect accord: whites and clears and chromes
luxuriously splotched warm with bright colors. Although the
chalet wasn't of imposing size, ten rooms only, plus servants'
quarters, it gave the impression of spaciousness. One of its
features was an arboretum, where, under glass and controlled
temperature-humidity, roses and violets and huge-faced pan-
sies were grown to supply the house with delightful fresh
touches during wintertime.

As soon as Maren and Chesser arrived, they took a long
sleep and woke up refreshed and hungry. No permanent help
served the chalet, and Maren hadn't arranged for any to be
there. For discretion, but more to please her whim.

They helped themselves, like playing house or being married. They made the bed together. Maren picked up, while
Chesser ran the sweeper. They walked to the village to do their

own marketing, and Chesser was secretly proud as he stood aside and watched Maren being highly selective about the vegetables and fruits she bought and the way she dominated the butcher. Confidently, she refused to buy bread and spent most of one night and half the next day preparing and baking four loaves. She messed up the kitchen terribly, but Chesser sat and watched and offered encouraging smiles along with sips of Scotch, while the flour flew and the dough stuck.

Maren definitely would not consult any of the recipe books that were right there, preferring to rely on remembering the ingredients and measures her own mother had used.

The result was four squat and very heavy, overdone lumps. Chesser relished a slice, feigning. Ate a thick one, even without butter. But Maren knew better, tossed away the entire batch and, determined, stayed up all night to produce four more loaves, these high and light and brown, smelling and tasting as delicious as they looked.

Then Chesser was truly impressed.

As a little sweet extra, Maren, with easy confidence, also baked some Swedish spice cookies, and Chesser thought he'd never tasted anything that pleased him more. While he devoured, Maren beamed, and they each wondered about the other's unspoken thoughts, and they both thought they knew.

At first, Chesser attributed Maren's domestic displays to her impetuosity, just another of her tangents, genuine enough but not to be taken seriously. She was, after all, one of the fortunates—that is, she could well afford to be waited upon, could demand and have, lavishly, and didn't need to concern herself with the menial or the trivial, no matter how romantically valuable such things might be. The fact that Maren didn't really have to perform these tasks, Chesser reasoned, was precisely why she could enjoy doing them. She was amusing herself, that was all, and any moment now he expected her to bring the phase to an abrupt end by summoning a housekeeper or two, and making use of her time with something more practical. Knife throwing, for example.

However, as the days passed, Maren settled even more into the routine of caring, and taking care. Her mood-range fluctuated only from contentment to exuberant buoyancy. Never below. Not once was she edged on, compelled to seek some adventurous distraction, as before.

And Chesser missed that.

Yes, he loved this Maren as much as the other. But he missed the other more than he ever believed he would. Actually, he found himself looking forward to the reversion.

Changes. Chesser misjudged the change in Maren, because it appeared too abrupt and therefore he assumed it to be superficial. But it had been simmering in her psyche more or less all her life, latently waiting to emerge when the time was ready. In that respect, it was more of a transition than a change.

Maren herself didn't realize that until she was into it. She didn't trust it any more than did Chesser. It required testing, such as the first good batch of bread and cookies and the satisfaction she had felt.

Reversing roles now, it bothered Chesser that they didn't have any guns. He felt it only a matter of time before The System or Massey zeroed in on them, came in force and found them defenseless. Every time they went into the village, Chesser anticipated it. He raised the subject several times, but Maren was little interested or concerned. She seemed purposely to avoid discussing the matter, and even when Chesser felt the need to review their recent adventures, she either ignored his starting comments or pointedly veered the conversation in another direction. For example: "Do you have any buttons off anything? I found a small blue one on the carpet today."

One morning Chesser got up early and drove to Geneva. He bought two Browning nine-mm. automatics. New his and hers. He brought them back, put them in the top drawer of his wardrobe, and felt much better. He said nothing to Maren about the guns, realizing that it didn't fit her present mood. But he was sure that when she came out of it she'd be very pleased. They'd go out for some shooting practice, he promised himself. He wondered if he'd lost his eye. He wanted to get more accurate from the hip.

CHAPTER 27

Massey's villa at Cap Ferrat.

Like an icon dedicated to luxurious leisure, it was set high on the altar of cliffs above the sea that seemed to wave in worship.

Massey was there, outside in the sun, the front of his blue velour robe thrown open for exposure. Patches of gauze soaked with a cooling solution comforted his eyes, and each of his hands enclosed a cube of ice, the melt seeping between his fingers, the substance gradually diminishing to nothing in his grasp.

Lady Bolding was nearby, completely surrounded by portable reflectors, to bake even quicker. Bees from the lime grove were attracted by the sweetness in the oil on her body. Eyes shut she heard them swooping and hovering ambivalently and she wondered if possibly one might light and probe her lower hair, believing it a blossom.

Toland had just arrived to report on the violent confrontation and the escape of Chesser and Maren. He stood above Massey and grudgingly told it all, admitting he had no idea how Chesser and Maren had managed to get off the Isle de Ste. Marguerite, certainly not via the public ferry, Toland said.

Lady Bolding was relieved to learn she'd not been seen rescuing them with the Riva. She privately celebrated by imagining the sensation of Maren in her arms. She wished there was no Chesser. Perhaps, she presumed, some day soon there wouldn't be.

Throughout Toland's report, Massey remained unmoved. "You cleaned up the mess?" he finally asked.

Toland said he had. He'd weighted Hickey's body and the other two, and dropped them overboard six miles out beyond the tide.

Massey stood abruptly. The soggy gauze patches fell from his eyes. It was expected that he would exhibit his fury, but, without a word, he walked into the villa, the robe hanging loose, its ties dragging, melt dripping from his fists. A heavy walk, as though all the blood in his body had gone to his legs.

Upstairs in his master suite, he locked the thick door. To enclose himself as much as to exclude anyone, everything. He'd not been struck like this in years. Actually, not since he'd lost to The System off the mouth of the Orange River. An overload of rage, too much for anything so commonplace as a tirade. Inside his skull a paroxysm of anger so potent there was no adequate human way to express it, so he could only turn it on himself, where it was converted into the dreaded black word. Death. His own.

He closed the double drapes over all the windows, preferring not to see living because there was dying in it, evading the sun which now only illuminated how ephemeral he was.

Letting the robe drop off, he turned the temperature control dial of his sauna to two hundred degrees, and went in. He lay face up and focused on the inconsequential grain of the wood ceiling, trying for the advantage of any distraction, hoping the heat would, meanwhile, sweat all the edges out of him. But quickly the sauna space became as small as an old coffin.

He fought that impression, not entirely sure it wasn't true, until he shocked himself with the squirt of icy water that ran reassurance down between his buttocks.

With less strength, and his anxiety increased, he left the sauna, went out and fell slick with sweat on the silk spread of his huge bed.

Helplessness.

His long-time, all-time, enemy.

The killer of power.

Helplessness.

The fear of being at anyone's, anything's, mercy.

Chesser, he pictured, trying to direct and spend his anger.

But Chesser became immediately vague, inconsiderable, compared to the fatal black word that was now lodged immovably between Massey's mind and Massey's eyes. He tried again for Chesser, but the force of his wrath betrayed him, was diverted to the image of his own slippery, worn internal organs. Pumping, filtering, pulling. So personal and yet unpredictable.

He put a finger, then, to his pulse.

Found it rapid staccato, as though it was striving not to stop. Additional alarm from that evidence made Massey crawl up and insert himself into the bed.

Perhaps if he slept, he thought. He closed his eyes to try, but his anxiety made sleep seem like death, the blackness, the aloneness, the complete loss of control. So he remained awake in order to know he remained alive. He lay there for hours, with time tightening him more and more. Suffering sequences of hysteria. Throat constriction, unable to take a deep breath. Ordinary tension headache suspected into the first symptoms of a stroke, accompanied by blurred vision and extremity tinglings. Vertigo.

Helplessness.

Knocks on his door and several more insistent, followed by Lady Bolding's voice speaking his name like a question, twice.

"Are you all right?" he heard her inquire and imagined that he answered, "No."

He lay there, cramped, and thought, with certain futility, that medical science eventually would announce the discovery of a simple solution, a mere pill or injection that would insure any man who could afford it another hundred years of life. But along with the announcement of that discovery there would also be the print of his obituary. He would die a fragment of time too soon. . . .

Lady Bolding knocked and called again, apparently afraid for him, seemingly corroborating the truth of his hopeless condition.

CHAPTER 28

"Do you know how they get married in Bora Bora?" asked Maren.

"Where?"

"Bora Bora," she repeated, as though it were the capital of the world.

Chesser guessed by the sound that it was somewhere in the South Pacific, although phonetically it was an appropriate name for a lot of places he'd been.

"To be married," informed Maren, "the woman builds a huge fire, and then runs away and hides." She paused to measure Chesser's attentiveness.

"Is that all?" he asked.

"Of course not. When the fire burns down to a glow, the man picks up some of the red hot coals with his bare hands and goes looking for his woman. If he finds her before he drops the coals, they're automatically married. Otherwise they just drop the whole idea."

"You're making that up."

"No, really. I read about it. Imagine, having to endure that."

"Getting burned before marriage, that's a switch."

She disregarded his male pessimism. "I suppose the woman helps."

"How?"

"By not hiding too well or too far away."

"That's the least she could do."

Maren agreed.

"How do they get divorced?" he asked.

277

A shrug from her. "Maybe they just never do."

"Or maybe what happens is one morning like every other morning the woman builds a big roaring fire and the man pisses it out."

"You're horrible." She laughed.

"Opposites attract," he declared.

They were in the high grass about two thirds of the way up Egli, one of the ski-sloped mountains around Gstaad. The town far below looked like a cluster of residue in a deep bowl. Little farms were scattered, patching the landscape with related shades of yellow-to-green crops, and the roads resembling minor stream beds, running, wandering.

Maren and Chesser had climbed up. The last half mile was a steeper climb, which made Chesser's legs complain some, and he was grateful that Maren hadn't wanted to go up all the way. They sat facing one another, apart by six or seven feet. She'd brought a book on psychic phenomena in Russia, which she now opened to any page and seemed immediately absorbed. Until she said, "They eat flowers in Bali."

"We had some in Munich," he said. "Remember?" They actually had—some special mountain flowers,, fried and sprinkled with powdered sugar. A Bavarian delicacy, they'd been told.

"I mean in Bali they get married by eating certain flowers. That's romantic, isn't it?"

"Some flowers are poisonous," he said. "Even some of the prettiest ones."

"I guess," she said vaguely, irritated.

She lighted two cigarettes. Chesser readied himself for an impossible catch. But she came to him, on her knees. She brought his cigarette to his lips. Then she placed her cheek on his chest and wordlessly requested an arm around. They were silent for a long moment. She was thinking back. He was wondering ahead.

"Remember the first time?" she asked.

He thought she meant their first lovemaking. He hadn't forgotten any of it, especially how he'd felt after, as though he'd reached a destination. But the first to which she was now referring was the time when they'd met.

"Your eyes were a different color then," she told him.

"Not true."

"They're browner now. They were more of a hazel."

"You just wanted them to be hazel. That's what you were looking for."

"I wasn't looking for anything." Accent on the next to the last word.

They'd met in Rome, in the Borghese Gardens. During a summer rain, large drops but not cold, and, while everyone else was inside avoiding it, they were outside, separately, strolling as if under sunshine. Chesser, drenched, the sky's water streaming from his chin and ears and nose, Maren, her long Viking hair matted wet, her dress soaked to her skin, clinging, defining. Although the Gardens were spacious, they had walked right into one another.

"It wasn't by chance, you know," she now claimed. "We were supposed to be there."

"Perhaps."

"It was our karmas."

Chesser suspected luck, or at best good, old-fashioned fate.

"What an advantage we have," she said, "knowing the reason we're here on earth, what our lesson is this time."

He wanted to talk out the Massey episode, particularly the killings. But he let her have her way. "Do you really know?" he asked, leading.

"Sure." No doubt.

"You've always known?"

"Possibly. But I haven't always known I've known. Every day now I get more psychic."

Every day, thought Chesser, I get edgier.

Maren lay back on the grass. As though revealing news she'd been withholding, she told him, "I've been in touch with Jean Marc again. On my own."

"Really?" He tried to sound impressed rather than tolerant.

"I had some help," she admitted, "but not much. From Billie Three Rocks and my Chinaman."

"Isn't it about time Jean Marc came back as somebody new or something?"

"He can. Whenever he wants. He told me he was happy we came here to Gstaad."

"Why?"

"He didn't say." She brightened suddenly. "But you know what else I was told?"

"What?" Chesser felt like a straight man.

"That there's a little girl, a beautiful child spirit, waiting on the other side for us. She wants to come over and be ours if we give her the chance. She'll be a ballerina."

"Jean Marc told you that?"

"No. Somebody else."

"Who?"

"I didn't ask who. Just somebody."

Chesser scoffed inside; a sigh came out.

"What day is today?" asked Maren, as though it were relevant.

"What's the difference?"

No reply from her.

He told her, "I think it's Monday. Because there were church bells yesterday."

"I mean what day of the month."

"Around the fifteenth or sixteenth, I think."

"You know what we're supposed to do next?" she asked.

He translated the invitation in her eyes and sensed that she was asking him to kiss, as a prelude to more when they returned home. Or right there, perhaps. Quite possibly right there, he thought, as impulsive as she'd always been.

He brought his kiss to hers, found her lips soft, compliant, and open. Right there also appealed to him.

"I love you," she said into him.

They were eye to eye, exchanging.

She told him, "Next what we're supposed to do is get married."

"People don't usually do what they're supposed to do."

"No. But they always do what they want to do most."

"As in Bora Bora?"

She nodded. "You've already carried your coals."

She meant it. He realized that, gave her a brief reassuring kiss, and sat up to think. It came to him that if they got married it would be the most costly wedding of all time, and, by some standards, probably the most foolish. He decided to keep it light, told her, "Maybe those French lawyers hired a telepath to do a number on your mind?"

She wasn't amused, didn't think so, said so.

"What about the money?"

She was waiting for that. She grinned. "Fuck the money."

Which made Chesser think of Massey. "We'll talk about it," he said.

"No."

"You're being impetuous."

"I don't want to analyze it."

"I'm trying to look after your interests."

She waited a moment for emphasis. "Mine?"

Her inflection hurt, hitting in him where he was most vulnerable. For another moment he stopped loving her. He looked at her and started again.

"Don't you want to?" she asked.

I do, he swore to himself, but said nothing.

She asked, measuring each word, "Will you marry me?"

"No," was his answer.

She left him there, picked up her book, and ran barefoot down the slope, and he watched the stream of her nutmeg hair and wanted very much to run after her, but he remained as though it were impossible for him to move. Soon she was only the speck of yellow that was the dress she was wearing, far down the mountainside, far away and going.

He told himself he'd done the right thing, the practical thing, for them. And she'd been wrong, her insinuation that he placed some ulterior importance upon her money. It was just that he wasn't going to allow her to chuck it all for something as unnecessary as marriage. Things were fine as they were. They were the same as married. What difference would a legal piece of paper make? Certainly not worth hundreds of millions.

To confirm his stand he imagined the changes their being married would cause. The main thing was he'd have to be completely responsible and, hell, he didn't have anything, not even any direction. Less now than before. When he'd been with The System at least he was going nowhere.

He stood, flexed some of the tension-tightness from his shoulders, glanced up questioningly at the unquestionable sky, and went down the slope to find her, thinking as he went how susceptible he was to suggestion, because his hands felt burning hot.

She told him she was pregnant, not from error but on purpose.

He suspected she was lying.

She also told him that he shouldn't let her condition influence how he felt about marrying her. She'd have the child anyway. Maybe.

He thought she was using emotional blackmail.

The doctor confirmed she wasn't.

That same afternoon they went to the town hall and located the official whose duties included marrying. A dour man with a paunch and a pate and an anonymous wear-and-wear gray suit. Behind an indestructible public desk. He exchanged his wire-rimmed glasses for a different pair in order to examine Maren and Chesser with greater disinterest. He considered their passports dubiously, removed a triplicate form from a drawer, and began asking questions in such a dry, unemotional manner that it could well have been the paper speaking.

The unreality Maren and Chesser felt from just being there was heightened.

Finally, all the spaces contained information, and the official, a Mr. Saltzman, according to the impressed plastic plate on the desk, reviewed the form carefully before turning it over to them for signatures. As soon as they'd signed, Saltzman demanded fifty francs. Chesser produced a hundred note, the smallest he had. Saltzman fumbled in a drawer for the fifty change, so much and so obviously that Chesser told him to keep it as a gratuity, causing Saltzman's thin lips to turn a smile on and off.

They'd both expected more of a ceremony, but it didn't matter. They were officially married, they believed, and were about to seal it with a nervous kiss when Saltzman told them to return Friday next.

Why?

Because medieval Swiss law required that banns be posted for three full days. In case anyone had any objections to the marriage and wanted to ban it.

Saltzman dismissed them with a look over his glasses, brought some documents before him and pretended busy.

Maren and Chesser went home, having taken only half the leap.

CHAPTER 29

On the afternoon of the fourth day of Massey's seclusion Lady Bolding was concerned enough to take drastic action.

Numerous times during the previous forty-eight hours she'd knocked on Massey's bedroom door and called loudly in to him. He didn't respond, and now she thought it was quite possible that he was unconscious, or even dead.

She summoned a locksmith from Cannes, who arrived toting a black bag much like a doctor's. With professional intensity he examined the lock on Massey's bedroom door and pronounced his diagnosis. *"C'est impossible,"* he said, his breath strong with the garlic and wine he'd had for breakfast and lunch.

He went on to explain that the lock was a very complicated magnetic type imported from the United States. He tapped upon the face of the door with his knuckles and suggested making an opening.

Lady Bolding agreed.

The locksmith used a rotating saw to slice out a circular chunk of the door. He reached in and released the bolting mechanism.

It was like opening a tomb. Stale air poured out. Vaguely discernible in the half light was Massey, nude on the bed, partially bound by twists of sheets and half buried beneath several punished pillows.

He appeared lifeless.

Lady Bolding hesitated, apprehensive. She went in and clicked on the bedside light.

A closed-mouth grunt from Massey.

She saw he was grizzly with a four-day beard, and his eyes were bloodshot, sunk, and raw-looking from no sleep. She knew he hadn't eaten in days.

"Are you ill?" she asked.

"No."

"You appear ill."

"Get out," he said, but weakly.

That ingratitude chafed Lady Bolding. For a moment she was tempted to strike back, but was quickly reminded of the equity she had in Massey and the future favors she expected from him.

She drew open the drapes of the nearest window. An oblong of sunlight slashed across the bed and Massey. He winced.

With sympathetic encouragement she pulled him up.

He resisted, grumbled obscene protests.

She tried to put his arm over her shoulder to support him, but he shook her off and walked into the bathroom, into the shower stall and turned on only the cold.

He dried and she made him sit in a chair while the bed linens were changed and the room thoroughly aired.

He tried to remember that he was one of the world's most powerful men.

She persuaded him back into the bed, propped him up with plumped pillows and, despite his whining refusals, induced him to drink all of a large mug of beef consomme that she'd laced with three sodium nebutals.

He felt more helpless than ever.

She sat on the bed's edge and massaged his fingers and felt them go gradually limp as sleep took over.

By then it was late afternoon.

Lady Bolding ordered tea served outside at the table beneath the arbor, where she sat alone to indulge mostly in thoughts of Maren, while studying the sexual shapes suggested by the leafy intermissions above her.

After tea, she put on fresh make-up, changed into a white sharkskin pants suit, tied her hair back with a true-blue, baby silk ribbon, and was driven to Nice to make the next flight to Paris.

Massey slept until the next noon. He opened his eyes upon Lady Bolding, and it was as though she'd been watching over him all the while. She smiled.

He was unsteady on his feet but felt considerably improved. He looked into a mirror and wondered if he was up out of it enough to shave and decided he was on the edge now, not yet surely balanced, and it was questionable whether he'd emerge or fall back. The black word was still there to contend with, he realized.

He splashed his face with double handfuls of cold water and returned to the bedroom. Lady Bolding held a bright silk robe ready for him and led him out onto an upper terrace, where a breakfast was waiting for him in the sunshine.

Hot, strong black coffee, perfect eggs, crunching toast, tiny country strawberries coated with powdered sugar, and more hot, strong black coffee to dissolve some of the black word.

I'm recovering, Massey told himself, not entirely trusting that impression.

"I flew to Paris last night," said Lady Bolding.

Massey concealed his disappointment that she hadn't been so vigilant as he'd thought.

"For us," she said.

"Oh?"

"I went recruiting," she smiled. "And I believe you'll agree I did exceptionally well this time."

She directed his attention to the area below.

There, nude in the sun, were two young girls, contemporary creatures with slender bodies, pleasingly firm as a result of their energies. Very pretty young girls not yet twenty. An authentic blonde with fresh, virtuous features, and a brunette more evidently suggesting experience.

The sight of them inspired Massey to alter the focus of his thoughts. They were to his taste, the physically fortunate sort of girls who unconsciously struck a desirable pose when in any position and, therefore, were all the more provocative in motion.

Lady Bolding excused herself to go down to them.

Massey ordered a servant to fetch his electric razor. And

while he was buzzing the gray stubble from his neck and face, he watched Lady Bolding approach the two girls, saw them move apart to welcome her between them. She said nothing, made no request, but the girls immediately brought themselves into contact with her, one on each side, sharing her, their cheeks resting on the planes of her shoulders. In that manner they were facing one another across Lady Bolding's breasts, while hands glided.

Without interrupting their attentions, Lady Bolding arched her neck back to look up above and observe Massey upside-down. He appeared interested.

That was Friday.

By Monday, Massey felt restored. The black word death had been erased. It was as though he had extracted some youthful essence from the weekend of erotic performances, for he now felt even more vigorous than before.

His enormous anger, which had attacked his potency, was hardly diminished. However, now he had control over it and was able to focus it even more directly on those who had provoked it.

Chesser.

And Chesser's Maren.

They would suffer, he vowed, pay for what he'd endured. He confided that to Lady Bolding, believing the perversity of it would appeal to her.

"Let's go to Venice," she said, pretending indifference, hoping to distract him. "I always do well for us in Venice."

"Perhaps later this month," he told her.

"You've given up on the diamonds?"

"By no means."

"Only they know where the diamonds are," she contended.

"What would you have me do?"

"I've only your interest in mind."

"You think I should let them live?"

"No. At least, not both of them."

A nod from Massey, indicating his understanding, if not necessarily compliance.

Lady Bolding was inclined to remind Massey of her recent and long-term loyalties, how much she'd done for him. However, she knew better than suggest he owed her this favor. A man as wealthy and powerful as Massey never owed anyone.

Still, she had to try. "I'll persuade Maren to tell where the diamonds are," she said. "It won't be a problem, I assure you. She'll want to tell me."

Lady Bolding had given much thought to her strategy. Her imagination had simplified it. Chesser would be dead. Maren would be grieving. She, Lady Bolding, would console. Tenderly, she would comfort Maren, soothe and sympathize. They would be alone, away together, some place remote, some ideal neutral sanctuary. She would nourish Maren back to feeling. Gentleness would work its art. Lady Bolding's tender heart would become Lady Bolding's tender hands would become Lady Bolding's tender body. But it all depended upon Massey's cooperation.

He agreed, without meaning it. Just that morning he'd received word about The System's investigation of Marylebone, Ltd., as well as Coglin's snooping visit to the Upland Bank. All The System had to do was uncover the fact that the common denominator between the two was Massey. He doubted that would happen, but being that close to incrimination made Massey uneasy.

His intention had always been to have Chesser and Maren killed after they'd served. Whether the robbery was successful or not. They were the only outsiders who could really connect him with it, and as long as they remained alive there was the possibility of his being annoyingly implicated.

He reasoned that neither Chesser nor Maren was the sort who could remain in hiding very long. Boredom would get to them, force them out and back into the milieu. Especially Maren with her penchant for the audacious. Massey had alerted his people everywhere. The moment Chesser and Maren emerged, he'd know about it. After that it would be simply a matter of capturing them and persuading them, painfully if necessary, to reveal what they'd done with those twenty million carats. He was sure they would cooperate. They'd tell, each to save the other.

Then would come the killing. Of both.

CHAPTER 30

The marriage banns were literally posted on a glass-enclosed notice board just outside the entrance of the Gstaad town hall. Chesser and Maren first went to see it together. They held hands and made light remarks, to take the edge off. Several other times each went alone to be more contemplative about it.

Chesser read the fine print:

Anyone possessing knowledge of any just reason why the above applicants should not be joined in wedlock must present evidence to the town clerk before midnight (date).

I know millions of reasons why not, thought Chesser. And he also wondered some about the origin of the word wedlock.

He felt the pincers of destiny tightening upon him. His undeniable love for Maren was taking him into impractical matrimony, while there was still the impending threat of violence, which Massey and/or The System would come to deliver at any moment. These were incompatible extremes, he believed, and on that basis he made a serious and tactful appeal to Maren for postponement, at least until they were in the clear, not hiding or on the run.

"Now or then, what's the difference?" was her reasoning.

"Exactly," said Chesser.

"Might as well be now," she declared decisively.

On the first night of the banns period, Chesser had an elaborate dream. A not impossible plot played by highly probable characters, with Meecham and Massey in feature roles. The action was set in and around the chalet and consisted of Chesser being murderously pursued. However, he performed various miraculous feats, such as disappearing and reappearing at will, jumping aside or up or ducking to evade bullets which he saw float harmlessly by in slow motion. Maren, content and child-bellied, sat nearby in a Swedish rocker while Chesser finished off a dozen or more of The System's most vicious enforcers, then Massey, and for a finale had a face-to-face sneering match with Meecham, who, realizing Chesser's clear superiority, sniveled for mercy, implored Chesser to accept a free million-dollar packet. Chesser propped Meecham up like a piece of life-sized cardboard and shot off his balls. One at a time. Which was a cue for Maren to exclaim, "Goodie!" as she popped a Swedish spice cookie into her hero's mouth.

Chesser awoke perspiring profusely, and with what struck him as an incongruous erection. He got up and went down to the kitchen for a cup of instant coffee. While he sat there sipping hot black coffee, he got to thinking about Thursday, and it came to him what he ought to do between now and then was face up to Massey and The System. At least, one or the other. His imagination played with the idea. The more he thought about it the more it lifted him, stirred him in a strange, strong, almost perverse way. Logic tried to intervene, but he wouldn't listen to it. Audacity was more appealing. Like a chemical stimulant.

At nine A.M. he placed the call. Circuits were busy. He hoped Maren would sleep late. He'd decided not to consult her. He was almost certain she would oppose it, now that she was pregnant, and almost married. She seemed now even less inclined to exert her old craving for dangerous excitement. Apparently, it was something she'd lost, and he'd found.

At nine thirty he tried to call again and got through to London.

After the usual three rings The System answered.

He asked for Meecham.

"I'll give you Mr. Coglin's secretary," said The System's flawless switchboard voice.

"I asked for Meecham."

"I realize that, sir. Perhaps Mr. Coglin will speak with you."

"I want Meecham," insisted Chesser.

"I'm afraid that's impossible, sir."

"Impossible? Why?" And why, wondered Chesser, was his call being directed to Security Section, when he hadn't yet even identified himself.

"I'm ringing Mr. Coglin's line, sir," said switchboard and clicked off.

Perhaps Meecham was on holiday, thought Chesser. He was tempted to hang up because he again felt cheated out of the satisfaction of getting to Meecham. But, at that moment, there was Coglin's secretary asking who. Chesser didn't hesitate, said his name with extra importance.

Coglin came right on with, "Ahhh, Chesser. Good of you to call."

"I thought I might as well."

"Yes. We've been wondering about you."

That's putting it mildly, thought Chesser.

"What have you been up to?" asked Coglin.

As if he didn't know, thought Chesser. It occurred to him that Coglin was stalling in order to have the call traced.

Chesser would save him the bother. "I'm in Switzerland," he informed. "Gstaad, to be exact."

"Our people must have located you."

"Not yet."

"Oh? Then you're calling on your own, is that it?"

"You think that's stupid?"

"Not at all. In fact, it's quite accommodating."

"I want The System to know where I am. I especially want Meecham to know."

"Meecham?"

"Yes. I hope he'll try to take care of me personally."

"Oh, come now, Chesser. I realize only too well what went on between you and Meecham, and I know how you must feel. Admittedly, Meecham singled you out for unfair treatment, but, I assure you, we're willing to make it up to you."

What the hell was Coglin talking about, wondered Chesser.

"Come to London on the ninth of August," invited Coglin.

"That's the first day of our next sights. Come and I'll see to you myself. I promise."

"You don't understand. I want . . ."

"Meecham. I know. But he won't be here," said Coglin firmly.

"Why not?"

"Well, it's not yet been officially announced, but I see no harm in your knowing. Meecham resigned from the organization as of Friday last. For his health. I am now . . ."

Meecham out? Chesser was stunned.

Only a select few would ever know the inside facts of the matter. Chesser never would.

After the Soviet crisis, and when all efforts had failed to turn up any trace of the stolen inventory, Meecham, deciding he had borrowed all the time he could, prepared his defense and summoned an emergency meeting of the board. A matter of gravest importance, was the way he put it. So, those directors who weren't already in London flew in especially to attend.

Meecham presided. He informed the members of the board of the recent robbery. They gasped. He stated his analysis of the possible, terrible consequences. They sickened. He placed the blame squarely on Security Section and condemned Coglin for flagrant dereliction of duty. They agreed.

Of course, Coglin, not being a board member, was not at the meeting. But he heard Meecham's every word and monitored Meecham's every gesture via a concealed closed-circuit television tap he'd had his staff experts install in the board room two years previous.

Coglin didn't appear noticeably upset by Meecham's accusations. He took them calmly, sat there tireless, shirtsleeves rolled up, drinking Guinness stout from the bottle. He listened and watched for a while, then guzzled down what was left of the stout, put on his tie and jacket and went to his own highly confidential files. He removed seven very fat dossiers. He took them, along with other substantiating material, across the street and directly to the board room. Politely excusing his intrusion, he proceeded to make his presentation to the board. Including motion pictures with sound, color slides with facts, tape recordings with an easily identifiable voice. Meecham's dossier.

Most of the evidence was pornographic, some of it perhaps subversive. Meecham, off balance, muttered a few outraged protests, squirmed some, and retreated hastily from the room. The other six board members saw no reason why Coglin should reveal any further information. Each eyed the remaining six dossiers and agreed that the board had already seen and heard enough. Quite. All were in favor of Meecham's immediate resignation. Putting an end to this nasty business, the board hoped.

Coglin was expected to leave the room then. But he didn't. He sat there self-confidently facing the directors. It was their move.

What, the board inquired uncomfortably, were Coglin's recommendations regarding the inventory crisis? How should it be handled, in his opinion?

Coglin said he didn't believe the situation was as critical as Meecham had suggested. There was no real danger of the stolen inventory being used to oversupply and ruin the world market. Because, he said, the very structure of the industry—those channels of distribution which The System still held under strict control—prevented such a catastrophe.

Coglin also predicted that the thieves would be apprehended as soon as they attempted to sell the diamonds in any significant amount. It would be impossible, he insisted, for anyone to make a large-scale transaction anywhere in the world without The System becoming immediately aware of it. It would be a relatively simple matter to trace the diamonds to their source and recover the lot.

The board was very impressed.

Coglin didn't stop there. He demonstrated ingenuity by suggesting that the robbery might actually be to The System's benefit. With its huge inventory gone, wouldn't The System be justified in announcing an increase in the price of gem-quality stones? Hadn't The System always determined value on the excuse of scarcity? Then why not take advantage of the lack of inventory? A *genuine* scarcity.

Indeed, why not?

Protests against the price increase, Coglin said, could be

dramatically overcome by permitting a few important buyers to take a convincing peek into The System's nearly depleted vault. Then the nature of the business would take over and spread the word around the world.

The board members pulled at their silk school ties, feeling relief.

Five minutes later Coglin emerged from the board room as Meecham's official replacement. President of The System. Despite the fact that he wasn't Eton or Queens or anything, the Board unanimously voted him lifetime cooperation. And, of course, he also maintained possession of all the dossiers. . . .

Now, via long distance, Coglin asked Chesser, "Shall we expect you on the ninth?"

No answer from Chesser. Too dazed.

"Or perhaps the tenth would be more convenient for you?"

"I don't know."

"There'll be a pretty packet waiting for you, I'll guarantee that."

"How pretty?"

"Say a hundred thousand. And that's just for starters. I have outstanding plans for you, Chesser."

"Why?"

"I recognize your potential. Meecham underestimated you. But business instinct tells me you're my sort of man."

Coglin was recruiting. A predecessor's enemy was usually a potential ally.

"You do want to be reinstated, don't you?" asked Coglin.

"Yeah, sure."

"I'd expected a bit more enthusiasm."

"I'm not feeling well today," Chesser told him.

"Nothing serious, I hope."

"Just a touch of fever."

"Well, get better and we'll look forward to seeing you on the ninth. Or did you say you preferred the tenth?"

"The ninth," Chesser said, to sound definite.

Good-byes.

Chesser put the phone back into its cradle. The System wasn't after them. Evidently The System hadn't even connected them to the robbery. He should have been greatly relieved about that but, instead, felt bitterly disappointed.

He went upstairs to tell Maren.

She was in the bathroom, soaking in the clear plastic tub. The water was fragrant, a baby-blue color. Chesser could see the exquisite bare line of her, slightly distorted, magnified. Her lower hair resembled a patch of delicate, glistening, nutmeg-colored weeds.

She didn't hear him enter. She had earphones on, connected by a long coiling cord stretched to the stereo outlet on the opposite wall.

"I called The System," Chesser told her.

Maren didn't hear.

"I just called The System," he shouted.

She smiled. She was listening to some medieval love ballads, very loud, while self-indulgently lathering her stomach with a frothy bar from Lubin.

Friday morning before breakfast, Maren and Chesser were at the town hall. Mr. Saltzman married them without even pausing for their "I do's" and "I will's," assuming they did and would. They didn't realize the ceremony was over until Saltzman turned his back on them. The plain gold band Chesser slipped on Maren's finger was the same one they'd been using for the past two years. Saltzman gave them a certificate he'd stamped and signed in advance, which they could sign later.

When they returned to the chalet they noticed the Aston Martin was not in front where it had been. Maren always left the car's keys in the ignition, so as not ever to need to bother searching for them elsewhere—a convenience that had resulted in three of her cars being inconveniently stolen during the past two years. Now Chesser could only hope she hadn't discarded the registration or bill of sale. He didn't, and was sure she didn't, remember the license plate number.

Maren wasn't at all upset by the missing car. Chesser's stomach decided that he'd call the police after breakfast.

They approached the front entrance of the chalet. It was locked. Had she locked it? No. Neither had he. They went to the nearest expanse of glass and looked in.

Looking back at them from inside were two men. It took a few seconds for Chesser to realize.

"Let us in," requested Chesser.

Both men raised their chins and shook their heads.

"Open up, goddamn it!" demanded Chesser.

"You're trespassing," defied the short lawyer.

"This is private property," informed the tall lawyer.

"They're right," Maren told Chesser, who was searching around for something to smash the glass. "They sure in hell didn't waste any time, did they?" Chesser said bitterly.

"Actually, all things considered, I think they've been quite patient," was Maren's opinion.

Chesser controlled his anger enough to tell them: "At least let us get our clothes."

"Nothing here belongs to you," said the short lawyer smugly.

His associate concurred with a pompous snap of his head.

That intimidated Chesser so much he thought if he did get inside the first things he'd go for were the guns. "Fucking French vultures!" he yelled at them.

"Go away," the short lawyer advised.

"Or we'll call the authorities," threatened the other.

"Let's go," Maren suggested, tugging Chesser's arm.

"We can't. They confiscated the car. Besides," Chesser just remembered, "we need our passports."

Maren smiled in at the two men. "We want only our passports," she told them in French, punctuating her attitude with a "please." A few minutes later a second-floor window opened and the passports were tossed down.

Chesser could just imagine the invisible Jean Marc floating around and gloating.

The only public transportation from Gstaad to Geneva is bus. Not a nice, comfortable, purring bus. Rather, a roaring, fumey vehicle, sick and tired from climbing mountains.

Maren and Chesser had to take it. And for the entire seventy-mile, three-hour ride, their empty stomachs were grinding and groaning right along with their conveyance. Their only funds were the eighty-seven francs Chesser just happened to have in his trousers pocket that morning. After paying for bus tickets, they were left with the equivalent of about three dollars.

Chesser believed everything would be better as soon as they got to Geneva. At least their immediate financial plight would be alleviated by the two hundred thousand fuck-you dollars he had stashed in the Geneva bank. Half of that would go for the packet Coglin had promised on the ninth. The other half would be enough of a cushion, if he could keep Maren, and himself, from living it up.

In his mind, Chesser had already accepted Coglin's offer of reinstatement.

Maren was set against it. "I thought we'd settled that," she said.

"Circumstances have changed," he said.

"Not so much."

"I have to make a living."

"Most people spend most of their lives making a living so that some day they'll be able to really live. That's stupid. Besides, it might be dangerous. They *might* begin to suspect you, for some reason."

"There's nothing else I can do," contended Chesser.

"You can just be with me."

Same old argument, thought Chesser, except now it didn't hold up.

There was no longer any bottomless Jean Marc fortune to support it. Maren was refusing to face reality, and it would doubtless take some time for her to adjust. All the more reason why he had to be practical. He had to go back with The System. Maybe he didn't want to but there was no choice.

Actually, the prospect of going back to receive the important treatment was rather appealing. The System would be different and so would he. He'd be serious about business, make every deal count, squeeze the most from every carat, prove to them that Meecham had been wrong about him. And in no time, he imagined, he'd be picking up packets as fat and perfect as Barry Whiteman's.

The most difficult thing was going to be looking them straight in the eye, taking their favors, without feeling a hypocrite. Still, there'd been the ten persecuting years he'd put in under Meecham. In a way, Chesser told himself, he and The System were restarting even. His whole life was restarting.

Not quite.

There was still Massey. He'd somehow have to square things with Massey before going back with The System. He knew it was naïve to believe Massey would let them off easily. Even if they put it straight on the line with Massey, told him the whole truth and nothing but, the old son of a bitch was going to want retribution. The most they could realistically hope was that he wouldn't come down on them again before they had a chance to tell their side of it, make their appeal. No matter, decided Chesser, they were absolutely finished with the running and hiding.

When they arrived in Geneva, they went directly to Chesser's bank on Stempenparkstrasse, a wide thoroughfare bordering the lake. Maren preferred not to go in with him. "I'm hungry," was her excuse.

"We'll have an elegant lunch after," he promised.

"I'm hungry now," she said, drooping forlornly so her hair fell forward, left and right, and all he could see of her face was her nose and some of her lips.

Chesser felt the pinch of his new responsibilities. He gave her all the money he had and told her, "Get a little something to hold you over."

She straightened, brightened, and hurried off down the street. He watched until she went into a bakery they'd passed along the way. Then he entered the bank.

It was typical of those Swiss banks which specialize in international accounts. That is, it didn't look like a bank. There was no name displayed on the entrance, or anywhere. It could have been any kind of business. Its reception area was carpeted deep red and paneled in dark, waxed walnut. A matching desk was situated at an unavoidable intercepting point in front of a solid counter that ran across the width of the room. About ten feet beyond the counter more paneling nearly camouflaged a pair of doors.

Seated at the reception desk was a young man, who did not request Chesser's name, discretion and anonymity being the rule.

Chesser asked to see someone concerning his account. The receptionist used the dark-brown phone, which was the only thing on the desk. Almost immediately an older, bald man emerged from one of the doors beyond the counter and offered his assistance.

"I want to make a withdrawal," Chesser told him.

The man placed a note pad on the counter top and accommodatingly unscrewed the top from a sterling silver pen, which he handed to Chesser.

Chesser wrote his account number on the pad, along with the amount he wished to withdraw. The fewest possible spoken words was normal procedure.

The bald man took the pad with him to the back of the bank. There he methodically checked the number against his registry of confidential accounts. He saw the name Chesser and immediately made a long distance call to Cap Ferrat, France. A few moments later he returned to Chesser and said to him, "We have no account by that number."

Chesser checked the number he'd written and saw it was correct. He'd memorized it, knew it as well as his name. "Look again. I'm sure you'll find it."

"Perhaps you're in the wrong bank."

"I'm in the right bank." Chesser was positive, although he'd only been there once before, six years ago, when he'd made his initial deposit. But nothing had changed since then. Same desk, same counter, same paneling, everything.

"There are a great number of banks on this street."

"Maybe one of your bookkeepers or someone made a mistake," said Chesser, and knew immediately he shouldn't have said it. There's nothing the Swiss dislike more than having their efficiency questioned. "I want to see the manager," demanded Chesser.

"I am the manager," was the man's curt reply. He ripped the sheet bearing Chesser's account number from the note pad, crumpled it in his fist, and dropped it with finality into a wastebasket on his way to the paneled door, which softly clicked him out of sight.

Chesser confronted the receptionist. "Tell that bastard to come back out here."

The receptionist sat as wooden as a carved music box figure.

"This bank's got my money and I want it!" shouted Chesser.

The receptionist blinked twice.

"Please?" begged Chesser.

The receptionist remained stiff, silent.

Chesser gazed futilely at the doors beyond the counter. He had the impulse to jump over and break in and make them give him his money, the money he now so desperately needed. But something told him if he jumped he'd eventually land in a tight Swiss jail.

He went out and looked for Maren; saw her across the way seated on a bench facing the lake. He crossed over and sat beside her.

She smiled, but he couldn't. She was just finishing off a croissant. She took another from one of the two paper bags she held on her lap. She bit off both crusty tips of the pastry and offered the rest to him. She always did that to croissants. Once in Chantilly she'd bought four dozen and indulgently nibbled only the tips from them.

When Chesser didn't accept, she asked, "What's wrong?" She knew he was hungry.

"Nothing," he mumbled. He sat tensely on the front edge of the bench, his elbows dug into his knees, his hands cupping his lowered head. He allowed a little spit to drop from his lips, making a darker wet spot on the pavement between his feet. He concentrated on that and thought what a fucked-up day it had been. Sacrificial wedding, French lawyers, bus ride, and the swindling Swiss for a topper. All on an empty stomach.

Things couldn't be worse, he thought. Now there was no way of financing that big packet on the ninth. No future, now. Not even enough money for a meal. And no place to stay. This wasn't just down. This was all the way out. How could he tell Maren they were broke? He thought maybe he could borrow some money, call someone for a loan and make up a believable enough lie to save the old pride. Who? His desperation suggested Weaver. Weaver had a million. Jesus, thought Chesser, how fast the bottom dropped out.

Maren got up and stood before him. She offered him another croissant. When he didn't take it, she kneeled down and put it to his mouth. She seemed to sense what had happened. Tenderly, she advised, "You'll feel better if you eat something."

He opened his mouth unwillingly. Took a bite. It did taste good.

She fed it all to him.

He swallowed and saw her loving smile. He managed a weak one.

She kissed a crumb from his upper lip and, still kneeling, offered the two bags up to him. He shoved his hand into one and brought out another croissant. He let her nibble off both tips before he devoured the rest.

"Have more," she urged, holding the two bags open.

"No." He decided it was time she knew.

"Do, darling. You deserve more."

He reached. Into the other bag this time.

It didn't contain croissants. Or anything similar. His fingers told him what they were feeling, but it was so incredible he had to see to believe.

Diamonds!

A whole goddamn bagful of diamonds.

Not rough stones. Finished ones, various shapes and sizes.

Chesser was speechless.

"I went to the bank while you went to the bank," explained Maren.

"I thought you didn't care for diamonds."

"I don't. Anyway, not to wear. But someone told me they were a good investment."

"I told you that."

"If you did I didn't hear because I already knew."

"Then who told you?"

"Jean Marc."

She'd been buying and dispatching diamonds to Switzerland all along, accumulating them in her secret safety deposit box. Ever since she'd received her first one as a gift from Jean Marc. Hidden assets. She was certain no one knew, not even those ferreting, foxy French lawyers.

Chesser took the bag of diamonds with both hands and held it as though his hands were a scale, weighing. About five pounds, he guessed. That would be around eleven thousand carats. Worth ten to fifteen million dollars, depending on quality.

He took one out. A five-carat round cut that flared magnificently in the sunlight. He examined it, approved, returned it to the bag, and looked in for another.

That was when he saw it. Right there on top, not to be missed. It stopped him for a moment, but his fingertips brought it out. He recognized it immediately.

Oval, one hundred seven point forty carats, cut by Wildenstein, perfect.

The Massey.

Chesser couldn't look at Maren that moment.

He sighted into the stone, as though looking for answers.

He now realized Maren must have known of Massey's game all along—at least early enough to prevent most of it.

He recalled now what she'd said about hoping she always cared enough for him to want to lie at least a little. But wasn't this a big and serious lie?

No bigger nor more serious than his own one-night infidelity with Lady Bolding, Chesser told himself. He also suspected that very night must have been when the diamond changed hands. From Massey to Maren. That same night. He remembered Maren coming up the stairs in diaphanous blue, carrying an innocent glass of milk and innocent bread and butter.

But why would Massey give her the diamond? What had Maren done to receive such an expensive show of gratitude? Perhaps, thought Chesser, she'd confronted Massey, told him what she knew or suspected, and threatened him with exposure. Massey had given her the diamond in return for her allowing things to proceed according to his plan. That would explain it. It fitted right in with her desire to prolong the excitement. The beautiful irony was that she probably wouldn't have told Chesser anyway, because then he would have refused to go ahead with the theft, knowing he'd been tricked into it by Massey. But Massey couldn't be sure of that, and so she'd gotten the diamond *and* her danger.

There were other possibilities, of course, but Chesser found them too painful to consider. His imagination started presenting them but he cut them off. He brought his look from the diamond to Maren, to Maren's eyes. She was his wife, carrying their child. He loved her.

"This one's a beauty," he said. "And so are you."

CHAPTER 31

Some 2,400 miles south, the revolutionary Harridge Weaver opened his eyes on the flaking ceiling of a prison cell in the African Free State called Mombi.

He was exhausted, but he sat up alertly and saw that Brother Spencer, who had been watching over him, was squatting against the opposite wall with an automatic rifle propped between his legs. Weaver asked the time.

"I was just going to wake you up," said Brother Spencer. "Man, you must have a clock in your head."

Weaver nodded. He did believe he could do anything he set his mind to. Despite the fact that his mind had played a mean trick on him when he'd awakened a few moments before—had startled him with the impression that he was in a different prison and not by choice. Thus, without showing it, Weaver was relieved by orientation and seeing Brother Spencer there.

He had slept with his shoes on, merely loosened the laces, which he now tightened and tied. He could have stayed at the Presidential Mansion, but during the negotiations he believed it more prudent to be in a cell near the goods. That was what he and his brothers had chosen to call them, the goods, a neutral, nonvisual term.

Weaver stood and went to the bucket in the corner. He took it up and drenched his head with water, reviving. There was no towel, but the African heat would quickly dry him.

He glanced through the interior bars to see that Brothers William and Davis were back-to-back sentries in the aisle of the cellblock, and two other Brothers were in the cell opposite, guarding the goods. All were armed with automatics. A contingency of twelve brothers had flown over to help. Four from the Bay area, six from New York, and two from the Midwest. They were upper cadre, dedicated to the end.

It had taken Weaver a day and two nights to convince President Bobu and his cabinet. Bobu, a thin man with a fat man's appetite, would have been easier alone. Prime Minister Moshiba and three appointed advisors had kept turning Bobu's head with selfish alternatives. The prime minister, for example, had been in favor of fast gain, dead set for extorting a huge sum in return for the diamonds. Weaver had persuaded tactfully, careful not to expose the Prime Minister's obvious personal greed and lack of imagination. It was necessary to avoid making an enemy of the man, for the time being.

After many hours of quibbling, the Prime Minister finally conceded part way and took an alternate stand. His compromise suggestion was that they sell the diamonds in large lots at undercutting prices. President Bobu thought that idea sounded reasonable and looked to Weaver for concurrence.

Patiently Weaver induced them further. He plowed their minds with words, planted and nurtured the seed of power beyond their most arrogant dreams. His persuasiveness was aided by the fact that he believed in power and had been the victim of it.

There was greater opportunity, Weaver maintained, in making Mombi appear to be a legitimate diamond-producing nation. Mombi would be to the diamond industry what Kuwait was to oil. Its leaders would be recognized, received, catered to, and even the indirect benefits of such a world position would exceed any short-term monetary gain that might be derived from selling the diamonds as the Prime Minister had suggested. The primary thing, said Weaver, was to make Mombi's sudden good fortune appear authentic. It could be done. The country was well located to make such a diamond discovery plausible. It was not far from Sierra Leone, one of the world's richest fields. In past years there had been some diamonds found in Mombi, and, although they were poor-grade stones suitable only for industrial use, that mineral history would serve as convincing testimony.

Weaver unrolled a map to show them what he proposed they

do. He'd come well prepared, had specifically chosen Mombi because that small country was both geographically and politically perfect for his plan. He called attention to the minor mountain range well within Mombi's borders—a few volcanic rises of varying heights called the Zalas, covering an area of about twenty square miles. It was arid land, ideally unpopulated. That entire section could be fenced off and restricted.

The diamonds would be scattered over the Zalas. Then the discovery would be made and officially announced. No outsiders would be allowed in, but government photographs and motion pictures would document and lend credence. Production would begin. Diamonds would be sold in increasing amounts through arrangements between the government of Mombi and the regular channels of international diamond distribution. Appropriately enough, The System, from whence they'd come. The money would flow into Mombi. It was a flawless plan. Didn't they agree?

Bobu, Prime Minister Moshiba, and the advisors exchanged measuring glances.

For a clincher, Weaver put a question to President Bobu. "How much does Mombi now have in its treasury?"

The president looked to one of his advisors, who replied hesitatingly, "Perhaps four hundred thousand dollars."

"Imagine twelve billion dollars," said Weaver.

And that did it.

Now, in the prison cell, Weaver strapped on a Smith & Wesson three fifty-seven magnum revolver and slung a bandolier, full and heavy, over his head. He put an arm through the bandolier and shifted it diagonally across his chest. He liked the feel of it.

He was then brought a tray of food that one of the brothers had personally prepared and no one else had touched. Taking no chances. Weaver was hungry but too full of visions of victory to taste what he forked into his mouth.

While he ate he thought of that part of his scheme that he hadn't revealed to the leaders of Mombi. The essential part, actually. He didn't intend to just let the great wealth accumulate and remain in Mombi's treasury as a symbol of power. Nor did he intend to allow the Prime Minister or the others to live high off the money. President Bobu would, of course, enjoy a share, because he was needed as a figurehead. Weaver was positive the president could be easily manipulated, kept content and distracted by such creature comforts as women and food and cars.

Weaver's ultimate goal was to finance the black revolution.

From Mombi's treasury he'd provide his brothers and sisters across the ocean with what they needed to rise up and fight for their color. He remembered himself having had to scrounge hard for enough money to buy a used rifle, and how he'd scrounged even more just to get out a few hundred propaganda newspapers. There wouldn't be any more of that. Not with twelve billion dollars backing them. That was for sure.

He hadn't yet analyzed what specifically could be accomplished with twelve billion dollars. But he'd done some preliminary figuring. He knew that twelve billion was only about one sixth as much as the annual United States military budget. But he reasoned that when all the influence and power of twelve billion dollars was concentrated in one direction for one purpose, without all that white bureaucratic bullshit skimming and waste, it could have the effect of fifty times that amount.

He visualized a quiet, gradual build-up of a secretly armed twenty million blacks, estimated that only four billion dollars would be required to supply every brother and sister in the United States with a rifle and ammunition, grenades, and explosives. That would still leave a balance of eight billion dollars with which to continue the fight.

It was a revolutionary's dream.

It could come true.

But its success, Weaver realized, depended upon secrecy. There could be no doubts, no rumors, certainly no investigations. The diamond discovery had to appear indisputably authentic.

He'd gotten the diamonds out of England without anyone knowing. Diplomatic cargo was the way they'd been classified. No questions. Without divulging anything, he'd been able to pull that off with the cooperation of a high-ranking North African official who was repaying a past favor. Weaver had led him to believe that what he was transporting via this privileged designation were four new, American-made refrigerators, merely to evade paying duty.

Since then Weaver had personally made sure the four large crates hadn't been opened, their supervaluable contents were intact, just as he alone had packed them.

It was absolutely imperative that no one should in any way connect him with the theft from The System. The cause was too important, the stakes too high to chance disclosure by anyone.

Three hours later, a cargo plane strained slowly across the cloudless African night sky. With its bay doors open, it made numerous low altitude passes over and around the Zalas mountain range.

Never, on the face of this earth had there fallen such a precious and potentially violent rain.

CHAPTER 32

They were in Monaco, staying in a corner suite of the Hôtel de Paris.

Maren and Chesser both regarded it as a legitimate honeymoon. However, neither mentioned it as such, because being there was not special enough, really, not a change from their customary life style. They couldn't even enjoy the self-conscious pleasure of making their newlywed status known to the hotel, for they'd often stayed there together before, and it would have been flagrantly tactless of them now suddenly to contradict the hotel's previously accommodating, if not sincere, assumption about their marital status.

They'd been there since midweek. The best of it was the two full days and nights they hadn't left their suite, had loved and loved, regenerated their bodies with long, any-time naps and excessive portions of their most favorite foods, and made more love.

Chesser found himself looking forward to Monday. That would be the ninth, the day of his return to The System.

Maren had given in to his attending the sight. She understood the personal satisfaction it would give him. But she had her terms: He would never go to London without her, and he must pick up his packet and sell it as quickly as possible, without even opening it.

He agreed to the latter condition because disagreement then might have caused her to withdraw her compromise altogether. In time he'd convince her that it was necessary for him to be doing something well besides loving her. Also, he could not forget those moments of anguish on the bench beside the lake in Geneva. That experience had hardened Chesser's determination never again to be caught having nothing. As yet he didn't know what that Swiss bank had done with his two hundred thousand fuck-you dollars, but he was sure Massey had something to do with it.

As for now, they had one more night in Monaco. According to their new perspective, it might be the last they'd ever spend there. So they decided to make the most of it.

They dressed for the evening and went to dinner at Le Régent. They ignored acquaintances and focused their attention entirely on one another. They discussed where they should have a house, make a home, and how large it should be. It came to them that the French lawyers might want to sell the place in Chantilly and that prospect delighted them.

After dinner they drove up the winding ribbon of steep road to Laghet, where they visited a small church they'd heard about. The church was a favorite of gamblers, and it remained open at night to facilitate pious incantations for protection against losing. Its feature votive attraction was The Little Black Virgin, a hard wooden statue with a virtuous black face carved and gessoed especially to transmit assurances to those who believed they could, with a bit of divine assistance, beat the odds. No doubt, some winners returned and inserted substantial gratitude into the slotted box that was a permanent fixture at the statue's base.

The Little Black Virgin had been credited with many divine accomplishments, such as miraculous cures, sixteen consecutive wins on black in roulette, and numerous rescues from sudden death.

Maren and Chesser disregarded the worn, velour-covered

prayer bench below the statue. They stood for no more than a couple of minutes. Chesser noticed that the black paint had completely flaked off the Virgin's feet, exposing them as chalky white. Also, disconcertingly, its dark, target eyes were out of alignment. Maren dropped a hundred-franc note into the offering box and lighted a candle. Just to do it.

Then they drove back to Monaco.

At that same time Toland and another professional killer named Riker were entering the Hôtel de Paris via the rear service entrance. They skirted the bustle of the kitchen and went up the back stairs to the fourth floor, unnoticed.

The hotel corridor was deserted, no sign of the floor waiter or chambermaid. Toland and Riker hesitated long enough to put on gloves and then proceeded down the corridor to suite *numéro quarante*. They unlocked the door with a master key and went in.

They went to work—quietly, efficiently creating the evidence of robbery. With purposeful carelessness they emptied and rummaged through drawers and cases, confiscating every valuable item small enough to be carried away in their pockets. Including the entire contents of Maren's jewelry chest and a thick fold of five-hundred-franc notes found tucked into the toe of one of Chesser's shoes.

By the time they had finished, both rooms of the suite appeared to have been hurriedly ransacked. Only a few additional touches were needed. A lamp on its side on the floor, its shade collapsed, the telephone wires ripped out, a table knocked awry with one of its legs splintered, the bed covers pulled off, a chair turned over, ashtrays thrown and spilled on the carpet.

Signs of struggle.

There would be no struggle, of course.

Chesser and Maren would enter the suite, and when they had closed the door behind them, Toland and Riker, from flanking positions, would shoot them with an immobilizing drug, noiselessly, using special compressed air pistols which accommodated dartlike syringes.

Under the effects of the drug, they would be bound and gagged. And as soon as the drug's effects wore off, Toland would give Chesser the opportunity to reveal where the stolen inventory was hidden. Chesser would be allowed one free hand to write down the information. Massey had no intention of relying on his representative's memory. If Chesser refused, Toland's instructions were to convince him by paying imaginatively crude attention to Maren. Riker was especially good at that, the sort who found sexual amusement in using objects as substitutes for his physical equipment.

Once the information was obtained from Chesser, Toland was to call Massey from a public phone. He was to call again every hour thereafter until Massey confirmed that Chesser had not lied. In all, it was estimated that Massey's people needed no more than three hours to check out the location of the diamonds anywhere in England. After getting the word from Massey, Toland was to rejoin Riker in the suite. Steel-spring garrots would be used. Noiseless, neat. Toland and Riker each carried one in his coat pocket. The simplest sort of lethal device. Merely a very thin woven-steel wire looped back, connected to itself and held cocked by a small but extremely powerful spring. The loop went over the head and around the neck. When the spring was released the loop contracted with tremendous force, strangling.

Toland and Riker had already taken their positions flanking the entrance inside suite *numéro quarante*. Toland, waiting, happened to notice a book on a near table. Book with a strange title that he assumed was Chinese. *I Ching*. Toland thumbed through it, saw it wasn't a story and wondered why the hell anyone would want to use three suit buttons to mark a place.

By then Maren and Chesser were just across the square from the hotel, entering the Casino.

In the *salle privée* Maren was ambivalent about whether to play roulette or chemin.

"Try both," suggested Chesser.

She shook her head and settled on roulette. She bypassed several active tables for the one deepest in the room, as if that choice was in some superstitious way significant. Chesser bought her chips—fifty thousand francs' worth. The amount they'd predetermined as her limit. She stacked them neatly according to denomination on the baize surface before her, but she didn't begin play immediately, waited to observe the fall of the ball for a while.

Her play was methodical, although it appeared erratic. Frequently she didn't participate in two or three consecutive turns and she always glanced left and right before selecting a number. She won her initial bet and continued to win more often than not.

Chesser stood behind her chair. He watched the green scattered with the wafers of hope, nearly every number covered despite the fact that only one could win. There was the frictional whine of the wheel and, finally, the plick-plick-plock of the ball skipping and falling. The croupier's rake was mercilessly precise, gathering for the house. Fingers, exhibiting the flashes of carats, placed mindless convictions here and there in large amounts. There was no laughter, the pleasure coming from the punishing intensity.

It occurred to Chesser that actually the players were wagering against one another, and the true stakes were preferential treatment by the god of chance.

He attended Maren, touched her shoulder encouragingly, took her hand when she offered it, lighted cigarettes for her and ordered champagne. From his vantage he could see down the front of her dress, her perfectly firm, bare breasts with their nipples looking aroused, as always.

He soon realized that the man beside him, a chubby Arab standing to play, was also enjoying that view.

Chesser glanced disapprovingly at him.

The Arab disregarded it.

Chesser sidled part way around Maren's chair, to obstruct the Arab's view.

But the Arab was a player, entitled to place his wagers. He nudged through and continued to steal from Maren's exposure. However, distracted as he was, the Arab gambled badly. And because he preferred not to relinquish his visual advantage, he continued to purchase more and more chips. Until he'd lost well over a hundred fifty thousand francs. Perhaps, according to his standards, it was worth it.

Chesser considered it nearly a fair price.

Maren was having a fortunate night. By early morning she

was ahead a hundred seventy-five thousand francs. Chesser suggested she stop.

"One more play," she said.

Only two other players remained at the table, both heavy losers trying to recoup. Maren summoned the head croupier and spoke privately with the man, who nodded politely to her and to the croupier serving her table.

She resumed. On the very next turn she looked right and left, paused unsurely, looked left and right again, shrugged, and pushed all her chips out into play.

"Number 11," she declared.

Chesser winced, but was silently appreciative.

After about fifty revolutions, centrifugal force gave way to gravity and the ball fell into number 13.

"Right next door," said Maren, blasé. She turned to Chesser, who was now seated beside her. She asked him to purchase more chips.

"No more," he told her.

He thought she would protest, but instead she admired him with her eyes and rewarded him with a kiss.

They left the Casino.

Maren was exhilarated, not sleepy. She didn't want to go back to the hotel yet. They'd drive somewhere. The Upper Corniche? No. She wanted to go to the harbor.

Chesser steered them through the one-ways of the town and down to the waterfront, out around where private boats and yachts were moored. Everyone else was sleeping. The only motion was the easy tossing of the vessels. He stopped the car and they got out to walk with arms around.

"Know why I was winning so much tonight?" she asked.

"The Little Black Virgin."

"Hell no. But I did have some help. Billie Three Rocks and my Chinaman were telling me which numbers to play. I relied completely on them."

"They certainly finished strong."

"They just couldn't make up their minds that last time," she explained.

"Oh, that was it," said Chesser, going along.

"Billie advised me to play number 11, but my Chinaman told me not to."

"You should have listened to the Chinaman."

"Obviously."

"If there was such a difference of opinion, why didn't you just skip that turn, instead of plunging as you did?"

"I had to play."

"Why?"

"I wanted to find out which one of them was right."

Chesser had to laugh. He imagined how many of their future decisions might be influenced by her two invisible and, evidently, not infallible mentors.

They walked out on the breakwater. Huge slabs of concrete placed one after another, slanted a few degrees to favor east and west alternately. This arrangement made the breakwater an attractive sunning place, and on any bright day the smooth slabs would be spread with nearly nude figures that shifted with the sun from the easterly slabs in the morning to the westerly ones in the afternoon.

Maren and Chesser strolled all the way out to the breakwater's tip. Dawn was just starting on the horizon. The sea was taking it calmly, gently lapping where it touched, but farther out it was incongruously vulnerable to a mere skim of wind.

"Back between," remarked Maren, gazing thoughtfully seaward.

"Hmmm?"

"That's where I'd like to go. Back between the sky and the sea. Not to live there, but for a while, at least, just to see how I see it now."

"Where's that?" asked Chesser, believing he knew.

She told him.

She seldom mentioned the place. From what little she'd ever said, Chesser had pictured it intolerably bleak and desolate. However, now she glorified it, reminisced brightly about how she used to look at the reflections on the placid surface of the fjord and pretend everything was inverted: the mountains sitting on duplicate mountains, birds on birds, her on her. Two of everything, so she could imagine not knowing which was real.

Describing it, her words came out coated with tender recall, as though they were slightly too large for her to express and her eyes grew moist. She asked him with her eyes.

"We'll go," he promised.

"Soon?"

"Soon," he told her.

She remained close to him for a long moment, then separated abruptly. She removed her shoes. Before he realized what she was doing, she'd slipped her dress off and down and had stepped away from the softly bunched circle of it. All she had on then were white bikini panties.

"A swim will relax me," she said.

"It'll be cold."

"All the more relaxing."

She went to the edge, looked down to the water, and hesitated. Then, making up her mind, she inserted her thumbs inside the elastic top of her panties and stripped them down, inside out. She kicked them in Chesser's direction.

The light was kind. Everything was gaining color now—the hills of the town, the water, her hair.

She was on the edge, poised to dive.

Chesser kept his distance, to enjoy the exquisite full length sight of her. He was suddenly very aroused, couldn't help calling her name.

She turned.

He went to her with arms extended, to take her in.

They held against one another, and, realizing his arousal, she pressured and moved to increase it.

"I love you," he said.

"I know," she said, "I *know*."

At that moment, the steel jacketed bullet entered her back. It came from a high-velocity rifle triggered by the finger of a black assassin, one of Weaver's brothers obeying. Making sure at any price that no one would ever connect Weaver with the twenty million carat theft.

The bullet went through her, all the way through, and into him, carrying some of her flesh into his.

Almost simultaneously, another bullet from another assassin's rifle entered Chesser's back and passed entirely through him, tore through, carrying some of his flesh into hers.

Her head fell back and her Viking hair streamed down.

"*Jag är rädd,*" she murmured. *I am afraid.*

He wanted to tell her not to be, and he felt that he could tell her.

But he didn't have to.

They were already dead.